Praise for
Catch Us When

"A gripping page-turner, *Catch Us Wh...* ...road to recovery in the shattering aftermath of a doomed relationship. Suffused with compassion, wry humor, and the unexpected grace of healing, it's a story not of angels or demons, but of two people struggling to find a safe harbor in the broken landscape of addiction. *Catch Us When We Fall* wrapped me in a blanket of hope and goodness."

—Randy Susan Meyers, bestselling author of
Waisted and *The Widow of Wall Street*

"*Catch Us When We Fall* is an emotionally rich, deeply satisfying novel that grabs you early and doesn't let go. With endearing characters, an expertly woven plot, and wonderful writing, Juliette Fay reminds us that no matter how tough we think we are, we really, really need each other."

—Matthew Norman, author of
Last Couple Standing and *All Together Now*

"A redemption story if ever there was one: Juliette Fay's *Catch Us When We Fall* gives us a character who seems almost beyond help, beyond reach, even to herself—but finds ways to prove us all wrong, one baby step at a time. A beautiful look at the strength it takes to save ourselves, the love it takes to save each other, and the hopeful truth that it's never too late to start over."

—Jessica Strawser, author of *A Million Reasons Why*

"A hopeful, poignant novel about the tenacity of the human spirit, our capacity for forgiveness, and all the ways a heart can grow when we least expect it. You'll want to curl up in bed with this heartwarming story."

—Allison Winn Scotch, *New York Times* bestselling author

"*Catch Us When We Fall* is a beautiful story about life's darkest demons—grief, addiction, and broken promises—but Juliette Fay's characters are so lovable and emotionally complex it left me suffused with light and hope. I read this book in a gulp, alternately crying, laughing, and cheering, and when I finished, I turned back to the first page so I could savor it."

—Ann Mah, bestselling author of *The Lost Vintage*

"When I'm done reading one of Juliette Fay's books, her characters always exist in my memory like people I've actually met. *Catch Us When We Fall* is full of hope and heart and genuine love. I already miss checking in with these beautiful people who are trying their hardest to heal and connect."

—Allie Larkin, bestselling author of *Stay,*
Why Can't I Be You, and *Swimming for Sunlight*

"*Catch Us When We Fall* by Juliette Fay introduces us to Cass Macklin, a former addict who finds herself alone and pregnant. Can Cass stop drinking and create a healthy life for herself and her unborn child? A novel about resilience and the power of human connection, *Catch Us When We Fall* is perfect for fans of emotionally honest women's fiction."

—Brenda Janowitz, author of *The Grace Kelly Dress*

Deep Down True

"When I wasn't inside the world of this book—because this is a book that you enter instead of merely read—I longed to be. I love it for its intensely human characters and for the way the author grants them their flaws as generously as she celebrates their daily decencies, their persistent hopefulness, their moments of personal grace."

—Marisa de los Santos, *New York Times* bestselling
author of *Love Walked In* and *Belong to Me*

"Sincere, powerful, and heartfelt, *Deep Down True* will resonate with women everywhere. I loved Fay's true-to-life characters and her ability to portray the intricate dynamics of friendship and family in such an immediately recognizable way. There is a 'me too' moment on every page, right down to the satisfying finish."

—Emily Giffin, *New York Times* bestselling author of
Something Borrowed, Something Blue,
Baby Proof, and *Heart of the Matter*

Shelter Me

"What a gorgeous paradox of a book: a deep, thoughtful exploration of a young mother's first year of widowhood that is as much a page-turner as any thriller. The translucent beauty of the writing and the sheer humanity of the characters pulled me along, often more quickly than I wanted to go. If it were up to me, I'd still be in the company of prickly, magnificent Janie and the people she loves."

—Marisa de los Santos, *New York Times*
bestselling author of *Belong to Me*

"*Shelter Me* is a richly told story that offers a keyhole into the pain and searing grief losing a loved one brings to a family. That pain is balanced against humor and the need to caretake life's day-to-day demands and relationships until one day, you realize you have the capability to love again. Fay writes with vivid dialogue and conjures up characters that feel real enough to be sitting in your kitchen."

—Lee Woodruff, *New York Times* bestselling author of *In an Instant*

"*Shelter Me* is the tender tale of Janie LaMarche, a young woman who is suddenly widowed and forced to find her way. She is guided by a searing wit, by her truth-telling five-year-old son, and by the unlikely sages of her suburban world. Juliette Fay can hit the high notes of emotion with unexpected moments of redemption and wry humor."

—Jacqueline Sheehan, *New York Times* bestselling author of *Lost & Found*

CATCH US
WHEN WE
FALL

Also by Juliette Fay

City of Flickering Light
The Tumbling Turner Sisters
The Shortest Way Home
Deep Down True
Shelter Me

CATCH US WHEN WE FALL

A Novel

Juliette Fay

WILLIAM MORROW
An Imprint of HarperCollinsPublishers

P.S.™ is a trademark of HarperCollins Publishers.

CATCH US WHEN WE FALL. Copyright © 2021 by Juliette Fay. All rights reserved. Printed in the United States of America. No part of this book may be used or reproduced in any manner whatsoever without written permission except in the case of brief quotations embodied in critical articles and reviews. For information, address HarperCollins Publishers, 195 Broadway, New York, NY 10007.

HarperCollins books may be purchased for educational, business, or sales promotional use. For information, please email the Special Markets Department at SPsales@harpercollins.com.

FIRST EDITION

Designed by Diahann Sturge

Library of Congress Cataloging-in-Publication Data has been applied for.

ISBN 978-0-06-307996-0

21 22 23 24 25   LSC   10 9 8 7 6 5 4 3 2 1

To my writers' group: Randy Susan Myers, EB Moore, Kathy Crowley, and Nichole Bernier, whose kind but honest literary insights are surpassed only by their kindness and honesty as friends

Chapter I

Ben McGreavy had been a very smart man. Cass cradled a secret pride for the way he always seemed to have the right answer to every question. That whip-speed intellect once landed him a spot on *Jeopardy!*, and his winnings had gotten as high as $22,400 after the first round. But before the next round he'd had a few belts of Seagram's scotch on his way to the set—just four or five, far less than a normal evening's intake—hoping it would soothe his nerves. The stakes were high. Depending on how long he could hang in there, he had hoped to pay off some debts.

Not the one to his brother, Scott. Cass knew Ben had stopped keeping track of that years before. He'd probably stopped even thinking about it, except when Scotty would get mad about something else and invariably add, *And what about all the money you owe me, huh? What about* that?

Ben would shame Scotty by pulling out his wallet and tossing his last few dollars on the floor. Or just by looking at him, a look that said, *You might be a big man somewhere in the world, but calling in a debt on your own brother, who hasn't had your luck—that's cold, even for you.*

Cass had seen variations of this interaction countless times in the eleven years she'd been with Ben, since she was eighteen. She hated that they often didn't have enough to live on—hated even more that it was their own fault. She'd been raised to work hard and follow the rules, and there had been precious little of that in the last few years. "We have to stop," she'd say. "We have to get jobs and stand on our own feet!" And Ben would agree. Till the job bored him, which was always. Till the whisper of alcohol in her brain surged to a voracious roar and she was plummeting toward a roiling ocean of pain and the only thing left to do was pull the ripcord on sobriety and let booze be her parachute, floating, drifting down, down, down into the glassy warm waters of oblivion. Drowning either way.

Ben lost on the Final Jeopardy! question, winning the third-place consolation of $1,000. No debts were paid, but Cass had taken a load of groceries to the single mother on the third floor, a lot of prepared foods so she didn't have to cook, and things Cass knew the kids had never had before, like clementines and blue-berries. Then she and Ben had had a few days of howling hilarity spending the rest of it.

On what?

She watched as the casket was lowered into the ground. It seemed too small, not nearly large enough to hold so much knowl-edge, such a commanding personality as Ben's. The winch let out its *crick-crick-crick* sound, and down he went into the stony brown earth.

God, he'll be so freaking bored down there.

But what had they spent the money on? All she could remember now was laughing and drinking fussy-sounding wine at a restau-rant with real flowers on the table. Real live flowers. Red ones, or possibly purple. Wherever it was, however long it lasted, it had been a good time.

"A wicked good time," Cass said now, loud and slurry, a half bottle of Seagram's having thickened her tongue. Her sudden ex-clamation destabilized her, and she lurched sideways for a step, as if she were on the deck of a storm-battered ship.

Don't act drunk. The silent chide came automatically, as it had for the last decade.

"Shut up," Ben's brother, Scott, muttered, his large face paler than usual, short hair tufting up like dead grass out of snow. His blue-gray eyes, dull and blank, slid momentarily toward the priest muttering prayers at the coffin.

Cass didn't care. Ben was dead. What else mattered?

"He was a good man!" Her finger wobbled at Scott, voice rising above the drone of cars whizzing unsympathetically by them on Market Street. "No matter what you thought of him."

"I'm warning you," Scott growled.

"Warning me? About *what*? What can you do to me now? Hit me with your big steroid muscles? Go ahead—I'm not afraid of that."

Scott glanced at the priest. "Thanks, Father, I think we'll wrap it up now. It's a nice spot." He handed over an envelope and nodded at the two guys in coveralls leaning against a tall, pointy headstone a few rows over. Through the blur of booze and tears it looked to Cass like an amputated church steeple stuck in the grass.

A broken hunk of God.

She felt her knees go loose again, and she stumbled forward. Scott grabbed her elbow; she could feel his grip through the only black coat the thrift store had had. It was a trench coat, size eight, and it swam on her like a tarp. The cuffs were frayed but she'd trimmed the wisps of thread and sewn up a hole by the elbow, right where Scott now laid his thick fingers.

"Don't rip it!" Her screech sounded like the caw of a crow, even to her.

"Just get in the fucking car," he muttered, taking her other elbow now and marching her toward his SUV, black, unscratched, and as clean as if he'd driven it off the dealer's lot and straight to the cemetery. He hoisted her into the passenger side like a sack of laundry, then slammed the door and went around to the driver's side, hopping up effortlessly, suddenly beside her, his finger thrusting toward her.

"First of all, I am not on steroids. And second of all, if he was such a goddamned good guy, why are you and me the only ones here? Huh?"

"People don't know he's dead!"

Scott heaved a long, aggravated sigh. "No, Cass. He's been low-life-ing it so long, people think he's been dead for years."

"Don't you say that! They all remember when he was on *Jeopardy!*"

"*Jeopardy!*? That was six years ago! The highlight of his life. The one time he used his brains for something other than trading risky stocks and the goddamned crossword puzzles."

Cass burst into tears again. Ben was so good at the crosswords. She'd gotten him a book of them once when she was trying to get them both off the sauce, and he'd stayed sober for two whole days till he finished them all.

Scott slumped back in his massive leather seat. "Where are you staying—same place?"

"Yeah." She inhaled a sniffle.

He reached past her, popped open the glove box, and tossed a couple of paper napkins in her lap. "Don't get snot on my car," he said. "And take those with you when you go."

She cried silently the whole way home.

Not home, she thought as they sped down Brighton Avenue. *Just back.* Back to one of the countless crappy places she'd crashed in over the past eleven years since she'd left her last foster home on her eighteenth birthday.

"DCF stops paying me today," her so-called foster mother had said when Cass got home from school that day. "Your ride's over." And she'd handed Cass a black trash bag with all her stuff in it.

"Can I have my pillow?" Cass had asked. She'd liked that pillow, it fit her just right.

"No, I need that for the next kid," the woman said and shut the door.

The social worker had helped her find a bedbug-ridden room and a job sweeping up old ladies' hair at Alba's Set and Go. But then she started dating Ben McGreavy, the smartest guy she'd ever met, older brother to her classmate Scott McGreavy, the best athlete at Brighton High. It had sure looked like a better deal than Alba's.

Scott pulled the SUV up in front of the crooked house, one end of the porch held up by a two-by-four. They lived in an illegal studio apartment in the basement. No, *she* lived there. Ben now had "a nice spot" in the Market Street Cemetery. Cass started to cry a little harder, her sobs painful and hiccup-y.

"Jesus, how hammered *are* you?"

"Screw you, Scotty!"

"Just get out of the car."

She had her hand on the door handle, but something stopped her. The sense of things changing, everything happening so fast. She'd lost Ben, and now Scotty would be gone, too. He wasn't really such a bad guy. Sorta big on himself, but athletes were like that.

"Scotty . . ."

"What?" He didn't even have the car in park, she noticed. It was in drive, and he had his foot on the brake.

"Just . . . thanks."

"For?"

"We owe you a lot of money, and you and I both know you're never gonna get it now."

He shrugged. "Ben owed me. You never asked for a thing."

"Still. Thanks. From both of us."

Scott stared out the window, up the street toward Brighton Avenue. "You gonna be okay?"

"Yeah." *No.* "You?"

He snorted a mirthless little chuckle, and it occurred to her that maybe he was glad about Ben. Nobody to bail out now. No more Ben drama. Cass knew Scotty hated the drama more than he hated handing out money.

But Scott said, "He was my brother." And his chin trembled. He blinked a couple of times, his blue-gray eyes shiny. Then he made his face go blank again. "You need anything? Groceries?"

"No, it's okay."

"I'm not giving you cash."

"I didn't ask for any."

He nodded. Then he looked at her. Cass realized it had been a long time since Scotty had made actual eye contact with her.

"You take care of yourself," he told her.

"You, too."

"If you ever want seats or anything, let me know. I'll leave them at the ticket window for you."

"Thanks." He'd been signed by the Red Sox two years before and had often gotten them tickets. Sometimes they'd loved sitting in the old park and screaming themselves hoarse when he got up to bat. More often than not, though, they'd scalped the tickets and gone drinking. Cass wondered if he knew.

When he pulled away, she stood on the sidewalk and watched his SUV accelerate. His brake lights went on at the end of the street. The black coat was so big she couldn't wrap it tightly enough to keep the damp March wind from whisking up and licking at her skin. Scraps of auburn hair lashed at her face. But it seemed important somehow to wait. It was a small vigil she held as she watched those taillights, glowing red, like votive candles. A prayer for the passing of her life with Ben.

Scott's SUV made a right turn. He was headed toward the Mass Pike, she guessed, west to that nice house she'd heard about, somewhere in the suburbs. Or maybe east to the airport to go back to spring training. Either way, that would be that.

Cass stumbled down the buckled flagstone path, around the back, and let herself into the basement. Her buzz dying, she focused only on getting to the half bottle of Seagram's she'd left on the table a few hours before.

Chapter II

The next time Cass saw Scott, she dropped a tray of strawberry daiquiris.

No! she thought as she watched all that liquor curl through the air with the beauty of an ocean wave. *Stop!* she wanted to scream. *Come back!* For a split second she felt as if she were surfing on that wave of rum-laced bliss, in the moment before being crushed beneath its power.

"God*damn* it, Cass." The manager crouched beside her, hissing into her ear like a fat little goblin as she knelt to corral the sticky shards. "These are expensive goddamn glasses, and I *told* you, one more drop and—"

"I know, I'll pay for it. Just don't—"

A shadow moved over them, and she almost yelled at the moron who was suddenly standing in her light, keeping her from cleaning up yet another mess.

"I'll take care of it." Scott's low voice placated the angry little man. "It's on me."

"Oh, no, Mr. McGreavy," the goblin simpered as he staggered up onto his feet, snapping his grimace into a smarmy grin. "We're just happy to have you and your friends—"

"It's Rogie's fault." Cass could hear the fake smile in Scotty's voice as she piled broken glass onto her tray. "Girls see him, and things get dropped. Happens all the time." He pulled out some bills. "That's why he keeps me around, to bat cleanup."

The goblin roared with laughter at this little play on words. "You're a prince, Mr. McGreavy!" he said loudly, calling attention to his thirty-second friendship with someone moderately famous. "A prince among men!"

It worked. The whole room clapped. Cass knew it would be talked about for weeks by the hardworking patrons and the sad sacks alike. For some it would be the most memorable thing that happened all year. A few would even claim to know Scott from his childhood here in Brighton. But they didn't, not really.

Scott shifted, his shadow moved, and one last shard came into view. She reached for it, but the goblin pulled at her arm to stand up. "*Thank* him, for chrissake," he muttered at her.

She stood and faced Scott. "Thanks," she said. And he was looking at her again, like he had in the car after Ben's funeral. He tipped his chin at her. *You okay?* his chin asked.

She gave the tiniest of shrugs. People were still watching and she had to keep her job. She always tried to keep her jobs, but now she really had to. So she went up on tiptoes and gave him a little peck on the cheek, playing the grateful damsel, the adoring fan. As expected, the crowd hooted and cheered.

"Go for it, Cassie!" called one of the regulars, and everyone laughed at the absurdity of Cass Macklin, a merely adequate waitress in a fairly run-down bar, kissing Scott McGreavy, a midlevel player on a world-class baseball team. Of course, they didn't know he would've flunked out of high school if his older brother hadn't written his papers for him. Cass and Scott had walked across the same stage to get their diplomas, one right after the other in alphabetical order. But Cass had written her own papers to get there.

"Isn't that sweet! Would you like her to be your waitress?" The goblin would've happily pimped out his granny for big-spending customers.

"Uh . . ." Scotty's face went blank like it did when he was trying not to react to bad news. Cass had seen it many times, usually from the vantage point of being the bearer of that news. "Sure."

She followed him back to the table, mentally prepping herself. *Tips, tips, tips*, she chanted silently. God, she needed the money.

Scott did not introduce her to his friends or even acknowledge that he knew her. His eyes darted around like everything else in the room required his scrutiny.

He's ashamed of me.

It shouldn't have surprised her, and yet it did. In her current state she was seeing all kinds of things more clearly.

Tips, tips, tips, she reminded herself as the sting of his disregard slowly faded. Big smile, hand to chest. "Oh my God, Nick Rogatelli! I didn't know if you were going to make it out alive, but you pulled it off. And Kep Miller! Wow, tonight's my lucky night." Cass did enjoy baseball and, like most true Bostonians, rooted devotedly for the Red Sox, at least till the end of the season, when that devotion might turn to disgust.

Rogatelli grinned back, milk chocolate eyes radiating sly charm. "Thanks to Scotty, here, for paying off your boss. He doesn't usually go all gallant like that." He slapped Scott's chest a couple of times.

Cass said, "Oh, I'm sure he's dropped some change in a few tin cups."

"Scotty?" Miller laughed. "I seriously doubt it. Dropped his *pants*, maybe . . ." Rogatelli burst out with a snorting guffaw and high-fived Miller.

Scott turned red and muttered, "Couple of assholes . . . never shoulda brought you here."

Cass took their drink order and left them to their teasing and trash talking. When she returned with three pints of beer, she was relieved to find no one at the table. Rogie and Miller were prowling the bar, signing autographs and chatting up a couple of women sporting the exact same overdone boob job. Standing together, their cleavage looked like twin glacial crevasses.

She lowered the pints carefully to the table, willing her hands not to shake. They jittered like windup toys these days. Scott came up beside her just as the last one nearly crash-landed. He raised his eyebrows at her but she ignored it.

"So you're slumming it?" she said. "Or is this a trip down memory lane?"

"Rogie likes the neighborhood pubs."

"He'll get more attention here than at the Ritz Bar, that's for sure."

He narrowed his eyes. "How'd you get this job? Pretty sure you don't have any references you can use. You know the manager?"

"No, but I flirted with him a little, and he gave me a chance."

Scotty hooked his fingers into little quotation marks. "'Flirted'?"

"Screw you."

"Hey, it's a fair question."

"I never did anything like that, and you know it." She flipped a couple of napkins onto the table and walked away.

The bar got crowded fast, as people called their friends to tell them Rogie Rogatelli, star Red Sox relief pitcher, was in the building. He and Kep Miller drank and danced and laughed. Scott mostly stayed at the table talking sports with a couple of obsessed fans.

What was it like to have baseball be your drug of choice? Cass wondered. It had to be a hell of a lot easier than her own.

". . . then he Bucknered!" sneered one of the fans.

"Hey," Scotty said, low and flat, the way he sounded just before he got really mad. "Don't you ever use his name like that. Billy Buckner was a great player, and all you assholes seem to remember is that one stupid play . . ."

The two acolytes nodded penitently as if they'd just heard the word of God from a really well-built Moses.

Everyone was happy. Tips were plentiful. Cass struggled to keep her tray steady as she wended her way through the press of bodies, and the smell of a hundred drinks flooded the terrain of her thoughts. But she kept driving her mind back to the growing wad of cash in her apron pocket and smiled as if she were having just as good a time as everyone else.

Occasionally she saw Scott watching her, which was infuriating. Going unnoticed was her preferred mode of travel—so much safer than attracting attention. His surveillance unnerved her, and she needed every last nerve to keep her eye on the prize. She made a *what-the-hell-are-you-looking-at?* face at him, and he turned away.

When it was past midnight and the working crowd had gone home, Scott came up to the bar and stood next to Cass while she waited for an order to be filled.

"What's with the shaking?" he murmured, eyes locked onto a commercial for discount mattresses on the bar TV. "You quit again?"

She was tempted to tell him to mind his own business, they weren't friends, they weren't even semirelated anymore. And he was ashamed of her, for godsake! But it was late and she was tired—so unbelievably tired—and that was a bigger speech than she had energy for.

"Yeah," she said, because what the hell, he already knew.

"How's it going?"

"It's rough." She took the drinks the bartender passed her and went to serve them.

He was still standing there when she came back for her next order.

"Why'd you quit?" he said and threw a couple of pretzels in his mouth.

Why? How little did he think of her that she had to have a special reason to stop doing something so utterly destructive that it had killed the only person on the planet who loved her?

"Because it's, um . . . *bad* for you?"

"Not buying it."

"Don't care." She walked away without collecting her drinks.

As the place thinned out, Cass had more time to stew on Scott's nosiness. Honestly, why would he bother? She figured it must be some weird residue from Ben's death. She remembered how Scotty's chin had trembled. They were brothers, and she knew there had been a bond between them once. Ben had told her about how they would do stuff together when they were younger . . . shoplift from the penny-candy store . . . play baseball in the vacant lot behind the gas station down the street . . . find new places to hide from their father . . .

He misses Ben, she decided. *How strange is that?* There was a word for it on the edge of her mind, a word Ben liked to use . . . *Ironic.*

As she cleared smeary glasses and pocketed tips, something occurred to her, just a thought, but over the course of the next half hour it wrapped around her like some sort of fast-growing vine. And then she couldn't *not* do it. It would be wrong—a bigger wrong than the vast variety of wrongs she was used to—not to say anything. Because Ben had loved him even when Scott had said *No, I won't help you, not this time* and *I wish to hell you weren't my brother.* That last one had hit Ben so hard, but he'd never spoken badly of Scotty, even after that.

Ben would want him to know, she realized. And that settled it.

When Scott headed down the hallway to the men's room, she waited for him. It was quieter back there, the music not quite so loud, the laughter not quite so invasive.

He came out adjusting his belt. When he saw her, he stopped short. "What," he said.

Cass took a breath and held it for a second. She hadn't told anyone yet. Maybe hadn't even completely accepted it herself, because words were powerful and she was hesitant now to release them into the realness of the world. She let out her breath.

"I'm pregnant."

Chapter III

The disgust on his face was worse than a full-windup backhand. "Didn't take you long."

Which didn't even make sense at first. Take her long for what?

"My brother's been gone a month and you've already dropped your panties for some other guy? Nice work, Cass. You're a class act."

Her empty tray clattered to the floor as she grabbed fistfuls of his shirt. "It's *his*, you idiot." She was up in his face, so close she could've bitten him. "You stupid, spoiled asshole. *Ben's baby.*"

She shoved him away from her, surprised that even at her size and on tiptoes, she had the momentum to send him staggering back a step. Her fist itched to hit him, but a strangely insistent urge sent her past him and out the back door into the alley by the dumpster. She stood there in her flimsy uniform, steam snorting out of her nose like a dragon in the cold night air. The stench of a week's worth of garbage filled her lungs, and she heaved the contents of her stomach off the end of the loading dock. She'd been nauseated for weeks, but this was the first time she'd actually thrown up, the dumpster and her own rage joining forces to overwhelm her.

When it was over, she pulled a couple of cocktail napkins out of her apron and wiped her mouth, and all she could think was how strange her own vomit tasted. She was perfectly familiar with its usual flavor. This seemed like it belonged to someone else.

Oh, right, she realized. *There's no booze in it.*

After another minute or two her heart stopped pounding quite so hard and she was getting cold. She opened the door and went back in. The hallway was empty. In fact, when she came into the main room of the bar, Scott was nowhere to be seen.

Rogie came up beside her. "He left with someone else."

"Oh," she said, not sure of how to respond. Rogie seemed to think she'd be disappointed.

"I saw you two chatting it up. I was sure he'd hang out till closing and take you home."

Boy, did you guess wrong, she thought.

"Better luck next time." Rogie laughed languidly. One of the women he'd been flirting with came over, and he put an arm around her as the two of them left.

The goblin, giddy about the night's stellar take, offered Cass some extra shifts and a ride home. "Or you could come to my apartment . . ."

In the interest of future tips, she smiled and said, "It's been such a busy night, I'm just too tired." But she did let him drive her "home" to a random house a couple of blocks away from her illegal room in the crooked house.

*   *   *

THE next morning Cass woke to the sound of knuckles rapping on glass. A hulking shape cast a blurry silhouette against the curtains in the cellar door window. Who in holy hell could it be? No one she knew got up this early. Unless of course they'd never gone to sleep at all, in which case they were either still wasted or jonesing for more. Either way, not good.

More rapping. "Cass, it's me."

She sighed, wrapped the blanket over her threadbare pajamas, and let him in. Scott's face was puffy, eyes bloodshot. *Rough night*, she thought. Not like he didn't deserve it after what he'd said. She went back to the twin bed and sat down cross-legged with the blanket around her. She pulled out a sleeve of saltines from the box on the floor.

There was a rickety chair she'd scrounged from someone's sidewalk trash and Scott sat down in it. "You gonna offer me any?"

"Why? Are you pregnant?" She popped a cracker into her mouth and crunched hard.

He shifted in the seat and it tipped onto the shorter leg, creaking under his weight. He was bigger than ever, muscles like ham shanks in his shirtsleeves. She'd heard steroids could make you sterile. *Probably just as well*, she thought. *He's so spoiled, he'd make a terrible father.*

He looked around, revulsion obvious in the twitch of his lip and the way he kept his limbs tucked close to him. As if shabbiness were contagious.

"So," she said. "Social call?"

"I was thinking . . . you know, about last night. I just wanted to offer to pay for it if you wanted to get it . . . taken care of."

"An abortion."

"Yeah. I don't know how much those things go for, but it's gotta be upwards of a couple hundred bucks, and I would spot you for that."

Spot her for an abortion. Like he was covering the cost of a hamburger or a bus ride.

Be nice, she told herself. *He means well*. And she knew he did.

"Thanks," she said. "But I'm going to try and make a go of it."

His eyes narrowed. "Why?"

"Because it's Ben's baby, and I want it. Why's that so hard to understand?"

"Um, let's see." He leaned forward, his elbows on his thighs. "Maybe because you're a drunk who can't hold down a job for more than a month? Or because you don't even *know* any kids, much less how to take care of one? And did I mention the drunk part?"

"I told you I quit—"

"Cass, for chrissake! How many times did you say you'd quit? Or cut down? Or do it only on the weekends? Huh? Like a million?" He stood up and raked his fingers through his hair. It had been blond when they were in high school, but now it was the color of wheat toast. "Jesus," he said. "This is the worst idea you ever had."

"Thanks for the vote of confidence, asshole, but if I recall correctly—and I do because I'm sober and have been since the day I found out—you have exactly zero say in this decision."

"Well, shit, that's great and all, and I wish you well, but how long's it been? A couple weeks? Can you keep it up for eighteen years? Because that's what it takes, Cass. Eighteen years without a sip is a fucking long time for someone who's as much of a lush as you."

She flew at him then, the blanket falling away, but he caught her wrists before she could hit him, and twisted her around so she couldn't knee him in the nuts, which had been her next plan. She stomped on his foot, and he grunted in pain, but then he simply lifted her off the ground so she couldn't do it again.

"GET OUT!" she screamed. "Just leave me ALONE!"

He dropped her onto the bed, and her pajama top came up, revealing the soft belly in her otherwise too-thin frame. He stared at it, then his eyes rose to hers. "Don't do it." The words came out threatening and harsh, but she could hear a plea in it, too. "Don't do to this kid what our parents did to us."

He turned and walked out the door. In a second she was up and running after him.

"My mother was a good mother!" she screamed down the broken flagstone path at his back. *"She was GOOD!"*

He rounded the corner at the front of the house, and in another moment she heard a car door slam and an engine roar. The monstrous black SUV rocketed into traffic and was gone.

The flagstones were like ice beneath her bare feet, and she ran back inside and sank onto her bed, furious, crying, exhausted. And missing her mother, even after all these years.

Chapter IV

That night, business was slow, even for a Monday. Patrons seemed to know that the bar couldn't possibly be hit twice by the lightning strike of fame. There would be no second coming.

Cass watched the game on the bar TV as she waited for orders. The Sox were playing the Baltimore Orioles and it was not going well, especially for Scott McGreavy, who whiffed every time he got up to bat. When the camera came in close, Cass could see the look on his face, that blank, bad-news face, like the pitcher had just told him his dog died. Not that he had a dog.

She remembered him saying once, *Dogs—I don't get the appeal. Why would I go out and purchase the opportunity to pick up shit? I don't even want to deal with my own shit.*

Cass didn't like slow nights. More time to think about all that liquor just inches away. She reminded herself that she had another human being inside her, for whom alcohol was poison. This single fact had helped her get over the hump of that first achingly painful week. *Are you going to poison Ben's baby?* she would chastise herself. *Might as well feed it Drano.*

Drano, Drano, Drano, she would chant silently. But it wasn't working as well as it had the first time she thought of it. She tried switching to *Lysol,* but it didn't sound as bad as Drano, and she wondered if drinking Lysol really would kill you, or just make you puke a lot.

It was right before closing, and she was working really hard not to imagine what size purse she'd need to hide a bottle of that beautiful Grey Goose vodka, when Scott came in.

There were only a few patrons left, four or five older guys at the bar and two middle-aged women in a booth. One was crying and the other was stabbing her finger at the table and making strong arguments for something. Occasionally Cass could hear phrases like ". . . because they suck!" or "his loss!" The word *lesbians* came up, and this made the crier laugh through her tears.

The goblin was at Scott's side as fast as his squat legs could carry him, but his gaze flicked several times to the door. In fact, Cass noticed that everyone glanced at the door.

"On your own tonight, Mr. McGreavy?"

They're looking for Rogie.

"Yeah." Scott glanced at Cass, then away. "Glenlivet, straight up," he told the bartender. "Mind if I take this table over here?" The one farthest away from every other human being.

Cass got his scotch, and in the ten or twelve steps between the bar and his table, she seriously considered downing it. He wouldn't rat her out. He disliked her, but he was no snitch.

If you drink this, he'll be right about you. It was the only thing that kept the glass on the tray. "Twelve dollars," she told him as she put it on the table. He pulled out a twenty and when she went to make change from her tips, he waved her off. She wasn't too proud to keep it.

"When do you get off?" he asked her.

She tipped her head toward the goblin and murmured, "Depends on who he thinks he's got a better chance with, me or Crystal."

Scott glanced at the other waitress, an ungainly, snaggletoothed girl leaning against the wall and picking a fleck of mustard off her apron. "Who's he have a better chance with?"

"Not me, asshole."

He downed the scotch and motioned to the goblin. "Looking

pretty slow. Mind if I give her a ride home?" he said, indicating Cass.

"Of course not! No problem at all!" The goblin leered approvingly at her.

If I start drinking again and decide to kill myself, thought Cass, *I am definitely going to take him down first.*

She got the awful black funeral coat and buttoned it up. Though it was April, it was still weirdly cold, as if after a taste of spring, the seasons had decided to go backward. Scott was quiet on the ride home, and Cass counted her tips. He pulled into a spot in front of her house and put the car in park. "How'd you do?"

"Not as good as last night. How about getting Rogie to come in after every game?"

He chuckled. "Rogie does what he wants. And if Guttierez's back magically gets better, they'll send me down to Triple A as fast as I came up." He shook his head. "If I have another night like tonight, they might prefer him, body brace and all."

She had a moment of sympathy for him then. He'd clearly gotten all the stress genes in the family. And she knew he'd worked hard, obsessively even, to get as far as he had. She admired that about him. "Tomorrow'll be better," she said.

"Damn straight it will," he muttered. "Look, that's why I came here. You've got me all screwed up with this baby thing."

And there went her sympathy right out the SUV window. "If you think I'm having an abortion so you can play better *baseball,* then you can go—"

"All right, all right! But, Jesus, Cass. How the hell are you planning to stay on the wagon? You know what fetal alcohol poisoning is? Because I looked it up, and it sucks."

"I know, okay. Don't you think I know?"

"So are you doing AA or something?"

"No."

"Why in the hell not?"

"Because it's for a bunch of God-fearing idiots, all about higher power and handing it over. To what? Something out there that doesn't exist? Oh, yeah. That'll work."

He studied her. "That's Ben talking."

"Yeah, and he knew a thing or two."

Scott crossed his arms. "Look, I know how smart he was—no one knows better than me. He was a fucking genius. But that didn't make him right about everything. Christ, if he'd been that brilliant, he'd be living it up instead of dead from a completely preventable thing. If he was so smart, how come he died from stupidity?"

Cass wanted to defend Ben, and several retorts came to mind. Ben didn't die from stupidity. He died from a disease. But it was one in the morning, and every cell in her body ached for sleep. And Scotty was maybe, just a little bit . . . right. Which really pissed her off.

"Okay," said Scott. "What if I got you into one of those programs where you stay for a month and get really dried out? I'll pay for the whole thing."

Angry and exhausted, Cass said, "Why the hell do you care so much? This is not your kid! You have no responsibility here, which is just the way you like it."

The look on his face was strangely desperate. "Exactly! And if you screw this kid up, he'll come to me, won't he? I'll be doing for him what I did for Ben—cleaning up the messes." He slammed his fist against the steering wheel. "Goddamn it, Cass! You're condemning us all!"

Cass got out of the car. She couldn't listen anymore.

* * *

THREE days later, she was clearing a table at work. Someone had taken one, maybe two sips of the most gorgeous tequila sunrise. And then they'd walked away as if it meant nothing. How did it feel *not* to be hopelessly in love with booze? Cass couldn't even remember.

It was so beautiful, almost perfect. She could imagine that it had been a mistake—the customer hadn't ordered the tequila sunrise. It had really been meant for her. Drinking it would right a wrong. And then her lips were on the glass, and she was swallowing beauty.

No one saw her. But she told the goblin she was sick, needed to go home.

She didn't go home. She snuck into the back office and used the phone to call Scott.

Chapter V

The team doctor gave Scott a list of places. It took a week to find an open spot. Cass called the goblin and said she had mono. She stayed in her room in the basement and Scott came by every couple of days with groceries, always surprised to find her sober. One time he brought books, which caught her off guard. Scott got defensive. "You *like* books, remember?"

"How do you know that?"

"English class, senior year. You even liked that *Jane Ear*. Christ, that was painful."

It was all she could do not to correct him on the title, *Jane Eyre*, but she did laugh about it after he left. Books. She'd forgotten about that. The ones he brought were mostly paperbacks with high-heeled shoes and shopping bags on the covers. But there was one called *GPS Set to Joy: How to Reprogram Your Life to Locate Happiness*. She didn't read it, but she had to hand it to the author. Way to cash in on people's joylessness.

Cass decided to move out of the dingy apartment when she went to rehab; without work she couldn't afford the rent, pittance though it was. She stuffed her things into a sports duffel Scott had loaned her. Anything that didn't fit in the bag got left behind. Almost everything fit in the bag.

Scott insisted on driving her to the Justin Prescott Center

himself. Apparently it was named for a rich kid who didn't make it, and his parents gave the place a load of money anyway.

"I can take a bus," she said.

"I'll play a lot better if I actually see you walk in and know for certain I'm off duty for the next four weeks."

You're not ON duty, she wanted to say. *I never asked you to be!* But then she remembered she'd been the one to call him. He could have told her to jump in a lake, but instead he'd come in for the save. She kept her mouth shut and focused on the landscape streaming by. Trees and hills and more trees. Connecticut. She'd never seen a place so unpeopled.

The car was becoming uncomfortably quiet. In the early years of her relationship with Ben, they'd hung out with Scotty quite a bit, laughing and shooting the breeze without a second thought. That time was clearly past.

Maybe Scott felt the weight of the silence between them, too, because he tapped the button for the radio just as a new song came on.

Cass recognized the opening chords right away. Soulful and uplifting somehow in its sadness, it was Joni Mitchell's "A Case of You." *Blue* had been one of her mother's favorite CDs, and she'd played it till the scratches became an insult to the great Goddess Joni. Then she'd gone right out and bought another one, even though they couldn't afford it.

"I could drink a case of you, darling, and I would still be on my feet . . ."

Maybe not the most appropriate soundtrack for a trip to rehab, though, thought Cass.

Scott must have come to the same conclusion, because he thumped the power button and the car went silent again. But Cass could still hear it in her head and imagine her mom singing along and swaying to the tempo in their tiny apartment all those years ago.

* * *

AT first Cass actually liked rehab. It was the best hotel she'd ever stayed at. She figured the place was pretty high-end if so many professional athletes went there. At six foot eight, the point guard was easy to recognize. The right fielder and tight end took an extra minute or two. Without their uniforms, and with the worn-out, zombielike quality that was pretty common in the place, you had to squint a little to remember what they looked like on TV.

Cass's room was clean and sunny. The bed was comfortable. People complained about the food, but Cass ate more than she had in years. She liked the woods outside her window, and the smell of budding things. She imagined that maybe it was like going to camp, except that the campers here were really screwed up, and there were no swim lessons.

But what she liked best about rehab was feeling safe. Even safer than she'd felt with Ben, because she had to admit, Ben was not into safety. Not even a little.

Memory is a stained and threadbare thing for a ten-year alcoholic, but she could never quite obliterate her awareness of the constant danger that had snaked through their lives. They had narrowly escaped countless dicey situations. Occasionally Ben had been beaten, she'd been groped and slapped, and they'd had their belongings and what little money they had stolen. Only six months ago they'd been sitting on a park bench on the Boston Common early one morning, shaky and hurting, working on a plan to score some breakfast booze, and a homeless guy had come at them with a broken golf club. *My bench!* he'd hissed, the stench of human rot spewing at them. *My bench!* The jagged end of the club had hit Ben's cheek. The apostrophe-shaped scar was a constant reminder of the precariousness of their existence.

Freedom means risk, Ben would say. What Cass had only recently figured out was that for him it wasn't a trade-off. It was win-win. He'd loved freedom and risk in equal measure, which upped the danger in their lives from merely moderate to precipitously high.

Here at the Prescott Center, Cass felt safer than she had since her mother died. After that she'd endured a series of foster parents and group home staff who ran the gamut from well-intentioned but overworked to bad-tempered and degenerate. She'd been thirteen then and she was twenty-nine now. Sixteen years of never knowing who was coming for you—or worse, knowing *exactly* who was coming for you. Who wouldn't drink?

What Cass did not like about rehab was therapy and groups and all the higher power stuff. Her reaction was—Ben's word again—*ironic*. It was supposed to help, but it only made her want to drink in the worst way. All these strangers talking about their feelings, like it was a good thing. It was not a good thing. Might as well dance naked through a minefield.

She was distracted from her intense aversion to therapeutic intervention, however, by her loathing for her roommate, Laurel.

Cass had been sitting on her bed, sucking on a lollipop and reading one of the paperbacks Scott had gotten her. It was about a clothing designer with a shoe-buying compulsion, a high-society boyfriend, and a cat named Manolo. *This shit is hilarious*, thought Cass. It was like reading about the kooky shenanigans of aliens.

The door to her room flew open and banged against the wall. Framed in the doorway like some sort of refugee from a fashion runway stood a woman wearing high leather boots, black leggings, and an impossibly soft gray sweater that swept to her thighs. Her manicured fingers gripped the handle of a monogrammed suitcase. Mahogany hair dangled into her eyes and foundered around her sharp shoulders. Mascara puddled in the hollows beneath her lower lashes.

Cass was wearing clothes she'd lifted from a Goodwill box: peach-colored jeans and a green T-shirt that said BOY SCOUTS, LIVING THE ADVENTURE.

"Hi, I'm Cass."

The woman stared at her for a beat and said, "Laurel."

"Do people call you Laurie?"

"No," said Laurel. "They do not." She let her suitcase bang to the floor, turned, and left.

Cass caught a whiff of alcohol in her wake. It was pretty common. Some folks showed up completely wasted, having swallowed every substance they could get their hands on in the hours before they stared into the abyss of sobriety. Cass was glad she'd gotten over the worst of the withdrawal symptoms before coming to the Prescott Center. She could enjoy it that much more.

* * *

IN the following days, Cass watched Laurel throw tantrums over not having a private room, at having to use Prescott toiletries (no outside containers allowed), the cleanliness of the TV room, and the lack of nutritional information for the food. She'd even thrown a piece of cornbread on the floor and hissed, "This is horrid."

Cass had taken a bite of her own cornbread and thought, *Tastes pretty damn good to me.*

The one place Laurel was silent was in group. Cass was also fairly closemouthed, and it was nice to have someone else for the group to peck at to open up. In private sessions, Cass would say a little more. The guy was a professional—she figured he was paid to keep his mouth shut. But when she tried to explain that it was dangerous for people to know your business, not to mention your weaknesses, he said she had "trust issues."

Um, yeah, she thought. *Why doesn't everyone?*

One day, the group lady got down to business with Laurel. "You have four kids, right?" she said, glancing at a piece of paper in her hand. The other group members eyed one another.

"Don't talk about my kids," Laurel warned.

"That must be a lot of work. Does that stress you out, Laurel?"

"No, it does not *stress me out*," Laurel snapped back.

Group lady looked down at the paper. "Your husband is an executive who travels extensively. That must be kind of lonely."

Laurel rubbed at the white spots where her rings used to be. No jewelry allowed at Prescott. "No, it is not *lonely*," she retorted. "He calls several times a day from wherever he is. In fact this is the only time in our entire marriage that we've spoken so infrequently."

You'd need a locksmith and a stick of dynamite to get her to open up, thought Cass. It was the only thing she remotely liked about Laurel.

That afternoon, Cass went for a walk in the woods. The grounds were surrounded by a high fence so there was no worry of getting the urge to head toward civilization and liquor stores. You could urge all you wanted, you just couldn't do anything about it. She heard something, a birdcall, she thought. Cass didn't know the first thing about what birds sounded like in the wild, having spent her whole life in a city. It was a *huh-huh-huh* sound, then silence. It repeated over and over.

Cass came over the rise of a hill and saw Laurel crouched behind a big rock, arms wrapped around her shins, crying, *huh-huh-huh*; the silence was an intake of breath. When leaves crunched under Cass's feet, Laurel glanced up, then buried her head farther into her knees, her arm slashing out, waving Cass away. Cass went back to the Prescott Center.

The next day was Visitors' Day. No one came for either one of them.

* * *

ON Monday, group lady said, "So, Cass. You're pregnant."

Shit, here we go.

"How far along are you?"

"A couple of months, I think."

"You think?" said Laurel suddenly. "You don't know?"

"I can't afford a doctor."

"You're at the Justin Prescott Center! How in the world did you get in here if you can't afford a doctor?"

"A friend helped me out." Cass glanced around the room. All eyes on her, like ghouls from a nightmare.

Laurel continued her barrage. "A friend who spent thousands of dollars on rehab and didn't even send you for a pregnancy checkup? That's utterly ridiculous."

"Okay, that's enough, now," said group lady.

Laurel ignored her. "Not to mention there are free clinics and government programs. How could you be so irresponsible?"

Cass stood up. "I'm sorry if I spent too much time trying not to poison my baby with alcohol to go score some pregnancy vitamins. At least I'm quitting *now*, before he's born. By the way," she said, "how screwed up are *your* kids?"

* * *

CASS went out to a little pond on the grounds and threw every stone, stick, and hunk of moss she could find into the water. "Oh, *I'm* irresponsible," she muttered. "Well, I'm not the one who left four kids crying for their mama so I could go dry out for a month . . ."

What she wouldn't have done for a bottle of something. She couldn't make herself stop scanning the area, hoping maybe someone had a stash out here. *Under this rock? No? Then into the water you go, you useless hunk of mineral*, and she'd hurl it into the pond.

She had to admit she wasn't just angry at Laurel; she was also mad at herself for taking a potshot at Laurel's kids. It wasn't their fault—Cass knew that all too well. And Laurel had a point about not finding a clinic. It had occurred to Cass, but she was afraid the doctor would somehow know she was a drunk and . . . she didn't know what could happen. But what people didn't know, they couldn't use against you. She'd learned that from Ben.

Ben, who was now resting peacefully in the Market Street Cemetery. She missed him so much, and yet she was mad at him, too. *Look at this mess!* she wanted to tell him. *What am I going to do now? How am I going to keep this up for eighteen years?* Maybe Scotty was right.

By the time she came back it was dinnertime, and her stomach gurgled for food. *Hungry little person,* she told the baby. *You must have your uncle's appetite.*

She got her tray and sat down at an empty table but was soon joined by a guy from the therapy group, Tate Hogarth. Cass had recognized him right away. He'd been with half the major-league ball clubs in the country, and now played third base for the New York Yankees.

"Mind if I join you?" His travels had sanded the edges off his southern accent, but it was still softly noticeable.

"Not at all."

"Man, you took her down a peg," he said, chuckling conspiratorially. "It was all I could do to keep from applauding."

Cass frowned. "She's a piece of work, but I shouldn't have gone after her kids."

"In my experience—which is extensive," said Tate, "there's different kinds of drunks. We all hate ourselves for drinking. But she's the kind that also happens to think she's smarter than everyone else. They tend to be a mite intractable."

"My boyfriend was like that." As soon as it was out of her mouth, she couldn't believe it. Cass hadn't said a word about Ben since she'd been at Prescott, except briefly in private therapy.

"Is he your baby's daddy?"

"Yeah. Was. He died a couple of months ago."

Tate shook his head. "Sometimes life is just too cruel. How'd he go?"

"Alcohol poisoning."

His smile was knowing and sad. "Cassie-girl, you got your work cut out for you."

* * *

WHEN Cass went up to her room after dinner, Laurel had moved out. Cass didn't know if she'd left the program entirely, or simply transferred to another unit. She was glad for the peace and quiet, but a little part of her worried that she had pushed Laurel over the edge.

The next morning, the therapist told her, "It's almost the end of week three, Cass. Who would you like to invite here to talk with you about your sobriety?"

"I don't have anyone." The guy knew she was a foster kid, that her friends were partiers, and that Ben was dead. Why was he asking?

"You make phone calls occasionally. Who do you call?"

"My friend Kate. But half the time she's bombed."

"Is this a close friend?"

"Sort of, I guess." Several years ago Kate had dated a buddy of Ben's, and they'd had some wild times together. Then the guy went to jail for cashing stolen checks, and Kate had nowhere to go. Cass had taken her in. She had sporadic work as a dog groomer, depending on how hungover she was when she woke up.

"Will you be able to continue this friendship and still stay sober?"

Cass thought about it. "Not likely."

"I see. What about Mr. McGreavy? I understand he paid for your stay here."

"He's got a series in Seattle next week. But even if he didn't, he wouldn't come. We're not really friends. He's the baby's uncle and he wanted to get me off on the right foot with the pregnancy, and all. But honestly, I can't ask him for one more thing."

The therapist furrowed his brow. "Cass, you've done very well here, but if you have no support when you leave, I'm worried you'll be right back where you started."

That night she called Kate, who happened to be only a drink or two in, and explained about the visit. "Do you think you could make it?"

"I can't afford the bus ticket—I'm barely scraping the rent together as it is."

"Shit," said Cass. "I'm supposed to get someone to come and be . . ."

"Be what?"

"I don't know. Like supportive."

"Of not drinking?"

Cass sighed. "Yeah."

Kate chuckled. "Um, do they have to do it with a straight face?"

Cass laughed. "Shut up, this is serious! I'm in fucking rehab!"

"I know, I know!" Kate said, still giggling. "It's just—"

It's just there's no one, thought Cass, and it brought her up short. This was not funny. And it was going to be really not funny when she got out.

Where would she go? How would she live? Clearly working in a bar was a bad idea, but the tips weren't nearly as good at places that didn't serve liquor. She had no real skills, no home, no money, no sober friends. All she had was an addiction that ran her every waking moment.

* * *

CASS and Tate started hanging out a little bit, taking walks and watching TV at night together in the common room. Tate was a fan of *Extreme Couponing*. He admired the organization and determination it involved. "My mama's like that. Sixty-two years old and never paid full price for a single thing in her life."

Cass was more fascinated by the quantities. What would anyone actually do with twenty-two bottles of laundry detergent, once the cameras stopped rolling?

"So," Tate said one night after the show was over, and they were still sitting there on the couch. "Looking forward to busting out of here?"

She looked at him, uncertain how to answer. He just smiled that slow, sad smile of his and said, "Me neither."

"How come?"

"Oh, you know. This is hard and all, but at least you're surrounded by people who get it, who won't say, 'Ah, come on, just a coupla beers—you'll be fine.'"

The ever-present ache of fear swelled in Cass's chest. She found herself telling him how she had nothing to go back to, and she couldn't ask the baby's uncle for one more favor.

"Whoever he is, you being sober must've meant something to him, or he wouldn't have sent you down here at considerable personal expense. He's got an investment in you now. Call him and see what you can work out. Think about what you can offer, and see if he'll make a deal. Heck, offer him a discount!" He smiled at her. "Everybody likes a bargain, Cass."

* * *

CASS kept up on Scott's series in Seattle. He played reasonably well, got some base hits, and in the last game, reached into the stands to catch a foul in the ninth for the win. She called the next morning.

"What's wrong?" he demanded.

"Nothing."

"You okay? Still playing by the rules?"

"Totally. Nice game, by the way. That was a great catch."

"Oh . . . thanks." He exhaled. "I almost didn't even go for it. It was over the stands and then the wind blew it in. Had to run like hell." They chatted about how lucky it was, and how all the guys thumped him black and blue when he got back to the dugout.

"So," he said. "How do you feel?"

"Squeaky clean. And hungry all the time. And a little bit . . . worried." She told him she didn't think she could go back to her friends in Brighton, couldn't trust herself to work in a bar.

"Where's this going, Cass?"

"What if I stayed with you?"

"Jesus!"

"I could clean your house, do your shopping, run any errand you want—for free! Just give me a place to stay where I can figure out what to do next. I'm offering you a bargain, Scotty. Please. Just give me a month."

Chapter VI

Scott did not drive to Prescott to get her. He met her at the bus station in Framingham. After scanning her for signs of slippage, he turned and let her carry her own bag to the car. Actually it wasn't even hers. It was the sports duffel he'd loaned her.

He lived in Wortherton on a leafy side street called Chickadee Circle. Cass had seen cul-de-sacs on TV, but she'd never seen one in real life. It had two houses at the end, and a basketball hoop on the edge of the circle of asphalt. Scott drove down the driveway to the right, as the garage door magically opened.

"Is that hoop private property or can anyone use it?" she asked. She had liked playing basketball in high school, though she'd never been on a team. She and Ben would shoot around sometimes, and it was one of the few things she'd been better at than him.

In fact, that's how they'd met. She'd been walking home from her sweeping job at Alba's Set and Go, past some guys playing a pickup game at one of the municipal courts. It was three on two. In a fit of . . . to this day, she didn't even know what—desperation for contact? a few bright moments in a gray-as-old-ladies'-hair existence?—she had called out, "Need another?"

The guys looked stupidly at one another as if she were speaking Latin.

"Nah," a chunky one had replied, at the very same time a tall, wiry one said, "How tall are you?"

Five foot four. That answer was not going to fly. "Tall enough to take you."

His grin—admiration for her cocky response laced with a touch of blooming desire—she would never forget it. He took her on his team, and when he missed an easy shot, he glanced at her with a look of apology and even shame at his own shortcoming. Ben was almost never ashamed, she would come to see, and that would turn out to be both a blessing and a curse.

"It's not your fault," she told him. "It's your hair. Keeps falling in your eyes."

"Who's got a knife?" he said, and all the other guys reached into their pockets.

"I've got scissors." She had filched a discarded pair out of the trash at Alba's. She cut his bangs, they won the game, and they fell hard for each other right then and there.

Scott broke her reverie. "You're not here to play basketball."

No, she certainly wasn't.

The house was a large center-entrance colonial, pale gray with black shutters, tidily kept but otherwise nondescript. They went from the garage into a little area for taking off coats. "No shoes in the house," he told her. "Now that you're here, you gotta follow the rules."

Cass slipped off her sneakers, thinking most of the places she'd lived lately she'd preferred to keep her shoes on, even in bed.

The kitchen looked like the set of one of those suburban-drama TV shows: honey-colored cabinets, speckled granite countertops, and a big island in the middle with three matching barstools. It opened onto a family room with an enormous black leather sectional sofa, and a TV that took up half the wall. A low glass-and-chrome cabinet beneath it held a stack of electronic components. This area looked more like something out of a beer commercial, except there were no bottles or pizza boxes. In fact the whole place was as neat as a furniture showroom.

"Hungry?" he asked.

She was ravenous, but she wanted to take care of business first. "I have a plan," she said, rooting around in the duffel bag and pulling out a piece of lined paper.

"Must be pretty complicated if you had to write it down," he snickered.

She ignored this. She and Tate had worked on the plan together, and the only part that was not written on the paper was *Do not fight with Scotty.* It was the most important part, so she was determined not to blow it before she'd even unpacked.

She smoothed out the paper on the cold granite. "Here's what I need to get done in the next month so I can go on my own. Some things cost money, but they're an investment." She looked him in the eye. "This whole plan is an investment in me being sober and a good mom, and you being free and clear with no drama. That's what you want, right?"

"Hell, yeah."

"Okay, so that's going to require a"—she glanced at the paper for the words—"an initial outlay of cash, but I'll pay you back every penny and work for free while I'm here." She looked up at him. "See, I made it a good deal for you. You get everything back and then some."

He made no effort to conceal his skepticism. "Right. Just get to the list."

"Well, the first ones don't cost anything. I have to get on the state health insurance and get a doctor, and I have to go to an AA meeting every day. I looked it up at Prescott, and there's a meeting at a church about a mile from here, so that's no problem. But depending on where the doctor is, I might need you to take me."

He nodded. She was glad the first part was easy.

"The next thing is a combo, it hits two goals with one stone. I need to get some job skills so I can maybe work in a day care, and I need to learn more about babies and kids. Like you said, I don't know anything about that." It killed her to admit that he'd made a good point, but Tate had assured her that telling a guy he was right stoked up his ego like nothing else.

"So I'm going to take an online course on child development. But you'd have to pay for it and let me use your computer."

He shrugged. She took it as a yes.

"Also, if I'm going to try and get a job at a day care center, I'll need some new clothes—just a few—and a haircut." Her auburn-colored hair was so split at the ends it created a sort of halo of frizz around her head.

"Fine," he said, glancing down at the paper. "What's that last one?"

"Oh, um, my friend put that on there. He says if you're a grown-up, you should know how to drive. But I don't have to. It's not critical."

"Friend?" His eyes narrowed. "You hooked up in *rehab*?"

Do not fight with Scotty, do not fight with Scotty . . .

She kept her voice low, but it was a tad menacing anyway. "Let's get one thing straight. I have not slept with another guy since I met your brother. Not ever, not even the times we were broken up. I was true to him. And even though he's dead and I am completely free to sleep with *whoever I want* . . ." She paused for emphasis. ". . . I have a baby coming. Trust me when I say, I am not getting distracted by some dude."

Scott got up and opened the fridge. He pulled out deli meat, mayonnaise, and mustard and got bread from a cabinet drawer. He put these and a plate on the counter by her list.

"I'll teach you to drive," he said. "Make yourself a sandwich."

* * *

UPSTAIRS there were three bedrooms, plus a master suite. Scott obviously had the master, so he pointed to the other three and said, "Pick one."

Cass chose the one closest to the bathroom and walked in. It had a four-poster bed, a dresser, and a photograph of dolphins jumping out of the ocean on one wall. The furniture was simple but elegant, made of some kind of blond wood. The walls were a soft blue, and the quilt on the bed had a blue-green pattern that she immediately loved.

"You picked out all this stuff?" she asked.

"Nah, the lady next door's a decorator. I gave her a budget, and she took the ball and ran with it." He chuckled. "I think I've only been in here once," he said. "Well, I'll leave you to it."

Cass ran her hand over the quilt. Tiny squares of teal and cobalt, emerald and chartreuse. An ocean of color. So beautiful. She opened the duffel bag and pulled out her ratty clothes. The pajamas were gray and threadbare. She wouldn't feel right sleeping in such a lovely room with nasty pajamas. Scott had said he would buy her some clothes . . .

"Hey," she called out. "You got a Walmart around here?"

* * *

SCOTT was not a fan of Walmart. "I hate to shop," he said on the way to the Natick Mall. "So if I'm gonna buy something, it better last."

It had been so long since she'd bought new clothes, Cass found it overwhelming. She went for the clearance racks, but even they were so jammed full of things . . . She looked at Scott.

He sighed. "Okay, what are you, a small?"

"I guess. But I'm going to get bigger, so I need things roomy."

"All right, here." He pulled a shirt from the mediums on the nearest rack. "And this one."

They went rack by rack, Scotty handing her things, Cass taking them to the dressing room, rejecting most based on fit or cost, but holding on to a growing pile of keepers. She particularly liked a loose pink top that made her cheeks look rosy and set off her green eyes. In recent years, she and Ben had washed their clothes less and less, and Cass had avoided pink. It got dirty too fast.

Next she needed a nightgown and underwear.

"You're on your own in that department," he said.

When she'd finished, Cass found Scott in the men's section by a display of sweaters. There was a heathered blue V-neck she liked, and it was marked down to twenty dollars. She pulled out an extralarge and put it with her pile.

"What's that for?"

"For you. It's like a bonus for helping me out."

"Yeah, except I'm paying for it. Am I giving *myself* a bonus?"

"No." She was about to get irritable, but then she remembered Rule Number One of her plan. "This all goes on the ledger of money I owe you. So while I'm not paying for it *now*, I will be paying for it someday. You can charge me interest if you like."

Sufficiently shamed, he rolled his eyes. "I'm not charging you interest, for chrissake."

"Thanks. And I hope you like your bonus. It's a good color for you. Goes with your eyes." They were blue gray, just like the sweater.

* * *

LATE that night Cass put on her new nightgown and slid beneath the covers in the four-poster bed. In the dark she could see moonlight sifting in around the edges of the curtains, and as her eyes adjusted, the outlines of the room came into view. Right angles, straight lines. Nothing lopsided or propped up. Everything set squarely where it ought to be. The opposite of life as she'd known it for a very long time. Cass started to cry.

She missed Ben, wished so much that he could be there with her in the crisp sheets, his long wiry arms around her, telling her secrets, making her laugh. His quick wit and wry observations had always softened the harsh edges of their existence.

But this room was no harsh life. And Ben might have enjoyed the comfortable bed, but he wouldn't have cared all that much about the rest of it. He had always been perfectly fine with the general lopsidedness and propped-up-ness of the world.

She'd admired that about him—his ability to be comfortable anywhere, to find humor in anything. She had strived to be more like that. But when his unwillingness to avoid harder times and harsher people led to serious danger, her anxiety had become unbearable, and she had left him to find shelter with more benign friends, like Kate.

He absorbed knowledge like a prodigy. She'd once watched an old guy in a park teach him how to play chess, and had smiled unsurprised when he'd won the second game, infuriating the older man. But he'd been disdainful of anything remotely status quo, always thinking he could game the system. Ben McGreavy had been too smart to live a smart life.

But, boy, did she miss him.

She sobbed quietly into her pillow, dampening it, ruining the crispness, and she desperately wanted something to soothe the hurt. That kind of pain seemed so wrong in such a beautiful room. She found herself wondering whether Scott had locked up the liquor.

She heard a door open, the muted creak of footsteps on the carpet runner in the hallway. It stopped outside her door. She left off crying and held her breath, more from habit than from actual fear. After a moment the footsteps receded.

He's like a cop, she thought, *driving slowly through a seedy neighborhood, snooping for trouble.*

He can't watch you every minute came the dark whisper of booze in her head.

There was an Alcoholics Anonymous meeting at nine the next morning at St. Vincent Church in Wortherton Village. It couldn't come soon enough.

* * *

Cass had been to AA meetings, even before rehab. Several times when things had gotten particularly crazy with Ben and she'd left him, she had tried to do something about her drinking. AA was free and meetings were everywhere. The first time she'd felt nearly paralyzed with shame and fear, having no idea of what to expect, but knowing one thing for sure: Alcoholics Anonymous was about facing facts. No more lying to yourself about how your drinking isn't that bad, you're in control, you're not really an alcoholic. You *are* an alcoholic. Hence the name.

The few meetings she'd gone to were not as bad as she'd anticipated. People were nice. But it had never quite taken. She'd found reasons not to like it. All that higher power stuff and saying the Lord's Prayer—it wasn't her. At least it wasn't her anymore. Her mother had taken her to church regularly as a child, and she'd loved lighting the little red votive candles and saying a prayer.

Her childhood prayers had been so simple. A new coat. Dinner at a nice restaurant. A trip to Canobie Lake Park up in New Hampshire. None of those prayers had ever been answered. Her clothes were hand-me-downs or things that people forgot to pick up at the dry cleaner where her mother worked. They never had the money to go out to dinner, much less buy tickets to an amusement park. But she kept praying; it was nice to imagine those things might come someday.

Cass stopped praying when her mother died. There was only one thing she wanted then; God had taken it, and He wasn't sending it back.

At the Prescott Center, though, AA was touted as the single best thing an alcoholic could do to increase the odds of staying sober, so Cass had resigned herself to just ignoring all the religion stuff. It seemed a small price to pay for better odds.

She rose quietly in the morning. Scott had a home game at seven that night, and he'd told her that he liked to get as much sleep as possible before heading in to Fenway. She went downstairs and looked through his kitchen cabinets and found the cereal: Cocoa Puffs, Honey Smacks, Froot Loops, and Apple Jacks. On the end was an unopened box of crunchy granola.

Maybe he's just using it as a bookend. She opened it and poured a bowlful.

By eight thirty she was on her way to St. Vincent's, walking through a misty rain with an umbrella she'd found in the hall closet. New sobriety was a delicate thing, and hers was only about six weeks old, as vulnerable and demanding as a newborn baby.

Cass tried to distract herself from the constant whine of her craving by taking in the scenery, focusing on some lovely red flowers as she passed a well-tended garden. But the color reminded her of red wine . . . vodka and cranberry juice . . . a maraschino cherry in a Manhattan. Booze seemed to be her brain's default setting. She wondered if it could ever be reset.

As much as she clearly needed the meeting, the sight of St. Vincent's stony exterior caused her anxiety to rise like a geyser. What if it wasn't like those other times? What if people looked at her with accusing eyes and said . . . What? Join the club?

She forced herself to march down the stone steps into the church basement. Scanning the room from the doorway, she saw things she'd seen at other meetings: the basket of raffle tickets, the blue velvet flags with the AA sayings, the coffee with the sugar packets and creamers. *Is there a kit?* she wondered. *Somebody wants to start an AA group, and they get this huge box in the mail with a coffee maker and signs and a roll of raffle tickets?*

A caramel-colored man with thinning white hair approached. "You are new?" he asked.

"No, I . . . Yes . . . I'm new here. But not to this"—she gestured vaguely—"concept."

"On vacation?"

"No . . . Well, sort of."

He smiled gently and made no sudden moves. "Welcome," he said.

Holy crap, pull yourself together!

"Come sit at my table. The old-timers." He made a small beckoning gesture. She followed him, trying to loosen her grip on the umbrella handle enough to maintain blood flow in her hand. She sat in the seat he pulled out for her. The others—three wizened gentlemen in various states of toothlessness, and an impeccably dressed older woman—looked up expectantly. From the corner of her eye, Cass saw the banner that said "Keep It Simple."

"I'm Cass," she said. They all greeted her warmly with names she forgot immediately.

On Mondays it was an open meeting, so anyone could come and listen to the speakers. Cass glanced around the room at the other attendees. Some were chatting or laughing with one another. Some were staring straight ahead, clutching their raffle tickets. A table of teenage girls did their best to lounge casually on the metal folding chairs and look pulseless. Their adult chaperone checked her watch and turned off her cell phone.

A middle-aged man in jeans and a T-shirt promoting Frissore Construction stood behind a podium. "Hi, I'm Angelo, I'm an alcoholic." The group responded with the customary, haphazard "Hi, Angelo." The girls said nothing, except for one, who just said, "Dude."

"Just for a surprise, we're gonna start with the preamble," Angelo said with a grin. This provoked chuckles from the group, except for the girls, and except for the older woman, who glanced at Cass and rolled her eyes. Cass smiled back.

The preamble, the joking, the all-walks-of-life-ness—it was like the other meetings she'd been to. She could feel her shoulders loosen just a little.

"Alcoholics Anonymous is a fellowship of men and women,"

Angelo read, "who share their experience, strength, and hope with each other . . ."

* * *

AFTER the first couple of speakers there was a break, and Cass got anxious. She didn't like coffee and didn't have to go to the bathroom; should she just sit there and stare into space?

"Cass, is it?" the older woman next to her asked in a round, elegant tone. Cass was somehow able to retrieve the name Jackie. The woman went on. "I'm always so discomfited when I travel and go to a new meeting." She ran a ringed finger over the table. Cass wondered if she would inspect it for dust. "But after a few moments, I find myself taken aback by the sameness of it. We drunks are at least reliable in that one regard, aren't we?"

Cass nodded. It was an interesting point.

"Are you new here in Wortherton?" Jackie asked.

"Yes, but I'm not staying long. About a month. Then I'll probably move back to Boston."

"I'm visiting, too. Dear friends. And loyal. My goodness, the first time my husband and I came, I became so inebriated that they rushed me to the hospital. I can't say I have fond memories, but it was a watershed moment in my life. I entered treatment—for the third time—and never drank again." She clasped her hands and set them on the table. "It'll be thirty years on December twenty-seventh."

"That's my birthday. No kidding, it's the actual day I was born. I'll be thirty."

Jackie placed her hand lightly on Cass's arm. "Then it was a good day for both of us."

* * *

THE meeting ended, as it had every time Cass had gone, and perhaps as it did all over the world, with the group forming a circle.

Hands were held, and the Lord's Prayer recited. Cass mumbled along. ". . . lead us not into temptation . . ." Jackie's hand was smooth and dry.

My mother's hand might feel like this if she were still alive, Cass thought. She glanced around the circle, and then her heart almost stopped. A familiar face.

Laurel.

No! Cass almost said out loud. *You can't be serious!*

Her mind reeled. Laurel had definitely not been there at the beginning. She must have come in late and sat in the back.

The prayer was over and people were turning to leave. "It was so good to meet you, Cass," Jackie said. "I'll think of you when you and my sobriety turn thirty. I'll wish us both a happy birthday."

Cass scurried out with her, desperate for conversation. "Are you going upstairs to Mass?"

"No, dear, I'm not Catholic. Not particularly religious at all, really."

"Does all the higher power stuff bother you?"

"It did at first. But then I realized I was grasping at anything that would keep the bourbon at hand. Besides, there has to be something greater than me." She smiled. "Doesn't there?"

Cass had to admit that the idea of humans as the greatest, wisest beings in the universe did seem a little depressing.

They said good-bye and Cass made her way quickly down the sidewalk. But someone behind her was faster, heels clacking aggressively against the concrete. "Just a minute, there."

What was Cass going to do, break into a sprint? She turned around. "Hi," she said evenly, but Laurel was already talking.

"You can't come here," she said. "This is my regular meeting, and I need it."

"I need it, too."

"Go somewhere else. Start drinking again, I don't care what you do, but for the love of God, don't come back."

Chapter VII

When Cass got to Scott's, he was in the kitchen eating Apple Jacks out of a mixing bowl.

"Does your trainer know how you eat?" said Cass.

"It's got vitamins and fiber and shit." He tapped the box with his finger, his mouth still full of little orange Os. "It's, like, healthy."

Cass rolled her eyes and dropped onto a stool next to him. She could tell he was looking at her in his peripheral vision. "Yes, I went to AA, okay? You happy?"

"Happy as a clam at high tide." He crunched on his Apple Jacks and eyed her. "I thought AA was supposed to be all supportive and everything. You look like you just got slapped."

Cass sighed. "I had this roommate at rehab . . ." She told him the whole story, even how she'd laced into Laurel about screwing up her kids.

"Ouch," said Scott. "That's pretty cold."

"I know. . . . So maybe I kind of owe her this. Except the next closest AA meeting is five miles away, and that's a lot of walking."

"Hold on." He tossed the spoon into the mixing bowl with a clatter. "You're actually considering walking five times farther just because this rich bitch doesn't want you there?"

"I feel bad—"

"She went after you first! She asked for it. And I don't know much about AA, but I'm pretty sure no one gets dibs on a group. Come on, Cass, you're tougher than that. Screw her."

Cass smiled. *Screw her. Sounds like a plan.*

Then she remembered Laurel's point about not having medical care. "All right, but I'd feel a lot better if I had health insurance and a doctor's visit scheduled."

He led her to the computer in the den, which was paneled in dark wood and had an entire wall of bookshelves. Cass was pretty sure Scott had never read any of the books, mostly classics. But there was one she knew he'd read: *Jane Ear*. She hid her grin at the sight of it.

The long curving legs of the huge desk had claws at the bottom clutching little spheres. Two leather armchairs sat by the window with a round glass-topped table in between.

Why does every room in his house look like the set from a TV show?

Cass had been on library computers fairly often, so she got the hang of it quickly. She filled out forms for the Massachusetts state health care plan, and found the Women, Infants, and Children's program. Scott checked on her occasionally.

"So I found a clinic—actually two clinics," she told him. "One's near here, and one's in Brighton. I won't be here long, so I guess I should probably start in Brighton."

Scott made a face. "I don't want to drive all the way in there. Besides, being back in the old stomping grounds so soon is a bad idea. Go to the one near here, and transfer your records to Brighton when the time comes."

Cass wanted to tell him to quit giving orders. But she reminded herself she was reliant on him for rides, no matter which location she chose. She should keep her mouth shut. For now.

She made an appointment at the Waverly Community Health Center, then turned her attention to finding an online course on child development. She had tried to get a day care job once, but centers generally wanted to see some relevant coursework. Cass hoped she could get a position that included child care for the baby as a benefit.

Around three o'clock, Scott popped his head in the door. "I'm heading to Fenway."

"Okay," she said, suddenly feeling strange about being alone all afternoon and evening.

"You all right?"

"Yeah, fine."

"I locked up the liquor."

Her back went up. She hated his constant suspicion, even if she deserved it.

"Don't wait up," he said. "I'll be home pretty late."

"I know. I'll probably watch the game."

"Yeah, uh . . . later than that. Like maybe not till morning."

"Oh."

"So . . ." He looked at the books, the desk, the carpet. Anywhere but at her.

"Got it," she said.

"See you tomorrow." And he left.

She wondered if he was seeing someone or just anticipating a postgame hookup with a random adoring fan. She knew he'd had occasional relationships, but usually during the off-season, and none for longer than a few months. Baseball always came first, and even when he was in the minors he refused to let anyone or anything become a distraction. In fact it had been his biggest gripe with "Ben Drama," as he called it. Not the money or the heartache of seeing his brother waste so much potential. Scott's greatest complaint was that it messed up his game.

Cass went back to her search for a child development course. After following what seemed like hundreds of links, she decided on Child Learning and Development at UMass Online. It had good financial aid potential and was part of a Bachelor of Arts program.

If she kept going, she could eventually become a college graduate. She smiled at the thought. Wouldn't that be something to add to her crinkled one-page plan!

Tate would be so proud. It was the first she'd thought of him in the twenty-four hours since she'd left the Prescott Center, and she suddenly had an urge to tell him about how much of their plan she'd already accomplished. But they had never exchanged phone numbers or email addresses. Cass didn't have a phone number to offer—she'd given up her cell phone a few years ago due to lack of funds and Ben's fury over the idea that "they" were tracking everywhere you went and everything you said.

Also, while there had never been any spark of attraction between her and Tate, exchanging information would have felt like opening that door, even if just a toe's width. Cass needed all her concentration to stay the course of sobriety and to prepare for motherhood. In that sense at least, she and Scotty had something in common. Neither of them was opening any doors for anyone.

* * *

By late afternoon Cass had officially signed up for the course, which began in a couple of weeks. Suddenly a huge racket started up in the backyard. Through the TV room window, she saw a kid standing next to a lawn mower, which was sending up puffs of smoke. He wore a knit cap from which sandy-colored curls escaped at the nape of his neck. Adjusting his earbuds, his head started to bob slightly. Then his whole body began to move, hips sliding back and forth, arms loose in their sockets, one foot coming up for a moment, then the other.

Cass watched him dance, smiling to herself. He seemed so . . . untroubled. Nothing on his mind other than the bliss of a good tune. There had been so few moments like that during her own teenage years, and it occurred to her that what she wanted most in the world was for her child to have countless moments of un-complicated, undiluted happiness.

If I can keep my act together, he has a chance.

After a minute, the boy's body slumped, and she knew the song must be over. He stared wearily at the lawn mower, then flopped his hands onto the handle and started across the grass. Cass went back to the computer to google books on pregnancy and child development. The library was a half mile away. She'd go tomorrow and see what she could find on the shelves.

By then it was five o'clock.

Happy hour.

How's that lock on the liquor cabinet? came the dark whisper in her head. *Pickable?*

She wanted to watch TV to distract herself, but there were too many remote controls with too many buttons, and she could not get the thing to work.

Just a sip.

Okay, she told the darkness. *You want to know for sure how strong that lock is? Let's go.*

The liquor cabinet was in the dining room, below a wooden plaque that held Scott's bat from high school, the one that had been signed by the whole team the year they won the state championship. The cabinet was glass and chrome like the one by the TV, filled with gorgeous bottles of happiness staring out at her, practically taunting her. It had a stainless-steel lock inset on the front, and Cass could tell that it wouldn't be easy to pick. Of course the glass would be *very* easy to break . . .

The sound of the lawn mower cut out. Cass continued to stare at the bottles.

The doorbell rang. She sighed and went to answer it.

The boy was startled to see her, clearly expecting Scott. "Oh, um, sorry, I thought . . ." His eyes were red. She figured it was allergies from mowing the lawn.

"Scott's at Fenway," she told him. "There's a game tonight."

He gave a little apologetic shrug. "I don't really follow the Sox."

"Is there something you need?"

"Well, he's supposed to pay me on the tenth, and that was yesterday."

"How much?"

"Twenty-five a week, so a hundred."

"Hang on." Cass went upstairs. She had about a hundred and twenty dollars left from her waitressing tips, which she kept in an envelope at the back of her closet.

When she came back and handed him five twenties, his face lit up. "Awesome! Thanks." He looked at her a moment. "So are you, like, living here now?"

"No, just visiting."

He nodded knowingly, and she wanted to say, *You don't know anything, you little twerp, so don't act all clued in.*

But that could get back to Scott, which would cause a fight, breaking Rule Number One. Instead she said, "Hey, what do you know about getting a really massive TV to work?"

They chatted briefly as he tried different combinations of button-pushing. His name was Andrew, but he went by Drew. He was almost fourteen, in eighth grade, and he lived next door. Soon he had the TV going and showed her how everything worked.

"I hope you have a nice long visit," he said on the way out.

"Thanks," she said. *Big huge thanks.* He'd gotten her away from the liquor cabinet, solved her entertainment problem, and reminded her of the innocence of youth. She made herself dinner and watched the game. The Sox won. Scotty would be out "celebrating." She locked up, set the house alarm, and got into bed, relieved to add one more day onto her count of sober ones.

* * *

WHEN Cass went downstairs the next morning, Scott was sitting at the kitchen island drinking coffee and reading the sports section.

"Reliving the glory?" she said with a smile.

He grinned back. "Never thought I'd get my name in the paper for anything good."

"You were in the paper all the time in high school. Scott McGreavy, sports miracle."

"Before that. I didn't get in trouble like Ben, but I only had half his brains. Probably would've ended up on the back of a garbage truck if I hadn't had a decent throwing arm."

"You lucked out."

Scott looked away. "Yeah, that's what Ben used to say. As if I didn't have to work hard, too. Like everything was handed to me with a glass of champagne and a bowl of caviar."

Cass didn't like where this was going. "Hey, have you ever actually tried that stuff?"

"Once." He laughed. "That is some disgusting shit—like you just took a bite out of Boston Harbor at low tide. I had to spit it in my napkin when no one was looking."

She grinned. "Oh, by the way, the kid was here mowing the lawn yesterday," she said. "He said you always paid him on the tenth, so I gave him a hundred from my tip money."

"You shouldn't have. His mom doesn't like him to have cash. She asked me to write checks to her and she puts it in a savings account for him."

"What's the problem with cash? It's his money, he earned it."

"She says he's been spending it on stuff she doesn't approve of. Sketchy video games, I'm guessing." Scott shrugged. "No big deal. I'll let her know what happened." He pulled out his wallet and slid the reimbursement over to her. "But don't let him scam you again."

Scott had an afternoon game and left the house around the

same time that Cass headed out to her AA meeting, so he gave her a ride. "Hang tough with that rich bitch," he said as she got out of the car. She would certainly try.

On Tuesdays it was a closed discussion meeting, which meant that they would be talking to one another rather than listening to speakers. The folding chairs in the church basement were set in a circle. There would be no avoiding Laurel's radioactive glare.

Jackie, the older woman from the previous meeting, was there, wearing a cream-colored suit, her French-twisted hair spun perfectly about her head like white cotton candy. Cass headed toward her like a shipwrecked sailor to a lifeboat. "I didn't think you were coming back!"

"Cass, how nice to see you again. We've had a slight delay, so I decided to come to one more meeting." Jackie gazed at her a moment. "Feeling a bit nervous?"

"Yeah. New meeting, new people. It's a little . . ."

"Daunting."

Yeah, really freaking daunting, thought Cass. *Like terrifying.*

Jackie took her hand and led her to two seats next to each other. Cass was sorry when Jackie's motherly hand released hers. Especially with Laurel sitting right across from them, eyes like twin machine guns trained on Cass, a hand to hold on to would've been nice.

The meeting began, and the leader asked if anyone wanted to share. Jackie leaned over and whispered, "I'll go first and then you follow."

"My name is Jackie," she began. "I've been sober for twenty-nine years."

"Hi, Jackie," the group responded.

"I'm here visiting friends with my husband, and he's taken ill. Just a cold, but he has a heart problem and I get so worried that he'll . . ." She took a breath, composed her features. "He's my champion. All these years, he's stood by me, but never let me get away with one bit of bad behavior. He confronts me fiercely, but with such love, such certainty in my ability to stay the course." She smiled sadly. "But one day death will part me from my dearest friend. I've been thinking about that a great deal lately. If he precedes me, I can't imagine how I'll continue. Twenty-nine years of sobriety will seem like tissue paper against the storm of my alcoholism. Who'll be there to halt my descent?"

"Thank you, Jackie," said the leader, a balding man whose paunch pressed out from his button-down shirt. "Just thinking about losing someone we love can sure bring on the demons. Would anyone else like to go?"

Jackie nudged Cass with her elbow.

"Uh, I'm Cass."

"Hi, Cass."

"So I'm new." She laughed nervously. "But you know that." She tried not to look in Laurel's direction, but her eyes felt like compass needles swinging uncontrollably toward Laurel's magnetic north. Cass took a breath. *One word at a time*, she told herself.

"I'm pregnant. Staying sober for the baby." They all nodded encouragingly—everyone but Laurel. "I've got thirty-nine days. Would've had fifty-three if I hadn't taken a sip off a customer's drink at the bar I used to work at."

Been-there smiles from a few of the group. A look of disgust from Laurel.

"The baby's father died two months ago. Alcohol poisoning. His brother sent me to rehab, and I'm staying with him for the next month, trying to get on my feet. I'll be leaving after that. But until then, I'll be here every day." She eyed Laurel hard. "Every single day."

* * *

AFTER the meeting Cass made her way to the Wortherton Public Library, an old building that had recently been gutted and renovated. A plaque named the major donors to the renovation. Scott McGreavy was not listed, nor did she expect him to be. But she checked anyway.

It was a palace compared to the city libraries she was used to—a Cinderella's castle of books. Cass liked the smell of all that paper, and the visual of the brightly lit, tidily kept shelves. As a child she had loved books. Strange that she'd needed Scott to remind her.

She found the pregnancy books she'd located online the night before and carried the stack over to a table. Sitting in a swath of sunlight, she was soon overwhelmed. Staying sober was a good start, but apparently, that was all it was—a start. There were special pregnancy diets and exercise regimens, music to be played and books to be read to her unborn child, and her personal favorite: stress to be avoided. (*Good fucking luck with that*, she told the book.)

One thing at a time. One stupid pregnancy rule at a time.

She shelved all the books but one, *The Normal Person's Guide to a Sane Pregnancy*. It had doable recommendations, like no bungee jumping or pie eating contests.

It was almost one in the afternoon, and Cass's stomach growled. After applying for a card and checking the book out (the librarian wanted some form of identification but gave Cass a break when Cass said she didn't have a driver's license and was just visiting), she stopped in the library foyer, suddenly uncertain about going back to Scott's. It was just so . . . empty there. Except for the liquor cabinet. That was full.

She dawdled, reading the community bulletin board. Lost cats, bikes for sale, Wortherton High School students performing a cappella. A poetry reading, a banjo concert, a fundraiser for a new playground. (What was wrong with the old playground?)

Finally she gripped the book in front of her like a battle shield, forced herself to venture out into the sunlight, and headed back to Chickadee Circle.

* * *

THE Sox lost, so Cass assumed Scott was unlikely to go out "celebrating." She tidied up the kitchen then pulled out the vacuum and ran it over the downstairs carpets.

Five o'clock. Happy hour.

She closed the door to the dining room, home of the evil glass liquor cabinet, and put a kitchen stool in front of it. She wrote the word *BABY* in big letters on a piece of paper, taped it to the chair back, and stood in the kitchen staring at it.

For the love of God, DO SOMETHING.

The pregnancy books had said that eating healthy was important. She would make dinner.

One seriously healthy-ass dinner, coming up.

She threw together a tomato sauce with ingredients she pillaged from the cabinets. Scott would be hungry after his game. She made a double batch. She could freeze the extra.

The bag of green beans in the freezer was dusted with frost, but the book said green vegetables were important, so she took a chance on their vintage. She improvised garlic bread from a loaf of sandwich white, slathering it with butter and sprinkling with garlic salt.

He should be home soon.

She set the table. Boiled the water for pasta. One pound didn't seem like enough, so she dumped in two boxes of spaghetti. As it turns out, pasta expands quite a bit. She'd never paid attention to quite how much—probably because she was usually pretty buzzed by dinnertime. It made a ton. She could feed a small village. And their goats.

It was six thirty. No Scott. The pasta kept expanding. Cass didn't even want it anymore.

She stood by the stove, dipping half-burned garlic toast into the pot of tomato sauce and eating it with her fingers. So quiet. As if there was no one in the world except her. No one to notice if she drank or didn't. It would be so easy. There would be no one to lie to.

Except yourself.

So what? She'd been doing that for years: *You're happy. You don't need the trappings of a normal life. Ben loves you—that's enough.*

She'd told herself these things so often they had folded themselves into the shape of truth in her mind. But now, in the high beam of sobriety, it hit her. They had been true . . . sometimes. But mostly not. Mostly she had just wished they were true.

Which meant that Ben, the one person who loved her, hadn't been enough. And if that was true, then she was screwed, because she was pretty sure no one would ever love her as much as he had. She was even more alone than she'd realized. . . .

She was alone *retroactively.*

Cass turned toward the dining room, with its ark of booze. But standing sentry in front of the door was the stool with the BABY sign taped to it.

And then she was in motion. She didn't even know where her feet would take her, but she found herself grabbing her coat, walking out into the simmering twilight, and striding quickly down Chickadee Circle.

Chapter VIII

The library was closed. Staring desperately through the locked glass doors into the foyer, Cass saw the poster for the high school a cappella concert. It was tonight at seven and it was free. Anywhere was better than being sucked into the vortex of Scott's satanic liquor cabinet.

Wortherton High School was not far; minivans and Suburbans streamed into the parking lot. Cass followed the crowd and was soon seated in a large, dim auditorium, waiting for the show to begin. The muscles in her neck, taut as bow strings, began to loosen. She felt unaccountably safe surrounded by strangers. They greeted one another, hugged sometimes, laughed occasionally. And no one seemed the least bit drunk.

It had been a long time since she'd been anywhere that the main activity was something other than drinking.

The principal, a tall Asian man with bristly hair, introduced himself and welcomed everyone. "We have three fantastic groups of talented young men and women performing for you tonight. The first is our all-female group, the Ruby Slippers."

Twelve girls filed onstage and none of them looked even remotely like Dorothy from *The Wizard of Oz*. Legs elongated like giraffes by perilously high-heeled red shoes, clad in short black skirts and dresses, the girls were all shapes, sizes, colors, and attitudes. The crowd reacted to them as if they were a collection of adolescent rock stars.

A girl with silky long brown hair stepped to one of the microphones and said, "Hi, we're the Slippers." The crowd burst into applause again, with hoots and calls of "Yeah, Slippers!" One boy in the back screamed, "I love you, Kelly!" and everyone laughed.

Kelly smiled serenely and said, "Love you, too, whoever you are. Okay, first Patrice is going to sing 'Black Horse and the Cherry Tree.'" Another girl stepped forward, and Kelly retreated, using her smartphone to give the others their notes. She murmured, "One, two, three, four," and began conducting with her hands. Suddenly the whole group came to life. "Woo-hoo, woo-hoo," they sang in three-part harmony.

There were no instruments. The group served as both band and backup singers to the girl in front, who belted out the melody. Cass couldn't imagine singing in front of a crowded auditorium without even the benefit of instruments. Yet here were the twelve of them, smiling and moving to the beat of their own sounds, the music completely self-made.

A few more girls got up and sang other songs and then Kelly came forward again. "Okay, this is our last song. At the break we'll be in the hall selling our CD, *Not in Kansas Anymore*, for only ten little dollars. I know you want them, so grab a bunch before school lets out for summer. Here's Mary; she's going to sing 'Blackbird' for you."

A girl stepped forward, short and squat with hips that rounded the sides of her snug black dress. Her dark hair was blunt cut, parted in the middle, and hung straight down on either side of her face like a pair of brooms. The applause for Mary was more subdued, and she looked slightly panicked, as if she were about to jump off a cliff and try to fly.

A couple of women in Cass's row clapped hard. They both wore cardigans, and one had a pair of glasses that hung from a beaded cord around her neck. *Teachers*, thought Cass.

The girls in back began humming a waterfall of chords, and then switched to da-da-da's. Mary took a breath and leaned into the first few words of the song, her voice soft and hesitant.

But then something began to change, as if Mary were slowly losing awareness of the audience and even the girls behind her. Her voice gained resonance and strength and by the time she was singing about broken wings, her eyes closed and her hands un-clenched, fingers spread. When she soared into the high notes at "Into the light of the dark black night," a murmur of surprise rippled across the crowd.

The teachers looked at each other. *Oh my God*, one mouthed silently, and the other nodded and mouthed back, *Told you.*

Mary came down clear and sweet onto the last line about wait-ing for this moment to be free, and it felt almost as if the entire auditorium was suspended in the embrace of that final note. There was a beat of silence. And then the place went completely berserk.

"Maryeeee!" came howls from the back, above the explosion of applause.

The girl blinked and gave a surprised little grin. Then she hurried back to her spot amid the twelve. The clapping went on. Kelly shot a quick, insistent nod toward Mary, who stepped for-ward for another bow. The teachers jumped up, still clapping, and the crowd followed, rising to their feet, applauding and hooting. The awkward girl; the amazing performance; the approval of her peers. Cass rose, too, clapping until her hands hurt, vicarious joy pulsing through her.

I'm happy, she thought, and wondered when she'd last been happy and sober at the same time. Did drunken happiness even count?

The following groups' performances were good, too; one or two of the kids were almost as talented as Mary. Cass clapped and smiled, still awestruck by the bravery of singing without music before hundreds of people. How did you come by that kind of courage?

When the concert was over, she merged with the crowd moving into the hallway. Parents mingled, waiting for their sons and daughters. When the performers came out a side door, the parents surged toward them, eyes searching for their own children, beaming when they were spotted. Cass watched a girl allow a hug from her father, rolling her eyes to her friends behind him, then kissing his cheek, nodding and smiling to him. Mary came out, and her mother, also short and round, gripped her as if she'd just returned from battle.

Cass felt her throat tense with emotion. A father to kiss, a mother to hug. How might that have changed the course of her own life?

As she walked toward the exit, she didn't dwell on her losses. Instead she found herself feeling grateful. Healthy living—they talked about that all the time at rehab. But when you'd done so little of it, how were you supposed to know what it looked like? Tonight felt like a clue, a small piece finding its proper location in the vast puzzle of living right.

Crossing the parking lot, she saw something catch the light of the streetlamp overhead; it was one of the CDs the girls had been selling. Cass picked it up and looked around to see if anyone was searching for it. "Is this yours?" she asked a woman getting into a nearby car.

"No, I've got mine right here. I guess it's yours now."

Cass slid it into her purse and walked home in the soft night air.

* * *

WHEN she opened the front door and went into the kitchen, Scott was waiting. He lunged toward her, grabbed her arm, sniffing at her. "Where the hell have you been? Huh? You go out drinking?"

"No, I—"

"You did, didn't you?"

"Get your paws off me!" She wrenched away from his grasp. "I didn't—"

"Don't fucking lie to me! You trash my goddamned house and just *leave*, and you're telling me you were sober? You think I'm some kind of moron?"

Cass took a breath to yell back. But there must have been some residual drops of joy dampening her fury, because no words came out. She looked around.

The pot on the stove surrounded by sputtered drips of sauce. The mountain of gelatinous spaghetti in the strainer. The burned garlic toast. And the stool with the BABY sign taped to it.

She could see how it looked: indicators of minor madness.

"Oh, geez, Scotty . . ." And she made the mistake of smiling.

Scott shook his head, furious. "You're a fucking head case, you know that?" And he slammed out of the room. In another moment she heard the angry growl of his SUV.

* * *

HE wasn't gone long, about half an hour. By that time she had cleaned everything up and stuffed the slimy spaghetti mush down the garbage disposal. She was tired and wanted to go to bed, but she knew it would only get worse if his anger festered.

When he came in, he went straight up the stairs, and she had to scurry to catch up.

"Scotty, wait."

He turned around at the top, looming over her. "Wait for what—for you to magically turn into a normal girl?"

She stared up at him. A normal girl—that was the price of admission? She leaned against the banister, so tired. This would never work. She had only ever been steering toward the distant shores of sober. Normal was on a whole other planet.

"I didn't drink," she murmured quietly.

"You trashed my kitchen sober?" Suspicious but not yelling. A good sign.

"Yes."

He crossed his arms. "You do that a lot? Make a mess and take off?"

"I made dinner. I thought you'd be home. Then you didn't show up and I started feeling crazy, so I just had to leave. I thought I'd be back to clean up before you saw it."

He considered this for a moment. "Why'd you feel crazy all of a sudden?"

She shrugged.

"Because of me? Because I didn't come home?"

"No, it's not your fault. I just . . ." She sat down on the step, weariness making her slouch against the balusters. "It's kind of like . . . like I'm the beach, and booze is the ocean. And I get a little bit of myself back when the tide goes out, but then it comes in again. Because that's what it does. It comes back. And I just have to hold on till it's safe."

He didn't respond, and she knew he couldn't truly understand. But somehow it felt better just to say it, to explain it to herself, if not to him. It was quiet, and she could smell the faint lingering fragrance of dish soap on her hands. A normal smell, comforting in its ordinariness.

He sat down on the top step. "Where'd you go?"

"A concert at the high school."

"That helped?"

"Yeah, it was nice. When it was over, all the parents waited for the kids to come out so they could congratulate them. It was sweet."

After a few moments he said, "I hated it when my parents came to my games."

"How come?"

"Because if I made an error or whiffed a strike, I knew I was gonna get a beating after."

She turned to look at Scott, sitting there so still. "Ben said your father was the angriest son of a bitch he ever met. And Ben knew a lot of angry guys."

Scott's face was blank. "Yeah."

"He threw a party when the old man died," she said. "He was completely bombed for a week straight."

Scotty looked at her finally, his gaze tainted with sorrow. "When I had a really bad game, Ben would do something to piss him off even more."

"Why?"

"So he'd get the beating instead of me."

Chapter IX

When Cass came down the next morning, Scott was eating Cocoa Puffs out of the mixing bowl. She went for the granola.

"Check the date on that," he said. "It's from a while ago."

"How come you never had any?"

"I don't eat that crap." He shoved another spoonful of chocolate corn balls in his mouth.

"Then why'd you buy it?"

"I didn't."

"Hold on—you let some girl bring groceries?" she said. "Must've been pretty serious."

"Well, we had a little difference of opinion about that." He chuckled. "Notice how it never got opened."

"Heartbreaker," she teased.

He shrugged, still grinning. The sell-by date was August. Cass poured herself a bowl and reached for the milk. "I can pick up some more of this," she offered, holding up the depleted carton. "Unless you've got a thing against girls getting groceries."

"Nah. Besides, you don't count." He pulled three twenties out of his wallet. "Pick up whatever you need." He slid them toward her, but his hand remained extended on the table an extra moment, as if he were second-guessing his decision to give her cash.

"I'll bring you the slip and the change," she said, and his hand retracted.

"I'm leaving early." He loaded the bowl and spoon into the dishwasher. "The cleaning lady comes today, and I don't like to get in her way."

The place was already so clean you could practically perform surgery right on the kitchen counter. *Waste of money*, she thought.

Scott was gone when Cass came back downstairs from brushing her teeth. The three twenties sat on the counter. As naturally as taking her next breath, her brain began to calculate: *Sixty dollars . . . that's five, maybe six bottles of the cheapest vodka, depending on the store . . . Do they have discount stores in Wortherton? . . . Probably just those snobby wine and cheese places . . . but there must be a bus that would get me closer to . . .*

STOP.

You do not buy alcohol anymore. You do not drink alcohol anymore. You and alcohol are no longer together. That relationship has ended.

But it hadn't, at least not in her mind.

It was sort of like her relationship with Ben. Even when they broke up and she didn't see him for weeks, she had still been Ben McGreavy's girl. And now that he was dead, with no possibility of a reunion, he was still with her, in her thoughts, even in the marrow of her bones, it seemed. And very much in the child that she carried.

It occurred to her that her attachment to both Ben and alcohol would never really be over. She would bear them with her for the rest of her life. A stunning thought.

She looked at the twenties.

Food, she told herself and sat down to make a grocery list. On foot she could only carry two bags, and based on the list, it wasn't likely to cost anywhere near sixty dollars. She didn't want to have any extra money with her—not today, not the way her brain veered toward vodka. She tucked the third twenty into a kitchen drawer full of takeout menus, put the other two in her purse, and headed off to her AA meeting.

* * *

WHEN Cass returned several hours later with the groceries, the cleaning lady was just leaving. Cass held the door for her. The woman, her age obscured by a bad dye job and baggy clothing, shot a quick glance at Cass and said merely, "It's all set," and hurried down the brick walkway to her car.

No doubt, thought Cass, *since it was clean when you got here.*

She put away the groceries, made herself a sandwich, and sat at the kitchen table reading the pregnancy book.

Your baby's ears begin to form at around eight weeks and are fully functional by about twenty-four weeks . . . Through ultrasound we know that a fetus responds to his parents' voices, sometimes turning toward them when they speak or sing . . . Consider reading to your baby and having your partner do the same . . .

Cass wasn't really sure when her last period had been, so she could only guess at how old the fetus was—maybe three months—which meant it should be starting to hear by now.

When she finished eating, she tidied up the immaculate kitchen and took the book with her to the huge leather L-shaped couch in the TV area. While she waited for the one o'clock Red Sox game to start, she read to the baby, her voice soft and sing-songy.

"'The fetus reacts to your voice and other nearby sounds, to light and darkness, and even tastes the sweet or spicy foods you've eaten.'" She pulled up her shirt and ran a hand over the roundness of her abdomen. "Sounds like you got a lot going on in there," she told the baby. "I'll try to stay off the spicy stuff in case you don't like it."

Cass watched the game, muting the commercials so she could continue reading aloud.

"If you can hear like the book says, you're gonna love me and the Red Sox commentators when you're born," she said, giggling. "Maybe we should invite Dennis Eckersley over sometime."

Scott got up to bat. "Okay, your uncle's in the box. Choke up a little, Uncle Scotty. He swings . . . and misses. That's okay, he gets two more strikes. You can't count yet, but just so you know, three seems to be a popular number on this planet. Here he goes again . . . Yay, a hit . . . and it's a double!" Cass threw her arms in the air. "Let's do the wave for Uncle Scotty!" She put her hands on her belly and flapped them up. "Good baby—way to root for the home team."

It was the most pleasant afternoon she'd passed in months. She could imagine how nice it would be to sit with a real child and watch games or read books together. A real child—and she would be a real mother. A good one, she hoped.

* * *

WHEN she woke it was almost dark. She remembered drifting off after the game ended, and now she was famished. The Sox had won; Scott wasn't likely to be home for a while, if at all. But she found herself preparing all the chicken anyway, feeling as if she could eat a whole coop-full. She was just sitting down, plate loaded with chicken, broccoli, and a huge steaming russet potato, when she heard the garage door open. A moment later, Scott walked in.

"Hey, what are you doing here?"

He tapped his broad chest. "Homeowner?"

"But you won. I thought you'd be . . ."

He shrugged. "I felt like laying low for a night." His gaze panned around the room as if searching for contraband, then back to her. "Got enough for two?"

She put together a plate for him while he refilled her water glass and got a bottle of Gatorade for himself. They were both so hungry, half the meal was gone in a matter of minutes.

"This is good," he told her. "Even the broccoli. I don't think I ever had it like this before. Plain, without any junk on it like they do in restaurants."

She laughed. "You eat like a five-year-old, you know that?"

"My mother could barely open a can. Heating up SpaghettiOs was a big night."

"I only met her once." Ben had rarely even mentioned his mother. When Cass had occasionally asked about her, he'd laugh and say something like, *World's biggest buzzkill*, and that would be the end of it. "What's she like?"

Scotty stared at the speckled granite counter for a moment. Then he shook his head as if to dislodge whatever his mind had conjured. "She's a piece of work."

"Like . . . ?"

"Like what." His tone said *Don't*, but she wanted to know.

"Like who was her favorite, you or Ben?" As an only child, she'd often wondered about sibling rivalry. It sounded kind of interesting, and she'd wished she'd had someone to try it with.

He snorted and said, "Ben. Till he met you."

This startled her. "What? Why?"

"He was so smart. Always getting awards at school and whatever. She had plenty to brag to the other mothers about. In her mind, she was the most important person in his life. Then you came along and he loved you for real, and she could finally see how he'd never loved her that much."

"Jesus. No wonder he never wanted me around them."

Scott heaped butter into his potato. "He didn't want you scarred for life like we were."

"I was scarred enough already."

He stopped mashing the butter into the potato and looked over at her. Cass wondered if Ben had ever told him about what she'd been through. "Foster care," she said.

"Oh." He seemed not to know what to do with himself.

"So, um, how come your mother didn't go to Ben's funeral?"

He resumed his mashing. "With her, you never know the real reason. She said she needed a knee replacement and couldn't get around well enough. But then I never heard about the surgery. And trust me, I would've heard about it."

"What do you think the real reason was?"

Scott pondered this. "If I had to guess, I'd say she knew no one would come. There was no audience to play the grieving mother to, so why bother? Also, she knew you'd be there. Her replacement."

Cass found this hard to believe, even considering the generally uncomplimentary few things she'd heard about Gilda from Ben. "That's pretty cold," she said skeptically.

"Yeah, well. Nice of Ben not to put you in a position to see for yourself. With any luck, you never will."

Cass considered this. After all, she was carrying Gilda's grandchild. Would her baby ever meet his only living grandparent? Would Cass want him to?

Scott shoveled a forkful of potato into his mouth and swallowed. "A really great meal," he said. "You had enough money?"

"More than enough." She reached for her purse on the counter to get the receipt and the change. "Here you go," she said.

He looked at the slip and coins. "Very funny."

"What?"

"Where's the other twenty?"

"Oh, I didn't think I'd need it, so I shoved it in the drawer with all the takeout menus."

She saw the look that passed over his face—wanting to believe her, but not quite getting there. She went to the drawer.

No twenty.

She rifled through the menus, then took them out and shook them one by one. Still nothing. Panic filled her. "I swear, I put it in here!"

His face was flat with anger. "Just give it to me and I won't make a thing out of it."

"Scotty, I'm telling you!"

"Did you buy the booze already?" He got up, the meal forgotten.

"I did not buy any booze, I swear on my mother's grave."

A snort of disgust. "That's a shitty thing to do to your mother."

"I swear to you!" She slammed her hand down on the counter.

"Hey, don't get pissy with me! I give you sixty bucks and you come back with forty dollars' worth of groceries. What the fuck, Cass? What am I supposed to think?"

"I don't know! Maybe . . . maybe the cleaning lady took it!"

"Oh, for chrissake. Really? You're accusing the cleaning lady? She's worked for me for over a year. Who should I trust—her or you?"

"Look, I *have* cash. Up in my room. My tip money. You know that. I paid the lawn guy and you paid me back. If I was going to get loaded, wouldn't I just use that? Why would I chance screwing it up with you?"

He looked away, shook his head. "Hell, I don't know. You and Ben screwed it up with me so many times, it just feels like normal."

It was true. She knew he had every right to think the worst.

"I'm sorry for all those times," she said. "But this isn't one of them."

She went upstairs and dug the envelope with her tip money out of the back of the closet. When she came downstairs again, he was in the study watching a video of today's game. She put a twenty on the desk.

He reached out and put it in his shirt pocket. His eyes never left the screen.

* * *

CASS had her first doctor's appointment the next day. When she walked back up Chickadee Circle from her AA meeting, Scott was idling the SUV in the driveway, thumbing through messages on his phone.

"You're gonna be late," he said, not looking up.

"I walked as fast as I could." *You could've picked me up*, she wanted to say, but didn't.

The drive to the Waverly Community Health Center was only about ten minutes, but the silence between them elongated the trip. Scott didn't even play the radio.

He pulled into a parking space. "Are you coming in?" she asked.

"No, I'll wait out here."

The building was dingy, but inside there was clearly a concerted effort to brighten up the place with colorful posters about "Happy Healthy Hearts!" and joining "Team Veggie!"

"Can I help you?" The receptionist's accent seemed Caribbean. Jamaica, Cass guessed.

"Uh, I have an appointment with Dr. . . ." Cass glanced at the scrap of paper in her hand where she'd written the name. "Tee-jeera?"

"It's pronounced *Teh-hair-a*, and she's a nurse practitioner. You'll like her. Everybody likes her—she's a beautiful person. First you fill out a whole lotta forms. You got insurance?"

"No."

The receptionist smiled. "Even *more* forms, then."

Cass hesitated. Ben had always warned her against giving information. *Then they can track you*, he would say. *It's a whole Big Brother thing.*

"You read?" said the receptionist. "Because if you don't read too good, that's okay, we got people to help you."

"Oh, no, I can read." Cass sat in a plastic chair and filled out the forms. It didn't take long, since many of her answers were *no*, and *I don't know*. She didn't even have a permanent address. Those forms told her just how broke and homeless she was. When she turned them in, she felt as if she should apologize. *I have nothing*, she wanted to explain. *Not even answers*.

A woman in scrubs came to take her back to an exam room. She gave Cass a johnny and told her to take off everything but her underwear. Also, she gave her a little cup to pee in and showed her to the bathroom. "We check for protein in the urine," the nurse explained.

"That's a bad thing?"

"Yeah, it's bad. But don't worry, it's not that common."

After Cass had changed and filled the little cup, the nurse had her step on the scale.

"That can't be right," said Cass.

"It's in the normal range for someone your height."

It was fifteen pounds more than she'd ever weighed in her life.

A gentle hand rested on her shoulder. "You look great. Very healthy." The nurse led her into the exam room. "Ana will be in soon."

Cass sat on the exam table and swung her legs. She hadn't been in any kind of medical building since she was fifteen. And it hadn't been for anything good, like she had now. But she remembered feeling safe in the hospital, so much safer than anywhere else at the time.

A woman entered, older, brown-skinned, with black hair that hung in gentle waves to her collarbone.

"I'm Ana Tejera," she said, holding out a knobby-knuckled hand to shake. "Most of my patients call me Ana." There was a clipboard with papers on it, but she didn't look at it. She sat down on the rolling stool. "So you're pregnant. How are you feeling about that?"

"Pretty good," said Cass. "I mean, I'm happy about it, if that's what you're getting at."

"That's exactly what I'm getting at. A woman who's happy to be pregnant will take her health and her baby's health seriously."

"I'm trying to be very healthy."

"Wonderful!" Ana clapped her hands together. "So tell me what that looks like for you. What are your efforts?"

"Well, I . . . I'm eating well. Vegetables and stuff. No junk food."

"Yes, I like to hear that! And are you staying away from alcohol, cigarettes, and drugs?"

"Completely." Cass suppressed a smile, not wanting to seem overly proud. She imagined that most women gave the preferred answer without a second thought.

"Terrific. Is there anyone in your life you're afraid of, who could hurt you physically?"

Cass almost laughed. The only person "in her life" was Scott, and he might get ticked off and grab her shoulder occasionally, but she was pretty sure he would never do anything worse.

"Nope, nothing like that," she replied.

"All good news," said Ana. Cass liked that comment very much. It had been a very long time since it had been "all good news" for her.

They continued to talk for a while. When was Cass's last period? Cass wasn't sure—her periods had never been regular. Ana wrote out a scrip for pregnancy vitamins and told her to make monthly appointments for well visits. The nurse came in and took a tube of blood from Cass's arm so they could run tests and get a sense of how far along Cass might be.

"Okay," said Ana. "I'd like to use the Doppler to see if we can hear the heartbeat. But if it's too early, before twelve weeks or so, and we don't hear it, I'm worried you're going to be upset. Would you rather wait until your next visit or should we give it a try?"

Cass thought for a moment. *Avoid stress*, the book had said, and not hearing the heartbeat would definitely stress her out. But what if they *could* hear it? "Let's try," she said.

Ana instructed Cass to lie back on the exam table and raise the johnny above her waist. "This is a Doppler," she said, spreading a clear, gelatinous substance on the end of a white handle. "It picks up the sound of the embryonic heartbeat through sound waves." She slid the slippery end across Cass's stomach, angling it this way and that, trying to track and capture some small indication of life. "Remember, don't worry if we don't hear it," she said quietly.

The Doppler made a shushing sound, like the oceanic whisper of a shell over Cass's ear. "Is that it?"

"Not yet," said Ana.

The shushing sound suddenly receded and there was a *wub-wub-wub*, soft but insistent.

"That," said Ana, "is your baby's heartbeat."

* * *

WHEN Cass got out to the car, Scott's head was tipped back against the headrest, eyes closed, lips parted. He looked older than his thirty years, like an old man dozing in his chair.

She opened the passenger-side door, and his head popped up, startled. She smiled at him—she couldn't help it—it was a smiling kind of day. He scowled, turned the key in the ignition, and revved the engine.

"When does your plane leave?" she asked. He had a series in Tampa.

"Tonight."

"You want dinner before you leave?"

"They'll feed us on the plane."

Cass put her head back. If he wanted to be angry still, she couldn't do much about it. Maybe it would be better to have him out of the house—he was a buzzkill. (Should she use that phrase anymore?) Anyway, he was stressful, and she wanted to enjoy her good mood.

"What," he demanded, glaring at the road in front of him.

"Huh?"

"You're sitting over there like the cat that ate the canary."

Her grin ripened into a full-cheek smile. "I heard the baby's heartbeat. It's really strong. Like a drum or something."

His gaze flicked to her, then back to the road. "That's good, I guess."

Cass chose to ignore the *I guess*. "At first she couldn't find it, and I was about to freak out, but then there it was. *Boom, boom, boom.* She says he's about four months, so I'm in the second trimester, which is great, because most miscarriages happen in the first trimester."

Scott still trained his gaze on the road, but he didn't look quite so irritable. "It's a boy?"

"Oh, I have no idea. I just say 'him.' But it could be a girl."

A girl. Cass's smile bloomed all over again. *A sweet baby girl.*

"Scotty," she whispered, "I've got two hearts in me."

And he smiled just a little. He couldn't help it.

Chapter X

Jackie came to the AA meeting the next day, but she did not look the same. Her soft white hair was in a severe ponytail instead of the elegant French twist she usually wore. Her eyebrows were penciled asymmetrically, her lips dabbed patchily with orange-red lipstick.

She looks like a drunk, thought Cass in horror.

"I'm Jackie," she told the group, then squinted at her diamond-trimmed watch. "I've been sober for about ten hours."

There was a moment of stunned silence around the circle.

"My husband passed two days ago," she went on, her voice hushed and scratchy. "There was a liquor store around the corner from the hospital. I noted its location as soon as he was admitted and headed there directly from his deathbed.

"My daughter and son flew in when he took a turn for the worse. I realize now that they never truly believed I was an alcoholic—they were too young when I stopped. It was ridiculously easy to slip away and buy the bourbon, and to play off my drunkenness as grief." Tears started to leak from her inflamed eyelids. "It certainly is that, too."

Cass took her hand, and Jackie gripped back hard. "This is the first time my daughter's let me out of her sight since she realized I was drinking." A mournful smile. "She's out in the hallway, and I do believe she's cased out all possible exits to this room."

The group nodded in sad solidarity. Being trailed by concerned friends and family members was a common story.

"My rehab bed will be waiting for me as soon as the funeral's over," said Jackie. "I can't wait to get there. As much as I've craved a drink over the past twenty-nine years, I can report that it doesn't feel as good as I thought it would. It's actually fairly sickening. And yet I can't stop thinking that if I have just one more, it'll feel the way it used to."

* * *

AT the end of the meeting, Jackie murmured to Cass, "Walk out with me?"

In the hallway stood a woman in her early thirties, stiff as a sentry. She strode purposefully toward them. Jackie introduced her to Cass.

"I'm very glad to meet you," said the daughter. "My mother has mentioned you kindly."

Cass felt her cheeks warm. "She made me feel welcome—I was so nervous at first."

Jackie took Cass's hand in both of hers. "I want you to know, I'll be thinking of you. I'll be sending good thoughts for you and your baby."

Cass struggled to keep from crying. "I'll be sending good thoughts for you, too, Jackie."

When they'd said their good-byes, Cass was left with a disheartened feeling she couldn't shake. Almost thirty years of sobriety—since the day of Cass's birth!—and it still hadn't been enough to keep her from drinking when things got too hard. Would Jackie have fallen off the wagon if she hadn't been so reliant on her husband's support? Cass pondered that as she walked home. Maybe it was better not to get too attached. She had loved Ben deeply, but she had known not to depend on him much. He'd made an art form of undependability.

Back at Scott's she found herself wandering from room to room, unable to shake the image of Jackie, so refined, with so many resources at her disposal, crumbling like any other drunk. Cass sat on the couch and closed her eyes, trying to resurrect in her mind the sights, sounds, and raucous joy of the high school concert. Then she remembered—the CD was in her purse.

She put it in the computer drive, and girls' voices filled the dark-paneled study; Cass leaned back in the leather desk chair and her shoulders relaxed for the first time that morning.

* * *

THE weekend passed slowly. Cass went to her AA meetings, read the pregnancy book out loud to the baby, and watched Scott's games on TV. She looked up how to get a driver's license. But boredom seeped into every corner of the day. She couldn't remember being bored when she was drinking. Time just . . . passed. Sobriety, she realized, could be So. Damned. Dull.

That bottle of Baileys in the liquor cabinet would liven things up, the dark whisper told her *Erin go bragh!*

She gave the dining room and its demonic liquor cabinet a wide berth and played the CD of the girls singing in a continuous loop. *It's my security blanket,* she thought and had to laugh at the absurdity of it. She'd heard the people in her AA group talk about their replacement obsessions—what they now did compulsively instead of drinking. One woman had gone from being completely sedentary to running marathons. Another guy was now a clean freak, joking that his vacuum had become his favorite dance partner.

The CD kept her calm, but it didn't do much to dispel the boredom or, she had to admit, her loneliness. Even though she seemed to fight with him as often as not, Scott offered the only reliable human contact in her life, and she missed that.

On Sunday she called her friend Kate, but only got voice mail.

Probably still sleeping it off, thought Cass. She left a message but had low expectations for a return call.

Monday the air was heavy and weighed on her like a physical presence. She knew a walk would do her good, but she sat on the couch as if tied down by invisible ropes. Outside the shed door slammed. She guessed that Drew was back to mow the lawn and almost got up to see if he would dance again, but instead she slid down even farther on the beastlike leather couch.

Then she smelled it.

Pleasant at first, tickling memories of lightness and laughter in her sluggish brain, Cass smiled at the smell. Then she sat up.

She went over to the window. Drew was standing on the shady side of the shed grasping a small white thing between his thumb and forefinger.

"Hey!" she called.

He flinched and slid his hand behind his back. "Just mowing the lawn!" he yelled.

"No, you're not," she called. "At the moment, you're smoking weed."

"Shit!" she heard him mutter, peeking around the side of the shed toward his own yard. He pinched the end of the joint and stuffed it into his pocket, striding toward her. "I wasn't!" he insisted, his voice low and panicked.

"Um, dude," said Cass, opening the screen. "You totally were."

He rolled his eyes. "Yeah, so? Can't you be cool about it?"

"Not really. I'm an alcoholic, and getting a contact high is not an approved part of the recovery program."

He squinted at her. "AA?"

She nodded.

"Might as well give up. It doesn't work."

Cass raised an eyebrow. "You have personal knowledge?"

He shrugged and looked away. "Personal enough."

She studied him for a moment. Tall and gangly, he looked like he'd grown recently and his weight hadn't caught up. His hands seemed oversized for his spindly arms, and he slouched to one side, as if he hadn't quite mastered control of his newly elongated spine. She felt sorry for him—for his awkwardness and his personal-enough knowledge of AA.

"Want to come in and have a sandwich?"

"I'm not giving you the weed."

"Did I ask you to?"

He gave her an ancient, tired look. "No, but you will."

"I really won't."

"How long you got?"

"All afternoon."

"No. *Sobriety.*" He said it as if it were a dubious concept, like alchemy. "How long?"

"Forty-five days."

"Pah!" he snorted. "That's *it*?"

She put her hands up. "Look, pal, I'm not asking for a round of applause. All I'm asking is if you want a sandwich. I honestly don't care either way."

He considered this. "All right," he said. "But I'm not even giving you a pull. Seriously. This stuff's expensive."

No wonder your mother doesn't want you to have cash in your pocket, thought Cass. "Couldn't care less," she said, and he came in.

Drew sat on one of the counter stools while she made him a sandwich, not asking anything more personal than whether he liked mustard or mayo. He seemed to be waiting for her to question him, almost disappointed when she didn't.

"So," Cass said, watching him wolf down a sandwich half practically without chewing, "I mean it about not smoking in the yard."

"I know," he muttered. "Why do you think I do it over here in the first place?"

"So you won't get caught."

"Yeah, and so my mother won't freak out and down a bottle of Courvoisier."

"Is she in recovery?"

"Barely."

"I'm sorry," she said. "My mother was a drinker."

"She ever quit?"

"No."

"Sorry," he said.

"Me, too."

He eyed her for a moment. "You think you'll really stop?"

"I hope so. But I won't lie. It's tough sometimes."

He studied her. "You're nothing like my mom."

"Alcoholics come in a variety pack—all different flavors."

He finished off the other sandwich half. "I guess I better mow the lawn. Unhigh."

She smiled. "Much appreciated."

* * *

LATE that night, long after Cass had tidied up, shut off the lights, and gone to bed, she heard the garage door go up. Scott's movements were neither noisy nor hushed, as if he were simply coming home to an empty house. As she listened to him climb the stairs she wondered if he remembered she was there. But then he stopped outside her door.

The knob turned carefully and his head appeared in the stripe of light from the hall.

"Hi," she whispered. "Good game."

"You okay?"

"Yeah, fine."

The door closed and his footsteps receded toward his bedroom. She wondered if he would ever stop doubting her, or if she would remain an object of suspicion for the rest of her life. At what point did a recovering drunk become worthy of trust?

Chapter XI

"Hi, I'm Laurel."

"Hi, Laurel!" they all said, their voices a shade more encouraging than usual. Laurel had come to every meeting since rehab but had yet to say a word.

This ought to be interesting, thought Cass.

"I've got thirty-seven days and I almost blew it this morning. I honestly came this close." Her burgundy fingernails hovered about half an inch apart. Cass wondered if it was advisable to wear nail polish the color of wine.

"I have a two-year-old," Laurel went on, "and he's just the sweetest, cutest boy." Her eyes went shiny, and for a moment Cass thought it was for love of her son. "But he's driving me up a wall! The messes, my God, he can trash a room in under a minute flat. And he's insisting on potty training—which he is *not* ready for—and he keeps taking off his diaper when I'm not looking. This morning while I took a shower, he ransacked the dressers until he found boxers. He stripped and put them on and went back into the family room to watch TV.

"When I came in he was so proud . . ." Laurel closed her eyes. "It's my fault," she sighed. "I should have taken control. That's what my husband always says."

She laughed, a sad, painful sound. "Control. You get the joke, right? Clearly control is something I have a little problem with.

"I just wanted to give him ten minutes of pride. Ten little minutes to wear the boxers while I made him breakfast. . . . He had a bowel movement. It leaked, of course." She closed her eyes as if to shut out the visual. "In between the cushions of the couch. He must have been uncomfortable and wiggled around."

Laurel started to cry. "I don't like messes." She inhaled raggedly, lacing her fingers together and squeezing till they trembled. "It felt as if he had purposely done it to hurt me, and I screamed at him and . . . I almost hit him. I was so ashamed and upset, and it felt like everything was crashing down on me. He was crying and saying, 'I sorry, Mama, I sorry.'"

Laurel's hands flew up to her face, and tears leaked out between her fingers. When she lowered her hands, her gaze was leveled at Cass. "It's hard," she said. "No matter how much you love them, it's really, really hard sometimes."

* * *

WHEN Cass got home, Scott was eating Frosted S'mores Pop-Tarts and looking over her list of goals. "Apparently you still need a haircut, a job, and a driver's license."

"It's only been a little over a week," she said defensively.

"I don't have a game today. Let's get some stuff done."

She wondered at his sudden motivation to help. *Probably trying to make sure he can get me out of here in three weeks.*

But driving to the Registry of Motor Vehicles, Scott was chatty and upbeat. The series in Tampa had gone well, the Sox had won two out of three, and his batting average had increased. "Management's happy," he told her. "I just have to keep them that way."

Cass told him about catching Drew smoking pot by the shed.

"Wow, I had no idea his mother's an alkie," said Scott. "She did a great job decorating my house. Always wicked organized and neat."

A strange little tingle ran across Cass's scalp, like half a memory, or the first three notes of a song she couldn't place.

"Kind of funny, though," said Scott, as he turned into the parking lot at the Registry. "You *stopping* someone from getting high."

"Yeah, it's hilarious. Sorta like you correcting someone's grammar."

He pulled into a spot and slammed the car into park. "I know you and Ben always thought I'm the world's biggest idiot. But I'm not. I'm smarter than you think."

"And I'm more sober than you think," she snapped back. "As in, very. As in, I'm working my ass off to keep clean, and you treat me like a career criminal."

"I treat you like what you are. Someone who's been drunk for a decade and has to put up a sign to remember she's carrying a baby." He got out, slammed the door, and walked away.

Rule Number One out the fucking window.

Cass sat in the car, waiting for the blood to stop crashing through her veins like a tiny tsunami. How had he made her feel so snarly so fast? It wasn't him, she realized. It was Laurel. That look she had, like some possessed oracle of doom when she'd said, *It's hard.*

It's hard. And yet all the alternatives are harder.

She found Scotty sitting on one of the benches and sat down next to him. "I'm sorry," she said. "There was a mom at the meeting today who told a very tough story, and I'm edgy."

He shrugged without looking at her and gave her his credit card. She went and processed her paperwork and got a numbered ticket indicating her place in the queue. Based on the much lower numbers blinking on the electronic signs above the registration desks, it would be a while.

"Hey," she said, returning to the bench, "can you test me?"

"Why should I?" Scott grumbled.

"Because if I don't pass, you'll have to drive me back here

again. And also because I'm an idiot and I need the help." They both knew she was no idiot; she hoped he would get the implied apology. She held out the study sheets she'd printed off the internet, her hand suspended in midair as he considered. Finally he took them. He quizzed her, and she did fairly well for a while. But then she got tired and hungry and missed six questions in a row.

"How many do you have to get right?" he asked.

"Twenty out of twenty-five."

"So you have to bat . . . what, eight hundred?"

She gave a wry smile. "Show-off."

He lifted a shoulder, feigning modesty. "Baseball stats. Easy."

They got slices of pizza and eventually Cass's number came up. Her heart started to race—she hadn't taken a test of any kind in almost twelve years. She wondered how she would make it through her online child development course without fainting at every quiz.

Ten minutes later she was getting her picture taken for her permit. She held up the little card for Scott to see when she came out.

"Congratulations," he said. "Glad I don't have to come back."

"Not till the road test, anyway."

As they drove home, Cass studied the picture on her new permit. She had smiled, but it was her fake smile, the one she put on for police officers and restaurant managers who might hire her. "Does my hair really look that bad?" she asked Scott.

"It's a little scraggly," he said, without taking his eyes off the road.

At a stoplight she saw a sign: THE BEAUTY SPOT. WALK-INS WELCOME. She pointed to it. "What do you think?"

"As good a place as any." He gave her his credit card. Cass hopped out, and he drove on to find parking. In the hair salon, there was a young woman at the reception desk texting madly. Her tar-black hair was cut shoulder length on one side and above her ear on the other.

"I'd like to get a haircut?" said Cass.

"Sure, no problem." The woman's eyes flicked to Cass's hair, then to an older woman in a black apron paging through a thick glossy magazine. "Denise, you want this one?"

Denise glanced over, an appraising look, then back to the page. "That's okay."

The black-haired girl didn't move for a moment. Then she set her hands on the desk and pushed herself out of the chair. "I'm Raven," she said. "Let's get you washed."

Cass was soon reclining with her head full of suds, Raven's strong fingers scrubbing across her scalp. "I like to give a little massage with the wash," said Raven. "That feel okay?"

"Yeah, great." It felt amazing, as if for those few moments the press of all her worries was replaced with the benign, physical pressure of Raven's hands. It had been so long since she'd been touched in any pleasant way.

Afterward, Raven seated Cass in front of a long mirror. "It's going to take a couple of inches to get all the split ends," she said, studying a handful of Cass's brittle locks. "I'm thinking shoulder length with some light layers, and angles around your face. How's that sound?"

"Go ahead," said Cass. Usually her friends cut her hair, or Ben had. It wasn't a situation in which you made style demands. She watched in the mirror as hunks of wet hair fell to the floor.

The bell on the door jingled behind them, and Raven stopped cutting and turned, about to say something. But it was Denise's voice they heard. "Oh my God! Oh my *God*!"

Cass twisted around in her seat. It was Scott.

Denise was standing now, coming up close to him. "I'm a huge fan," she said breathily. "You're my favorite. I always say that. I always say, 'Scott McGreavy's the most underappreciated player on the team.'"

"Thanks," he said, eyes darting as if searching for some sort of weapon to defend himself. A hairbrush, maybe, or some defrizz-ing spray.

"You need a haircut?" Denise offered. "Because I am excellent at men's cuts. Aren't I, Raven?"

Raven nodded. "She's pretty good."

"No, I just wanted to tell her . . ." He indicated Cass. "I had to park a few blocks up."

Denise's head swiveled around fast, like an owl's, eyes glaring incredulously at Cass.

"Okay," said Cass. "I'll find you." Scott left quickly.

Denise stalked over and came to rest against the product coun-ter in front of Cass, studying her as if she were an unlikely animal for these parts—a platypus maybe, or an iguana. "Are you, like, cousins or something?" she demanded.

"We're . . . friends. From high school." This wasn't true. Scott had hung out with the jocks; Cass had kept to a loose circle of slightly awkward unfortunates like herself. The roster changed with pregnancies, extended truancy, unexplained relocations, worsening drug use, and bouts of depression. But the list never varied so widely as to include Scott or any of his crowd.

Denise was clearly skeptical. "You stayed in touch all that time?"

"Yep." This, of course, *was* true. They'd had Ben in common.

"Huh. So, what's he like?"

"He's, um . . . he's a nice guy."

This was not nearly enough for Denise, who spent the rest of the haircut peppering Cass with questions about his training sched-ule, food preferences, and of course, his social life. Annoyed, Cass kept her answers brief and unrevealing. It was a relief when Ra-ven switched on the blow-dryer and the noise made it impossible to talk. Denise drifted back to her magazine.

After a minute, Raven turned off the blow-dryer and leaned forward to whisper, "Should I know that guy?"

Cass laughed. "Nah, he's just a baseball player."

When Raven was done, she gave Cass a hand mirror and spun her around so she could see the back. Without all the split ends, her hair looked a shade darker—more like cinnamon nutmeg, less like a sandy auburn. And it had a silky shine to it that Cass hadn't seen in a very long time.

"I cut it so you don't have to blow-dry it," said Raven. "In case you don't always have time." Apparently it was obvious that hair care wasn't Cass's top priority, but Raven had offered this kindness in a respectfully veiled way. Cass tipped her well.

When she located Scott's SUV and got in, he looked then glanced away. "Nice," he said.

"Thanks," she said. "It feels really good."

"Well, I'm not going to run my fingers through it," he said, pulling out into traffic.

"That's not what I meant," she said. "What I mean is, it feels good *to me*."

* * *

IN Wortherton, Scott didn't turn down Chickadee Circle. He drove right by.

"Where are we going?" she asked.

"That shut-down electronics store over on Route 9."

"What for?"

"Big empty parking lot." A hint of a grin flashed across his face. "It's a good spot for your first driving lesson."

Chapter XII

The vast asphalt emptiness of the parking lot was a very good thing, because if there had been so much as a tricycle parked along the weedy curb, Cass would've hit it.

Scott yelled "Jesus Christ!" so many times, he might have been at a religious revival.

"Jesus Christ, turn!"

"Jesus Christ, don't cut the wheels so hard!"

"Jesus H. Christ, *stop*!"

Cass bucked the SUV to a halt just short of a light pole. Between Scott's yelling and the panic of trying to control the huge, disobedient vehicle, her heart was thumping maniacally, reverberating against her ribs like blasts from fireworks. She thought of the pregnancy book—it said the baby could hear everything. *Poor little guy, you must be freaking out with all this racket.*

"Jesus Christ!" Scott said, breathing hard. "You fucking *suck* at this!"

"That's enough," she snarled.

"Enough of what—you driving? Because I am totally on board with that."

"It's enough of you screaming and using bad language! The baby can *hear* you, you know. His ears *work*. So I would appreciate it if you would not teach him to swear like a . . . a gosh darn sailor before he's even born!"

Scott's face exploded with incredulity. "You just nearly killed us—*and* the baby—and you think the biggest problem here is *swearing*? Christ, Cass, have you lost your fucking marbles?"

"I'm serious! It's not good for him. And it's . . . it's unnecessary!"

"Oh, it's necessary, all right. When I see my fucking life flash before my eyes, it's necessary as *shit*."

He was doing it on purpose, she decided. Baiting her like booze baited her. No—booze baited her much worse. And if she could withstand that, Scotty shouldn't be so hard to handle. She took a breath, tried to relax her muscles like she'd learned in that yoga class at rehab.

"Scotty," she said evenly. "I am asking you nicely—will you please not swear in front of the baby. If he was born, and he was in another room or something, you could curse me out all you want. But he's not—he's inside me. So for the next two and a half weeks, could you please keep a civil tongue in your head?"

He stared at her for a moment. Then he burst out laughing. "Cass, the baby is like the size of a jalapeño. I really don't think he's starting to potty-talk in there because of me."

She shrugged and tried to keep a straight face, though the image of the cursing jalapeño was tough not to smile at.

Scott held up his thumb and forefinger, pinched together. Then he opened them a little and squeaked, "Shit . . . fuck . . ." She couldn't help it; she started to giggle. He pulsed his fingers open and closed. "My uncle Scotty is one fucking foulmouthed bastard," he squeaked. "And I'm gonna grow up to be *juuuuuust* like him!"

Cass burst out laughing. Scott grinned broadly, satisfied at getting the best of her, and that made her laugh even harder. He started to chuckle, and this grew into gulps of laughter.

"Ah, geez," he said, sighing, wiping his eyes. "You are too funny."

"*I'm* funny? You started it!"

"No, you did. 'Gosh darn'? I never heard you say that in all the time I've known you."

"Well, get used to it, because I'm gonna need to say a whole lot of gosh darns to make up for not swearing."

"I think I'll go with 'freaking.' Like 'You are a freaking terrible driver.'"

She smiled at him, grateful for his consent.

"Hey, don't look so happy," he said.

"Why not?"

"Because I value my freaking life, so this is the last freaking driving lesson I'm ever gonna give you."

* * *

CASS was more than a little surprised, then, when on Thursday, Scott said, "Time for a driving lesson."

She had just walked home from her AA meeting, and he was waiting at the end of the driveway, the SUV growling its warning at her. "Really?" she said.

"Yeah, really. Get in." He seemed vaguely annoyed.

The driving lesson went only slightly better than the first one, and there were no gales of laughter to cut the tension. Scott gripped the armrests as if they were flotation devices and he was trying to survive a mid-Atlantic hurricane. He muttered, "Geez!" a lot, and a couple of times started to make the "f" sound without ever quite completing the thought. She was grateful for that and felt she actually drove a little better—but not much. He also kept checking his watch.

"We can stop if you need to get to Fenway," she offered.

"No. Keep driving."

Finally, he gave his watch one last glance and said, "Okay, that's enough."

They switched seats and he drove home. When they arrived, the cleaning lady was just putting away the mop and broom. Cass hadn't realized she was coming. Scott didn't even acknowledge the woman but took the stairs two at a time up to his room. Then he came back down again just as quickly.

"Helen," he said, and Cass felt a prickle of fear when she saw the look on his face. "You mind emptying your pockets?"

Helen froze. "What for?"

"I'm asking you to empty your pockets. Is that a problem?"

"Not at all. I'm just not used to being ordered around."

"Sorry about that, but if you do what I ask, we can put this behind us." It didn't seem to Cass that he intended to put anything behind him. He looked steaming mad.

Helen put the contents of her pockets on the kitchen counter. A button, some change, her car keys, and a five-dollar bill. Scott ground his molars, the muscle bulging in his jaw. "How long you been stealing from me?"

"What are you talking about—I had that bill in my pocket when I got here."

"I put sixty bucks on my dresser—"

"I didn't take any of that!"

"—now there's only fifty-five. Before I left I took a pen and gave a black eye to every guy on every bill. So tell me, Helen. Does your Lincoln there have a black eye?"

Holy smokes! thought Cass. *He believed me!*

Helen narrowed her eyes at him. She collected everything but the five and put it back into her pocket, turned, and walked out of the kitchen.

"Just to be clear, you're fired," Scott called after her. The front door closed with a *thunk*.

Scott slammed his fist on the counter. "I gave her a huge tip at Christmas."

"Thanks for believing me," said Cass.

"I didn't believe you." He blew an annoyed sigh. "But then I started thinking how when I'd leave money around, sometimes there'd end up being less than I thought."

"You never leave money around."

He glanced at her.

Oh, she thought. *Not with me here, you don't.*

"So," he said. "You want to fill in until I can get someone else? I was shelling out a hundred a week to that thief."

"Absolutely," she said. "I told you I'd clean just for living here."

"No, I'll pay you. We'll put it against what you owe me."

When Scott left for Fenway, Cass took a look around. There was some grout behind the sink faucet that was starting to go gray. She took out the cleanser and hit that grout until it was snowy white. It was her first job since getting sober. She had no intention of blowing it.

* * *

THE next morning's AA meeting was small. It was a closed meeting, so it was generally less populated than the open meetings, where anyone could show up. But still, there were only seven people, about half the usual number. It was mostly men and a few older women.

"The moms aren't coming," she heard someone say. "School let out yesterday."

Laurel wasn't there. Cass found herself wondering how she was doing with all four of her kids at home. That could be a lot of messes.

During the meeting a few people talked—some were okay, some not so great. And then toward the end there was a long silence, and no one said anything. Cass had only spoken once before, when Jackie had been there to prod her. The silence drew longer.

"I'm Cass."

"Hi, Cass."

"I've been sober forty-nine days, and what I notice is, even though I'm still thinking about drinking all the time, I'm able to get things done now. I never realized how much I didn't get done when I was drinking. I'm almost thirty and I never learned to drive. Which is probably a good thing, come to think of it."

There were knowing nods from the group.

"So I went online and found out how to get a permit, and I got it, and now a friend is teaching me to drive. And I am so terrible at it. But I know that if I stay sober and just keep practicing, eventually I'll learn. I know this isn't new to most people but it is to me, and I'm glad I got the chance. And thanks to this group for helping me stay sober."

At the end of the meeting, they held hands and said the Lord's Prayer. When it was over, the person on her right didn't let go. "So," said the hand's owner, "the quiet girl speaks."

Cass looked up. He was older than her, maybe in his forties, bright blue eyes, wavy black hair, very nice suit. He released her hand.

"Oh, I, uh . . ." she stammered. "I'm still not, you know, totally comfortable talking . . ."

"Hey, you're here. That's ninety percent of it. Talking's just a bonus feature." He smiled—his face full of humor and warmth—and she felt her anxiety downshift out of overdrive.

"So I have a guess about you," he said. "I'm guessing that you're recently out of rehab and you don't have a sponsor."

"I know I'm supposed to have one, but it's weird to just go up to someone . . ."

"Of course it is. It should be like speed dating so it could be sorted out with less fuss."

She laughed. "I think if it looked anything like dating, I'd be out of here in a shot."

"Me, too," he said. "I'm very happily married." His smile softened, and his pale cheeks turned slightly pink. "In fact, we're newlyweds. I'm a very lucky guy." He glanced down at her. "And so is he."

Good, she thought. *Now I don't have to worry about getting hit on.*

"Congratulations," she said. "That's really nice."

He nodded. "Thanks. I'm Patrick, by the way. And now my portion of the speed date is over. What about you?"

She told him about the pregnancy, and Ben being gone, her temporary living arrangement, online class, and hope of working at a day care.

"Wow," he said. "Those are some serious changes, all in a very short time. I'm impressed you're doing so well. But I have to tell you—even Wonder Woman needed a sponsor."

"Wonder Woman?"

"A total lush. All the superheroes were." He lowered his voice conspiratorially. "Half the squad was falling out of the sky every other day—think of the pressure they were under! The Justice League kept it very hush-hush, of course."

Cass laughed. "So are you offering, or do I need to ask?"

"This is AA, hon. Asking for help is a critical skill, so yes, you need to ask."

Cass took a breath, finding herself strangely nervous, even though he had brought up the idea himself. "Patrick," she said. "Will you be my sponsor?"

He smiled that warm smile. "It's already a done deal."

* * *

WHEN she got back to Chickadee Circle, Drew was in the cul-de-sac playing basketball with two younger boys. As Cass got closer, she could see it was him against the two of them, but as tall and long-armed as he was, he was still besting them. The younger one shot the ball toward the basket; Drew slapped it back, and it hit the boy on the top of his head.

"Owwww!" he whined.

Drew gave the boy's head a rub. "Don't be a baby—you're fine."

"Hi," said Cass, stopping to watch. "School's out for the summer, huh?"

"Oh, hey," said Drew. "Yeah, these are my brothers. I'm 'keeping them occupied.'" His fingers made little quotation marks in the air.

Cass introduced herself. The middle boy was Matt and he was twelve; the younger one was Luke, age ten. "Looks like you might need another player to even things up," she said.

"You want to play?" said Drew. "Seriously?"

"Sure. Unless you're worried I might make you look bad."

"Ha! You're on."

Cass teamed up with Matt, and Drew with Luke. The game started friendly and loose, for which Cass was grateful. Though the baby might still be small, she had never been so heavy in all her life. It took her a while to get used to maneuvering with her no-longer-wiry figure, and not being able to really jump. Soon enough she got in stride, however, and made a few baskets, narrowing the score gap to a couple of points.

Matt high-fived her and made a face at Drew. "Better watch your back," he sneered.

"Watch your own, little man."

The game heated up. Fouls were alleged, baskets were cheered, names were called. After a while, Matt held on to the ball, chest heaving. "Time out!" he called.

"For what?" Drew demanded, his face flushed with exertion.

"For my lungs to stop collapsing."

They all stood there catching their breath, and in the silence a voice shrill with irritation yelled, "Boys! Boys, I've been calling you!"

A woman came barreling down the driveway toward them, a toddler bouncing precariously on her hip. "Lunch was ready ten minutes ago, and—" She stopped short and stared at Cass. "Oh, my God," she murmured. "What are *you* doing here?"

It was Laurel.

Chapter XIII

Drew's eyes flicked back and forth, mouth open slightly as if he couldn't decide whom to address and what to say first. Finally his confused gaze landed on Cass. "You know each other?"

"We've met," said Cass. She watched Drew silently put the pieces together.

"Boys, get in the house," said Laurel.

"Can't we play for a few more minutes?" said Matt. "We were almost—"

"Please go in the house and eat your lunch." Laurel's voice was taut as a high wire.

Drew glanced at Cass. Cass gave him a *do-as-your-mother-says* look.

The boys galumphed up the driveway; Laurel handed off the toddler to Drew as he passed. She put her now-empty hands on her hips. "Well?"

"Well, what?" said Cass dryly. "I'm staying with Scott."

"Let me get this straight. Scott McGreavy is the *friend* who paid for rehab?"

"Yep." Cass didn't like the snide way she said "friend," but for the boys' sake, she didn't tell Laurel off. They didn't need their mother any more tense than she already was.

"But you're not staying long," said Laurel.

"A couple more weeks."

Laurel squinted off across the cul-de-sac. "Okay, let's just agree to stay out of each other's hair. You keep to your yard and I'll keep to mine."

"Fine."

Laurel's finger came out. "And stay away from my kids."

It was too bad. Cass had enjoyed the game, and the boys seemed to like it, too. But they belonged to Laurel. "Okay," she conceded.

She could feel Laurel's agitation, that newly sober, frayed-nerve irritability with all of life's little difficulties—all those things you didn't have to think about, or even know about, when you could just keep a good buzz going.

"Laurel," said Cass. "They're nice boys."

This seemed to hit Laurel like a slap, rather than as the compliment it was intended to be. "Yes, I *know*," she said tightly, turned, and strode back up the driveway.

* * *

THAT night, it was all Cass could do not to tell Scott that the woman she'd described from rehab was his next-door neighbor. She knew she couldn't—revealing the name of a member went completely against the code. It wasn't called Alcoholics Anonymous for nothing. But she was still reeling from the encounter, and it would've been nice to talk to someone about it.

Afraid she might blurt it out, she made herself go for a completely different topic. "I should probably start looking for a room somewhere."

Scott was eating the cheeseburger she'd made him, and he stopped midchew. "Huh."

"I don't want to go back to Brighton. I know too many people there. I was thinking maybe Hyde Park or Roslindale. Somewhere near a T stop."

He laid his burger down. "Makes sense."

"So I'm going to start looking through the paper, making calls.

You've got a night game tomorrow. Think you could drive me to a few places in the morning?"

He considered this, then shook his head. "I don't want to get to the ballpark too late. Let's wait till next week when I have a day off."

"Scotty, I'm moving out two weeks from Sunday. I have to get going on this."

"You'll find something. That's plenty of time."

* * *

"HELLO?" The voice was slurry, and Cass felt a fright go through her—was it possible that her new sponsor was drunk?

"Oh, uh, it's Cass," she stammered. "I'll call back tomorrow."

"Cass, what's up?" His voice gained an edge of clarity. "Wait. Let me go out in the hallway." She heard the click of a door latching, and Patrick clearing his voice. "Are you okay?"

"Oh, my gosh, did I wake you?" It was only nine o'clock.

He chuckled. "Yeah, I was a late-night drinker, so now I go to bed early and avoid all the alcoholic mind chatter."

"I can call back—"

"Cass. Day or night. That's how the sponsor thing works, honey. You call, I answer."

"This isn't a crisis or anything . . ."

"I'm in the kitchen making peppermint tea now. Am I going to have to drink it all by myself?" he teased.

She told him about Laurel, and it was an enormous relief to get it off her chest. "I still feel so bad about accusing her of screwing up her kids back in rehab, so I tried to be nice today—and she took it the wrong way!"

"Cass, you get what this is, right? It's called drama, and it's the opposite of serenity."

"Patrick, this stuff didn't happen to me because I'm bored."

"Of course not. Drama happens all the time. It's how you participate in it that matters."

She rolled her eyes. "I'm not participating—it's just *happening*."

"Cass, you have taken an enormous amount of responsibility for the course of your life in the last month and a half. It's mind-boggling what you've achieved considering where you started. It's agency. You are the agent who guides your own life."

Cass felt a little bloom of pride, though she was still unsure of what he was getting at. "Um, thanks," she murmured.

"Some things are within our agency, some things aren't. How you behave—and how you let others' behavior affect you—is. Other people's behavior and how things affect *them* are not."

"So you're saying I'm not responsible for Laurel."

"I'm saying you're responsible for your own actions and for not getting sucked into other people's drama. And I'm saying it's always better to err on the side of kindness, even if the other person doesn't get it."

* * *

THE weekend sputtered along. Sometimes hours passed quickly—after her AA meeting Cass went to the library, got another book on child development, and spent the morning reading in a cushy chair by the children's section. But when she got home, the afternoon dragged its heavy heels and she found herself wondering whether Scott had any alcohol-based cough syrup.

At dusk she heard the boys in the cul-de-sac playing basketball and longed to go out and join them. From the window, she saw Laurel sitting in a beach chair at the end of her driveway, watching them while keeping an eye on the toddler, who was rolling a toy lawn mower across the lush green grass of their yard.

I told her I'd stay away, thought Cass. *Why does she have to go all armed guard on me?*

But then the toddler stumbled and fell, the little plastic mower toppling onto him, and Laurel jumped up at his cry. He seemed startled rather than hurt, his wails more insistent-sounding than painful. Cass had just read about that in her book, how a child's need for reassurance and attention can be just as psychologically important as the need for help. She watched as Laurel picked him up and danced him around the yard, galloping to make him laugh.

"More, Mama!" he yelled when she slowed down, and she made one more circuit around the front lawn, then crumpled carefully onto the grass with the little boy on top of her, hugging him, using her body as a kind of rocking chair to jostle him back and forth.

Shoot, thought Cass. *This makes it a lot harder to hate her.*

Luke, the ten-year-old, suddenly broke from the basketball game and flopped down next to his mother in the grass. His older brother Matt jogged over and faked a knee-drop. The two boys began to play-wrestle and the toddler crawled off his mother and into the melee. Laurel sat up and said something to Drew, who was dribbling the ball lazily.

He shrugged, then shot a basket. It bounced off the rim toward Scott's yard, and when he went to retrieve it, he looked up at the house and caught Cass in the window. His gaze lasted only a few seconds, but she saw something in it. Weariness. Wariness.

He's weary of being wary, she realized, and it dug into her so hard. Her own mother could be loving and fun, but then the booze would make her stupid and unpredictable. You never knew which you were going to get.

She remembered that feeling. It was exhausting.

* * *

THAT night Scott left for a series in Toronto. Five minutes after he was gone, Cass knew she couldn't stay in the quiet house. There was nothing to distract her from thinking about that look in

Drew's eyes . . . and cough syrup. Searching the calendar section in the local newspaper, she found a free concert at the Wortherton Senior Center.

As it turned out, it was more of a variety show put on by the seniors themselves. There were several duets, some silly skits, and a barbershop quartet of elderly men in straw boater hats. The last act was a tap dance troupe called the Happy Tappers: eight women in black tuxedo outfits with canes and top hats. One or two of them needed a hand getting onto the stage, but once they were dancing, those ladies' feet flew. They did "Me and My Shadow" in pairs, mirroring each other. The big finale was "Singing in the Rain," with the dancers in a line, doing their most complicated steps. On the last few notes, one lady turned the wrong way, into the woman next to her, and they collided, hanging on to each other to keep from falling down. In another beat they began to waltz together, as if this had been their intention all along. The crowd laughed and clapped at their quick thinking.

I want to be like that when I'm old, Cass thought as she walked home afterward. *I want to be active and funny and have some kooky hobby like tap dancing. I want to have friends who'll catch me when I stumble, and help me turn my mistakes into something that's okay in the end.*

The night was cool, the soft darkness blending in and out between pools of light from the streetlamps. She felt calm and whole, imagining herself as a happy, tap-dancing old woman. Maybe she would even be a grandmother. It was so much more pleasant to think about that than cough syrup, and she wondered if someday her brain might stop veering toward alcohol every chance it got.

When she walked in the door at Scott's, the phone was ringing. The landline almost never rang, and when it did, Scott never picked it up. He had a cell phone—anyone he wanted to talk to had that number. There was an ancient answering machine attached to the landline he must have gotten years ago and never upgraded, because why bother if you weren't going to actually use it?

But the voice murmuring through the answering machine speaker was familiar.

"Um . . . I'm looking for Cass Macklin? If this isn't the right number, I'm wicked sorry."

Cass picked it up. "Kate?"

"Hey! It's you!" she said. "Where are you? Where am I calling?"

Cass had given Scott's landline number when she'd left a message for Kate the previous weekend. (Thank goodness he still had one—there was no way she could currently afford a cell phone.) Now she explained how she'd worked out a deal to stay with him for a month.

"In *Wortherton*?" said Kate.

"Yeah." Cass chuckled. "You'd think they would've stopped me at the border."

"Is it all Teslas and designer handbags?"

"There's a bit of that, yeah."

"I thought Ben and his brother hated each other."

"No. They just fought sometimes," said Cass. "What about you? It's Saturday night, how come you're not out?"

"Trying to quit." Kate's voice went low. "Emphasis on trying."

Cass knew that the happier she sounded about it, the more Kate would feel it as pressure. "It's hard, huh," she said quietly.

"Wicked hard."

"Are you all shaky and nauseated?"

"I feel like hell. I tried to taper off because they say that's the best way, but I don't think it mattered. It's like getting hit over and over by the same eighteen-wheeler."

"Go to an AA meeting. It really helps."

"I have been. That's why I'm calling you."

Cass smiled. "Good girl. That's how it works. It's like the buddy system."

"Huh." Kate snorted. "Because we're such losers we can't make a move without holding someone's hand."

Cass thought of the two ladies at the senior center. "Someone to notice if we go off in the wrong direction and tug us back? Maybe everyone needs that."

They stayed on the phone for over an hour. Cass walked around the house, the phone wedged between her shoulder and ear, putting things away, setting the house alarm, and locking up. At one point they each put their phones down, changed into pajamas, then talked some more, then brushed their teeth and got into bed and kept talking. Kate was staying with her cousin in Cambridge, on the strict condition that she stayed sober. The cousin had helped her get part-time work at a pet-grooming place with an unfortunate company name: Hair of the Dog.

"You're kidding me," said Cass.

"No lie," Kate said, chuckling.

"You like it there?"

"Yeah, I'm really good on the days I go in. I just love the dogs, you know? They calm me down." Unfortunately Kate was only working a day or two a week, when they were shorthanded. She asked Cass if she'd found anything that helped.

"I'm a big fan of free performances." Cass laughed. "The more amateur, the better."

Eventually Kate got sleepy. "I think I made it through another day," she said. "Six down . . . a zillion to go."

"Don't think about it like that," said Cass. "It's too overwhelming. Just be happy you got this far, and tell yourself you'll try again tomorrow."

"Okay." Kate yawned. "You're the expert."

* * *

THE week was going pretty well until the ceiling collapsed.

Cass started her online course on Monday, and she pored over the readings three separate times and took pages of notes. This made it fairly easy to complete the first brief assignment and helped to stifle the doubt about whether her formerly marinated brain could find its way to the finish line of a college course.

Scott was coming home from Toronto Tuesday night, and she hoped he'd take her to look at some studio apartments on Wednesday. She had scoured the newspaper and spoken to several landlords. She wasn't looking forward to asking Scott for more money, but she figured he'd be motivated to get her out of his house finally. Then she could begin a job search and, with a little luck, become self-sufficient in the not too distant future. Well, maybe with a lot of luck.

She was watching his game in Toronto Tuesday afternoon when the ceiling came down. Just a couple of little pieces of ceiling plaster at first, falling like volcanic ash onto the L of the couch next to her. Then a chunk of wallboard hit her in the elbow.

There was a large tea-colored stain on the ceiling that she could've sworn wasn't there the day before. Water poured through the hole and onto the couch. She ran into the kitchen, grabbed a bowl, and positioned it on the couch cushions. After the initial deluge, the water continued to trickle steadily.

"Scott McGreavy at the plate," said the TV announcer. "Taking a couple of practice swings . . . He came up from Triple-A at the beginning of last season. . . . So far he's having a good year, giving him a fair chance for retaining his position on the roster. . . ."

Which is nice because he's gonna need the money to fix his freakin' house! thought Cass frantically. He was such a stickler about everything being tidy. This would put him over the edge. She ran to get another bowl and switched it just as water reached the rim of the first bowl.

As she watched the second bowl fill, she realized she couldn't do this all afternoon and evening till Scott came home; she had to get help. Did he have a plumber? She certainly couldn't call Scott and ask. What was he supposed to do, hold up a hand to the pitcher, *Sorry, pal, I got a call coming in*, and whip out his cell phone at the plate?

She ran into the office, found a phone book, and bolted back to the TV area just in time to switch the bowls. Over the next ten minutes, she called a handful of plumbers but either got answering services or receptionists saying they would try to get someone there in twenty-four hours.

Outside she heard voices and the *thoink, thoink, thoink* of a ball hitting the pavement. She ran to the living room window. It was just the three older boys, no Laurel in sight.

"Drew!" she called. "Come here a minute!"

She saw him glance at his own house, calculating the risk, and she hated putting him in that position. She was about to tell him never mind, but he was already approaching the window, Matt and Luke trailing behind him.

"Hey, sorry, but there's a weird leak in here," she told him. "I'm having a hard time getting a plumber. Do you guys have someone you use?"

"No clue," he said. "You want me to ask my mom?"

Cass considered for a moment. "Just tell me your mom's cell phone number and go back to your game."

Drew was visibly relieved. He rattled off the number and herded the boys back toward the cul-de-sac. Cass heard Luke, the youngest, say, "She *seems* okay."

"Shut up!" hissed Matt.

What were the chances that Laurel would help her? Approximately the same chance as aliens landing on the front lawn, with smiles on their little three-eyed faces and plumbing wrenches in their seven-fingered hands.

She switched the bowls again.

Whatever, she thought. *She hates me anyway.*

When Laurel answered, Cass spoke very quickly, "Hi, it's Cass next door. Can you give me the name of a plumber?"

Laurel got flustered. "What? How did you get this number? What are you talking about?"

"There's a leak, and Scott's not here. I called a bunch of plumbers but no one's available."

"What kind of leak?" Laurel demanded. "Did you break something? You broke something, didn't you?"

Cass took a breath. *Leak, leak, leak,* she reminded herself. *You have to get it fixed.*

"I think it's a pipe or something, because all of a sudden chunks of ceiling fell on the couch and now there's water coming out of the hole. Do you have a plumber I could call?"

"Oh, my God. *Which* couch?"

Which couch? What the . . . ? Who CARES *which couch?* Cass wanted to yell.

"The couch in the TV room."

"I'm coming over." And the phone went dead.

Chapter XIV

Cass felt as if she had suddenly been tied to a railroad track with a train hurtling toward her. She wanted to hide. But in another minute there was rapid-fire knocking at the door, *one-two-three-four-five*, and what was she going to do—not answer? Keep switching bowls for the next six or seven hours till Scott got home?

When she turned the knob, Laurel pushed the door open and ran in as if she owned the place, right to the TV area. "Oh, no! Not the . . ." She turned to Cass. "This is a Giuseppe Giordano—I had to special order it from Italy! You couldn't have moved it?"

Cass stared at her, dumbfounded. Because, really, was she supposed to answer?

"Never mind," Laurel muttered. "Where's the water main?"

"The . . . ?"

"The water main! Where is it?"

"I don't even know what that is." Cass started to switch the bowls, now deeply regretting the call to Laurel. For the life of her she couldn't remember why that had seemed like a good idea. Laurel grabbed one end of the couch and angled it out of the way of the falling water. "How can you not know what a water main is, for goodness' sake?"

Cass set the bowl down hard on the floor under the leak. "Because I only ever lived in apartments before, okay?"

Laurel blinked distractedly, digesting this. "It's in the basement somewhere. Come help me find it."

Cass followed her to the basement and looked around at the stuff there. Scott's weight lifting set and treadmill. A bunch of boxes. A half bathroom with a really small sink. Did a water main have a sign or a label of some kind? Because even if it was staring right at her, that was pretty much the only way she was going to find it.

"Here it is!" called Laurel from a small room in back. She stuck her head out the door. "Well, come here so I can show you, in case this happens again."

There was a long handle with a yellow rubber coating sticking out sideways from a pipe. Laurel raised it to parallel with the pipe, then pulled it down again. "Okay, now you do it."

Cass gave her a dead-eyed glare. "But you just did it."

"Yes, but what if this happens again? You have to do it yourself and know how it feels, so you'll remember. That's how you learn."

As smart and accomplished as Cass had felt completing her course assignment, she felt the exact degree of stupidity grabbing that handle and twisting it upward as Laurel watched.

They went back upstairs and Cass was counting the seconds until Laurel left. But Laurel did not leave. She stayed and helped sop up the puddles on the couch, then took the cushions off and stood them on end to air, saying, "He's lucky you were here. In another hour the leather on that couch would have been completely compromised."

Well, we sure wouldn't want our leather compromised, thought Cass snidely though she was grudgingly grateful for Laurel's help, and for the number of the plumber she wrote down.

"Tell him you're my neighbor," said Laurel, "and that I *strongly* recommended you contact him." She wrote down the name of a carpenter to repair the ceiling, too.

"Thanks," said Cass.

Turning to go, Laurel flicked her hand, as if to say *It's nothing;*
I would've done it for anyone. Even you.

* * *

THAT night, Cass perched on one of the stools at the kitchen island, strategically positioned between the door to the garage and
the TV area. She wanted to prepare Scott before he saw the ceiling
and flipped out. Possibly his flight was delayed. Possibly the little
jalapeño inside her had soaked all her energy into its own tiny
form, as it often did, and her head had sunk lower and lower until
it rested on the open pages of her book.

Somewhere above the watery surface of a dream, she heard
noises, but they were not loud or strange enough to make her swim
back up. Then she felt a presence near her—warmth, breath—and
her head bobbed up fast.

"Ow!" Scott had his hand to his mouth, where the side of her
head had hit it.

"What are you doing, hovering around like that?" she snapped,
rubbing her scalp.

"Trying to figure out why you passed out in my kitchen, is
what!"

"You were *sniffing* me?"

"Yeah, I was sniffing you. How else am I supposed to—" His
gaze shifted suddenly behind her, upward. "What the . . . ?"

Cass started talking fast. "There was a pinhole leak in a pipe
from your bathroom, and it soaked the ceiling, but we turned off
the water main, and then the plumber came and fixed it, and the
carpenter's coming on Friday to patch up the ceiling."

Scott glared at the hole, then took in the stripped-down couch
and the cushions leaning upright against the wall.

"It leaked onto the couch," Cass explained. "We didn't want
the leather compromised."

He squinted at her uncomprehendingly. "Okay. . . . Wait, who's 'we'?"

She told him about Laurel. "You have a day game Friday, so I'll deal with the carpenter."

Scott nodded and seemed to relax with the knowledge that his house would soon be in order again. He studied the ceiling. "Good thing you were here."

"That's what Laurel said. After she threw a hissy fit about the couch."

"Yeah, she's wound pretty tight, but she's wicked efficient."

And she hates me. "Well, she found the water main."

"Yeah?" he said. "Where is it?"

Cass smiled, vindicated. "I'll show you tomorrow."

* * *

CASS had a list of seven apartments to see in Boston. Scott crossed off three right away. "Those are bad neighborhoods," he said.

"No worse than where I was living with Ben."

"Yeah, no better, either. You're going to have a kid, Cass. You want to carry a baby around those streets?"

"I'm trying to find something affordable—I already ran up my bill with you."

He was quiet for a while, driving through Newton toward Boston. "Don't worry about the money," he said finally. "Just don't take a place near a bar."

Everything's near a bar, for godsake. You think that would matter? Like I couldn't find booze anywhere? Cass bit her tongue.

The first place was actually pretty nice. Second floor, sunny, no obvious bug or rodent problem. The landlord took one look at Scott's car and the rent was suddenly two hundred dollars higher than advertised.

On the way to the second place, Scott's cell phone jingled. He looked at the caller ID. "Ah, *ffff*-frig." He turned to Cass. "What's the date?"

"June twenty-seventh."

He answered the phone. "Happy birthday, Ma. . . . No, I didn't. . . . I remembered. . . . No . . . No . . . You just beat me to it." The fingers of his free hand tapped agitatedly against the steering wheel. "I'm sorry to hear that. . . . I'll call the condo manager. . . . So what's up for your big day?" He listened for another moment and then put the phone down onto the console between their seats.

After a minute he picked it up again. "Uh-huh . . . Sounds nice. . . . Did you get my flowers? . . . It's still early out there, they just haven't delivered them yet." He rolled his eyes. "I'm pretty sure they don't make the rounds at seven in the morning, Ma, that would just piss people off, don't you think?" A tiny muscle bulged in his jaw as he ground his molars. "Okay, I'm at Fenway now, I gotta go. . . . I'm *not* lying. . . . You're right, I don't have a game today, but they're calling a special practice. . . . There's Rogie, I gotta go, he's waiting for me. . . . Yeah, you too."

He stabbed his thumb at the end button as if he were squishing a bug and dropped the phone onto the console. Cass could feel his irritation pulsing around the car, trying to find a way out. Trying and failing.

At the next stoplight he picked up the phone again and scrolled through the contacts. "Yeah, hi, I need a dozen roses delivered today. . . . Gilda McGreavy, 257 Aloha Boulevard, Unit 12 C, Honolulu. . . . Just put Happy Birthday, Scott. . . . I really could care less what kind of vase. . . ." He rattled off his credit card number and expiration date.

Cass waited until his breathing evened out a little before asking, "She lives in Hawaii?"

"Yeah, I got her a condo a couple of years ago."

"That was nice of you."

"Not really. She wanted Florida."

"That would be a lot closer."

"Exactly."

* * *

THE next apartment they looked at was above a pawnshop, the whole front window crammed with a display of guns and ammo belts. The one after that was two doors down from a big discount liquor store.

The last place was on a side street a couple of blocks from a T station. The landlady seemed nice, though suspicious of Scott and his car. The apartment was listed as a studio but had a separate room the size of a walk-in closet that could eventually be used as the baby's room. It was shabby and inexpertly patched in places, but it was fairly clean and the price was reasonable.

"I'll leave you two to consider," the landlady said and stepped outside.

Scott and Cass stood in the room and looked around. It reminded Cass of any one of a number of places that she and Ben had lived in. Actually it was better than most of them, and the neighborhood seemed far quieter.

But for some reason Cass felt tears pinching behind her eyes when she envisioned a life here with her child. In the vast unknowable scheme of the world, this was what she got. This was what she deserved. It was actually better than she deserved, since she couldn't even pay the rent yet. Scotty would be taking care of that until she found work.

And when the baby came, what then? Would she keep struggling along, fending off the dark whisper in her head telling her how much easier it would all be with a drink or ten?

This place is not so bad, she chided herself. It was about as nice and almost as big as the apartment she'd grown up in. And suddenly a wave of missing her mother washed over her so hard that she thought she might weep. *Mom*, she called silently. *Mom, where are you?*

Gone. And would Cass turn into her mother, grinding along every day just to stay a step ahead of poverty, the only contentment to be found at the bottom of a wineglass, until it was finally over?

The enormity of the task she had taken on, having this baby alone, with no money and no real job skills, fighting to stay sober every hour—it felt like cinder blocks on her shoulders. And it occurred to her in the abyss of that moment that it would be so much easier . . . so much simpler . . . if there was no baby . . . if there was no her . . .

"I don't think so," said Scott.

"What?"

"I don't like it."

"Scotty, this is the last place."

"There'll be others." He put his hand on her back, and it seemed that his fingers spanned the entirety of it, from shoulder to shoulder. He nudged her forward and out the door. "Thanks anyway," he said to the landlady waiting in the hall and continued to guide Cass to the car.

"You hungry?" he said as he threaded the SUV down narrow side streets out to the main boulevard. "Let's stop and get a bite."

"Scotty," she murmured to hide the quavering in her throat. "I have to find a place."

"No hurry."

"What do you mean, no hurry? I've got no—"

He cut her off. "You could stay a little longer. I been thinking about that leak. Would've been a whole lot worse if you hadn't been there. And you're cleaning the house now. It'll take a while to find a replacement as good as Helen. Without the stealing, I mean."

A temporary reprieve.

The tears pressing behind her eyes broke free, and she couldn't speak for a moment. She felt Scott glance over, then quickly turn back to the road. She wanted to thank him, to give some expression of gratitude, a promise that he wouldn't regret his kindness, but her vocal cords refused to cooperate, so she reached over and squeezed his forearm. She felt his muscle tighten under her hand, and in another moment she released him and put her hand back in her lap.

"Pizza or burgers," he said. "What's it gonna be?"

Chapter XV

Things changed after that. Cass could still feel Scott's watchfulness, and it still annoyed her. But now that he was willing to take a chance on letting her stay, she sensed that in his mind the odds had shifted. Before, he'd been betting she would fail. Now he seemed to think it was better than fifty-fifty that she might make it.

The obvious unspoken agreement was that the minute he found her drinking, she was out.

But with imminent departure no longer looming, Cass felt less panicked about how she would manage. And she found herself thinking about drinking slightly less often than constantly.

The calls with Patrick helped. It had been a very long time since anyone thought she was worth guiding. And his advice was always sound, even though it often took her a day or so to see that. Strange how irritating good advice could be in the moment.

And strange how the calls with Kate helped her, too. Kate was a mess, often about ten seconds away from chucking everything and sucking the dregs out of wine bottles in the neighbor's recycling. But Cass seemed to be able to help her steer away from those bottles, and Kate's relief buoyed Cass's own resolve to stay clear of it, too.

"You have a nice voice," Kate said to her one night.

Cass laughed. "I do not!"

"You do. It's very sweet, like someone singing me a lullaby."

"Rock-a-bye, Alkie," Cass warbled. "Don't take that sip . . ."

Kate giggled and sang back, "When your life blows, it won't help a bit . . ."

* * *

THE next morning, Scott said, "How come you're always on the phone?"

The petulance in his tone made her snap back, "I'm not always on the phone."

"You're on it a whole lot more than you used to be."

"I have friends now."

"Alkie friends?"

"Yeah, Scotty, alkie friends. And calling each other is part of the secret alkie code."

"Okay," he said, hands up in surrender. "You just never used to be much of a talker."

"But I used to be a hell of a drinker, didn't I? More talking, less drinking. That's how we roll." She gathered up her purse. "And now I'm off to a meeting to talk a little more."

Actually she had no intention of talking at the meeting. Speaking in public still made her feel like some sort of endangered species. *Keep a low profile*, Ben had said countless times. Talking about herself, about her feelings and experiences, felt dangerously high profile.

That morning, it was an open meeting, so anyone could come. As she walked up to St. Vincent's, she saw Angelo, one of the group's leaders, waiting outside. After greeting her, Angelo looked over her shoulder.

"Waiting for someone?" she asked.

"Buncha guys from Dedham are supposed to come for a commitment. Looks like they're no-showing."

"A commitment?"

"It's when people come from other places to tell their stories. That way you don't always listen to the same ones."

"Maybe they're just late," said Cass. Angelo didn't seem to think so.

She went inside and saw an open seat at the old-timers' table. "Is this taken?" she asked.

"Nah," said Kenny, who had an impressively jagged scar on his lip. "There's always room for more, right? No such thing as a sold-out alkie show!" He let out a bark of a laugh.

Angelo came in looking none too pleased and made a beeline for Cass. He squatted down in front of her. "Listen, they aren't coming. Bozos thought it was next week. Any chance you'd speak? No one here's heard your story before, and we're all bored to death of each other."

"I'll do it," offered Kenny.

Angelo glanced at him then back to Cass.

Cass looked around. There had to be forty people there. Talking in front of a few people at a closed meeting was hard enough. This was unthinkable. "I . . . I can't," she said. "I'm sorry."

"I know it's hard, and I sprang it on you out of nowhere," said Angelo. "I just really hate to let these folks down."

"I'd be really bad," she said.

"Well, we're gonna throw rotten fruit at Kenny, so no matter how bad you are, you'll probably win an Academy Award."

"What kinda fruit?" asked Kenny. "I'm a big fan of grapes." He let out another barking laugh at his own joke. Cass smiled despite herself.

"Atta girl!" said Angelo, taking her smile as a yes. "You're up after Kenny." Before she could protest, he turned quickly and walked up to the podium. "Hi, I'm Angelo and I'm an alcoholic," he said.

"Hi, Angelo!" they all called. Except for Cass, who was considering throwing up in her purse.

* * *

To keep her mind off the impending disaster, she glanced around the room. Six or so teenage girls languished at their table, looking anywhere except at the speaker. But they didn't giggle or chat, so it was possible they were listening. She guessed they were from a nearby foster care group home. Cass remembered girls from her own group home in Brighton going off to meetings. An older woman sat with them, probably a staff member.

A little girl sat on her mother's lap eating a donut. A man who was likely her father had his arm across the back of the woman's chair. Every few minutes the child held the donut up to her father, who pretended to take a huge bite, and the little girl would giggle. Cass wondered if someday she'd be bringing her own baby to meetings. It was better than not going at all.

Focusing on anything but Angelo at the podium helped slow the pounding of her heart, but suddenly he was talking about her, and how lucky they all were that someone new was willing to jump in at the last minute. "But first," said Angelo, "Kenny's gonna talk."

Kenny hopped up from his seat and jogged to the podium. He grinned affectionately at the group. "I'm Kenny, and I am one sorry alcoholic.

"I started drinking when I was twelve and I got no one to blame for it but me. I didn't come from hard circumstances or nothing. I grew up in a nice neighborhood, nice family. Mother, father, aunts, uncles, the whole nine yards.

"I just liked to have fun and clown around and be a big shot. Drinking made it easier. Crazy, funny things would come into my head to say and do when I had a few belts. It felt great so I did it more and more. Other kids thought I was hilarious. It was fun, goddamn it. Everyone here knows it's fun.

"Being a fun guy, I had lotsa buddies. Lotsa girls, too. The ones that hung on through the wild times, it was strange, but I had no respect for them. *I* didn't really wanna be with me, so what was wrong with them, huh?

"Damned if I know how I ended up married to such a girl as Marion. She was different, and I always had respect for her, even if I didn't show it for years at a time. We had a few kids, and I think she kept me around so they would have a father, even such as I was.

"She kicked my ass for me on a regular basis, I'll tell you that. And I think that's what kept me going, kept me working, trying to do right.

"I tried to stay sober. I tried really hard. And I could—for about four days. That was my limit, then I'd have to make up for lost time. And she would know. The minute I'd walk in the door she could tell. That really pissed me off, let me tell you.

"And she tried to get me to AA a million times, but I always threw it back at her. I was too damn what they call functional for my own good. I always worked, even if I didn't get promoted too often. I always picked up the yard, paid bills, did my duty, so I thought.

"Then my eldest, Billy, comes to me right after my first grand-baby was born. I was in love with that little girl. Made me feel like the whole world was right, just looking at her. Billy says, 'Dad, about the baptism. You can come to the church, but you're going home before the party.'

"I was stunned. I was speechless, which, as you might guess, is a pretty rare thing. 'Why?' I says. And I remember his words exactly. To this day it punches a hole in my chest to admit it. He says, 'Come on, Dad. We all know what'll happen. You'll get tanked and make an ass out of yourself in front of my in-laws. I let you come to the wedding reception and that was a mistake. I can't let you ruin any more important events in my life.'"

Kenny stopped talking then. He stood gripping the podium, gazing over the heads of the members. He cleared his throat, stretched his neck from side to side.

"That night I called a guy I knew who went to AA. I told him I didn't think I could do it, but I would take a look. And when I went, everyone was wonderful to me—like good buddies I hadn't met yet. It made me realize just how pissed off my family was, because I hadn't been treated that good in a long time. It was a hell of an eye-opener.

"That was two weeks before the baptism, and Billy, God love him, he let me come. It was the best day of my life, no lie.

"Now, I won't tell you it's all peaches and roses and Sunday afternoons on the swan boats. I tripped up a few times since. And it's hard. Sometimes I'm hard. Just because I don't drink now doesn't mean I turned into Mr. freakin' Rogers. Everything seems fine, and then I blow up about something small. The difference is now I say I'm sorry. AA taught me that.

"And it's not like I lost my appetite for booze. No sir. The desire's always crackling at the back of my head.

"But one thing I know. Alcohol did to me just what it's supposed to do to us drunks. Beat me down. Turned me into something shameful and embarrassing. And I'm not going back there today. Maybe tomorrow. But not today."

* * *

WHEN the break was over, Angelo stepped up to the microphone. "Back to your tables, boys and girls," he said. "Our next speaker has been coming here for a while now, but she's never been up in front of the mike before. Her name is Cass and she's a real angel because she agreed to talk to us, even on such short notice." He started clapping and everyone else did, too.

"Good girl!" she heard Kenny say as she stood up.

Breathe, breathe, breathe, she chanted silently. As she turned to walk toward the podium, she saw Laurel sitting at the side of the room with her littlest boy on her lap.

Cass stepped up to the microphone. "Hi," she said softly, as if her lungs couldn't quite let go of the air inside. "I'm Cass. And I'm an alcoholic."

"Hi, Cass!" they shouted warmly. The teenage girls adjusted their slouches to look in her direction.

"Lately," she began, "I've, um . . . I've been thinking about my mother a lot." Her eyes began to ache as soon as her lips formed the words. *Hi, Mom*, she thought. *Look at me. Can you believe it?*

"My mother was from Nova Scotia, and she came to Boston a few months before I was born, all by herself. I was never sure why she did that—came all that way, alone and pregnant. But she must have had a reason. And I think it must have been something very bad.

"She was sad. Very sad sometimes." Cass's voice quavered. She let the air flow in and out of her mouth for a moment, then pushed on. "And she drank every day, three or four glasses of wine. She had rules for herself: never before five, always from a clean glass. I can't tell you how I knew these rules, but I knew them the way I knew the sound of her voice.

"When I was thirteen, she died of a heart attack. Suddenly. Right in front of me."

A tiny, collective gasp went up in the room.

"My mother was very shy. She worked in a dry cleaner, and she had a few friends there, but no one who could take me in. So I went into foster care.

"The first place I went was bad. Very bad. They were so"—she took a breath—"bad to me. Especially the man. He said things and tried to do things that a man should not want to do to a young girl. I was certain I would never be happy again until I was dead. Then maybe I could see my mother. And I would be safe. I don't know if I ever really admitted that to myself, or whether I see it now, from the distance of time. But death was what I wanted more than anything.

"So I stopped eating. Nothing tasted good, anyway, so that was pretty easy. When I got so thin I couldn't do much for myself, they put me in the hospital. When I got a little weight back on me, they put me in a group home until they could find another foster home for me."

The teenage girls perked up at this. She could feel the force of their attention accelerate toward her, like a flock of birds changing course as one.

"I liked school. I liked reading—a friend reminded me of that recently. And I got by. But then foster care was over and I was on my own. I had started drinking in high school, like a lot of kids do, but when I was on my own, the fear got to me. I was always scared since my mother died, but it got so much worse when I had no one. I was terrified all the time.

"Then I met Ben. And he loved me, he really did. But he was an alcoholic too, and so we just let each other be drunks. As much as we loved each other, I'm starting to realize just how unhealthy it was. God, there's so much you see when you're sober that you never saw when you were drinking, isn't there? It's like suddenly being buried in an avalanche of the truth.

"But for good or for bad, Ben was everything to me. His love probably kept me alive, even though it almost got me killed a couple of times, too."

Oh, Ben. She missed him. But she didn't miss those years. Not anymore.

"He died a couple of months ago. Alcohol poisoning."

Sad head shakes. A moment of silence for one of their own who didn't make it.

"Sometimes I wonder how I ended up . . . like this," Cass said. "I think I was born okay. I remember being happy as a child. I remember laughing with my mother one time when we only had cereal left to eat. And I remember the feel of her cool hands on my face when I had a fever.

"But I think slowly her sadness seeped into me. I absorbed it the way if you stick a pen in your pocket without the cap, eventually the ink will stain your shirt. The pen doesn't mean to stain you, but that's what ink does."

She felt herself caught in the laserlike beam of Laurel's attention for a moment. Laurel's face was hard, almost angry, but Cass had the strange feeling that it was just possible Laurel wasn't angry *with her* this time.

"I've been thinking about my mother more than usual because I'm pregnant. In the hospital when I got so thin, they told me that I probably wouldn't be able to have kids. So this is like a miracle. I've been sober for almost two months now, and that's the longest time in over a decade, and I have this baby to thank for it."

The tears caught behind her eyes started to wiggle free.

"Just as this baby makes me happy, I realize now that I made my mother happy. I was the reason she got up in the morning and worked in that hot smelly room, cleaning other people's clothes. I remember how she looked when she would first lay eyes on me when she came home from work. Like I was the most beautiful thing in the universe.

"And here I spent so many years scared and drunk and squandering that beauty. Sober and pregnant with my own child, I get that now, and I'm ashamed of it.

"But I'm trying to focus on the good: all the stuff I'm learning, now that my brain isn't in a constant fog . . . the friends I'm making . . . the help I can give others. And the hope that I can keep my own sadness from seeping into my child.

"Even in sadness, I know I've been given a chance. And I thank you all for listening."

The applause went on for a while. Several of the teenage girls were openly weeping. People reached out to touch Cass's hand or pat her arm as she walked back to her seat. The little girl's father wrapped his arm tightly around the mother's shoulders.

Cass sank into her chair, exhausted, but she couldn't help but turn to look for Laurel, sitting off to the side of the room, her little boy now asleep in her lap. She cradled his limp body against hers, lips brushing lightly against his forehead. Laurel's gaze lifted to find Cass's and held it for several moments. Then she stood gingerly with the child and walked out.

Chapter XVI

That afternoon there was a knock on the door, and Scott went to open it. Cass was in the study, working on her next class assignment, and she heard him say, "Hi, Laurel. Come on in."

Cass sat straight up, straining to hear.

"Thanks for helping out with that leak," said Scott.

"Cass handled most of it," Laurel said. "Is she, uh . . . is she here?"

"Yeah, hold on." In a moment she heard his voice in the hallway. "Cass!" he called.

A prickle of apprehension ran through her as she rose and went to the foyer, and she braced herself for a new Laurel-launched assault.

Laurel's gaze was intermittent, as if she couldn't make eye contact for more than a second at a time. "Hi there," she said. "I just wanted to invite you both to our annual Fourth of July barbecue tomorrow. I know it's last minute, and you probably have a game, Scott . . ."

He nodded. "Eleven o'clock start."

"Oh, great. The barbecue doesn't even begin until four. I hope you can both come."

Scott glanced at Cass, and she knew he was as unenthusiastic as she was. Small talk, people wanting autographs. He wasn't like

Rogie Rogatelli, happy to bask in the attention of public life. But how could they reasonably decline?

"Thanks," he said. "We'll stop by."

"Wonderful." Laurel stood there twisting one of the rings on her fingers. "Um, Cass, do you think we could speak for a moment?"

Oh, God no, thought Cass. "Sure."

Scott said a hasty good-bye and strode back in the direction of his massive television.

"Do you want to come in and sit down?" asked Cass.

"No, no," Laurel said quickly. "I just wanted to say that, um . . . well, I thought you were very brave today, talking in the meeting. I don't know if I could ever do that. And . . . um . . . I'm glad that I know. About you, I mean. I'm sorry you went through all that." Laurel shook her head, as if just knowing that a child was forced to bear such burdens made her mad.

Cass softened. "Thanks," she said.

"Also, I just wanted to tell you . . . well, to warn you . . ." Her eyes leveled at Cass, then away again. "There'll be alcohol. At the party. My husband and his friends like to have a few beers to celebrate the birth of our country." She smiled, attempting a lightness she clearly didn't feel. "It seemed unpatriotic of me to say no."

"Thanks for telling me."

"Oh, and please don't feel the need to bring anything. I'm having it catered, so there'll be lots of festive food," she said brightly. "And a magician for the little ones. But you don't have to worry about that. Not yet, anyway."

This was Laurel, trying. Cass barely knew what to make of it.

"Sounds nice. Are you going to the meeting at ten?"

"Oh, no, I'll be getting ready for the party. I won't have time for that."

After she left, Cass called Patrick and told him about Laurel's invitation.

"Well, how do you feel about it?" he asked. "Do you want to go?"

"Laurel and I aren't exactly buddies, so that'd be stressful enough. Add open containers of alcohol, and I'll probably have a heart attack right there in the yard."

"So don't go."

Somehow it wasn't the answer Cass was looking for. "Do you think it's weird that she's being nice to me all of a sudden?"

"I could speculate, but I could easily be wrong, so it's sort of pointless. The real question is, how do *you* want to handle this? And what's your backup plan if things get tricky?"

When she got off the phone with Patrick, Cass went into the TV area and sat down on the couch. Scott was in his usual spot with his legs up on the L, watching *Deadliest Catch*. A patchy-looking fishing boat bounced around in a vast gray ocean. The camera flicked to a close-up of big orange crabs being tipped from a trap. The deckhands yelled to one another, bleeps obscuring every fourth or fifth word. Scott muted it after a minute.

"What was that about, with Laurel?" he asked.

"She wanted to warn me there'd be booze at the party."

"How's she know you're an alcoholic?"

Cass didn't answer. On TV the crabs scuttled around a big plastic bin trying to escape.

Scott waited. "Oh, I get it." His eyes widened, as if he'd solved a riddle of some kind. "You can't tell me . . . which means you've seen each other at AA meetings."

Cass gave him a withering look. "Don't be a jerk about it, okay?"

"Hey, you were the one who told me she was a drunk."

"Because Drew told me, and I didn't even know who she was then. I shouldn't have said anything, so let's pretend I didn't."

"Whatever." He picked up the TV remote, but didn't push any buttons. "Are we going or aren't we?"

"Do you want to?" she asked.

"Not really, but I should probably drop by. They're neighbors and she decorated my house, and everything. Plus she knows I don't have an excuse." Scott looked at the huge screen filled with the image of a guy in foul weather gear talking agitatedly to the camera, but he still didn't unmute it. "What are you going to do?"

"I think I should go. It was nice of her to ask, and she and I haven't been all that . . . friendly. I feel like she's making an effort."

"What do you mean you haven't been all that friendly? Are you duking it out at meetings or something? Like that bitch from rehab—" His face went wide with understanding. "Holy crap! It's her, isn't it? The one from rehab!"

Cass grabbed the sleeve of his shirt. "Listen to me! You cannot say anything, you can't even *look* like you might know! It is so not-cool that I told you any of it."

"All right, all right," he said, tugging his sleeve away. "Don't flip out. Besides, you have a bigger problem than what I might or might not know."

"And what's that."

"Getting through the party."

* * *

STRANGELY, it wasn't the easy access to alcohol that occupied Cass's worry that evening. Instead she found herself perseverating on what to wear. Laurel always looked like she'd just walked off the pages of a perfume ad, even at her worst. Cass had spent the last decade filching clothes out of Goodwill boxes. It was a challenge for which she was wholly unprepared.

She found Scott in the basement doing curls with an absurdly huge weight, and for a moment she wondered if it could possibly be as heavy as it looked, or if it was a fake like the ones they used in movies. "What are you going to wear?" she asked him.

He switched hands with the weight and gave her an obtuse look. "Wear?"

"To the party."

His face was red and sweaty and he needed a shave. "Um, clothes?"

"Can you put that thing down for a minute and answer me?"

He clunked the weight down onto the stand. "I'm wearing clothes, Cass. Shorts and a polo, something like that. Are you worried I'll embarrass you?"

"No, I'm worried I'll embarrass *myself*. I've never gone to anything this fancy before."

"It's not fancy, it's just a Fourth of July barbecue."

She rolled her eyes. "Think about it, Scotty. Think about Ben, and how we lived for the last eleven years. When I say I've never been to anything fancy, I'm not kidding, am I?"

He lay back on the bench and slid his head under a barbell. "Wear that pink top we got you," he said, positioning his hands on the metal crossbar.

Cass pictured this, assessing it. "I think that's starting to get a little snug." Her breasts, previously small enough not to bother with a bra if she wasn't in the mood, had miraculously blossomed with the advancing pregnancy.

"It looks like it finally fits." He lifted the bar off the struts, grunting a little.

"How would you know? Are you checking me out?" Cass stepped forward, looming over him. She poked him in the ribs. "Are you?"

"No!" Scott's face went plum-colored, and Cass suspected it wasn't only with the effort of raising the barbell again.

"Checking out pregnant girls," she teased. "Wow, McGreavy, you've really hit rock bottom."

"I'm not . . . I didn't—" he stammered, trying to fit the barbell back onto the struts.

"Very pathetic," she said, walking back up the stairs. "Hope the papers don't get ahold of that one. . . . What's the number of the *Boston Herald* sports desk? I need to make a call."

"That's not even funny!" he called after her. "Cass!"

* * *

THE next morning Cass woke to the sound of rain slapping aggressively at the leaves of the oak tree outside her window, and relief made her sink deeper under the covers, smiling secretly to herself. Laurel would probably call off the barbecue now. Problem solved.

But when Cass walked back to Chickadee Circle after her AA meeting, the rain had tapered into a messy drizzle. By noon it had stopped altogether, though the sound of dripping leaves and trickling downspouts didn't end for another hour. Then while she was studying for her class, Cass saw the catering truck pull into the cul-de-sac and turn down Laurel's driveway, and she put her elbow on the desk, leaning her head into her hand.

Darn it, she thought. *Darn the freakin' heck out of it*.

"You don't have to go," Scott had told her before he left for the game. "Laurel will understand. She probably doesn't want to be there, either."

It was that very comment that made Cass feel certain she *did* have to go. Laurel was crazy to throw a party with alcohol this early in her recovery. The least Cass could do was show up and maybe give her a little support if she needed it. Cass remembered the one time Laurel had talked at the AA meeting about the baby pooping on the couch, and how she liked things clean and orderly.

This barbecue was not likely to be either.

* * *

SCOTT got home at 4:30 and they went right over, in hopes of avoiding the majority of the guests and their ensuing alcohol intake, intending to stay no longer than the bare minimum of politeness. A tall man with a pointy chin answered the door. After a moment, Cass realized he was not that tall, he was just standing ramrod straight. Scott had several inches of height and muscularity on the guy, and yet he looked slightly less consequential by comparison.

"Adam Kessler." The man thrust his hand toward Scott's belly.

"Scott McGreavy." Scott took the hand and pumped it once, hard.

"Great to finally meet you," Adam said, though it didn't seem as if it were actually all that great as much as appropriate, as if Scott had somehow owed him something and that debt had finally been discharged. Then he looked to Cass and thrust out the hand again, eyebrows raised, an invitation to be introduced.

Scott blinked at Cass, and she wondered in that moment if he'd forgotten her name. "This is . . . my sister-in-law, Cass Macklin," he offered finally.

"Ah," Adam said, seemingly satisfied with this explanation. "Come on in and get yourselves something to drink. Beer in the cooler out on the deck; wine, hard lemonade, and other ladies' drinks in the fridge."

Another couple was coming up the walkway, and Adam turned his attention to them. Cass and Scott stepped into the foyer and continued toward the back of the house.

"Sister-in-law?" Cass asked.

"What was I supposed to say?" he murmured. "My dead brother's pregnant girlfriend?"

"At least it's the truth."

"You saw him. It wasn't gonna fly."

Cass peeked into the living room as they passed, and she

wished she could go in and sit for a moment. The room was beautiful, bathed in buttery yellows and soothing blues. A large, bulbous-based lamp, checkered prettily with a mosaic of colorful tile chips, sat on a honey-colored side table. It was elegant yet inviting.

In the kitchen, two aproned caterers set bite-size snacks on trays. Baby quiches, tiny pizzas, skewered shrimp, and other things Cass couldn't quite identify. She smelled bacon and maple, and it was tempting to swipe a snack or two before they were presented to the guests.

"Keep moving," murmured Scott, his hand on her back.

In the family room, there was a passel of children, the younger ones driving matchbox cars across a carpet printed with streets and buildings. Older kids were slumped on couches, playing or watching a video game that involved snowboarding down neck-breaking slopes and around obstacles that seemed to crop up nightmarishly fast. Drew gripped a controller, his upper teeth sunk hard into his lower lip.

His concentration broke, however, when he glanced up and saw Scott and Cass. His guy crashed into the side of an overpass (*on a mountain?* Cass wondered), and his hovering onlookers let out a gleeful chorus of grunts and yeahs.

"See ya!" his brother Matt crowed, grabbing the controller from his hands.

Drew got up and went over to where they were standing. "Hey," he said uncertainly.

Scott chuckled. "Don't worry, we were invited."

Drew threw a skeptical look at Cass. "My mom said . . ."

"Guess she changed her mind," said Cass lightly. "Where's the soda?"

He led them out the sliding glass doors onto an expansive deck still dewy from the morning's downpour. There was an enormous hulking stainless-steel grill, a cushioned wrought-iron patio set, and coolers each neatly marked with signs: beer, soda, juice boxes, water.

Laurel stood at the far end of the deck, chatting with another woman. She glanced over, and Cass could sense her hesitation. The woman was still talking; Laurel crossed her arms and aimed her attention back at the woman, smiling and nodding.

Cass opened up the soda cooler and pulled out a Fresca. Scott's gaze flicked across the signs, as if he couldn't decide. "Juice box?" said Cass.

He shot her a *ha-ha-very-funny* look.

"You don't drink in your own home because of me," Cass murmured. "You should at least be able to have a beer at someone else's."

Still he hesitated, seeming to weigh the wisdom of her words. Drew glared down at his black canvas high-tops.

"It's okay," she said, aiming the comment at both of them.

Scott reached into the beer cooler, pulled out a can, popped the top, and took a swig. He grimaced and studied it. "Light beer—I don't even like this shit." He glanced over at her and then down at her belly. "Sorry," he told the baby. "But I don't even like this *stuff.*" He turned toward Drew, man to man, and rolled his eyes. "She won't let me swear in front of the baby."

Drew's face went wide with alarm.

"I'm pregnant," Cass explained gently. "You want to go back in and play video games?"

Drew didn't wait for a second opportunity to escape.

Suddenly a voice was raised across the deck. "Sweetie!" the woman called out across the yard. "Try not to get your shoes too muddy!" She huffed a little sigh, said something to Laurel, and stepped down the deck stairs to the yard.

When the woman was a few yards away, Laurel strode quickly across the deck toward them. "Hi," she said, smiling tightly. "I'm really glad you came." And it seemed to Cass that it was directed more toward her than Scott.

There was an elongated moment when they all seemed to need time to digest the weight of this comment, and then Laurel glanced down at the can in Cass's hand. "You like Fresca?"

"Uh, yeah. You?"

"I practically live on the stuff now. Some days I think I can smell artificial grapefruit flavor leaking from my pores." Laurel didn't appear to see the humor in it until Cass let out a laugh, and then she laughed, too, and the air around them seemed to lighten. "That's a pretty top," she told Cass. "The pink sets off the warm highlights in your hair."

"What about mine?" said Scott, pulling at the collar of his golf shirt. "Does green set off the highlights in *my* hair?"

"Well, now that you mention it, yes it does!" said Laurel, grinning.

"Geez," he said. "I gotta go find some guys to talk to."

He wandered off and the two women smiled awkwardly for a moment.

"So," said Laurel. "How are you feeling?"

"Okay," said Cass. "It's a little weird, though. I haven't been around people drinking in so long. It feels like . . . I don't know, sort of like an obstacle course or something."

Laurel's smile dimmed a watt or two. "I meant your pregnancy."

"Oh, that! Um, it's good. Except I'm eating a ton."

"Well, you're in the right place—I overordered, as usual, and Adam will be grilling hamburgers soon. Why don't you go in the dining room and have a little snack to tide you over?"

"I'll do that," said Cass, nodding. "And thanks for inviting me. This is a really nice party."

* * *

AFTER sampling everything in the dining room except something that looked and smelled like chopped seaweed, avoiding conversation with other guests, and snooping through a few more of the lovely rooms on the first floor, Cass was ready to go. She looked around for Scott, but didn't see him and decided to head home on her own. She made her way out to the cul-de-sac, where Drew and Matt and a couple of other boys were shooting baskets.

"Hey," said Matt as she approached. "Wanna play?"

Cass was so full of little cheesy spinach pockets and chocolate-chip-studded brownies, she knew she probably shouldn't. But the expectation on his face made her consider.

"A *mom?*" said one of the other kids.

Cass had certainly never been mistaken for a mom before, and she felt a tingle of terror-laced delight at the sound of it.

"She's pretty good!" Matt insisted.

"For a *mom*," muttered the kid.

Game on, you little brat! Cass thought and put her hands out for a pass.

There were enough players to sub in and out, so Cass always had a chance to catch her breath when she needed to. Kids came and went from the game, running around to the back deck to grab a burger, the rich, savory smell of grilled meat filling the damp air. They trudged through the house for treats and back out the front door to the street to watch or play.

Cass didn't know how long it had been—half an hour, maybe?—when ten-year-old Luke came out, no plateful of food in his hands, a worried look on his face.

"Drew," he said, coming to stand on the sidelines next to Cass.

"What?" Drew jumped for a lay-up but it tapped across the rim and over the other side.

"Drew."

"What? I'm playing!" He looked over at Luke, then stopped.

Sullenly he passed the ball to a kid waiting to sub in and came over to his brother.

"Mom's cleaning," said Luke.

Drew's eyes narrowed. "Like a lot?"

"She's got the Dustbuster."

"Shit," Drew muttered and strode quickly up the walkway toward his house.

Chapter XVII

Without being invited, or even thinking, Cass followed him. She wasn't sure why dust busting was a problem, though she could imagine it was probably a little annoying to the guests. But there was that look on Drew's face, the weary/wary look, and she wanted to help if there was any reason or means to do so.

Inside the front door they could hear it immediately—the petulant whine of a tiny motor. They followed it to the formal living room, where Laurel was on her knees working the small machine back and forth across the carpet. She glanced up and launched a short-lived smile.

"The kids came in here," she explained. "They tracked dirt all over the rug."

"I'll help you clean it after the party," Drew murmured.

"It'll be rubbed in by then. I'll just take care of it now." Her tone was offhanded, reasonable. But there was a stiffness to her face, as if she were holding every muscle in check.

"Mom," Drew said with forced calmness. "Let's get something to eat. There's a lot of good food out there. Let's go have a brownie."

She turned off the Dustbuster and sat back on her heels. "I'll just stay in here for a bit."

"Mom, please don't sit in here."

"Hey," said Cass, patting his arm. "If I lived here, I'd sit in this room all day. Why don't you go get yourself something to eat while your mom and I hang out for a few minutes."

Doubt stained his features.

"It's okay, honey," said Laurel.

He gave Cass a warning look, and then left.

Cass sat down on the rug with her back against the ivory canvas of the couch. Laurel stared at the round mosaic lamp. The sounds of the kids in the cul-de-sac rippled in the windows, layering with women's voices in the kitchen.

"Are we out of beer?" someone called.

"There's more in the fridge downstairs." Adam's voice.

Laurel exhaled. "He just wants everything to be normal."

Cass nodded. It was the only response she could come up with, given the fact that she had no idea what might constitute normal for a family of six in Wortherton. In fact, normal was a concept that had eluded her for most of her life. It must be nice to have an idea of what things *ought* to be like, even if you couldn't quite make it happen.

"This is a beautiful room," she said. "How'd you learn how to do this?"

Laurel took a breath and let it slide out of her like the tide. "I studied design in college."

"That must have been fun."

"It was."

"You have an eye for it."

"Thanks." Her chin lowered slightly. "I should probably go back and join the party."

"I don't really think you should just yet."

Laurel stared at her hands, her chin almost resting on her breastbone. "I have guests."

"They're fine. They aren't hungry, that's for sure."

"My boys don't like it when I disappear."

Disappear. That was the word for it. Whether it was into the bottle or a compulsive coping mechanism like dust busting . . . or something more permanent, like death . . . kids don't like it when parents disappear.

"You're right here, Laurel. In your own home. Sober."

Her voice was barely audible, like a little girl with a fever. "I don't know how long I can hang on."

One day at a time, Cass thought. One minute at a time. One breath at a time.

"What time is it?" she asked.

Laurel looked at her watch. "Quarter to six."

"How about six o'clock? Can you hang on till then?"

Laurel looked up at her for the first time, as if to gauge whether this was some kind of joke. Cass let the beam of Laurel's gaze pass over her like a searchlight.

"Where'd you get that lamp?" she asked.

"At a trade show in New York. I was interning with a design firm."

They went on like this for a while, Cass asking about things in the room, Laurel giving brief histories and explanations. Eventually they ran out of things, and Laurel looked at her watch. "Six-oh-three," she said.

"Nice job." Cass grinned. "Three bonus minutes."

A hint of a smile passed over Laurel's face. "Okay," she said. "Now what?"

Good question. Cass was just making it up as she went. Laurel seemed calmer, but Cass knew it could turn at any moment. "What about going over to Scott's for a little bit?"

"Cass, that's very nice, and I see what you're trying to do. But I can't. It's one thing to sit in my own living room. It's another to leave the building entirely."

"Okay. How about we go watch the kids playing basketball? I think you need to get away from all this . . . this . . ."

"From all this."

"Yeah. Just for a little while."

They took beach chairs from the garage and set them up at the edge of the yard. Drew eyed them peripherally. He stood on the foul line poised for a shot, but Cass could feel the heat of his attention. "Miss!" she teased, and he turned to stare at her, wide-eyed with indignation.

"You can make it, honey!" Laurel called.

Drew shook his head, muttering to himself. His shot barely reached the rim.

"*Oooooh*," sneered the gaggle of boys.

Drew grabbed the ball on rebound and bounce-passed it hard to another kid. "Sub," he said and came over to collapse onto the grass a few feet from his mother. The frequent flick of his eyes toward her belied his loose-limbed pose.

"You'll make it next time," Laurel said.

* * *

THE light slid down, hiding behind the leafy boughs until it snuffed out altogether and the streetlights came on. Adam came out on the front step, calling, "Who wants to see the fireworks?"

The basketball game broke up immediately, as kids ran to find their shoes and their parents, piling into minivans and SUVs, calling to one another, "See you there!" and "Save us a spot!" The fireworks would be set off in the farthest soccer field at Wortherton High, with the whole town crowded into the parking lot, sitting on the hoods of their cars to watch.

"Are you coming?" Laurel asked Cass.

"I'm really tired," said Cass. "I'll head home and watch the ones in Boston on TV."

"Come on, Mom!" called Luke.

"Are you sure?" said Laurel. "We have room."

"I'm sure."

Laurel hesitated and then pulled Cass toward her for a hug. "Thank you," she whispered.

"Good job," Cass whispered back.

The last car was leaving as Cass reached Scott's front door. When she went in, she found Scott sitting in his favorite corner of the leather couch with his legs up on the L, watching *Pop Goes the Fourth* on the Esplanade in Boston. "Where you been?" he asked. "I thought you went home and then you weren't here."

"With Laurel."

"You two BFFs now?"

Cass let out a tired laugh. "Yeah," she said. "We're going for manis and pedis tomorrow. Then we're getting matching tattoos."

She dropped onto the opposite corner of the couch—the corner that was starting to feel like it belonged to her—curled her legs, and let her head sink back into the soft, supple leather.

Eventually Keith Lockhart, the conductor of the Boston Pops, led his orchestra into the 1812 Overture, as meteors of color pierced the sky over the Charles River on-screen. Scott turned the volume up, "so it's like you're there," he said, and they felt the booms of the detonated explosives and the crashes of the cymbals in their chests.

Cass wrapped her arms across her stomach as insulation, not wanting the baby to be scared by the violence of sound. He could hear, after all. And maybe just as he heard these explosions, he'd heard her help Laurel eject from the nosedive of her alcoholism before she hit the ground this afternoon. She hoped that he had, that right from the get-go he would have something to be proud of in his mother.

Chapter XVIII

The next week was the July All-Star Break. Players from each ball club were voted onto two teams representing the National and American leagues to play against each other. Scott was not chosen, nor did he expect to be. "It's partly about being the best of the best, and partly about acting like you are," he explained as they ate lunch one day. "I don't qualify in either category."

Cass had watched almost every game he'd played this season so far and found this to be an accurate assessment. He was a pretty good ballplayer. But he wasn't killing it. And he didn't have the kind of star-shine that Rogie Rogatelli had, either. Still, she said, "You're a solid player, Scotty. And you could still make All-Star."

He shrugged this off, but he didn't say *Whatever*. Instead he let out the tiniest hint of a sigh and admitted, "It'd be nice." She appreciated that he'd trust her with this glimpse of his dreams, even if he thought it was probably hopeless.

In seemingly different, but essentially similar ways, their childhoods had taught them not to hope too hard, not to seek recognition or even attention. This alone would hold him back, she knew. Scott McGreavy would never be able to muster the bravado, the public fascination that Rogie Rogatelli could conjure on a hitless day with a head cold. (As it turned out, in the end Rogie hadn't made it either. But that was his problem.)

Cass smiled and reached out to squeeze Scotty's forearm for a moment. "It'd be awesome." She grinned. "And hey, maybe you could be a groomsman at the fan wedding." Last year a lucky couple was chosen to hold their wedding on the grounds of the All-Star Game, with baseball-themed flower arrangements and food. Players showed up to kiss the bride and shake the groom's hand. One or two had even been honorary members of the wedding party.

Scott snorted. "Now *that* I could do without."

Of course you could, thought Cass. Which was partly why he'd never have the chance.

"So," he said, riffling the pile of mail on the kitchen counter with a randomness that made her listen a little more carefully. "The All-Star Game's on Tuesday. I was thinking of having some of the guys over."

"Oh." She'd been thinking it would be just the two of them.

Cass had watched more games this season than she ever had in her life, and consequently she'd learned a bit about each of the players, developed opinions about their skill level and sportsmanship. Every one of these games had been viewed alone, with no one to comment to or ask questions of. It would be a big night for her, having someone else there—a player, no less—someone who could confirm or deny whether Kep Miller had a bit of a teenager-y temper, for instance, or clarify the difference between a no-hitter and a perfect game.

"Hey, that's fine," she said. "I can clear out." It was the last thing she wanted to do. She really wanted to watch that game, and where could she go? A bar?

"You don't have to leave," he said quickly. "I mean, it's up to you. There'll be beer and probably some scotch. And a lot of screaming and swearing, of course. Kep only has a ten-word vocabulary, and half of them are variations on the f-word."

"I don't want to put a damper on things."

"No, it's all right," he said. But that was exactly what she'd be—a big wet blanket thrown onto the campfire of their guy-fun. And Scott needed some guy-fun. One thing she'd noticed in the past month was that he didn't have much in the way of buddies. Other than postgame carousing with his teammates, he didn't see people. Didn't call people on the phone. He worked out, ate highly processed food, watched reality TV, and went to Fenway. Period.

"Maybe I can go over to Laurel's," she said. But she wasn't at all sure about that. Since the Fourth of July party, she and Laurel had been going to meetings together, chatting amiably in her mini-van to and from. But there was always a hesitance to Laurel, as if the intimacy of an AA meeting, bookended by a five-minute car ride, strained the limits of her friendship capacity with an unwed mother-to-be, formerly derelict ex–foster kid.

"Great idea." Scott nodded, as if he hadn't commented to her recently that he didn't think the Kesslers were "baseball people," more likely "lacrosse types," and had wondered aloud if Adam Kessler was "military." Cass knew from Ben that their father had been in the navy.

In the end, Cass never got a chance to ask Laurel if she and her family might be planning to watch the All-Star Game, and if so, might she join them. Laurel preempted this with the announcement that they'd be leaving on Saturday to spend two weeks on Martha's Vineyard, sharing a rental house with Adam's brother.

"It should be fun," she said unconvincingly. "His wife is very nice, and they have kids around the same ages as ours. Oh, but I feel bad that you'll have to walk to meetings again." As if this might be a viable reason to cancel their vacation plans.

"I don't mind," said Cass. "I'm getting so fat, I need the exercise."

"You are not!" insisted Laurel playfully, and Cass imagined that this was the way affluent women spoke to each other about their lesser insecurities (as opposed to their greater ones about phi-landering husbands and underperforming children and getting sloshed at company picnics). "You look rosy and healthy," Laurel went on. "In fact, I brought you something."

She pulled into her driveway and parked. Reaching into the back seat she pulled forward a big cloth bag. "These are my maternity clothes," she said. "I won't need them again. Adam got a vasectomy as soon as he heard I was pregnant with Timmy." She rolled her eyes and muttered, "Practically that *day*."

"Wow, that's so nice of you!" said Cass, having no idea what to say about Adam's behavior. At almost five months pregnant now, her belly was beginning to press uncomfortably against even the looser pants she'd purchased a month before with Scott. She'd been dreading another shopping trip, especially since maternity clothes would be expensive and their use short-lived.

"It'll be nice to see them get some wear again," said Laurel wistfully. "I loved being pregnant."

"You did?"

"Oh gosh, yes. I felt so powerful. Creating another whole person, who'll someday walk this earth, making their mark—it's so . . . important. And everything is clear. You have to take care of yourself for the sake of the baby. You *have* to." She gazed through the windshield up at her house. "My alcohol craving was almost nothing. I was too busy craving the child." She sighed. "And now . . . I clean."

"Hey," said Cass. "A cleaning habit isn't so bad. At least it gets you something."

"What?"

"A clean house! I go to performances—there's nothing to show for that."

"What kind of performances?"

"Any kind. Last night I went to a poetry reading at the library. I didn't understand half of what the guy was getting at. Something about a brown dress and a tin bucket and rage. People were nodding, and I was like, 'Huh?'"

Laurel laughed—a real, truly tickled, loud guffaw—and Cass realized how rarely that happened, which made it particularly gratifying.

Two weeks without Laurel. Who could ever have predicted that would end up being a *bad* thing?

* * *

SULLEN as an unfairly punished child, Cass trudged to St. Vincent Church on the evening of the All-Star Game. St. Vincent's, as it turned out, was home to a recently renovated, particularly old and unusual type of pipe organ. Cass had seen the notice for the concert posted on the church bulletin board as she left her AA meeting that morning. She had absolutely zero interest in organs, or for that matter, dusty old blue-haired church music. But she needed somewhere to go, and it was between that and sipping a ridiculously expensive cup of tea very slowly at Wortherton Tea and Spices.

She sat slumped and irritable in the pew, spindling the photo-copied program between her fingers. But when Father Whatever-His-Name-Was stopped thanking the seemingly endless list of people who'd contributed to the renovation fund, and gushing about Professor Who-Cares and how lucky they were that he'd deigned to grace them with his talent, the guy finally began to play the damned thing.

And in a way Cass had never experienced before, the music filled every last crevice of the church, from the highest corners of the vaulted ceiling to the pads of the kneelers tucked under the pews. It reverberated along her clavicle and hummed in her ribs, great mountains and valleys of sound, whole continents stirring and moving at the hands of one little stoop-shouldered man, his comb-over flapping as if it, too, could hardly keep from rising in awe.

When the concert was over, the little professor's face shone with joy and sweat, and he had to keep dabbing his flushed cheeks with a handkerchief as he bowed. "An honor to play such a venerable instrument," he said, breathing heavily. "And a workout!"

Cass didn't know what time it was when she left the church to walk home. She felt she had had a full evening and assumed the rest of the world had, too. So she was surprised to see two trucks and a sports car, all late models and expensive looking, parked in the cul-de-sac when she got home. She stopped, wondering momentarily what to do, realizing very quickly that, short of sleeping in the shed curled up between the lawn mower and the Weedwacker, she would have to go into the house and hope to avoid the scene by going straight up to her room.

She opened the door to find the foyer full of Rogie Rogatelli yelling into a cell phone. His opposite hand waved so far afield from his body that his fingertips seemed to brush the walls.

"You don't listen!" he was shouting. "I told you all this already, but you only hear what you want to hear!" He saw Cass and his free hand dropped to his side as he held her gaze with his own. "Look," he murmured into the phone, suddenly conciliatory. "I don't want to fight anymore. I'll call you in the morning. . . . Okay, baby, I love you, too."

He pocketed the cell phone and smiled at Cass. "Hello," he said, and she could see how anyone—man, woman, or child—would want to please such a person. Those big dark eyes, flashing with fury only moments before, were suddenly full of all the happy times there were to be had in the world.

"Hi," she said, smiling foolishly. "I, uh . . . I'm just going . . ."
Upstairs.

That had been the plan, but before she had quite retrieved it from memory, Rogie had his arm around her, guiding her toward the back of the house, where the TV blared and men laughed, and one in particular screamed, "Fuck, no! Aw, for fuck's sake!"

Three men stood in front of the TV—Scott, Kep Miller, with his wandering blond curls sticking to his forehead, and Cory Macia-Rojas, a catcher with thighs as thick as tree trunks.

The kitchen and TV area were barely recognizable. Empty beer bottles stood along the counters amid containers of Chinese food and packets of soy sauce half used and dripping. A box of Klondike ice cream bars that no one had had the sense to return to the freezer sat leaking milky fluid off the counter and onto the floor. Half-empty bowls of chips lay abandoned on the coffee table next to a tipped jar of salsa.

"Look what I found," said Rogie, his arm still firmly around Cass's shoulders.

The men turned, Cory grinned stupidly, and Kep said, "Whoa, whozat?"

"Cass. She's my sister-in-law," said Scotty, louder than necessary. "She lives here." He wasn't as drunk as Kep, but Cass could tell he was working hard to enunciate.

"That true?" Rogie asked, his voice a purr by her ear.

"Yep," she said, because what was the point in splitting hairs with this crowd?

"Well, come in and watch the game with us, Scotty's sister-in-law that we never even heard about before," he said wryly. She was glad that in her newly plumped state, he didn't recognize her from that night at the bar when she'd dropped the daiquiris.

The scoreboard on-screen said it was the top of the ninth, and she really wanted to catch just one inning. She looked at Scott for the okay, and he looked at her for the same. "Maybe for a minute," she said and moved forward, out of Rogie's grasp.

The men started to settle back onto the couch, Kep taking up Cass's usual corner. Scotty told Kep, "Get up, that's her spot." Then he sat down next to her, effectively barricading her from the men and the booze. There was a glass of amber liquid on the table—scotch, Cass guessed from the bottle of Glenlivet on the counter—and Scotty began to reach for it, his eyes on the TV screen, but then seemed to catch himself and sat back without completing the action.

"So you're Scotty's brother's wife," Rogie asked her amiably, as if he weren't being nosy, just passing time with some conversation. But she could feel him sizing her up, speculating about her place in this scenario: Scott's house, Scott's life.

Cass nodded at Rogie and turned back toward the screen, hoping he'd get bored with her and watch the game. But apparently he was still interested enough to ask, "The brother Scotty's always yelling at on his cell phone? Telling him to get his shit straight?"

Cass cut her eyes toward Scotty, who told Rogie, "He's dead now, so leave it."

Rogie let out an *"Ohhh,"* more of a sigh than a word. "Sorry, man." It rang with sincerity, and Cass saw that there was understanding for the magnitude of the loss in his eyes. "Sorry," he said to her, and she nodded her thanks and went back to watching the game, because what else could she do? That's what they were all there for.

The camera zoomed in on a pitcher Cass didn't recognize. "Shoulda been you, Rogie," Kep proclaimed loudly. "That guy's such a douche."

"He's National League," said Scotty. "He didn't take Rogie's spot."

"All's I'm saying is he ain't as good as Rogie. In fact, he ain't fit to—"

"Kep," growled Rogie. "Shut up, for once."

"Rogie, I'm just sayin'— Shit, how is *he* up again!" Kep jumped up from the couch, flinging his arm in the direction of the TV screen, which showed a player from the Yankees taking a practice swing. "They're screwing with the lineup!"

"Sit down!" the others yelled. "You're drunk! They're not screwing with anything!"

"I HATE that guy!" howled Kep. Turning to the TV, which

now projected a close-up of the player's face, he let out a stream of recommendations for Mr. Yankees to bite, suck, and chew on various parts of Kep's anatomy, which he now wagged wildly in front of the screen.

Cass tried to keep a straight face, but when she peeked over at Scotty, she caught him glancing at her, and the two of them burst out laughing.

The others stared at them, Kep whipping his loosely hinged body around and demanding, "What?," which sent the two of them into another fit of hilarity. Loose with scotch, Scott reached out, patted her stomach, and chortled, "Cover your ears, little Ja-lapeño! Hal! I like to call him Hal"—he stopped to laugh and gulp in air—"or possibly Hallie!"

Kep put a hand on his hip and turned to the others. "The fuck is he talking about?"

Which made them laugh all the harder.

* * *

WHEN the game ended, Cass made a hasty exit, her stomach muscles still aching from laughter. On the way up the stairs she heard Rogie's voice. "She seems like a nice girl," he said. "What the hell's she doing with you?"

Stopping to listen, Cass heard Kep's raucous "Ba-ha-ha!" and hands slapping together—a high five, she guessed.

"She's just staying here till she finds a place."

"What—you're running a homeless shelter now?" Rogie razzed him. "You finally found a cause to support?"

"That's right," Scott retorted. "So when Miss July kicks you to the curb, come on over."

"Ah-ha-ha!" Kep cackled. "Wait—it's July?"

Cass went upstairs to bed. As she drifted off to sleep she heard voices raised briefly about car keys. When she came down the next morning, Kep Miller was snoring on the leather couch, a throw blanket reaching only to his knees. The place was still pretty messy, but the beer bottles had all disappeared. She tossed out the rest of the detritus and wiped down the counters. She would vacuum later when Kep was gone. She was the house-keeper. That was her job now.

* * *

No one calls in the middle of the night to give you good news, thought Cass a week later when the phone rang at two in the morning. She was returning from one of her frequent nighttime bathroom trips, and the harsh jangle seemed to scream through the quiet of the house.

She went downstairs, hoping it was a wrong number. When she answered in the kitchen, Scott had just picked up the extension in his bedroom, his voice gravelly with sleep and annoyance. "Hello?" he said. It sounded like *Ho?*

A woman began to cry on the other end, gasping, straining to control herself. "Thank God," she whispered, her words slightly slurred. "Cass? Is Cass there?"

It was Kate, and she was drunk.

Dammit, thought Cass. *If you have to jump off the wagon, don't call in the middle of the night to tell me about it. And for godsake, don't wake Scott before a game.*

Cass let out an annoyed huff. "Are you okay?"

"No, I'm . . ." She started to cry again.

"Where are you?"

"I think . . . I think I'm at that crappy motel on Soldiers Field Road," Kate groaned. "Wait, let me get to the window."

Cass heard Scott on the extension. "Jesus," he muttered.

"Yeah, that's it," Kate said, panting. "You know that one?"

Worry began to override Cass's annoyance. "Kate, what happened?"

Kate's voice rasped painfully. "This guy, he seemed *nice*, Cass. I swear to you he seemed like a good guy." She had sounded drunk at first, and she probably was. But Cass realized that her words weren't slurred so much as malformed, as if her lips and tongue were the wrong size. "But he was . . . Ow! I think my ribs are broken . . ." And she started to cry again. "I have to get out of here before he comes back, Cass. Please, you have to get me out."

"I'm calling the police."

"No!"

"Why not, for godsake?"

"Because he said he'll come after me! Please, *please* come get me. I'm begging you!"

Scott was still on the line; Cass could hear his breath in the receiver. Things had been so good between them—far better than she ever could have imagined. She not only had a safe place to live, but they were even slowly becoming (she was shocked to admit) friends. But he'd made it clear there was only one thing other than her drinking that he absolutely would not tolerate: anything that messed with his game. No drama. No friction. No stress.

Asking him to go to Brighton in the middle of the night, when he should be getting sleep before the game, to bring home her drunk, beat-up friend . . . That was drama. Stressful drama. And it would cause plenty of friction. How soon before he'd had enough? How soon before she'd be living in some rattrap apartment, alone, broke, and unprotected?

"Is there anyone else you can ask?" Cass said. "How about your cousin?"

Kate began to weep. "It's okay," she choked. "I shouldn't have called."

Self-hatred swept through Cass like a sandstorm, grinding away any pride she'd felt at helping Laurel get through the party or counseling Kate on the phone. Easy to do when there was no personal cost, no sacrifice involved. Now with a friend waiting to see if her attacker would return, Cass was actually considering whether to turn her back.

I suck, she thought. *I really do.*

"We'll come." His voice was so low Cass wasn't sure if she'd heard correctly. "We'll be there in fifteen minutes," Scott murmured. "Open the door a little so we know where you are."

"Thank you!" Kate wailed. "Oh my God, thank you so much!"

They hung up and Cass quick-stepped up the stairs. Scott was already coming out of his room, zipping up the fly on a pair of jeans, bare-chested, holding a T-shirt in his hand.

"Scotty, I'm sorry——"

His look was cold. "You were gonna leave her there?"

It was like a slap, and Cass felt herself reel from the blow. "I——"

"She's your friend, right?"

"I didn't want to ask you—you've got a game tomorrow——"

He squinted at her in disbelief. "What kind of a selfish prick do you think I am?" He looked away. "Jesus, get some clothes on."

On the way to Brighton he drove as if they were being chased, though the roads were mostly empty. Cass couldn't tell if it was because of his hurry to get there or his anger at her.

At a stoplight she said, "I don't think you're selfish, Scotty. I'm just trying not to screw it up."

The light changed and the car lurched forward, engine roaring up to the gear change, then roaring up to the next. But the rope of muscle in his neck stopped bulging quite so much, and the air between them stopped vibrating with his anger.

He pulled into the low-slung Beauty Rest Motel, the parking lot scattered with an odd array of cars, from beaters to a few fully loaded high-end models. Scott's SUV crawled along, searching the poorly lit walkway for a door that was slightly ajar. They saw it on the end, and Scott double-parked. With the motor running he opened his door. "Stay here," he said.

"Why?"

"Because if the guy's back, you'll be in the way."

"But—"

"Just do it." And he got out and closed the door.

It seemed to take lifetimes, and Cass felt her blood pounding in the vein in her neck. *Get her and get out*, she practically chanted. *Just get her and get back here.*

The motel door opened wider now, and for a brief second Cass couldn't tell what she was seeing. She grabbed Scott's cell phone, ready to dial the police.

It was a set of bare feet coming through at doorknob height. Then arms. Then Scott was hurrying toward the car carrying Kate cradled against him. Cass jumped out, opened the car door, and helped him guide Kate onto the back seat. Cass got in with her. In another moment Scott was in front, and the car was in motion.

Kate was barely recognizable. One eye was swollen shut. Her lips were purple and huge like a clown's, the lower one split and her chin dark with blood. Her pale dress was splattered. At the angle she was lying across the seat, Cass could see she had no panties on.

Kate began to weep. "Thank you!" she choked over and over.

"It's okay." Cass soothed, gripping her hand. "You're okay now."

Scott turned off the highway, and shortly they were pulling up to the Emergency Department at Woodland Hospital. Kate looked out the window and saw the sign.

"I can't go in there!"

"You don't have to tell them who did it," said Scott.

"No!"

He wrenched around fast in his seat. "Okay, where should I drop you, then? Because if you won't get checked out, you're not coming home with us."

Chapter XIX

The emergency room was nearly empty. Nevertheless, between the x-rays, the rape kit, the bandaging and bone-setting, they were there for hours. At first Kate refused the rape kit that would gather DNA evidence of her attackers and involve pictures of the damage they'd done. But then the nurse took her hand and murmured, "Sweetie, all this does is give you options. You never have to use them if you don't want to." Kate acquiesced like a child.

Cass had sent Scott home to sleep, but when he returned to get them, he looked bleary-eyed and pale.

"Broken?" he said to Kate, nodding toward her ankle.

"Yeah, but it's a clean break. It'll heal up quick."

"Ribs?"

"Hairline. Just two."

Cass held Kate's crutches as she slid herself gingerly onto the back seat of the SUV. At the house they got her up to a bedroom on the second floor. She was asleep in moments. Scott went back downstairs and Cass followed.

"You're not going to bed?" she said.

"Day game," he told her, tearing into a packet of Brown Sugar Cinnamon Pop-Tarts and loading them into the toaster. "Have to be there by ten."

"You could sleep for a couple of hours. I'll make sure you get up in time." Cass was so tired she could have lain down right there on the floor tiles, but she had to take every opportunity to reduce the cost of last night's rescue mission.

"Nah, it'll just make me foggy. Better to stay up," he said. "You should sleep, though."

She didn't move and neither did he. The smell of synthesized brown sugar and cinnamon wafted over from the toaster as they sat on stools at the island, gazing wearily in different directions.

"I'm trying to figure out how to thank you," she murmured into the air.

"I don't want to be thanked."

"You did something big last night."

"I did what I shoulda done. What anyone would do. It's not big, Cass. It's normal."

That word again.

She turned and looked at him, because it was clear that whatever she said would be the wrong thing, that in his head it would always somehow mutate into an insult. But she wanted him to see her face, in hopes that it might say the right thing without saying anything at all.

He glanced up and met her gaze, and she thought, *I know you're a good guy.*

His features relaxed, still dead tired but the irritability seeping away. "So don't thank me," he said, as if continuing his previous thought.

"Okay," she said, still gazing into his face. "I won't."

* * *

Cass couldn't sleep. The image of Kate's battered face—the wrongness of the colors that now laid claim to her cheeks and lips—kept popping into her head. Filled with panic, Kate had wanted Cass to stay during the medical examination. Cass had seen beatings before, and she'd seen the resulting damage. But she hadn't been prepared to witness what had been done to her friend when the blood-spattered dress had been cut away. Evil was alive and well, having feasted on the rotted hearts of Kate's attackers.

Sickened, she'd closed her eyes and listened to her CD of the girls singing. But even that couldn't keep her from thinking about how nice one drink—*one little drink*—would feel right about now. She kept her distance from the dining room liquor cabinet.

Kate continued to sleep. Cass watched Scott's game. He played terribly, bobbling the ball, throwing wide so Kep Miller at first had to jump for it, and whiffing every at bat. After his third strike-out, he stalked back into the dugout and thunked down hard onto the bench. The camera caught the manager going over to sit next to him, elbows on knees, talking blank-faced while looking out onto the field.

"Uncle Scotty's having a bad day," Cass murmured to the baby. "It's what you get for being a good guy sometimes."

"Who're you talking to?" Kate's voice was weak and parched behind her. She was still in the hospital scrubs the nurse had given her after the dress was cut off.

"I didn't hear you come down," said Cass, turning off the TV. "How're you feeling?"

"Sore," said Kate. She hobbled gingerly over to one of the kitchen stools and sat down, leaning her crutches against the counter.

"Food?" Cass got up.

Kate shook her head. "Maybe just water."

The doctor had given her some antibiotic salve for her split lip, and she'd applied it before coming down. The shine amplified the bruising to an angry eggplant color.

"I should call my cousin," she said.

"What're you going to tell her?" Cass filled a glass from the tap.

"The truth."

Handing over the water, Cass raised her eyebrows.

"Believe me," said Kate, "I've got the lie all worked out." She gave a tight, sad smile. "But I haven't lied in twenty-six days. And you know, it was kind of nice. It takes so much less energy when you don't have to keep track of which bullshit you fed to who."

Cass nodded. She hadn't thought of the correlation between drinking and lying. Other than the fib about being Scott's sister-in-law—which was his fabrication, not hers—she'd had no reason to twist the truth in seventy-six days. And Kate was right; the truth was just easier. Or could be.

"You can use the phone in the study," she said.

"If you don't mind, I'll use the one in here. Then I won't have to say it all twice."

She took a couple of gulps from the water glass, picked up the phone, and dialed. "Melanie?" she said. "Yeah, I'm fine. Well, actually I'm pretty banged up, but I'm okay now. I'm with my friend Cass." Kate glanced over, and her eyes went a little shiny. "Yeah, the one who's been helping me keep it together." She nodded and said to Cass, "Mel says thank you."

She reached out and rested a hand on her crutches, studying them for a moment, as if they were a clue to some mystery. Her voice quavered. "I need to tell you what happened last night."

Kate's evening had begun benignly enough with a call to an old friend named Sofie. She'd been bored and lonely and Sofie had a wicked sense of humor. "Sofie's not a drunk," Kate told her cousin, "but she's got that same crazy kind of funny. And she can sure drink, if you know what I mean."

Cass knew exactly what she meant. Sofie was one of those lucky souls who could drink heavily, and then not think about alcohol for a week or a month, or until the next party fired up.

Sofie had invited Kate to come out with her and some girl-friends to a club in Allston, insisting that she wouldn't let anyone give Kate a hard time about not drinking. And she had kept that promise. "It was weird, though," said Kate. "I've never been out sober. I didn't know how to talk to people with just a Diet Coke in my hand. They were all so nice, but I couldn't figure out how to be part of it."

The girl sitting next to her at the table was drinking rum and Coke and must have taken the wrong glass when she got up to talk to someone at the bar. Kate picked up the remaining drink and took a big gulp. Suddenly she had that silky-easy feeling where everything loosens up and gets pliable.

Just one, she told herself. *I'll just have the rest and then go back to Diet Cokes.*

Kate spoke into the phone, but she was looking at Cass. Cass gave a sympathetic nod. It was like being at a meeting. The stories were all different . . . but they were all the same.

"These guys asked us to dance," she told her cousin. One of them seemed to like Kate, dancing only with her. His name was Beck Breen, and she thought it was the coolest name she'd ever heard, especially once he started buying her drinks. Under cover of loud music, no one knew she was telling him to get rum and Cokes. It was all so easy, as if the cosmos had given her a free pass.

And then people were pairing up and leaving. Sofie questioned her several times about going off with the guy. *You okay?* she'd asked. *You sure about him?*

"I was as sure as I ever was when I was drinking. Which means too stupid even to ask myself the question in the first place." He had said simply, *Let's get out of here*, and she'd said, *Okay*, and they went.

Breen made a drug run. "I'm not even sure what he picked up," said Kate. She took a couple of breaths. Her fingers gripped the edge of the counter.

"Then two of his friends got in the car, and we drove to that shitty motel, and they did drugs and raped me and beat the shit out of me when I tried to fight back, and then they left to go score some more drugs, and I didn't know if they were coming back, and I called Cass and she came and got me."

The phone clattered onto the counter as her shaking hands came up to cover her face, and she began to sob, her body hitching back and forth. Cass wrapped her arms around Kate. She picked up the phone and said, "We'll call back," and hung up.

"They raped me," Kate choked out, her voice sounding scorched and blackened, as if by wildfire. "They beat me up so bad—and not just to control me so they could rape me some more. They did it for fun, Cass. They were laughing. They thought it was funny."

* * *

SCOTT came straight home from Fenway, eyes half lidded with exhaustion and self-disgust.

"Sorry about the game," Cass said.

He shrugged. "How's she doing?"

"She's in tough shape." Cass met his eye. "In every way."

He glanced off, staring unfocused into middle space, as if envisioning the many ways in which Kate was not okay. "She going home?"

"Her cousin has little kids." A simple declarative statement, but with repercussions for all of them. After Cass had gotten Kate calmed down, showered, and into a set of borrowed clothes, she went down for a nap like a cried-out child. Then Cass had called Melanie back. Melanie was sympathetic, and even willing to overlook Kate's drinking this one time, since she'd already paid for it far more than just getting kicked out of the house. But Melanie was firm that she didn't want to traumatize her kids with the sight of their beloved auntie Kate's bludgeoned face. Could she stay with Cass until the bruises faded?

"I can't let her be alone," Cass told Scott. She'd already decided to ask him for the money so she and Kate could stay at an inexpensive hotel somewhere. It would put her further into his debt, but she could still feel the shame of her hesitance to go get Kate in the first place. She couldn't abandon her a second time.

"Will her cousin let her go back at some point?" Scott asked.

"When she doesn't look so scary. Maybe a couple of weeks."

Scott sighed. "Okay," he said.

Cass was puzzled. *Okay, what?*

"She can stay." He rubbed the back of his neck. "She's not a slob or anything, is she?"

Cass flew toward him before she could think. Kate could stay. Which meant Cass could stay. Here in this house that had become a home for her, the first she'd had in almost seventeen years. Her arms were around the broad girth of his chest, her cheek against his collarbone, squeezing him as hard as she could, breathing in his soapy, postshower smell, still liberally mixed with the salty scent of skin that sweat every day.

In another moment, his hands were on her back, patting her. She could feel the rumble of laughter in his chest. "Hey, you're pretty strong for a skinny pregnant girl."

She looked up at him, grinning, feeling maniacally grateful. He gazed down at her. "You haven't slept yet, have you?" he said. "You're crazy tired."

Thank you, she mouthed.

He smiled and chided, "Ah, go to bed."

* * *

THE next morning Scott drove Cass and Kate to the AA meeting at St. Vincent's. There were muted gasps when they entered the room. This was predictable, of course, but it sent a jolt through Cass. In the twenty-four hours since Kate had been at the house, Cass's brain had slowly acclimated to the hideous sight of Kate's face, dropping a sort of mental veil between them. It was the only way she could talk to Kate without feeling sick. Now the barely hidden shock in the room had the effect of lifting that veil, and Cass felt the queasiness return. Selfishly, she was glad she could sit next to Kate in the circle and not have to look at her.

When it was time to share, Kate said, "I'm Kate. I've been sober for a day and a half." She glared down at her casted foot. "I'm not ready to talk about it yet. Maybe tomorrow."

After the meeting, Scott was waiting to take them to Cass's five-month pregnancy checkup. Kate slid into the back seat of the SUV and began to cry quietly, taking little sips of air with her hand over her eyes. Scott glanced warily toward Cass. She gave an apologetic shrug. *There's going to be a lot of crying,* she thought. She hoped it wouldn't bother him too much.

She was surprised when he followed them into the waiting room at the Waverly Community Health Center and raised her eyebrows at him when he held the door. "It's hot in the car," he said and took a seat in the corner under a poster that proclaimed *Condoms = Smart.* He put earbuds in and was soon engrossed in thumbing through items on his phone.

"Come with me?" Cass said to Kate. "I want you to hear the baby's heartbeat."

They approached the desk and the Caribbean-sounding receptionist pressed her lips together at the sight of Kate, but otherwise betrayed no concern. "Hello, ladies," she said brightly. "And how you feeling this fine day?"

Cass smiled back. "I have an appointment with Ana."

The receptionist checked her list. "Cassandra Macklin, that's you." Her eyes took in Kate in a full gulp, as if daring herself to face danger. "And how may I help *you*, miss?"

"She's with me," Cass said quickly. "But I was wondering if someone might be able to check the dressing on her bandages?"

"I think we can arrange that, yah. You go on back now, and I'll work my magic."

In the exam room, Cass introduced Kate to Ana.

"Very nice to meet you." Behind Ana's pleasant smile, Cass could sense her assessing the damage. "I see you've had some bad luck."

Kate's eyes found Cass with a *what-do-I-say?* look. Cass tipped her head toward Ana.

Kate sighed. "I got beat up."

"I'm so sorry," Ana said gently. "No one should treat you like that."

Kate's nod of agreement was completely unconvincing. That's when Cass understood: *she thinks she deserved it.*

"Are you talking to anyone about this beating?" Ana's soothing voice softened the edge of her direct questioning.

Kate shook her head, but then she corrected herself. "I talk to Cass," she said.

Ana warmed Cass with her approving gaze. "Is always good to have a friend to talk to." She turned back to Kate. "But, *mi hija*, a beating like that, it's too big for just a friend. You deserve more help than that."

Mi hija. Cass had heard it before. It meant *my daughter*, a Latina way of showing motherly concern. It made her throat tighten with sadness.

Kate nodded, her head lowered in shame, as if she had been thoughtless to put so much on the shoulders of a friend. Tears began to leak down her face. Seeing the depth of Kate's self-loathing, Cass realized Ana was right. *She needs more help than I can give.*

"We have counseling services here," said Ana. "I'd like to get you an appointment as soon as possible. Should I do that, *mi hija*?"

"Okay," Kate whispered.

"I'll be right back." Ana strode quickly from the room.

"I'm sorry." Kate wiped tears from her chin with the back of her hand. "I shouldn't—"

"Hey." Cass cut her off. "You'd do the same for me."

Kate looked up uncertainly. "I would?"

Cass smiled. "Well, you would *now*."

The barest whisper of a smile passed over Kate's face. "That's a fact."

* * *

AFTER Cass's appointment, one of the counselors at the clinic
skipped her lunch hour to talk with Kate. While they waited, Cass
and Scott went and got something to eat at a nearby diner. It was
built out of an old railway car and sat on actual tracks that ended
abruptly on either side of the lot. The menu looked like it had
been conceived sometime in the 1950s, with entrées like Salisbury
steak and liver and onions. They sat at the counter on red vinyl
stools. Scott ordered pot roast with mashed potatoes and gravy;
Cass wanted chicken pot pie.

Comfort food, thought Cass. *Just what we need*.

"This place is awesome," Scott murmured. "Old-timey. Like
the worst problem you could have is whether your loafers are
scuffed."

Cass laughed. "You don't even own loafers."

He nodded solemnly. "And I never will."

The food came and they ate in soft, agreeable silence. Cass tried
to keep her mind off Kate—she needed a break from the horri-
fying bleakness of it. But she found herself thinking about Ben,
and all the times they'd faced violence. "Ben got beat up like that
once," she said to Scott. "I mean, he got beat up a bunch of times,
but only once that bad."

"I know," he said. "He looked like he'd picked a fight with the
Klitschko brothers."

"You saw him?"

"Yeah."

"I didn't know."

"He didn't always tell you when we got together. We fought
a lot, and he didn't want you in on that." Scott shook his head.
"He kept coming, though. I could be really hard on him, and he'd
keep coming back to see me."

"Asking for money?"

"Sometimes. Mostly not, though." Scott gave a sad little chuckle.

"He'd say he was checking up on me. Making sure I stayed out of trouble. As if I was the screw-up, and not him."

How had she not known this? It was heartbreaking. "You must have hated me," she said.

His head spun toward her. "Why would you think that?"

"Because I enabled him. He was happy, even though our life was such a disaster. Maybe if he hadn't been so happy he would have gotten clean."

"No." Scott shook his head. "I think it was the other way around."

"What?"

"Cass, I knew you. You weren't that messed up before you started seeing him. And you were never as messed up as he was, ever. If anything, he kept *you* down. We fought about that sometimes, too."

Cass was stunned. She had never suspected any of it—that Ben was sneaking off to see his brother, or that Scott had thought anything of her, much less lobbied Ben to take better care of her. All this going on behind her back . . . it made her wonder what else she didn't know.

Scott picked up his fork again, and Cass did the same, though in the end she couldn't finish the rib-sticking pot pie. Scott switched their plates and finished it off while she picked at the last few bites of his roast. He asked the waitress to fill their water glasses.

"Not me," said Cass. "I can't take another sip or bite of anything."

"You need to stay hydrated," he said, licking a drip of gravy off his lip. "You and Hal got a lot of fluid needs."

She gave him a wry smile. "Thank you, Dr. McGreavy."

"I read it somewhere."

"My pregnancy book, maybe?" she teased.

"No." He wiped his hands on his napkin for a moment, then admitted, "You left it in the bathroom. I needed reading material."

"Busted!"

He rolled his eyes. "Yeah, major felony." But a flush rose in his cheeks.

When they went back to the Waverly health clinic to pick up Kate, her eyes were very red, as if a lifetime of tears had washed over them in that one hour. But she also seemed calmer, her load just a straw or two lighter.

"I brought you some takeout," Cass said.

"Thanks. And thank you, Scott. I know you probably foot the bill."

"My pleasure," he said.

"Hey," Kate told him, inhaling a sniffle. "Next time you should go in with Cass and hear the baby's heartbeat. It was really cool."

"Yeah, and maybe you can read up on it first," Cass teased.

"Maybe I will." He stuck his chin out at her. "Maybe I'll just do that."

* * *

ON Monday, Scott had to fly out for back-to-back series against the Detroit Tigers, the Minnesota Twins, and finally the Los Angeles Angels. He'd be gone for eleven days, the longest trip of the season. In the foyer, as he waited for the car to show up to take him to the airport, he handed Cass two hundred dollars "for food and Ubers and whatever."

"Not Uber. No phone to download the app, and even if I did, I'd need a credit card. No surprise, I've never qualified," she said wryly. "I'll call a cab." She tucked the money in her pocket. "Thanks for this."

"Keep track of it."

"I'll give you the receipts."

Scott shook his head. "I don't care about that. It's not you I'm worried about," he said. "If I were in her shape, I'd want to drink, and I don't even have a problem."

Cass gave a little nod of concession.

"And if stuff gets out of hand," he said, "you'll call me, right?"

"I'm not going to bother you on the road, Scotty. If anything happens, I'll handle it."

"I know you can handle it, Cass. I'm just saying you could call if you needed to."

"But I won't."

"Geez, were you always this stubborn?"

She grinned up at him. "Yeah, pretty much."

A long black car pulled up in the cul-de-sac. She opened the front door for him and he walked out, pulling his rolling suitcase. She watched for an extra moment as he made his way down the front walk. The driver loaded his bag into the trunk, and Scott turned to look back at her. He made a face and wagged his hand by his ear, thumb and pinkie extended to imitate a phone. She made the same face and gesture, but then dropped her hand in a mime of hanging up. His grin broke wide with laughter and he got into the car. She was still smiling after it pulled away.

Chapter XX

The next morning, Laurel called. "We're back!" she said.

"Welcome home," said Cass. "How was your trip?"

"We're back!" Laurel sang out again, this time with a trill of half-crazed relief.

Cass laughed. "That good, huh?"

"I made it," Laurel said with a sigh. "And that's all that matters. So should I pick you up for the ten o'clock meeting?"

"Um, well . . ."

"Is everything okay?"

"Everything's fine with me. But I have a friend staying here who's, um . . . she's in tough shape." Cass was unsure of how to explain it. Laurel was more of a high-stress, can't-win-the-game-of-perfection drinker. Cass and Kate were more life-handed-us-a-bum-deal drinkers. And Cass was fairly certain Laurel had never set foot in a crappy motel in her life, much less with drugged-up rapists.

Cass decided to go with "She went drinking and ended up in the wrong situation. She got beat up and she looks really bad, Laurel. Like *really* bad. We'll just take a cab to the meeting."

"That's absurd," Laurel said matter-of-factly. "I'll be out front at quarter to ten."

Ironically, Cass was even more hard-pressed about how to explain Laurel to Kate. She decided less was better. "A neighbor's picking us up for the meeting," she said. "She's kind of . . . *Worth-erton*, but she's a good person, so don't judge."

Kate let out a snort. "I look like I just took on the Hulk, and you're worried *I'll* judge?"

But when they went out to the car, Cass felt as if she could see Laurel through Kate's eyes. The crisp tan capris, brightly colored belt, and peach "peasant" blouse that no actual peasant could ever afford. The turquoise Chanel purse, the tasteful makeup, the delicate scent that wafted by whenever Laurel moved her arms.

"Oh, you poor thing!" breathed Laurel, the minute she saw Kate. "Does it hurt very much?" It was well intentioned, but Cass cringed at the directness.

"Not much anymore. Just throbs sometimes." Kate answered neutrally, but she caught Cass's eye with a look behind Laurel's back.

Laurel tried to make pleasant conversation as they drove to the meeting. "What do you do for work, Kate?" Cass held her breath.

"Dog groomer." Kate stared out the window, watching the manicured lawns of Wortherton go by.

"Oh. That's nice. You must be an animal lover."

"Mm-hmm." After an echoing silence, Kate asked, "What do you do?"

"I used to be an interior designer, but I don't work much anymore, with the kids and all."

With the piles of money my husband makes and all. Cass could practically hear Kate's derisive thoughts.

"The last project I did was Scott's house, as a matter of fact." Laurel smiled at Cass. "Not much creativity there, though. He basically wanted the house to look like the set of a TV show."

Cass grinned. "That's so funny, because that's exactly what I thought."

"I hope you didn't assume that was my taste!"

"Not after I saw your house, I didn't." She turned to Kate. "It's really beautiful."

Kate widened her eyes, a forced look of interest.

Laurel pulled into a parking spot by St. Vincent's. They all got out and made their way, pleasantly, politely into the meeting. But when it was time to share, none of them said a thing.

* * *

As happy as Cass had been that Kate could stay at the house, part of her had dreaded the energy it would take to follow Kate around every minute and make sure she didn't drink. Like Scott, she'd assumed that Kate was at high risk for a relapse. But other than the tension with Laurel to and from meetings, it went surprisingly smoothly. They made meals together. They laughed and talked and cried and talked some more. In the warm light of Kate's good company, Cass saw how lonely she herself had been. How lonely she'd always been, even with Ben.

"I know we've been friends for years," Kate said one night, "but I feel like we're just getting to know each other."

Cass smiled. "Yeah, I know. Funny how not being wasted makes it easier to remember the details of somebody else's life."

A couple of days later at an AA meeting, Kate said suddenly, "I'm Kate."

People sat up, their attention merging toward her. *They're finally gonna get the dirt*, thought Cass. *They've heard it all, but they still like to know the story*. Laurel perked up, too.

Very briefly, Kate told what had happened to her. Then she said, "What's weird is, I only have five days, but my craving is, like, over here." She held her hands away from her, off to the side. "It's still attached to me, but . . . I don't know. Separate. Every time I think about having a drink, it's like knuckles are smashing into my face all over again. I always knew my drinking was a bad thing, but now it feels like life or death."

* * *

IN the car, Laurel said, "I know this is going to sound crazy, Kate, but I envy you."

Cass froze. Kate said nothing.

Laurel went on. "You *get* it. Life or death," she said. "I wish it was that clear for me. But it's not." She sighed. "It's just not."

* * *

KATE went to her counseling sessions at the health clinic twice a week by cab. Each time, she came home exhausted but calmer. For the third session, the cab didn't show. Waiting by the front door that afternoon, Kate started to panic. "I have to get there," she told Cass. "I have to!"

Cass called the taxi company. They'd have someone there in twenty minutes. "That's too goddamned late!" Kate yelled. "Wait. Where are Scott's keys? I can drive myself."

"No way," said Cass. "Absolutely not."

Kate paced like a caged animal. "You have to get me there!"

"Hold on. I'm calling Laurel."

Laurel was willing to drive, but Timmy was taking his afternoon nap and the older boys had gone swimming at the community pool across town.

"I'll stay with Timmy," said Cass. "You take Kate."

Cass brought her pregnancy book to Laurel's and sat on the couch in the family room to do some reading. But shortly after she got there, she heard footfalls thumping slowly down the stairs. The little boy stopped at the bottom, his eyes barely registering her, a threadbare blanket dragged behind him. He wore shorts and a T-shirt with tiny boats sailing across his chest.

"Hi, Timmy," Cass said softly. "I'm your mom's friend Cass."

"Basketball," he mumbled.

"That's right, I play basketball with your brothers sometimes. You remembered."

He stuck his thumb back in his mouth and raised the blanket to rub over his nose.

"You hungry?" she asked.

He shook his head.

"Thirsty?"

Again, no.

"What do you want to do?"

The boy said nothing, just lumbered forward until he hit her knees. Upon impact, the top half of him slumped over onto her lap and he began to slurp noisily at his thumb, pulling his little blanket up to cover his face.

Cass had never spent much time around small children. She had no idea what to do until he growled, "Pick me up," from under the blanket.

Cass got her hands under his armpits and hoisted him up to a sitting position on her lap. "You smell like cake," he murmured as he snuggled his head against her chest and closed his eyes again. Then he resumed his thumb-sucking.

She held on to him, worried that he would slide off her lap as his body began to slacken and his breathing drew heavy and regular. His thumb slid from his mouth and his hand dropped to his narrow lap. But his mouth retained its soft O-like form, as if he were perpetually just about to comment on something fascinating.

She ran her cheek lightly across his silky hair and smelled his baby-shampoo-and-cotton smell. She traced his delicate fingers, the impossibly tiny fingernails, the skin plump and warm. She studied his feet and pencil-thin toes and contemplated the utter perfection of a small child.

An hour later when Laurel got home, they hadn't moved. Laurel gazed down at her.

"This is heaven," whispered Cass.

"It is," Laurel murmured, a wry smile playing across her lips. "Every child's an angel when he's sleeping, Cass."

Laurel went into the dining room and made a phone call. Cass could hear the cadence of her voice rise and fall, and an occasional word or phrase: *"Really?"* and *"Oh, that's perfect!"* When she came back she handed Cass a piece of paper with the words *Second Chances, Elise Giles* and a phone number. She leaned down and carefully disentangled Timmy from Cass, positioning his legs around her waist, his head nestled against her shoulder.

"Can you give that to Kate?" she said. "Please tell her Elise is waiting for her call, and I'd be happy to drive her over there if she decides to try it."

When Cass walked into Scott's house, Kate was sitting in her favorite chair in the corner of the living room, the one she retreated to after counseling sessions. The upholstery was a subtle brocade of rust and cranberry. "It feels rich," Kate had told Cass earlier in the week. "Like only good things happen to someone who sits in a chair like this."

Cass handed Kate the piece of paper. Kate groaned. "I shouldn't have said anything."

"What is it?"

"It's a dog shelter. Her friend *volunteers* there." Kate made little quotation marks in the air. "Not cleaning the cages, I'll bet. Wouldn't want to get her Gucci flats dirty."

"What did you say to her?"

"I came out of counseling and I was still all . . ." Kate made a face. "Emotional. I told her I missed the dogs from my old job. And she starts getting all excited about her friend and some shelter she goes to."

"You know," said Cass, giving her a level gaze. "Just because Laurel suggested it doesn't mean it's a bad idea."

Kate crossed her arms. "Yeah. It actually does."

"What's your problem? She's always nice to you."

"You don't see it."

"See what?"

"How happy she is driving us around. Like we're orphans and she gives us hand-me-downs so she can go back to her *Real Housewives of Wortherton* life and feel good about herself."

It had been a heck of a morning, and Cass certainly didn't want to get into a snit with Kate. She'd been through enough.

But one thing Cass had heard over and over at meetings was the critical importance of humility. Once you put yourself above someone else—even by sneering at his own high opinion of himself—it was a slippery slope toward thinking you were "good enough" to have a drink.

"You're right," she said to Kate. "She likes it. And we happen to be *actual orphans*, and we do need her handouts. But helping each other is what we're supposed to do. I've helped her, and I feel good about that."

Kate's eyes narrowed skeptically. "What did she have—a nail polish emergency?"

"You know better."

"How would I know better?" Kate snapped back.

"She told you! When she said she actually envied you? When she said she wished she got it that it's life or death? She wasn't making small talk, Kate. Why would a woman with so much to lose envy a broke, beat-up, out-of-work dog groomer? Think about that."

Chapter XXI

Dinner was quiet. Kate didn't seem angry, just pensive and maybe a bit ashamed of herself—which had not been Cass's intention. But she did hope that Kate would think twice before looking a gift horse in the Chanel bag. And she hoped Kate could find a little compassion for Laurel. Because she needed it. They all needed it.

They watched *America's Cutest Pet* on Animal Planet and laughed at the antics of a turtle trying to eat a tomato bigger than its head. At ten, Kate rose. "You coming up?" she asked.

"Nah, I'll watch the game." The Red Sox were playing the Los Angeles Angels at 10:05, which was 7:05 on the West Coast.

"Too late for me," said Kate.

"Me, too. But I've watched every Sox game since I got here." Cass chuckled. "It's like a religion at this point."

"For you and the rest of Red Sox Nation." Kate yawned and headed for the stairs.

Cass flipped the channel to catch the first pitch. She liked when the camera caught the players in the dugout or the bullpen. It was interesting to see who stood with whom, who smiled and enjoyed himself, and who paced like a boxer about to enter the ring. Rogie Rogatelli stood with his buddies in the bullpen, arms hung over the right-field fence, grinning, talking. Kep Miller was on the dugout steps, chewing ferociously on a wad of gum. A questionable call by the umpire brought on a torrent of silent but wholly recognizable curses.

Scott sat alone on the bench, elbows on his knees, watching the game intently. Cass must have seen him do this countless times in the past two months, but tonight it caught her attention.

He's a loner, she thought. He'd been fairly popular in high school, but even then, there was a separateness about him, as though things and people would come and go in the random manner of the universe, and he didn't get too attached to their temporary visits.

She hadn't paid much attention to him in the years since, in part because she couldn't see so well through the dense fog of her drinking, and in part because when she could, he was not a pleasing sight. He scowled a lot, his disappointment in Ben reeking like a bad odor from every pore. And sadness. She could see that now in retrospect.

There was that time . . . when was that? Years ago. Their partying had still been a mostly hilarious thing and hadn't yet tipped toward pain avoidance and desperation. They were having breakfast with Scott at some greasy spoon somewhere, and he came right out and asked them to quit. He was prepared with reasons and options and offers of help. But she and Ben had smirked and squeezed each other's hand under the table at the ridiculousness of it.

Scott had rightly lost hope over the course of that breakfast when it had become clear that Ben didn't see himself as a guy with a problem—he was in love and as happy as he'd ever been in his short, grim life. He had put it in a funny way, Cass remembered, a uniquely Ben way: *I got no problem with happiness. I'm happy with happiness. And if you're unhappy with my happiness, you're the one with the problem.*

Sitting on the fancy Italian sofa in Scott's big house, watching him on TV, Cass could see in her mind's eye that younger Scotty as he had looked in that moment: heart-stoppingly alone.

Until that moment—that precise moment—they had been friends. They had hung out together off and on, the three of them. But they almost never did after that. And then to find out that Ben had been going to see Scott after all, without her . . . as if somehow he'd known that Scott would need the company, even if it was just the two of them fighting.

Scott had said that he hadn't blamed her for Ben's state. But Cass had to wonder . . . if she hadn't been so willing to drink right along with him, would Ben have stopped? Would Scott have gotten his brother back?

* * *

SCOTT played well, fielding grounders like a human vacuum, his arm arcing hard and graceful as he threw to get a runner out. His body, thick and muscular, seemed to compact itself into something sleek and streamlined when he ran. He wasn't as fast as the gangly, stork-legged Kep Miller, but then he didn't look like an ostrich with his tail feathers on fire, either.

It was a tie score at the top of the ninth with two outs and no one on base. The Sox seemed to have lost their starch, popping flies and grounding out for the last few innings. Scott stepped up to the plate and took a practice swing.

"Come on, Uncle Scotty," Cass whispered to the baby. "Let's get a hit."

He stretched his thick neck from side to side and got into his stance. The first pitch came at him and he swung. *Thwap*, into the catcher's mitt.

"Bad pitch," murmured Cass. "Uncle Scotty needs to make an appointment with the optometrist, I'm thinking."

Scott let a couple of balls go by. Then he swung again.

"High and outside." Cass shook her head. "Maybe Uncle Scotty wants this game to be over so he can go have some juice and cookies with his friends."

The pitcher had apparently come to the same conclusion—Scott was done—because his last pitch was a fastball straight down the middle. Scott cocked back and swung his body around like a whip, the bat slamming into the ball with a ferocity that sent it screaming into the air.

Cass jumped up. "Oh my God! Go!" she yelled at the ball. "Go! Go!"

Scott ran with his head craned toward the outfield.

The low droning voice of the announcer was suddenly loud and clear. "McGreavy has sent that ball into space! And . . . it's . . . gone!"

"Woo-hoo!" screamed Cass, jumping and clapping. "Way to go, Scotty! Way to go!"

Scott began to lope around the bases, and she could tell he was trying to be cool about it. But she could feel his joy beaming through the TV screen, and she got a little choky with pride on his behalf. When he got back to the dugout, his teammates were waiting for him. They patted his head and slammed his shoulders and crowded him until he was lost from view for a few moments, as they paid their respects to one of his very rare homers. The camera showed him sitting down on the bench, rubbing a towel over his sweaty face and head, still trying not to smile. And maybe the rest of the world didn't see a smile, but Cass sure did.

Kep Miller grounded out and they were left to see what the Angels would do about being one run behind in the bottom of the ninth. As it turned out, they weren't up to the challenge. Rogie Rogatelli was on the mound, and smooth as satin, he struck out the side. The Red Sox had won.

"Interview Scotty," Cass told the camera crew on-screen. "He's the guy with the winning homer, for crying out loud. Interview him!"

And sure enough, there he was, wheat-toast-colored hair sticking up at funny angles, blue-gray eyes gleaming at the reporter, an attractive blonde with enormous horsey white teeth. "Scott McGreavy, you're a dependable player, great on backup and base hits, but not known for the big money plays. How's it feel to hit the game-winning homer?"

Cass didn't like that at all. It sounded like *You're okay, but not great. How's it feel to be great this one time?* She wanted to pull that horsey-girl's hair. But Scott gave a little grin and said, "It feels good. I'm just happy to help the team any way I can."

And that was it. The reporter very quickly moved on to Rogie, flashing her equine smile and gushing about his flawless performance. Cass made a gagging sound and turned off the TV.

She sat there grinning, so happy for Scott. He was a good guy, and sometimes—not always, but sometimes—good guys got what they deserved.

There was a funny little pain in her stomach. Not a pain so much as a poke. She waited. There it was again. She pulled up her shirt and looked at the speed bump of her belly, put her hands on it. She couldn't feel anything on the outside, but on the inside . . .

Poke . . . flutter . . . poke . . .

"Hey!" she whispered at the baby. "Hey, I feel you! Are you doing the wave in there?" This baby was getting realer and realer. She could imagine little fists and feet dancing around in its warm, watery world, and she was dying to tell someone. If it hadn't been past midnight, she would've told Kate or Laurel, or even called Patrick, her sponsor. But they were all asleep. She picked up the phone.

He answered after one ring. "What's wrong?"

She could hear men's voices in the background. "Nothing!" she said quickly.

"Are you sure?" Before she could answer, he was calling out, "Go on—I'll catch up!" and then he was speaking into the receiver again. "What's going on?"

"Nothing, I swear."

"It's almost one in the morning there. Why are you up in the middle of the night if nothing's wrong?"

"Because I watched the game—"

"Why?"

This was getting annoying. Why did she watch the game? The real question was why he was so suspicious of everything she did. "For crying out loud, Scotty, I watch *every* game!"

"You do?"

"Yes, of course, and tonight was unbelievable—you hit that ball so hard!"

He didn't say anything for a moment, but when he did, she could hear the smile in it. "Felt really good," he murmured.

"You won the game!"

"Actually Rogie won the game . . ."

"Rogie nothing—it was *you*."

He laughed. "Yeah, okay."

"I'm really proud of you, Scotty."

"Thanks. Thanks for calling. It's nice to . . . like, talk to someone . . . real about it. Not just some player knuckle-bumping me and saying 'Nice one, dude.'"

"Glad you think I'm real."

"Oh, you're real, all right," he teased. "A real pain in my—"

"Fine, I'm not going to tell you *my* big news, then."

"You know you're going to tell me, so just tell me."

"I felt the baby kick."

"Really?"

"Yeah, it was right after the game, and I was jumping around and yelling so much, it must have stirred him up, because then there were all these little punches and pokes."

"Wow," he said. "That must feel so weird."

"Totally. But in a good way. He's doing just what he's supposed to do."

"Way to go, Hal. If I was there, I'd knuckle-bump him."

"Also . . . um, there's something else." In the excitement of the moment she'd almost forgotten. "Tomorrow I've got ninety days sobriety. It's kind of a big deal."

"I know it's a big deal, Cass. Congratulations. I'm real proud of you, too."

"Thanks."

And then it felt a little weird. Cass didn't really know why. Like too much somehow. "You better go catch up with your friends."

"Yeah. I'll be home day after tomorrow."

She knew this, of course. "Okay, see you then."

"Bye." And he was gone.

* * *

ON the day Scott was to arrive home, Cass walked to the grocery store and bought pork chops, Yukon potatoes, heads of broccoli, a round loaf of crusty bread with olives in it, and a strawberry rhubarb pie. She would have liked to bake the pie herself, but the ingredients would've made the grocery bags too heavy to carry. Kate stayed home, of course. She couldn't be much help on her crutches. But the doctor at the clinic said the break was healing nicely and soon she'd be in a walking cast.

"Does aluminum burn?" she'd asked Cass after that visit. "Because it would feel so good to torch these stupid crutches."

"Um, how about if we just donate them to one of those places that gives away medical equipment to people who can't afford it?"

"That'd be good, too. I mean, not as good as watching them melt, of course . . ."

Cass had patted her shoulder. "Goes without saying."

When Cass got home with the groceries, Kate was gone, and Cass felt a twinge of worry. Then she found the note. *Went to the dog shelter with Laurel's friend. Back at five.*

Scott got home at three, wrinkled and unshaven, dragging his bag behind him. Cass noticed a slight infiltration of silver in the short whiskers on his chin and wondered when the rest of it would go gray. The Sox had won the final game in L.A. in the twelfth inning the night before, and he'd gone out with the guys until the early morning hours.

"Forgot to shave?" she asked.

"Couldn't find the razor. Or my face." He squinted at her. "How's it going around here?"

"Fine. Laurel's got Kate volunteering at an animal shelter."

He raised an eyebrow. "That's a weird combo."

Cass chuckled. "Yeah, it's definitely got a *Fresh Prince of Bel Air* feel to it."

"How's she look?"

"Better. The bruises are turning yellow and her lips are the right size. She's getting a boot cast next week, doctor says."

"Going home soon?"

Cass stuck her hand in her pocket and gave her new ninety-day chip a rub. "She's . . . um . . . I mean, she can go whenever you want. It's your house."

"But . . ."

"She's been going to a counselor at Waverly. And she's still a little, you know . . ."

"Messed up."

"Yeah."

He stood there looking at her for a moment, and she waited to feel the electric pulse of his irritation, but it never came. He inhaled and let it out slowly. "How long you think?"

She considered how much she could reasonably ask for. "Another week would be nice."

He nodded.

"Thanks," said Cass. "I know she'll be really grateful."

"In a week I'll be out of town again. She could stay while I'm gone, too."

"Really?"

"Sure. What do I care, as long as she's no trouble to you."

"She's no trouble. She's actually pretty good company."

"Better for you not to be alone so much." He gazed down at her belly pushing out below her crossed arms. "Hal's getting big," he said.

"That's his job." She smiled. "Go crash for a while, and I'll call you when dinner's ready."

* * *

KATE loved the Second Chances Dog Shelter and went every day with Laurel's friend Elise. Now that she was in a walking cast, she was able to help more and had made a name for herself as the volunteer they could count on to clip the nails of the vicious dogs.

"*Vicious* is really the wrong word," Kate explained to Cass and Scott over grilled chicken and asparagus one night. "They're vicious on the outside but they're just boring old *angry* on the inside. I tell them, 'Hey, I'm angry, too, so simmer down and let me get your nails done.'"

Scott flicked a look at Cass and shoveled a forkload of rice into his mouth. Cass nearly laughed out loud. Later, when they were alone, he said, "Kate's a little kooky about the dogs."

"Yeah, and you're not even here that much. You missed the one about pulling burrs off a pit bull's privates." Scott squinted in disgust.

"It's good, though. It's the perfect place for her to put all that addictive energy. And she gets a lot of love in return. The dogs don't care what she looks like or how screwed up she is."

"She talks about it all the freakin' time!"

"And you'd talk about baseball all the time if you were that much of a talker."

He lifted a shoulder, conceding her point. "What would you talk about?"

She thought for a moment. "The baby."

"Kicking a lot?"

"Yeah. Now that I know what it feels like I notice all the time. He's doing it right now."

"Could . . . would someone be able to feel it? From the outside?"

"Probably not. But you could try." She took his hand and held it against the thin cotton of her maternity top. "Okay, there. Right then. Did you get it?"

"Not . . . no. I don't think so."

She moved his hand down to the underside of the bump. "How about that one?"

"Nope." He pulled his hand away quickly. "I'm gonna go work out."

She looked up at him. "It's kind of late. Aren't you tired?"

"Nope." And he headed for the basement.

* * *

AFTER a two-game series in Boston, Scott left for back-to-back series against Cleveland and then the Baltimore Orioles. That's when Kate brought Bunny home.

When she came into the kitchen, she was momentarily dogless. "Hey, um . . ."

Cass was chopping carrots, but something about Kate's tone made her look up.

"So, uh . . ." said Kate. "I did something."

"Like what?"

"Like I brought a dog home from the shelter."

"Are you crazy, Kate! I cannot have a dog in here—Scotty'll hit the roof!"

"It's temporary! Until she gets placed! Or until I can get my cousin to decide she wants her kids to have a dog."

"How likely is that?"

"Not very," Kate admitted. "The whole family's allergic."

"For crying out loud!" Cass knew only half the dogs got placed; the rest had to be euthanized.

"You have to see her. Her name's Bunny and she's the most lovable thing . . ." That was apparently the cue for Laurel's friend Elise to bring in the dog. And with its speckled brown fur, short nose, and long floppy ears, it did look a little like an overgrown rabbit. But it was the eyes that got you. Big and dark and soulful. Bunny's eyes were a lot like Rogie's.

When Cass looked at her, Bunny cowered behind Elise. "What's that about?" asked Cass.

"We feel *certain* she was abused. She's the most *fearful* dog I've ever seen." Elise was in her fifties with thick graying hair twisted into a clip at the back of her head and always seemed to put her quiet, elegant words into italics. Whatever she said, she *meant* it.

"The other dogs pick on her because she's so submissive." Kate bent down and Bunny ventured out a few inches toward her. "I couldn't leave her there. She'll die of terror."

What do you say to a friend who's been terrorized and abused and wants desperately to comfort another terrorized, abused creature? Cass dropped her chin. "Kate . . ."

"I'll find her a place before Scott gets home. I promise."

"What if you don't?"

"I will."

"What if you *don't*, Kate?"

Elise intervened. "Let's all agree that the dog will be gone by then and work out the details as best we can."

Cass sighed. "You've got five days." She was sure she would live to regret it.

* * *

BUNNY spent most of dinner quivering under the living room chair, the "rich" one Kate always sat in. "She can smell me in that chair," Kate explained.

"She could smell you a whole lot better here in the kitchen with us."

"Yeah, but you're in here, and she assumes you're a danger until you win her over."

Cass dropped her fork onto her plate. "I am not 'winning her over.' I am putting up with her until she leaves. Then I'm going to vacuum this house down to the studs. That's *my* contribution to this scenario."

"Okay, okay." Kate got up to put her dishes into the dishwasher, booted foot clonking on the tile floor. "I'm taking her out for a walk." She glanced at Cass. "Want to come?"

They didn't get very far. The Kessler boys were out in the cul-de-sac playing basketball, and with all the yelling and bounding around, Bunny refused to go anywhere near them.

"Do you think we could ask them to go inside for a few minutes?" Kate murmured.

"No, I do not. What are we going to do—make everyone in our path clear the way so Bunny doesn't freak out?"

They walked around the yard until eventually Bunny seemed to accept that there was no imminent threat to her life. The sun was blushing through the trees, casting splashes of pink and orange onto the clouds. They sat down on the front step and watched the boys play. Bunny curled her small, pliable body into Kate's lap and sniffed at Cass.

"Don't pet her," whispered Kate. "Let her come to you."

Cass rolled her eyes.

After a while the three boys approached, and Bunny started to quiver. Cass got up. "Hi, guys. I see you're perfecting your dunk shot, Luke," she said to the youngest.

He grinned, accepting her teasing. "I got one in, though!"

"You did not!" and "Liar!" insisted the other two.

The boys had met Kate, but they were intrigued by the dog. "Can we pet her?"

"No, sorry," Kate told them. "She's scared of everything."

"Why?" Drew asked. "Something happen to her?"

"We don't know for sure, but we have to figure she was abused."

The boys plunked down in the grass and speculated on the bad things someone could do to a dog, which made Kate visibly uncomfortable, though they never seemed to notice. Bunny stayed tightly curled in Kate's lap. Eventually Laurel called the boys in, and Kate and Cass went in to watch TV. Bunny went back under the chair in the living room, but after a while she slunk into the TV room. She sniffed at Cass and then gave her hand a lick.

"Look at that," said Kate in wonder. "That's the fastest she's taken to anyone. She knows you're pregnant. Maybe that makes her feel like you're less of a threat."

"She knows I'm pregnant?" Cass said skeptically.

"Dogs have a wicked sense of smell. They can tell all sorts of things—like if someone's sick and stuff. Some dogs can tell when a person's going to have a seizure."

"Oh, come on."

"No lie. They have like a three hundred times better sense of smell than people do. And Elise thinks Bunny's part hound, so that makes her like a professional smeller."

Cass gave the dog a wry look. "So, Bunny, what do you think— boy or girl? Do you smell stinky feet or fruity lip gloss?" Bunny laid her head on Cass's knee.

"Now," said Kate, "you can pet her."

Cass looked down at the strange dog. Those chocolate eyes gazed back up at her. *Just like Rogie*, she thought. *Hard to resist.* And she smoothed her hand over the soft, furry head.

* * *

ON Tuesday, the night before Scott was due back, there was still no plan for Bunny. Kate was moving back in with her cousin, who had declined to adopt a mutt into her allergy-ridden family. No one who'd come to the shelter in the past five days had claimed her.

"What are you going to do?" said Cass.

"Stop asking me!" Kate snapped. "Something will work out."

Cass was annoyed. *Things don't always work out!* she almost yelled. *Don't we both know that well enough by now?*

And yet a little part of her was heartbroken, too, and this annoyed her even more. Didn't she have enough to do just looking after her own survival? And now she had the death of Bunny—a sweet, healthy, yes, even lovable dog—to anticipate. She wanted badly not to care.

The phone rang, and she went into the kitchen to answer it.

It was Drew. "Um, Cass? Could you like . . . come over? My mom's . . ."

"Is she cleaning?" It was nine o'clock. Late-night cleaning was a bad sign.

"No."

"What's she doing?"

"She's drinking."

Chapter XXII

Cass and Kate ran barefoot across the yard, damp grass clinging to their feet. Drew was waiting for them at the front door. "I tried to call my dad," he said. "But I think his cell must be dead. He always answers, no matter when I call. Even if he's in a meeting."

He must know things are dicey with Laurel, thought Cass. "Where is he?" she asked.

"Japan."

So much for tracking down his hotel and telling him to get his ass home.

The other boys migrated into the front hallway. Matt had little Timmy on his hip.

"Hey." She smiled. "You guys should be in bed."

They stared back at her, as if she'd just suggested there were pink llamas in the backyard and they could all go ride them. It was the weary/wary look. Even on the toddler.

"Mama crying," he said solemnly.

Cass heard it then, a low wail coming from upstairs. She shot Kate a look. "Okay," she said. "I'll deal with your mom, you guys go next door with Kate and try to get some sleep."

The boys looked at one another, conferring silently. Drew tipped his chin at Matt, second in command. "Matt will take them over," he said. "I'll stay here."

"No," said Cass. "You'll all go."

"She's my mother."

"And you're a great son to her," said Cass. "But this is grown-up stuff now."

Drew snorted. "Grown-up stuff. Really. Then why've I been dealing with it for years?"

She leveled a gaze at him. "This time, you don't have to."

He stared back at her, and she could see his eyes start to fill. "Let's go," he said gruffly, and they all marched out.

Cass followed the wailing sound upstairs to the master bedroom. The door was locked.

"Laurel, it's Cass. Open the door."

"Oh, Cass! You should'n be here," Laurel slurred. "You're *pregnant*. You need sleep!"

God in heaven, thought Cass. "Open the door, Laurel."

"I'll jus' stay in here," called Laurel. "I'm oookay."

"You open this fucking door right now!" Cass slammed her hand against it.

The wailing resumed. "Don' be mad at me!"

"I'll stop being mad as soon as you open it!"

"No you won't!"

Damn straight I won't, thought Cass, her mind speeding to Scott's house, where four heartsick boys were trying to get the thought of their alcohol-sodden mother out of their heads.

I need to remember this, she thought. *When my baby comes, and I feel like drinking, I want the memory of this night to beat some sense into me.*

"I promise to stop being mad."

The door opened. Laurel stood, legs apart as if she were on a ship's deck in stormy seas. There was an empty bottle of Courvoisier and a brandy snifter on the dressing table, surrounded by creams and perfumes. Half a bottle of Gilbey's gin sat on the floor next to the bed.

"You have a foul mouth, you know that?" said Laurel, shaking a limp finger. "You're gonna have to stop that when the baby comes."

Leave it to a drunk to get hammered and still feel fully justified in pointing out your flaws. Cass picked up the gin, strode into the master bathroom, and poured it down the sink. "Where's the rest?" she said.

"Downstairs."

"Downstairs where?"

"In the liquor cabinet, silly. Where else would you keep it?"

Cass sighed. "Can you make yourself throw up?" It would stop the liquor that was still in her stomach from hitting her bloodstream and get her sober sooner.

Laurel wrinkled her nose. "Messy."

"I'll clean your toilet after."

"What products do you use?"

Oh, for chrissake . . . Cass steered her into the bathroom. When Laurel was done, she sat on the tiles and watched Cass swish lavender-scented bleach around the inside of the bowl.

"I like that smell," said Laurel. "Do you?"

"Yeah, it's awesome. Let's go downstairs and get some food into you."

Cass made Laurel do everything she could think of to sober up: drink glass after glass of water to flush her system and walk miles on the treadmill to metabolize the alcohol faster. She didn't know if that actually worked, but it felt better than just letting Laurel lie around enjoying her buzz.

"I'm tired!" whined Laurel.

"Keep walking," said Cass.

Several hours later, when Laurel was significantly more sober, they went upstairs and got her showered and into clean pajamas. As they left the bathroom, Cass stumbled and lost her balance, her hand going out to the door in front of her, which slammed with a wall-shaking bang.

"Are you okay?" asked Laurel. "I hope that didn't wake the boys."

Cass looked at her. "The boys aren't here."

"What?" Laurel was alarmed. "Where are they?"

Cass told her about Drew's call, and how she'd sent them to Scott's with Kate. Laurel started to cry in earnest then—real tears, not boozy waterworks.

"They'll never forgive me," she said. "They *shouldn't* ever forgive me."

Cass put her hand on Laurel's shoulder. "Let's not worry about that now. It's the middle of the night, and we both need some rest."

"I need to say good night to Drew. He won't sleep until he knows I'm okay. I'll just sneak over for a quick minute."

"You'll sneak over and stay. You don't think I'm letting you come back here, do you?"

"Oh, that's so nice of you, Cass, but I don't want to put you out."

Put me OUT? Cass took a breath before responding. "Laurel, tomorrow there'll be a whole lot of things to sort out. Tonight, you're staying at Scott's, so don't make a thing of it."

When they got to the front door, Laurel saw the grass clippings that Kate and Cass had tracked in. "I should get these up before they stain the carpet," she said.

Cass guided her out the door. "I'll find you something to clean at Scott's."

It was almost two in the morning, but as Laurel had predicted, Drew was still up, sitting on the leather couch watching a movie with Kate. When his mother came in, he turned at the sound of footsteps, but reversed himself to glare at the TV as soon as he saw her.

Laurel sat down on the couch with Drew. Kate and Cass went into the living room.

"How'd it go?" Cass asked.

"Fine. We watched TV for a little while and I gave them a snack. Then I put the younger three upstairs in beds. Drew wouldn't go."

"She knew he wouldn't."

"What made her drink?"

"I didn't ask. She was loaded, and I wasn't in the mood to listen to drunken bullshit."

Kate nodded. "Kinda weird being on the other side, isn't it?"

"You think you're so sparkly and fascinating when it's you." Cass shook her head. "But, my God, it's just unbelievably boring."

Laurel came in, face ashen. "He won't talk to me."

Good boy, thought Cass. "Everyone's tired," she said. "Kate, can you put Laurel in one of the empty bedrooms?"

Laurel stood there looking like a motherless child on a dark street. "Thank you," she said to Cass. "I don't . . . I can't lose them."

You're absolutely going to lose them if you don't stop, thought Cass. But this wasn't the time to start that conversation. She nodded, and Kate walked Laurel up the stairs.

Cass went back in and sat down next to Drew.

"I hate her." He stared at the TV as if his glare was the only thing keeping it attached to the wall. "I'd run away, but Matt's such a baby, he could never handle it."

"They rely on you."

"She's the worst mother in the world."

"No," said Cass gently. "There's worse."

He turned on her, rage pulsing through the tears now rolling down his face. "What could be worse than this!"

"If she was a drunk who *didn't* love you."

The boy gritted his teeth so hard, Cass thought he might break a molar. But even that couldn't keep him from weeping. He put his hands up to his face, and sobs racked his gangly, still-growing body. Cass put her hand out and stroked his head and his shoulder, and he allowed this until he calmed himself into hiccups and sniffling, wiping his nose on the arm of his shirt.

"Will you help me?" he murmured.

"All I can," she said.

*   *   *

OF the four bedroom doors upstairs, only hers was still open, and Cass guided him through it. He climbed under the covers, and she grabbed the extra blanket out of the closet and went back downstairs to sleep on the leather sectional.

Though it was full of people, the house was quiet. Cass wondered if it had ever had so many sleeping bodies in it. She liked the thought of this and wondered if someday she might have a house that sheltered more than just her and the baby. It wouldn't be this big, of course. But maybe someday she might find another man to love, who would love her back, and give her more babies.

It was too much to hope for, really, and she stopped herself, worried that if she wished for the world, she'd be cheated out of even what she truly needed: sobriety, a safe place to live, steady work with enough income, a good school for her child. And just a little bit of luck.

Safe, she thought as her mind wandered toward the outskirts of consciousness. *And lucky.*

There was a distant humming sound that grew steadily louder, as if someone had turned on a small motor, and Cass wondered dopily if Laurel had found the Dustbuster after all. Then there were two thumps somewhere outside, and the motor sound went away again. When she heard footsteps coming up the walk, Cass sat upright, every nerve on alert. Her brain, always on hair trigger for anxiety, told her, *This can't be good.*

She tiptoed into the room she hated most in the whole house: the dining room, with its siren-call liquor cabinet. On the wall was the wooden plaque that held Scott's bat from high school. She lifted it off its cradle and stood in the darkened foyer, waiting for whoever, whatever was coming up the walk.

The bolt slid back and the knob turned. . . . The door opened and the lights flicked on.

"Holy crap!" Scott put his arms up to protect himself. "What the hell are you doing?"

Cass lowered the bat. "What am *I* doing? What are *you* doing home early?"

"There's a storm in Baltimore—they rain checked. Geez, give me that." He took the bat away from her.

"Sorry, I thought . . ."

He exhaled and let out a chuckle, setting the bat against the wall. "Least I know the house is well protected."

It was the most exhausting evening Cass had had in a long time. She yawned widely.

"Yeah, me too," he said. "I'm going straight up. I'll see you in the morning."

She thought to warn him about all the extra bodies, but he was halfway up the stairs, and he'd probably sleep late tomorrow. She could get them all out of the way and tell him about it in the past tense. *That'll work out way better*, she thought.

She was back on the couch, about to turn off the light when she heard footsteps descending the stairs. In another moment Scott was looming over her.

"So," he said. "You want to tell me about the two sleeping boys *and the dog* in my bed?"

Chapter XXIII

Cass stared up at him. Had Kate actually put two of the boys *and the dog* in Scott's room? Cass could've killed her. Better yet, she'd throw Kate out of her own bed, move the kids and the freaking dog into it, and then change Scott's sheets. This day was getting longer and longer . . . She tossed the blanket off. "I'll get them out."

"No," he said, coming around to thump down in his corner of the couch, with his legs up on the L. "Who are they, Laurel's kids?"

"Yeah, Laurel fell off the deep end. I can move them, I just have to—"

"Holy smokes, what happened?"

She gave him a brief rundown, expecting him to say, *Whatever*, but he kept nodding and asking questions. "And the dog is in my bed with the boys, because . . . ?"

Cass shook her head. "No idea. Honestly, I could kill Kate."

He picked up the big blanket off the floor and tossed it over her, pulling the end of it down over himself as he curled his long body to fit onto the L of the couch. "Turn off the light."

"Scotty, for godsake. I'll get you a bed. If I'd known you'd be home, I never would've—"

"Stop. It's fine. Just go to sleep."

She turned off the light. In the dark there was a little snort of laughter. "What?" she said.

"It's like some kind of halfway house. McGreavy's Home for Lost Women and Dogs."

She laughed; though it wasn't exactly flattering, at the moment it was all too true.

The quiet descended again, and Cass lay there thinking this really was the most bizarre night. Crazy stuff had happened all the time when she was drinking. But it was always the *same* crazy stuff. This night had been one surprise after another.

* * *

THE back of the house faced east, which became abundantly clear when the rising sun glared through the windows and onto Cass's face. She shaded her eyes with her hand and raised her head to peek down the couch at Scott. His eyes were open. "You snore," he murmured.

"I do not."

"You do. Like a bear."

"You're lying."

"Check your teeth. They're probably loose from all those snores barreling through."

"Shut up!" She nudged his chest with her bare toe.

He grabbed her foot, grinning sleepily up at her. And she had the strange thought that it was nice, being close like this. She'd had so little physical contact in . . . how many months was it? Almost five. Since Ben.

Scott looked down at her foot in his hand, as if he wasn't sure how it had gotten there, and let go of it. "I'm starving," he said, rolling off the sectional. "I'm going out for bagels." Still in his clothes from the night before, he put on shoes and went out to his car.

Cass got up. It was only six, and she hoped everyone would sleep for a while—everyone but Kate, whom she had a few choice words for. But first she had a job to do.

When she let herself into Laurel's house, a phone was ringing, a perky little trill that she recognized as Laurel's mobile. It was on the foyer table, and Cass checked the caller ID. *Kessler, Adam.* She answered it.

"Who's this?" Adam demanded.

"It's Cass from next door. I'm here because—"

"Why are you answering Laurel's phone?"

"I'm *here because* there was an incident last night. Everyone's fine but—"

"What kind of incident? Where's my wife?"

"I'm trying to tell you. Laurel got drunk last night."

"Oh, God."

"Drew called me, and I got Laurel sobered up. They're all sleeping at my house."

Silence on the other end of the phone. *This is where you say thank you*, thought Cass.

"If they're all at your house, what are you doing at my house?"

You're welcome, jerk. "I'm pouring out all your booze."

"Well, you can't just . . . there's some expensive . . . that's a lot of money down the drain."

Are you joking? she wanted to scream. *Are you fucking kidding me?!* She stalked over to the liquor cabinet and grabbed the most expensive-looking bottle she saw.

"Just come home as soon as you can," she told him as she emptied it into the kitchen sink. "Your family needs you."

* * *

WHEN Cass got back to Scott's house, Luke and little Timmy were on the couch watching TV, with Bunny across their laps. Timmy was scrunched up against his brother, thumb in mouth, stroking his threadbare blanket against the dog's tail.

"I see you guys made friends with Bunny."

"Yeah, she liked us when we came over last night," said Luke.

"Yeah," said Timmy around his thumb. "She liked us."

"She liked you so much, she slept with you."

"Oh, that was funny," said Luke. "Kate kept trying to get Bunny out of the room, but she wouldn't go. Then Kate dragged her out, but she sat outside the door and barked, and she wouldn't stop until she came back in with us. Kate said Bunny thinks we smell good."

You probably smelled terrified and Bunny recognized kindred spirits. Cass sighed. Kate was off the hook, at least about the dog. She went up and changed the sheets on Scott's bed. When she came back down, Scott was walking in with bags of bagels and cream cheese.

"You guys hungry?" he said to the boys. They blinked at him silently.

"You remember Scott, right?" said Cass. "He's a baseball player."

"In real life?" Luke asked skeptically.

Scott shot a glance at Cass and grinned back at the boy. "More or less."

The two of them shuffled out from under the dog, Timmy clutching something in his chubby little hand. He held it out to Cass—a square packet with something ringlike inside.

"Is dis candy?" Timmy asked.

Scott's hand shot out. "That's, um, medicine," he said and put the condom in his pocket.

"Yuck," said Timmy.

"Where'd you get that?" Cass asked him.

"Under da big bed. Can I have a bagel?"

Cass raised an eyebrow at Scott as she spread cream cheese on a bagel for the little boy.

Scott raised his own eyebrow and said, "I guess we know where you're not vacuuming."

"And now I never will. Some things even the cleaning lady won't clean."

He mumbled something about getting a little sleep finally and went up to his room. Drew and Matt came down and ate a couple of bagels each. When Laurel appeared, the three younger boys swirled around her like butterflies in a flower garden. She hugged and tickled them, all the while casting furtive glances at Drew. He ignored her so hard he might as well have slapped her.

Cass moved up next to him. "Can you hold down the fort this morning?" she murmured.

"Like always?" he grumbled.

She turned back to the huddle of motherly love. "Laurel, we have a meeting at ten."

Laurel's smiling face went slack. "I'll be ready."

* * *

At quarter to ten they were parked in front of St. Vincent Church.

"Why did we have to come so early?" said Kate.

"Because today we don't want to miss even a minute of it, do we, Laurel?"

Laurel stared out through the windshield into the drizzle of rain, a remnant of the storm that had made its way up the coast from Baltimore in the night. "No," she said blankly.

"You have two things to accomplish," Cass told her. "You're going to get a sponsor—"

"How am I supposed to do that?"

"You're going to walk up to some reasonable-looking person and ask."

"What if there aren't any reasonable-looking—"

"You pick one, or I'll pick one for you. And I'm picking the toughest one I can find."

Laurel kept her eyes on the rain. "What's the second thing?"

"You're going to talk. A lot."

* * *

"Hi, I'm Laurel."

The group was small. Cass suspected it was the rain—fair-weather alkies didn't always come. But those who were there sang out "Hi, Laurel" loud and sweet, as if they knew encouragement was in desperate need.

"I got drunk last night," she said. "I don't even know why. Not like it matters, I guess. But it started when my husband said he'd be on a business trip this weekend, and I'd have to cancel my plans to attend the Design Expo in Boston. I'm used to having my plans canceled by my husband's ever-changing travel schedule," she went on bitterly, as if the frequency hadn't improved her acceptance of it one bit. "I was disappointed. A little angry. And then I just calmly walked over to the liquor cabinet and took out a bottle of Courvoisier and went up to my room. I watched myself do this, as if I were watching a movie. Like it wasn't me doing it."

Nods from the group. Everyone could relate to "the other me" getting the booze.

"It's never me," Laurel said, encouraged. "It's always that other woman. Because I'm perfect. I. Am. Perfect." She said this, tasting it, trying it on . . . copping to it.

"My parents are musicians. First chair cello and viola in the Santa Barbara Philharmonic. They play *perfectly*. I"—she laughed sadly—"I'm tone-deaf. I know this for two reasons. One, I played the violin, practiced until my fingers bled, until tenth grade when, two, my mother told me to stop. 'You'll never be great,' she said. 'We don't want to pay for the lessons anymore.'"

Laurel sat there for a moment, absorbing her own words. "I

really wanted to be perfect. But I was visual, not musical. I can see the most infinitesimal differences in color. So a little part of me—the only part that wasn't horribly ashamed—was relieved. There was more time for art. I drew and painted and sculpted. I had my first design job when a friend's mother asked me to help her pick out art for her office. It was heaven.

"But to my parents it was useless. Visual art meant nothing to them. I might as well have said I wanted to run away and join the circus. To appease them, I tried to be the perfect girl. It's addictive, perfection. It lulls you into thinking it's attainable, and if you work really, really hard, it almost is. I dated perfect men, wore perfect clothes, traveled to perfect places.

"I married the most perfect man—strong, kind, smart . . ." She smiled wryly. "One who earns enough to support my high-end tastes." Her head turned ever so slightly toward Cass. "He seems rigid and clueless sometimes, but he comes through in the end."

Hope so, thought Cass, *because today, not so much*.

"And then I became a mother. Four times." A couple of eyebrows lifted around the circle. "All so different, my boys. All equally fascinating to me. I want to know each of them—the real boy, not some reflection of who they think I want them to be. I want *so much* for them to be exactly who they are." Her eyes welled, and tears escaped her lids. "And I, of course, want to be the perfect mother. But if there's one thing I've learned, it's that motherhood is exquisitely, painfully imperfect. Nothing can bring you face-to-face with your shortcomings as quickly as your own child. It's the paradox of my life. I love my children so much, I hate myself."

Laurel took in a long, slow breath and let it out again. "I'm an alcoholic," she said. "And by the way, I need a sponsor."

After the meeting a short, round woman with frizzy gray hair and clunky brown shoes came over to Laurel as she stood with

Cass and Kate. "I'm Belva," she said with a gracious smile and a slight lisp. "I'll be your sponsor. I think we're an excellent match."

"I'm sure we are," said Laurel. "Thanks very much."

* * *

THE Kesslers kept Bunny.

"I'm not in favor," Cass told Laurel. "Dogs can be a lot of work, and you don't need any more stress in your life right now. Besides, you're clearly doing it out of guilt."

"Belva disagrees," said Laurel. She didn't actually roll her eyes, but her tone implied it. "She says pets are good for the soul. She has three cats, a dog, and a parakeet."

"Of *course* she does," said Cass, and both women laughed. Belva, they'd soon learned, was a former head nurse with a will of steel and a penchant for long, squeezing hugs. Laurel was a little bit afraid of her, which as it turned out was working just fine.

"She's kicking my butt!" said Laurel. "Two meetings a day for two weeks! And once a day every single day afterward. If I did that with ab workouts, I'd look like Kelly Ripa."

Laurel was working hard on her sobriety and it made it easier to be with her, which was nice, because she was Cass's only woman friend in the area now. Kate had moved back in with her cousin, but took the train out to Wortherton to volunteer at Second Chances Dog Shelter as often as she could. One night, when Cass walked her back to the train station, Kate asked, "How come you live with a Red Sox player and you never go to any games?"

"I never had anyone to go with. Also, there's beer everywhere."

"True," said Kate. "But it would be kinda fun to go. I haven't been in years. If we went together and one of us got tempted, we could just leave."

The next day, on the way to her six-month checkup, Cass mentioned it to Scott.

"Sure." He held open the health center door. "You know all you have to do is ask."

"My class ends next week, and I've got some babysitting hours lined up." She'd started sitting for Timmy when Laurel went to the Design Expo. "Maybe in a couple weeks?"

"Anytime you want." He took a seat in the waiting area when she went up to the desk.

"You got your ultrasound today, Miss Cassandra," said the receptionist. "You ready to see that beautiful baby of yours?"

Cass was so ready she almost couldn't bear it. She was finally going to *see* those poking fists and feet, that tiny body . . . that face. The face of her child. The only thing that felt off was seeing it alone. She glanced back at Scott. "Hey, do you . . . Are you at all interested in seeing, you know . . . the baby?"

He sat up in his chair. "Um, yeah. I mean, do you want me to, or is this, like . . ."

"Like what?"

"I don't know. Private. You and the baby. I don't want to be an extra guy in the room."

"You're his uncle, Scotty. You're not some extra guy."

He got up and strode toward her. "Let's go. I mean, do I go with you?" He looked at the receptionist. "Do I go with her?"

"Yah, man." Humor crinkled around her eyes. "There's nothing to see out here."

In the ultrasound room Cass lay down on the exam bed and pulled up her maternity top to expose her growing abdomen, stretched smooth as a polished stone over the baby's watery nest. Scott aimed his gaze anywhere but at the most interesting thing in the room, as if looking at her belly was akin to checking out her burgeoning cleavage. "You cold?" he said. "It's like the North Pole in here. You'd think they'd crank up the temp if people are going to have their skin exposed."

"Pregnancy makes you hot, anyway. You burn a lot of calories growing a person."

"Huh." Scott nodded hard, as if he found this profoundly interesting.

But Cass knew he was profoundly uncomfortable. *I should let him leave.* But then the tech came in, a young guy with a close-cropped beard. He introduced himself and started tapping at the ultrasound keyboard, confirming Cass's name, birth date, and expected due date.

"November twenty-fifth," she said.

"Around Thanksgiving?" said Scott.

"It's *on* Thanksgiving this year." She smiled up at him. "Pretty cool, huh?"

He nodded and stepped closer to the exam bed to scrutinize the screen on the other side. It was just static, Cass's name and a bunch of numbers. He leaned down and murmured in her ear, "This is modern medicine? It looks like one step up from an Etch-a-Sketch."

She turned to grin back at him, and his face was so close she could smell his aftershave.

"Hold on, Dad," said the tech, as he squeezed gel onto the ultrasound wand. "You're about to see what this Etch-a-Sketch can do."

Scott stood to his full imposing height. "I'm his uncle."

"Got it," said the tech as he applied the wand to Cass's belly. A vague image came into view, oblong with an uncertain number of appendages. The heart was a little pebble of a thing, but it throbbed rapidly. "Normal heart rate," said the tech, typing quickly into the computer.

The face! Cass practically hollered. *Show me his face!*

The baby moved and suddenly a ghostly outline of eyes, nose, and mouth filled the screen. "Well, hello," said the tech. "Couldn't wait to say hi to Mom and Dad. Uh, I mean Uncle."

Cass slid her hand over to the side of the exam table to find Scott's. It was large and warm and wrapped quickly around hers. "There he is," murmured Scott. "That's Hal."

Cass felt a tear slide out of the corner of her eye and down into her hair. *That's my baby*.

"Want to know the gender?" asked the tech.

Cass had thought she'd want it to be a surprise—that moment when the doctor says, *It's a boy!* or *It's a girl!* But now, with the answer so close, she wasn't sure anymore. She looked up at Scott, who was still staring with fascination at the screen. "What do you think?" she asked.

He gazed down at her. "Up to you."

"I can't decide."

They looked at each other for a few beats, and he said, "I'd kind of like to know."

"Tell us," she said to the tech.

He drove the scope across her belly until they could see two longish things—legs, he told them. "And you have . . . a girl!"

Cass gasped. And then tears flew down her face so fast she hardly knew where they'd come from. She reached up for Scott, and his arms slid quickly around her neck and back, pulling her toward him, his cheek next to hers. "A girl!" she said. "A girl!"

He laid her back down on the table and put his hands on her cheeks to wipe the tears. "A girl," he said, grinning so broadly his cheekbones disappeared. "A little girl."

It was the happiest moment Cass could ever remember.

Chapter XXIV

Scott started coming home after every game.

This became clear to Cass when they kept running out of food. He'd show up for dinner after one o'clock games and was generally home by midnight after a night game. Then he'd be up early in the morning, eating bowls of cereal or towering plates of eggs.

"Helps me keep my weight down," he said. "Restaurant food is rich. And expensive. Paying for all those drink rounds adds up, too."

"You're going to have to come shopping with me, then. I can't carry that many grocery bags home on foot."

"Oh, I'm happy to help," he teased. "We ran out of Pop-Tarts a couple of weeks ago, and you keep missing it on the list."

"I didn't miss it," she said. "I ignored it."

He laughed. "Come on, I'll let you drive."

Driving lessons were going only slightly better than they had at the beginning. Scott was patient with her, though he still gripped the armrest like it was his only chance for survival.

Cass liked having Scott around. He didn't get in her way or interrupt when she was studying, which Kate often had. But he was there to talk to in the mornings when Cass felt most energetic and chatty, and to sit with in companionable silence after lunch as he read the sports section and she read the latest child development book she'd picked up from the library.

He got her a set of hand weights and showed her how to use them. They would go down to the basement and lift weights together, and he'd make cracks about how he'd have to be nice to her or she'd take him down with her mighty muscles. Then he'd curl the enormous black dumbbells that made her little weights look like toys by comparison.

He got used to her pressing his hand against her belly when the baby was active, and telling him random facts about fetal lung development or rare genetic conditions. She liked when he came in late after a night game and sat on the edge of her bed in the dark to talk for a few minutes. Sometimes Cass wished he would put his head on the other pillow and keep talking.

When she'd first moved in, there had been a sort of sibling physicality between them. He'd grabbed her shoulders when he was mad or suspicious. She had poked at him or shoved him in frustration. Over time this had given way to rarer but gentler contact. His hand on her belly. Her hand squeezing his arm. The occasional hug, sudden as a summer thunderstorm, retreating just as quickly.

It was confusing. But there were moments, brief flashes, when it wasn't confusing at all. When it was perfectly clear.

Cass hated those moments.

Don't screw it up, she told herself. Rule Number One was "Don't fight with Scotty." But there was another rule forming, this one not quite codified in words, but it had to do with not letting things get messy or ruined by feelings that were trouble waiting to happen.

Rule Number Two: "Just don't."

* * *

"You're talking about Scott a lot these days," Patrick commented as they sat at Wortherton Tea and Spices one day.

"Well, I live with the guy." Cass tried to sound offhanded. "He figures prominently."

Patrick dunked his teabag a couple of times, then pulled it out and set it on his spoon. "It's really better to stay out of relationships for at least six months of sobriety, hon. And when I say six, I really mean eight, at which point you might as well round it up to a year."

"I'm not in a relationship," she said with finality. "And I won't be anytime soon."

"Good," he said. "If it goes bad—or even too well—it can spark a relapse."

"Too well?"

"All that giddy happiness. You feel like a new person. A better person. Someone who can drink without everything going to shit."

"I hope I'd be smarter than that," Cass muttered.

"None of us is smarter than that, Cass. Some of us might be luckier than that, but none of us is so wise that we can see every pitfall before we step in it. None of us."

* * *

At the end of August, Cass got her grade for the child development course. She'd been hoping for a B; after all, she hadn't completed so much as a magazine quiz in eleven years. When she logged into her class account there it was. An A minus.

She called Kate, but got voice mail. Kate was getting more hours at Hair of the Dog pet groomers, going to meetings every day, and occasionally volunteering at the dog shelter. "Busy is better," she said in a pointed way that suggested maybe Cass could be a little busier herself. Cass had complained about this to Patrick, who'd said, "Sometimes when people see the light, they try to shine it in everyone else's eyes, too. Just be glad for her. And then ignore it."

Cass called Laurel, who was thrilled of course. But it was seven o'clock, and she was putting Timmy to bed. There was yelling in the background, and Laurel called out, "Matthew Robert Kessler, I said stop teasing him!" and had to get off the phone.

It was Patrick's wedding anniversary. Cass couldn't even think about bothering him.

None of this mattered, though. The one person she really wanted to brag to wouldn't be home until at least eleven.

In the top of the ninth the Sox were up by one, and Rogie was on the mound. All he had to do was close it with no runs and the game would end early. "Come on," Cass told him. "Let's get this over with." But with two outs, he let the most worn-out player on the Detroit Tigers get a hit, and the guy on second went home. Rogie struck the next guy out, but the score was tied.

"Rogie, you big goon!" she yelled and threw a pillow at the screen. He flashed those big brown eyes, full of highly attractive fury, and stalked off the field with the score tied.

One after another, the best of the Red Sox lineup flied out, grounded out, and struck out, which put the game into extra innings. Cass went to put her pajamas on, hoping that when she came back, the score had changed in either direction. At this point, she really didn't care which.

She must have fallen asleep out of pure aggravation during the thirteenth inning. The next thing she knew, Scott's hand was on her shoulder. "Come on, Sleeping Beauty, up to bed."

"Who won?" she mumbled.

"The other guys. Rogie was spitting nails, so I had to take him for a beer. Then Miss August showed up, and I headed home."

"Miss August?"

"The girl he's dating this month. Next month he'll have a new girl, and we'll call her Miss September."

Cass smiled as she stood up. "Maybe Miss August will last more than a month."

"Nah. It would, like, throw off the earth's rotation and stuff. Can't have that." He put an arm around her back, and it remained there as they went up the stairs and into her room.

"Hey," she said. "I got my class grade. An A minus." She slid under the covers and scooted over so he could sit down.

"I never got an A in anything but gym and math," he said.

"You liked math?"

"Loved it. It's so clear. No worries about whether the teacher likes your answer. You either got it right or you didn't. Cut and dried. No drama."

The guiding principle of his life, she thought. *He's got Rule Number Two down cold.*

"You gonna take another course?" he asked.

"I'd like to. Not sure where things stand on our ledger . . ."

"Screw the ledger."

"Really?"

"You're improving your life, Cass. Why would you think I'd say no to that?"

"I just don't want to make assumptions. It's your money, and you can say no anytime."

"I'm saying yes. So which course?"

"I can't decide. Either Child Development 2 or Fundamentals in Education."

"Take both. You can handle it."

"Really?"

"Stop saying 'really'!"

She laughed. "Well, I'm kind of limited—you won't let me say 'thank you,' either."

"Just say, 'This time I'll get A pluses.' Piece of cake for a smart girl like you." He tucked the sheet up around her shoulders and suddenly it was all she could do not to reach for him. She clutched the sides of her pajama pants. He sat there for another moment; Cass held her breath.

Scotty, please just go before I grab you.

"Well, g'night," he murmured.

"Night."

* * *

WHEN Scott left a couple of days later for consecutive series in Miami and Tampa, Cass was bereft. As full as her belly was, she felt a weird emptiness in her chest, as if certain critical organs had gone missing.

But another part of her—an equal part—was relieved.

Without his physical presence she focused on sorting it out. *It'll pass*, she told herself. *You haven't had sex in almost six months, you're just horny.* The pregnancy book said hormones could amp up your sex drive. *Besides, he's Ben's brother, for godsake. It's too weird.*

But the most compelling reason for Rule Number Two was that she just couldn't afford it. Scott was the source of all stability in her life. He kept her housed, fed, clothed, educated, and safe. What if they did get together? She could sense his affection, and despite her current rounded state, he might just be up for it. *But be honest*, she told herself. *It would never actually amount to anything.* He practically had a policy about not keeping a girlfriend for more than a couple of months. So was he likely to sign up for something long term with a recovering alcoholic and her baby? Not a chance. Which meant it would be just a hookup. And then what?

Then it all goes bad, just like Patrick said.

Eventually, probably sooner rather than later, it would get uncomfortable and weird, and she'd end up moving out. To where—some rathole apartment? How would she even pay for it? Her pregnancy was obvious now. No one would hire her. She and her baby would be up the creek. A place where anything could happen. Homelessness. Drinking. Losing her child.

That was it. There could be no Cass and Scott. End of story.

* * *

SCOTT was gone for eight days, and in that time, Cass adopted Kate's mantra of "Busy is better." She started the reading assignments for her two courses, planning to complete them early, with plenty of time before the baby came. She babysat for Laurel, took Bunny for walks, and scrubbed the house from top to bottom.

She still watched Scott's games, but now they served a new purpose: practice controlling her feelings. When Scott got up to bat, she watched the way his powerful legs tensed at the oncoming ball, his hips engaged and twisting, his shoulders whipping around to complete the swing. Under such scrutiny, she was almost able to persuade herself that he was no more appealing than any of the other players. Well, maybe more than Kep Miller.

By the third night, Cass felt she had it down. Scott's body, no big deal.

As if he somehow sensed this, he called. Her heart pounded when she saw his number on the caller ID. She waited a few rings, telling herself to *calm down for godsake, what is wrong with you.*

"Hello?" As if, unlike every other time he called, she didn't know exactly who it was.

"Hey," he said, "it's me."

"Oh, hey!" She reminded herself not to let her voice get too quiet. They had a tendency to murmur to each other, as if their heads were on the same pillow.

"Um, so . . . how was your day?" he asked.

It was horrible, Scotty. I missed you so much.

She squeezed her hand, sunk her fingernails into her palm, and told him all about her reading and exercising and her long walk with Bunny. "How about you?" she asked brightly.

"Why are you yelling?"

"Oh, sorry . . . I didn't . . ." She shook her head, made herself relax. "Sorry."

"Is everything okay?"

"Yeah, fine. Where are you—out with the guys?" What a stupid question. If he were out with the guys, he certainly wouldn't call her.

"No, I'm in my hotel room. The bar scene's kinda boring. Same old, same old."

"Okay, well, I'll let you get some sleep."

"Cass, are you sure everything's okay?"

"Totally. I'll see you when you get back. Knock 'em dead in Miami." She hung up and sank onto a kitchen stool. It was going to be so much harder than she thought.

The next night she called him, her voice soft but not cozy. She joked around, but didn't tease him like she usually did. He wasn't in the mood for that anyway. He'd had a bad game.

The conversation was choppy. They talked over each other or left weird, gaping silences, neither of them quite sure when to jump in. A tentative tone crept into Scott's voice as if there was something he could sense but couldn't quite grasp the meaning of.

At the end of the call, she told him about Timmy finding a box of Laurel's panty liners and sticking them all over the dog as bandages for imaginary boo-boos. They got laughing about that, and it felt almost normal. Almost, but not really. When they said good night, she set the phone down into its cradle, put her hand over her eyes, and cried.

Practice, she told herself the next night. It was a little like recovery from alcoholism, learning to deal with a craving you could not surrender to, teaching yourself healthier habits.

There were two main differences, however. The first was that there was always someone you could talk to about not drinking: there were meetings and sponsors and friends in recovery. She couldn't talk to anyone about this thing with Scott. She just couldn't.

And second, she could avoid alcohol completely—in fact, that was the goal. But she couldn't avoid Scott. She needed him. The trick was to be with him without letting it get out of hand, without, as she was beginning to think of it, getting Scott-drunk.

"*I could drink a case of you, darling,*" went Joni Mitchell's song, "*and I would still be on my feet.*" But Cass would not be on her feet. She would be out on her ass.

* * *

SHE called the next night, honing the balance between distant and intimate, and was surprised at how quickly he followed her lead. He pulled back precisely as much as she did; it was sexless, siblinglike. Safe. Maybe it had never meant anything to him in the first place.

Afterward, she cried again. It had worked a little too well.

Cass called one last time before Scott got home. She felt sad and empty afterward, but she did not cry. This gave her hope that she was prepared, at last, to face him in person. Rule Number Two was firmly in place. He would be home tomorrow. It would all be okay.

Chapter XXV

"I got those tickets for you," Scott said over lunch the day after he got home. "They're for Thursday. Field box, third baseline, just before the visitors' dugout."

"Wow, thanks." These were far better than the ones he used to get for her and Ben, which tended to be on an upper deck, or out by right field, a position Scott never played. She and Ben had laughed over the fact that he clearly wanted them as far away from him as possible. He was a third baseman. She'd be sitting right near him. "Who are you playing?" she asked.

"Yankees."

Cass had second thoughts. The Boston crowd that came out for Yankees games tended to be a little rowdier and more committed to their beverage intake than usual. She wondered how Kate would feel. Surprisingly, Kate had no problem whatsoever. "A Yankees game by the visitors' dugout? Are you kidding? I wouldn't turn that down for a trip to Nantucket."

Cass rode in to Fenway with Scott to meet her. When they pulled up outside the players' parking lot, he took out his wallet and held out sixty dollars.

"That's okay," she said. "I have money."

"Whatever you brought, trust me, it's not enough. A burger costs like a filet mignon." When she hesitated, he dropped it in her lap. "It's on me," he said. "A night at Fenway."

"Thanks," she said. "That's really generous."

He gave her a look. Soft, like before. But then it was gone. His gaze turned toward the growing numbers of people striding down Jersey Street toward watering holes like the Cask 'n Flagon to get a head start on their revelry. "I'll meet you here after."

Cass and Kate strolled around a bit and chose a pizza place that didn't serve alcohol. They chatted and ate, Kate teasing Cass about her huge appetite.

A group of young men, all sporting various well-worn Red Sox caps, stopped outside the restaurant window to wait for a lagging friend. "We don't have all day, asshole!" called out one wearing a YANKEES SUCK T-shirt. The friend retorted with something out of earshot, but the men outside howled with laughter, and the YANKEES SUCK guy grabbed his crotch in response.

Cass rolled her eyes. It was so familiar, just like half the guys she grew up with. Kate, however, seemed frozen in panic, ready to run if the small herd of men suddenly decided to stalk their prey in the pizza place. Cass studied her. "Have you been out at all since . . ."

"I go to meetings and out for coffee, and stuff. But, you know . . . not *out* out."

Cass knew that Kate was going to a counselor in Cambridge. "You like the new person you're seeing?" she asked.

"She's great. But it's not like it goes away overnight. I don't know if it'll go away, ever." She leveled her gaze at Cass. "I have to tell you something. I think I'm going to press charges. Those guys could do it to someone else—what's to stop them? They got off scot-free with me."

"That's not your fault, Kate. You were petrified."

"Yeah, but I'm not anymore. I mean, I'm scared, but I'm not begging for my life. I have to *do* something or it's just left as it was: me all beaten up . . . them laughing."

The terror of that night rose up around them: Kate's guilt at having gotten herself into the situation in the first place; Cass's guilt for hesitating before rushing to help.

Fear and shame. An alcoholic's constant companions.

"I've thought about it a lot," Kate went on. "If I do nothing, I live like a victim for the rest of my life, knowing I didn't have the guts to try."

"I get that, and I think it takes a lot of courage, but I have to ask . . . what if he comes after you for trying?"

"He said he would, if I ever went to the police. Said he'd kill everyone I love, too. But I have to do what I can to keep this from happening to someone else. Besides, he was so messed up, it was probably just the drugs talking."

Jesus, I hope so, thought Cass.

As they headed toward Fenway, Cass pondered Kate's choice. She was proud of Kate for reclaiming the power those sociopaths took from her, and trying to spare some other poor girl the same fate. But a rape trial. They would dig around in Kate's messy personal life and try to make it her fault. And if the guy got off, as so many of them did, that threat he'd made . . .

Cass felt slightly ill at the thought of it and tried to distract herself with gratitude for this day right now, a warm September night, and the feel of a ticket to Fenway in her pocket.

The gates opened and they had to stick close not to lose each other in the erratic surge of the crowd in the cool, dark underbelly of Fenway. Walking up the ramp toward the park itself, Cass remembered the few times she and Ben had actually gone to the games instead of scalping Scott's tickets; how the dimness below would morph into a scene so saturated with color that it took a moment for your eyes to adjust.

And there it was: the impossible green of the field, the rusty red of the warning track, the feeling that you'd finally arrived at the Emerald City after trekking through the dark forest.

Their third-row seats were between home plate and the visitors' dugout, and Cass guessed that they were some of the best seats in the house. So generous of Scotty.

She walked down to the low wall that separated the fans from the field. Yankees players were scattered across the grass taking turns batting and fielding. When the current batter finished and turned toward the dugout to get his mitt, his face was in clear view.

Tate Hogarth, her friend from rehab!

She knew he'd strained his back early in the season and had been on the injured list ever since. But apparently he was back in the lineup because there he was heading right for her. She said his name and he looked up.

"Cass?" His grin was wide as he strode over and hugged her across the wall. "My Lord, girl, what're you doing here?"

"Well, I guess I'm about to watch you play!"

His gaze dropped down to her protruding belly. "Look at you, all round and rosy." He glanced back up, his look purposeful. "How's it going? You doing okay?"

"Good," she said. "Really good, Tate. You?"

He nodded but looked away. "Better, now that I'm playing."

Fans started to congregate, invading their little bubble of reunion with baseballs and tickets for Tate to sign with proffered Sharpie pens. He shot a pointed look at Cass. "You got anything for me to sign?"

She rooted in her purse and pulled out a grocery receipt. He wrote something on it and handed it back. He waved to the fans, called out, "Thanks, folks!" and headed into the dugout.

Cass looked down at the receipt. He'd written a phone number and the words *Call me when the game's over so we can get together and catch up.*

When Cass went back to her seat, Kate was staring at her. "What was that all about? You're buddies with everyone in the league now?"

"An old friend," said Cass. "He gave me a push in the right di-rection when I needed it." It was just cryptic enough for Kate to know not to ask more questions.

Cass continued to think about it, though. Tate had been the one to get her to approach Scotty with the bargain plan. Other than a few glitches, it had worked out better than she ever could have imagined. Cass wondered where she'd have ended up with-out Tate's advice.

Nowhere good, that's for sure.

*   *   *

A little before seven o'clock the Fenway Code of Conduct was an-nounced, including "please avoid balls in play" and "drink re-sponsibly" and "watch your language." The three guys in the seats behind Kate and Cass hooted at "drink responsibly" and Kate stiffened.

Cass murmured, "These idiots need that tattooed on their bod-ies somewhere."

"Preferably their dicks," said Kate. Cass let out a loud laugh, and even Kate chuckled.

They were still smiling when a family took the seats in front of them. The little boy eyed someone's bag of popcorn as he scram-bled past. "I want one of those," he said, though he was already holding a hot dog and a drink.

"What are you, kidding me?" joked his father. "I'm gonna have to take out a second mortgage if you keep eating like this. The game hasn't even started yet, ya locust."

"What's a mortgage?" the boy giggled.

One of the guys behind Cass and Kate said, "What's a locust, is what *I* wanna know."

"Isn't it one of those yoga moves?"

The third said, "For chrissake, it's a bug. Like a grasshopper."

"Grasshoppers don't eat that much."

"Yeah," said the other. "And what do they eat? Grass? That's cheap."

"You two are officially stupid," muttered the third.

The Red Sox players' names were called as they sprinted onto the field. "On third base, Scott McGreavy!" The announcer's voice echoed out over the park. Cass and Kate cheered and screamed his name. He didn't look over, but he tossed a little wave as he jogged by. When he got to third, he squinted toward home plate, a little smile playing around his lips. Cass could feel it as if he were grinning right at her. Happiness. Scott was happy she was there.

For a moment she felt her chest swell in response and then tighten as she reminded herself, once again, of Rule Number Two. She gritted her teeth waiting for the warring emotions to pass. Joy and sadness. Real life. This was how it felt when you weren't in a constant state of anesthetization.

And alcohol was everywhere. It seemed half the crowd was holding clear plastic cups filled with amber liquid that sparkled like melted gemstones in the waning sunlight . . . drawing her in like the goddamned Holy Grail . . .

"Come up with any names yet?" said Kate.

"Names?"

"Yeah, there's this funny custom of naming babies—maybe you've heard of it?"

Cass forced a wan smile. "Oh," she said. "I was just going to call her Baby. Or maybe Pumpkin, for the very attractive shape of my stomach." She patted the hard roundness of her belly, and the urge to medicate her emotions began to dissipate.

Everything passes, Patrick had told her once. *And the stuff that doesn't pass doesn't get better by drinking. It only gets worse.*

Cass gazed out across the park, at the tens of thousands of people who had come to watch a bunch of guys play with a stick and a ball. So much of life defied explanation. People wanted what they wanted, often without having any idea of why they wanted it. They just followed their fascinations, their obsessions, their hearts.

And here we all are, she thought. *At Fenway.*

Chapter XXVI

Scott was having the game of his life. A fly off the Green Monster for a double that brought Kep Miller home; a diving third-out catch; and in the third inning, a home run into the bleachers. As he jogged down the third-base line toward home plate, he looked over at Cass and grinned. Beaming, she pointed at him and mouthed, *Way to go!* She saw her words land on him like a kiss, and he tucked his head so the crowd wouldn't see him smile. But she saw.

In the fifth inning things got a little strange. Like Scott, Tate also played third base, a coincidence that was not lost on Kate. "If we sat here next week," she said, "you think whatever guy was playing third base would suddenly be your friend?"

"Yeah, it's a contractual thing. You play third, you gotta smile at the pregnant girl three rows back."

When Scotty got up to bat in the fifth inning, he hit a high foul that dropped down right in front of them. Tate ran forward from third for the catch and got him out. Then he turned and tossed the ball to Cass. One of the guys behind them reached out to snatch it, but missed.

Kate flinched, as if expecting to be hit. "Watch it!" she snarled at them.

"Whoa, sorry," said one. He turned to the unsuccessful ball-snatcher. "The fuck's wrong with you?"

"I never caught a ball at Fenway before!"

"That's nice, trying to steal it from a pregnant lady, moron!"

The mother of the little boy in front of Cass and Kate shot an annoyed look at her husband, who shrugged and murmured, "It's a ballpark. There's language."

Cass leaned forward and handed the ball to the little boy, and his face went wide with happy surprise, a look that was caught on-camera and projected onto the jumbotron. Applause went up all over the field. "Look," the father said to the boy. "You're on the big screen!"

He shot his little hand into the air. "It's me!" he yelled. "And my ball!"

The man grinned over at his wife, who smiled back with a little conciliatory eye roll. The look between them almost made Cass's eyes water. What would it be like to feel so certain about your love that you could project it like a beam of light, not caring who saw? She glanced over at Scott in the batter's box. He had seen Tate toss her the ball, and her subsequent gift to the little boy, and nodded at her. *That was nice*, his look said. His face was so beautiful in that moment, she had to look away.

At the beginning of the sixth inning, the Yankees were up by two runs. The Red Sox pitcher was struggling, and the catcher and manager went out to talk to him. The batter at the plate took some practice swings. Tate was in the visitors' on-deck circle right in front of their seats waiting for his at bat. "Enjoying the game?" he said to the crowd, but looking at her.

"No batter, no batter!" sneered one of the guys behind her, and Tate shook his head. He looked tired. He was in his midthirties, Cass remembered. It was a rare ballplayer who was still on the roster at forty. She wondered what he would do when all this was behind him.

The usher came down the aisle and said, "You're getting too loud, boys. Settle down or I call security, understand?"

They made acquiescent noises at the usher and muttered at one another after he left. "These tickets cost a mint, asshole. You get us chucked and I'll beat the living shit outta ya."

"Fuck you."

"No, fuck you, and I'm not kidding."

Cass was distracted from this brilliant interchange, however, by the way Scott, standing at third base, was scrutinizing Tate. Cass wondered if maybe they knew each other.

The game resumed, but Scott was still looking at Tate when the batter hit a line drive toward third. Scott's glove went up a split second too late, and the ball went by him, skittering into the left-field corner; the runner made it to second. The replay on the jumbotron showed Scott's late effort in humiliating detail, and the word *ERROR* scrolled across the screen.

Tate was up next, and he slammed the ball toward the gap in right-center field. The center fielder grabbed it up but bobbled it for a moment before sending it to second, by which time Tate was on his way to third. The second baseman shot the ball to Scott, who snatched it from the air and swung low to tag Tate as he slid hands-first toward the bag. Tate's shoulder clipped Scott's leg, knocking him over like a bowling pin. Both men sprawled in the dirt.

The dust eddied up around third base for a moment. The crowd was hushed, waiting for the umpire's decision. His arms slashed out to the sides. Tate was safe.

The two men got up. Cass saw Tate give Scott a quick pat on the back and say something. Whatever it was—"Y'alright?" Or maybe "Close one"—Scott ignored him. It wasn't uncommon for opposing players to give a brief greeting to each other. Cass knew Scott didn't tend to be chatty on the field, but to give no answer whatsoever . . . it seemed off, even for him.

Rogie Rogatelli was called out to take over on the mound. During the pitching change, Kate went off to the bathroom and came back with soft serve ice cream swirled into two little plastic batting helmets. Cass tried to repay her, but Kate just said, "Are you kidding? This is the most exciting game I ever went to! It's my treat."

Cass was surprised that Kate was so enthusiastic, given the men sitting behind them. "These guys aren't bothering you?" she murmured.

Kate shrugged. "They made me nervous at first. But they're like the Three Stooges—harmless except to themselves."

In the middle of the eighth inning, the crowd sang along with the traditional "Sweet Caroline," thirty-five thousand voices belting out "Oh-oh-oh!" The Three Stooges sang their hearts out. When it was over one of them said, "I *love* that song." He gave Cass a tap on the shoulder. "Hey," he said. "Not trying to butt in or anything, but if it's a girl, you should call her Caroline."

"I'll keep it in mind," said Cass.

"Also, that was really nice, giving the kid the ball. Sorry I tried to grab it from you."

"That's okay."

"And I hope everything goes smooth with the baby and all. My sister's kid took two days coming down the chute, the little bastard. Hope it goes better for you."

One of his buddies leaned in. "I apologize for Jimmy, here. He gets wicked chatty when he's had a few."

"Hey," said Jimmy. "I'm just being nice and you had to ruin it, talking like that."

"Sorry, chatty." And the third guy burst out laughing.

In the top of the ninth inning the light breeze that had kept Fenway pleasantly cool suddenly strengthened into erratic gusts, and balls that were expected to go one way ended up on different trajectories altogether. The score was now tied, with two outs and no one on base.

Tate Hogarth stepped to the plate, and Cass could see Rogie relax a little. *Old Tate*, she could just imagine him thinking. *This'll be quick.*

Tate's first two swings met air. His third sent a ball foul toward the right-field stands, but he ran hard for first base nonetheless. The outfielder, assuming the ball would end up in the hands of a fan, stopped running for it just as it curled away from the stands and onto the warning track in the right-field corner. He scrambled awkwardly to get his mitt on it, losing precious seconds, then flung it toward the second baseman. But Tate's long legs had carried him past second by then and he was heading to third when the second baseman fired the ball to Scott.

The throw was high. Scott leapt up to pluck it out of the air, but the ball sailed over his glove, bounced off the wall behind him, and ricocheted into left field. Tate hit home plate as his teammates sprinted out of the dugout to meet him. A rare inside-the-park home run.

A collective groan went up at Fenway. Kep Miller stomped his foot like a five-year-old. Rogie's handsome face darkened with fury. Scott crossed his arms and stood there like a seawall, as waves of fan disappointment crashed over him. His face was utterly expressionless. Cass imagined that this was what he might have looked like facing his father after a bad game.

The Red Sox had last ups, but the batting was lackluster. It was as if Tate's unexpected success had demoralized every last one of them. The game was over. The Yankees had won.

The Three Stooges stood and wiped the peanut shells out of the wrinkles in their pants. "Hey, um," one said to Kate. "You want to grab a drink somewhere?"

"No," she said flatly.

"Maybe a bite to eat?"

"No."

"How about ice cream? I know you like ice cream—you practically ate the helmet!" he teased.

"Really," she said. "No."

The guy gave Cass a *what's-with-her?* look.

"She just doesn't want to," said Cass. "And she doesn't have to if she doesn't want to. It's up to her, right?" He stared at her, trying to decipher the meaning of this little speech. "Right?" Cass repeated, nodding her head.

"Absolutely." He nodded back uncertainly.

"Also, a little advice," said Cass. "Don't swear so much. You'll have better luck."

She followed Kate down the ramp, and when the crowd thinned, Kate turned to her, grinning. "'Don't swear so much'? When did you turn into Little Miss Proper? I think Wortherton's rubbing off on you."

"Oh, they swear in Wortherton, too. Trust me. Can I borrow your cell phone a minute?" Cass pulled out the grocery receipt with Tate's number, and Kate handed her the phone.

"I was waiting for your call," he said.

"Great game!"

"My best this season. 'Course I only played five, but this was definitely the highlight. So can I take you out for something to eat? I can't wait to hear how our plan worked out."

"I'd love to, but my ride's leaving soon, and I don't have any way to get home after that."

"I'll get you an Uber," he assured her.

"I live kind of far away."

"Listen," he said. "I gotta see you, Cass. I mean . . . I'm okay, but . . . it's hard, you know? Especially on the road. It'd be so great to sit and talk with someone who understands."

Scott had told her about being on the road, how some guys had a hard time with the loneliness and boredom between games. To pass the time, they played cards a lot, and with the card playing there was drinking. Separate yourself from that and there wasn't much else to do.

Tate had been there for her. In fact, his advice had set her on a much better path. She couldn't let him down now. She knew, of course, that Scotty would not like this. He'd suspect that she was going out to drink. But he would get over it when she got home sober and everything was back to normal.

"Okay," she said. "Where should I meet you?"

She called Scott next. "Hey," she said, "I bumped into an old friend and we're going to catch up for an hour or so. I'll meet you at home." She saw no benefit in offering up the fact that her friend was the guy who had made Scott look incompetent tonight.

"Christ," said Scott. "It's Tate Hogarth, isn't it?"

So much for keeping that to herself.

"Don't tell me," Scott went on, his words sharp as metal shards. "You met him in rehab. Everyone knows he's a lush."

Cass sighed. He could be such a jerk sometimes. "I won't be out late. I'm tired and—"

"Whatever," he said and hung up.

Kate gave her a look. "What's with you two?" she said. "You're like an old married couple, fighting and pecking at each other."

Cass shook her head. There were only two rules: don't fight with him and don't love him. But no matter what she did, it seemed that if she wasn't breaking one, she was breaking the other.

Chapter XXVII

It was 10:30 by the time Cass had said good-bye to Kate and taken the T over to the Ritz-Carlton, where the Yankees were staying. Tate met her in the lobby, freshly showered and shaved, his thinning black hair still slightly damp.

"You don't wear a cap or anything to keep people from recognizing you?" Cass asked.

He laughed. "That'd be a nice problem to have. I played so little this season, I'd be mighty surprised if anyone in Boston even remembered who I am."

"They'll remember you after tonight."

"Huh. Scott McGreavy will, that's for sure. Started out so well for him, but it was straight downhill after that."

Cass felt her ire rise. "He's a solid player."

Tate lifted an eyebrow. "I see you're a fan."

She looked away. Was there a reason not to tell Tate about Scott? She was so used to keeping things private she didn't know what was fair to reveal anymore. But Scott had been nothing but good to her, so there was no reason to keep his help a secret.

"Where do you want to eat?" she asked. "I need to get off my feet."

"Me, too," he said. "My back's killing me."

They ended up in the hotel restaurant, eating double truffle fries and drinking ginger ale. Cass told Tate about Scott and how well their bargain plan had worked out.

"I have to hand it to him," said Tate. "He's a bigger man than I thought."

"What's that mean?"

"Oh. he's all right, doesn't have a big head or anything. But he isn't known for magnanimous gestures, either. Some of these guys visit sick kids in the hospital or show up at all the fundraisers. Years back, when I was a bigger name and stayed in one place longer, I always found something to support. Special needs and cancer research and such."

"Yeah, Scott's kind of shy. Not with me, but in general. He hates to be in the public eye. He doesn't even go out with his buddies after games anymore."

"What does he do?"

"Comes home."

"And?"

"I don't know—hangs out with me, I guess."

Tate picked up a french fry and twirled it between his fingers. "You two together?"

"Just friends," Cass said quickly. "So it must feel good, being back on the team."

Tate shifted in his seat, wincing a little as he changed positions. "Relieved is what I feel. The injured list is purgatory for a guy like me. Just hanging in limbo, bored outta my mind." He let out a long breath. "And yeah, if you're wondering, I slipped up some." Silence hung between them for a moment, as if Tate's sobriety were a friend who'd fallen on hard times. "But I'm better, now that I'm playing," he said. "Almost got my thirty-day chip."

"You want to go to a meeting with me tomorrow?" she said. "You could Uber out to Wortherton. It's a really nice group."

He nodded, seeming to consider this. "'Course I don't sleep that well, with the pain and all. I can't get anywhere too early. Then there's practice."

Clearly he wasn't enthusiastic, but Cass persisted. "I could find you a meeting near here."

"That's a great idea," he said wanly. "In fact, I'll look it up myself when I get back to my room." He slid a hand into his pants pocket and pulled out a small pink tablet. He popped it into his mouth and washed it down with ginger ale. "Oxycodone," he said. "For my back. That slide into your buddy Scott wrenched it all up again."

Cass's chest tightened. Alcoholics in recovery tended not to take pain medication for fear of weakening their resolve. "How often do you take it?" she asked.

"As needed. But don't you worry, I'll stay away from the minibar in my room." He was so unconvincing Cass could've cried. She knew the minibar would be his first stop.

* * *

ON the ride home she did shed a tear. Tate's attention had wandered and his speech slowed as the medication took effect. He'd left her with the hotel doorman and hadn't remembered his offer to pay for her ride home. Too eager to get to that minibar.

Such a terrible shame, she thought and wondered if anyone had ever thought the same thing about her when she was drinking.

When she came in the door, something seemed off. There was a strange sound in the distance, sort of like when the washing machine got off balance and the drum knocked against the housing. But it didn't seem to be coming from the laundry room in the basement. Also, there was a faint smell, sweet like overripe fruit.

Too tired and sad to investigate, Cass dropped her purse on the hall table and began to trudge upstairs. The sound got louder. The smell got stronger. There was a white satin tank top hanging over the railing at the top of the stairs. It reeked of that sweet smell.

Holy Mother of God.

In the upstairs hallway, another sound rose in concert with the knocking. It was soft at first, like a stuffed animal that squeaked when you squeezed its stomach over and over . . .

Cass froze, trying desperately for a brief moment to come up with any explanation other than Scott having sex with someone in his bedroom.

No luck. Cass felt as if she might vomit.

She went quickly to her bedroom and closed the door, but the sound got louder. The knocking—of his headboard against the wall, she guessed—sped up, and the squeaking grew more emphatic, like the yelping of a very small, very agitated dog.

Cass grabbed the pillow and a blanket off the bed and ran down the stairs, stumbling at the bottom and falling onto one knee. Pain shot up her leg, but she couldn't let it stop her. She had to get away from the sound. Limping into the TV room, Cass collapsed onto the couch. Her knee throbbed, and on inspection she saw that there were drops of blood seeping through a hole in her favorite maternity jeans.

There was a screech from upstairs. And then it went quiet.

Cass lay on the couch, shaking.

* * *

SHE heard murmuring, and then a soft gasp. "Who's *that*?"

"My sister-in-law."

"What's she doing here?" The voice had a slow laziness to it, as if still half asleep.

Cass fluttered her eyelids against the light and looked up. Long black hair. Dark eyes smeary with mascara looking down at her. The face disappeared. "She's awake."

Cass would've given her last dollar to simply disappear, vaporizing into the sky like a cloud. The thought of seeing them—him, *her*—was nauseating. She rose quickly to make her escape up to her bedroom. "I'll give you some space," she murmured, avoiding eye contact.

"What's with your knee?" His tone said he really didn't care, and yet he stood in her way.

"I fell."

"Ohhh," he said knowingly, as if it were predictable, as if she deserved it.

That one word, thick with derision, turned her despair into rage. She had worked so hard, followed all the rules, and tried to be so fucking *good* every minute of the day—for what? So he could disrespect her in front of some nameless piece of ass he'd brought home?

She flicked her eyes at him, then at the girl, who was rummaging in the kitchen cabinets, stretching to reach a glass. Her shirt came up to reveal a thong rising out of her tight, low-slung jeans. Above the thin lacy string was a tattoo in curling script that said simply *Yes*.

Cass turned back to Scott and launched a look so loaded with contempt that it felt like firing a gun at point-blank range.

"Yeah, I guess we all fall down sometimes. . . ." Pressing past him she hissed, "Don't we."

* * *

TWENTY minutes later Cass heard the rumble of an engine pulling away—an Uber, she guessed. It was 9:15. She needed to eat and get going if she was going to make it to her ten o'clock AA meeting. Almost seven months pregnant, she walked so slowly these days.

Scott was in the kitchen drinking orange juice. "Have a nice date?" he said sarcastically.

He just won't quit, she thought.

"Well," she said, pouring cereal into a bowl. "I didn't have sex with a Chihuahua, so I guess I can't complain."

"Least she's not eligible for the senior discount."

"And she can spell, too, so that's a bonus. Oh, wait, that was the guy at the tattoo parlor."

"You're just jealous because your wild days are gone."

"Jealous? I had more wild days than anyone should have in a lifetime. All I want now are tame ones." Sorrow tightened her throat and she swallowed hard. "That's the whole point of this arrangement, if you've forgotten. No drinking, no drama." And though she had no right to, she couldn't keep from muttering, "Nobody squealing like a dying pig in the next room."

"It's my house," he snarled, "and I'll bring home whoever I want!"

"And this is my life, and I'll sit in a restaurant and have ginger ale and overpriced french fries with whoever *I* want." She pulled three twenties from her wallet and flicked them onto the counter. "Thanks for the tickets," she said dryly. "Kate had a really nice time."

* * *

HE's going to kick me out.

As Cass trudged toward the meeting, she was sure of it. And a little part of her was relieved. As much as she wanted to kill Scott, the feelings were still there. How was that possible? She had never hated Ben like this. She'd been angry enough to break up with him a couple of times. An argument could be made that he'd done more hateful things than Scott ever had. He'd left her in dangerous situations and discouraged her when she'd tried to stop drinking.

She thought of the time he was on *Jeopardy!* and lost all that money. The irony of it—jeopardy was his middle name, the story of his life. She had never expected anything different.

Scott was reliable, if not always pleasant. He'd not only encouraged her to better herself, he'd funded it. And she was safer here than anywhere else. How could she give that up, now that she'd come to expect it? She wouldn't likely have a choice. Scott was furious, that was clear.

But where could she go? Racking her brain, she was caught off guard when a car pulled up next to her and the passenger-side window rolled down.

"Hey, how come you left without me?" It was Laurel.

"Oh, I, uh . . . I just needed to get some air." Cass opened the door and got in.

"What happened?"

"Nothing, I—"

"Oh, come on," scoffed Laurel. "Nobody ever actually 'needs to get some air.'" Her fingers made little quote marks above the steering wheel.

Cass looked out the window. She wanted so much to talk to someone—not just about her impending housing crisis, but about Scott and the miserable things that had happened. How you stopped falling for someone you really shouldn't fall for. How you stopped being so angry.

Laurel pulled into a parking spot by St. Vincent's. Cass said, "Is this close enough to the meeting to consider it part of the meeting?"

Laurel studied her. "If you want it to be, it is."

"Honesty, confidentiality—the whole package?"

"Absolutely."

Cass told her everything. The relief was enormous. She wondered if this might be what having a big sister was like. A snobby big sister with a drinking problem, a cleaning compulsion, and overly expensive taste, granted . . . but one who listened. Laurel was really listening. Cass could tell. When she finished, she asked, "What do you think?"

Laurel didn't answer right away, pursing her lips as she considered. Finally she said, "I think Scott's in your life and you're in his."

"Not if I move out, I'm not."

"That wouldn't solve it."

"What? Why not?"

"Because you have a connection, a history. And you really do care about each other."

"I don't think he cares too much about me, at the moment."

"For goodness' sake, Cass. Open your eyes. You moved into his home. You've become a part of his daily existence. You think he'd put up with that for one minute if he didn't care about you? The man's practically a recluse."

Cass let out an irritable sigh. "He certainly doesn't have any problem going out and finding sex when he wants it."

"At this particular point in time, that is not your business. Your business is to figure out how the two of you can stop being so nasty to each other."

They never did make it to the meeting. But Laurel wanted to hold hands and say the Lord's Prayer anyway. "Can we not?" whined Cass. "I hate all that religious stuff."

Laurel slid her smooth hand into Cass's and started, "Our Father, who art in heaven . . ." She raised her voice a little when it came to the part about "forgive us our trespasses as we forgive those who trespass against us . . ."

When they were done, Cass asked, "Do you have anything to eat? I'm starving."

"Of course I do. Open the glove box." There were cereal bars, some trail mix, a small bag of pretzels, and several juice boxes.

"You're such a mom," Cass teased.

"Yes," said Laurel, raising her chin. "Apparently I am."

* * *

CASS asked Laurel to drop her off at the library; she'd head to the grocery store afterward.

"Don't stay out all day until he leaves for the ballpark," said Laurel.

That was Cass's plan exactly. "Why not?"

"Because things fester."

Or they cool off, thought Cass. It was midafternoon when she left the grocery store, and she hoped he'd gone to Fenway early. But Scott was upstairs, packing for the next series in Chicago. He came down to the kitchen as she was putting away the food and almost turned away when he saw her. She forced herself to make eye contact. He stood in the doorway, filling it up with his size and his anger. "This isn't working out anymore," he said.

And there it was.

Breathe, she told herself. She thought of Bunny the dog sensing the feelings of the people in the room. Scott was a little bit like that. Not so good with words, but good at sensing. Cass tried to emit a truce vibe. "I'd like to stay," she said.

He shook his head. "We fight too much. It's bad for my game."

Truce, she thought at him. *Truce, truce, truce.* "I'm not going to fight. I'm going to clean the house and buy the groceries and stay out of your hair."

He narrowed his eyes. "What if I bring someone home."

She pressed her hand on the cool granite countertop. "That's your business, not mine."

He looked away. But he did not leave. Cass felt some small hope in that. He was considering. Then he shook his head. "Why should I let you stay?"

Because I've got nowhere to go. Nowhere.

Then she thought of Laurel's point about connection. "Because we're friends, Scotty. More than friends, really. The baby's your niece—that makes us family. You're important to me, and I don't want to mess that up. If I leave now, it's on bad terms."

His blue-gray eyes unfocused as he pondered this. She wondered if he had any close friends. Kep Miller was too stupid. Rogie was too in love with himself. As for family, there was only his mother, and you couldn't get more distant than Hawaii and still be in the same country. He shook his head. "I don't know. I can't think about this now."

"Should I start looking for apartments?"

"I said I don't know, Cass." He looked at her finally and ran a hand back through his hair. "But yeah, maybe that's not a bad idea."

She nodded, feeling the fear curl around her chest like a serpent. "Okay," she said and went back to unloading the groceries.

Chapter XXVIII

Cass scanned the online apartment sites every day. Desperate, she broadened her search beyond the neighborhoods of Boston and found an ad for a room in the home of an elderly man near the Wortherton Library. The rent was free in return for caretaking and housekeeping.

More or less the same deal I have now, she thought. *Without the fighting.*

She called immediately. Nancy Kulch, the man's daughter, answered. Her voice was warm and encouraging, and Cass found herself responding with surprising confidence. She said she'd been housekeeping for a Wortherton homeowner who traveled on business, but there had been some uncomfortable incidents lately, and she wanted a position with less drama.

"I understand," said Nancy knowingly. "All too well, my dear. All too well."

"There's something you should know, though. I'm pregnant." Cass pressed her lips together hard, waiting for Nancy to shut her down.

"How wonderful! Dad loves babies. He'll be delighted just to sit in his BarcaLounger and watch you two play. My goodness, that'll be the most pleasant activity for him." As it turned out, the elderly Mr. Kulch was also hard of hearing, so a crying baby wouldn't bother him in the least. "Now I should mention that my father has Alzheimer's, and sometimes he wanders. He's not angry or uncooperative, but he can't be left on his own."

"Okay . . ." It didn't sound so bad, but Cass got a funny feeling about it.

"With a new baby, you'll have your hands full. Are you sure you're up for this?"

For free rent in a safe neighborhood—and near the library, too?

"I'm absolutely sure." They discussed references—Laurel would give her one for babysitting, and she knew Scott would say something nice, if only to get her out of the house. An interview was scheduled for the following Saturday, September 15.

"A baby!" said Nancy. "Wait till I tell my sister. She won't believe the luck."

* * *

LAUREL was not enthusiastic about the caretaker position. "With a new baby?" she said. "Between the postpartum hormone storms and sleep deprivation, you'll be out of your mind for the first month, at least. You can't look after a wandering old man on top of all that."

But the baby was not due for another two months. Cass figured that if it wasn't going to work, at least she'd have some breathing room to figure something else out.

When Scott got home, he didn't ask about whether she'd found an apartment, or even if she'd looked. He just worked out, watched *Hoarders* and *Pawn Stars* and ate his Pop-Tarts.

On the morning of the interview, Cass woke early. She picked out her best maternity outfit and researched interview questions for caretakers and tried to come up with answers to the questions. If they asked for a résumé, she was sunk. Her work history was a tattered patchwork of short stints, and none of her former bosses could be used as references.

But Nancy Kulch wanted this to work, which made Cass hopeful that somehow it would.

"Where you going?" Scott asked. "Lunch with your sponsor or something?"

"No, I have an interview." She explained the position to him. His face stayed passive, but she knew that, if anything, it was an indication of some sort of heightened emotion. The harder he tried not to feel anything, the blanker he looked.

"Huh," he said. "That was fast."

I'm leaving, and that's all you have to say? She felt the blow as if he'd slapped her.

The phone rang—the landline, which he never answered anymore. She wondered if he would start answering it again when she was gone. Or get rid of it altogether.

"Hello?" she said. Scott wandered off to the office to check his email.

"A Miss Cassandra Macklin, please."

"This is she."

"Miss Macklin, this is Myra Kulch, Nancy's sister. I'm afraid she may not have given you the full picture." Her words were apologetic, but her tone was not. "We're looking for a seasoned home health aide for my father. His condition is deteriorating rapidly. And with your pregnancy, I'm afraid I just can't see how this would work."

Cass's breath froze in her chest. She managed to let out a crippled little "Oh."

"I'm sorry for the misunderstanding. My sister is kindhearted and was quite taken with the idea of having a baby in the house again. I hope you'll accept my apologies." She wished Cass the best of luck with the delivery. "I envy you," she added wistfully. "Just starting out at the beginning of life, with so much to look forward to and so many memories to make."

It's not like that, Cass wanted to say. *You have no idea of the mess I'm in.*

Afterward Cass stared out the window into the backyard. The

grass was long. *Drew must have forgotten to mow it this week.*

So strange the things that came to mind when your best chance has just turned to cinders. The lawn. The lunch dishes in the sink. The towels in the dryer.

Scott came into the kitchen and started sifting through the mail on the counter, though she was pretty sure he'd already looked at it.

"They wanted someone with more experience," she told him. "And not pregnant."

"Oh," he said, studying a flyer from a house painting company. "You tried, though."

She was so tired. She wanted to go up to her room, with its soothing blues and greens, and lie down for about a month. But someday soon she would be . . . somewhere else. Hard to imagine that the new place would be nearly as nice, or safe, or encouraging. Safety, of course, was the most important thing, but she was also coming to truly appreciate the encouragement.

He was still standing there, holding a supermarket circular.

"I'll keep trying," she said quietly. When she looked up, he glanced away.

He tossed the circular in the recycling and went back to the office.

* * *

It was hard to get her class work done. Cass spent a lot of time on the internet trolling for housing. She wanted to be near Laurel and Patrick and her regular AA meeting. It was all she could think about now: how to remain near those who made her feel safe.

She even wanted to be near Scott. As uncomfortable as it was between them, the idea of losing contact with him made her think about drinking.

You're too dependent! she railed at herself. *He's just a guy! Stand on your own two feet, for godsake.* But her own two feet were swollen and sore.

If I had my mother . . .

She tried not to think of it. She would never have her mother back. She would *be* a mother, and have to be strong and sheltering for someone else. But as the days passed the thoughts of her mother came more and more, and the schoolwork got done less and less.

"We're out of milk," Scott told her. It was not accusatory or demanding, just a simple statement of fact.

"Okay," she breathed and hurried from the room so he wouldn't see her eyes fill. Crying over milk. Not even spilled milk, only the fact that it would have to be carried home from the store a mile away, the simmering ache in her back blown into a full boil by the extra weight.

On Thursday, Scott drove her to her checkup. He walked in, and she hoped he would come with her to the exam room, like he had for the ultrasound. But he just slumped into a seat in the waiting area and took out his phone.

"You want to come in and hear the baby's heartbeat?" she asked.

"Nah, that's okay." His thumb dabbed at the tiny screen like a nervous twitch.

The receptionist gave her one brief, bright smile—as if she hadn't noticed that the man who'd been so anxious to go with Cass a month ago now preferred to sit in a molded plastic chair, likely covered in an impressive variety of germs, and play with his phone.

Probably Angry Birds, thought Cass. *How appropriate.*

Ana was kind, as usual, and sprinkled questions throughout the exam as to how Cass was feeling. "And you're being treated well at home, *mi hija*?"

My daughter. Cass could have wept.

"Yes, fine," she said. Because she was. He did not yell or grab her. In fact, he kept at least an arm's distance between them at all times. She would have given anything to feel his hand on her back as she walked up the stairs, or on her belly when the baby kicked.

Ana didn't seem satisfied with her answers, but those were the only ones she had to give.

* * *

SHE asked Kate about getting an apartment together. Kate was sympathetic, but not ready to move out of her cousin's house. "I'm still not making that much money," she said. "Also, it's just really good for me here. Stable. Melanie's so . . . you know . . . normal."

Normal, as in not a recovering drunk or about to have a life-changing event. Or both.

Kate kept apologizing.

"Hey, it's okay," said Cass. "I wouldn't leave, either, if I were you."

"But you saved my life!"

"I helped you out," said Cass. "But I didn't do it so you could turn around and put yourself at risk again, even if it's for my sake."

It felt very noble, and Kate was grateful for her understanding. When Cass hung up the phone, she picked up the can of pencils from the desk and hurled it across the room.

She even broached the subject with Laurel. "Any chance you're interested in having a live-in nanny?" she said, grinning as if it were a joke, although it was certainly no joke.

Laurel sighed. "Oh, Cass. I've thought of that, of course. I even got Adam to agree. But Belva went into orbit. She says it's too early for me to take on something this big, a new mother with a baby. I told her that you'd be helping me, too, but she didn't buy it for a minute."

Cass nodded and smiled and made noises about Laurel being

a good friend even to consider it. But it took every ounce of self-control to bite back a nasty comment about how Belva might be sober when it came to alcohol, but she was obviously drunk on her own power.

* * *

THE next afternoon, after she'd dissected the housing classifieds down to the thinnest, driest artery, Cass's memory failed her. She could not remember why one drink would be so bad. She knew she should talk to someone to remind her, but she didn't feel like talking.

She felt like drinking.

Chapter XXIX

There was a restaurant just past the library called Marco's. It had a large brick front and small windows. It would be dark inside. And there would be a bar.

Tattered shreds of clouds hung beneath the sky as she walked, diffusing the light into something gray and colorless. Inside Marco's it was even dimmer, and it took a moment for her eyes to adjust. She spotted the sign that said *Lounge* and walked up to the bar, sliding onto a low-backed stool. The darkness was brightened here and there by clusters of faces and the sounds of their midafternoon lounge chatter. Cass sat at the far end of the bar and ignored it all.

The bartender headed toward her. His cheeks were jowly when they weren't lifted into a professional-grade smile. His gaze took in her belly. She didn't care. Let him look.

"What can I get you?" he asked.

Those words. She'd been waiting to hear them for so long. But now the wait was over.

"Vodka rocks, wedge of lime," she said.

His gaze remained on her a second too long. "House brand?" he said.

"Grey Goose." Because what the hell. If you were gonna fall, it might as well be worth it.

In the early years, back when she and Ben were better at holding down jobs, they'd gone to bars all the time, and bartenders like this guy had served them. She'd always liked vodka, and usually ordered it with cranberry or orange juice or sometimes with tonic and lime.

But as time went on, the juice and soda took up room she needed for more vodka. The brand stopped mattering. They'd drink anything they could get. Cheap wine, Everclear. Beer pilfered out of the back of a distributor's truck while the driver wasn't looking.

The jowly bartender let a cocktail napkin settle onto the bar before landing the short stocky glass onto it. Water condensed on the sides, and she watched a drip roll slowly, seductively down to the napkin. The lime bobbed like a tiny boat in an iceberg-ridden sea.

It was beautiful.

She slid her hand around the icy dampness of the glass, holding it until her fingers began to get tingly, then numb. Numb was good. For years it was all she'd wanted.

She brought the glass up, the tang of the lime and sharpness of the vodka filling her head. She inhaled it like perfume, wanting to eke every last bit of pleasure from the fragrance before she sipped.

Beyond the rim of the glass, her gaze caught on the bartender, his arms crossed over a slight paunch, sleeves rolled to the elbow. He was looking at her.

Wrenched from her reverie, she set the glass down on the napkin, but she didn't let go.

He ambled toward her as if he didn't have a thing in the world to do but take a stroll. "You ever tend bar?"

She narrowed her eyes. "No."

"You should try it sometime." He gave the high-gloss bar a slow wipe with his towel. "Very different perspective from this side of the keg taps."

Stop talking, she wanted to say. *Don't ruin it.* She gripped the glass, waiting for him to amble on back.

"You see people, you know?" he went on. "You really see 'em. And they hardly see you at all. It's like being a ghost." He smiled, pleased with this analogy. "A ghost that serves."

You think you see me? she wanted to scream. *You have no fucking idea what it is to be me! You don't see shit!*

Maybe it was the laser-hot rage beaming from her eyes, or maybe the other end of the bar truly needed its umpteenth wipe. He blinked, stepped back, and walked away.

Good! Go! Take your judgment and your x-ray vision and go fuck yourself.

She lifted the glass to her lips, ready to down the whole thing just to spite him.

But then she felt it. One sharp kick to the ribs.

No one, *no one*, could keep her from drinking. Not this asshole bartender. Not AA, with its stupid meetings and sayings and Lord's Prayer. Not even Scotty, who would surely waste no time tossing her into the street so he could turn his attention to someone more deserving. Less fucked up, less pregnant. Someone who didn't make him feel things he didn't want to feel. Probably bigger boobs, too.

No one could stop her . . . except someone she'd never met before. A little girl who'd just done what all kids are born to do: demand attention. Insist with their kicking feet and squalling lungs and relentless cuteness that they be protected and cared for.

Hand shaking, Cass lowered the glass. It slid from her fingers before she could set it down, and it spilled into a glistening puddle, the little wedge of lime run aground against cubes of ice.

She looked around the bar. It was warm and safe and it smelled like the most convincing kind of fake comfort there was in the world. But this wasn't where she and Ben would be if he were alive today. No, they'd be in a liquor store parking lot somewhere, passing a bottle of whatever back and forth, trying to stanch the pain of being momentarily sober.

If he were alive today.

She remembered waking up and Ben was on the floor—the bed was a twin; one or the other of them almost always fell out. But that morning, he didn't nudge her over and climb back in. He didn't get up at all, even when she screamed and cried and begged him not to be dead.

They'd gotten so trashed the night before, she couldn't remember how they'd gotten home. What was the last thing he'd said before he died? What were the last words he'd heard from her? She hoped they were loving and sweet, but they had probably been mumbled and stupid. If there had been any at all. Such a pitifully empty, wordless death for a man like Ben.

That was her life with alcohol. It had not been beautiful.

She put some cash on the bar next to the mess she'd made, slid off the stool, and walked home.

Not home, she reminded herself. *Scott's. You're homeless.*

"Hey," she said when Patrick picked up on the other end. "I almost drank."

"Did you, though? Be honest with yourself, if not me."

"No, I caught myself."

"Ok, hon. Let's get you to a meeting."

* * *

"It's been tough around here these days," said Laurel, handing Cass a cup of herbal tea.

Join the fucking club, Cass thought darkly.

"Drew is acting so strange," Laurel went on. "You never know what you're going to get—he can be sweet, like when he was little. Then he'll snap like his head is about to pop off."

"Sounds like standard teenage stuff."

"You're probably right," said Laurel.

But Cass was not right. This became clear on Saturday when Laurel and Adam went out to celebrate their anniversary with a fancy dinner and tickets to a revival of *The Sound of Music*.

"Adam's a good sport," Cass had said when Laurel asked her to babysit.

"About the play? It was his idea." Laurel's smile had had a hint of triumph, as if finally proving a point. "He played the captain in *The Sound of Music* in high school." She cocked her head smugly. "Get him to sing 'Edelweiss' sometime. It'll bring you to tears."

"Seriously?"

"I told you not to rush to judgment on him. People can surprise you."

Yes, but mostly in a bad way, Cass had thought at the time.

Now it was Saturday night and she was surprised, all right. She'd just gotten Matt and Luke into bed. Timmy had been asleep for hours. Drew was supposedly at a friend's house.

Then the phone rang. "Is this . . . ?" Then the caller hissed at someone nearby, "What's his name again? Just tell me—you're in enough trouble already!"

Oh, God, thought Cass.

"Is this Drew Kessler's house?"

"Yes," said Cass. "Is everything okay?"

"No, it's not," said the woman, obviously shaken. "We've called an ambulance."

Drew was supposed to be at his friend Aaron's house. But this was not Aaron's mother. This was the mother of some older boy who had thrown a party while his parents were out. The parents had come home early, found their house full of inebriated teenagers, one of whom was Drew Kessler, lying on the patio, throwing up into their pool. "He's so drunk he can't sit up!"

Cass's head was spinning. "I'm the babysitter," she said. "I can't leave the other kids. I'll call his parents and tell them to meet the ambulance at the hospital."

There was no answer—Laurel had probably turned her phone off for the show. Cass left a message: "Please call home as soon as you can. Drew is sick."

She wanted desperately to get to the hospital, but how could she leave the other kids alone? She almost called Scott. He was probably on his way home by now—if he wasn't going out. And he'd been great when Kate was in trouble. Heroic, really. But this was different; he was already so sick of Cass, and Drew's rescue was already in motion. Cass could only be there while he sobered up . . . If he sobered up.

Alcohol poisoning had taken Ben's life, and he'd been an adult who drank regularly. Drew hadn't even gotten through puberty yet. *I have to get there!*

She ran upstairs to twelve-year-old Matt's room. "Get up, buddy." She gave his shoulder a little shake. "I have to go help Drew. Can you answer the landline if your parents call?"

Matt sat up quickly, ready to assume command. "Yeah," he said, scratching his chest. "I can do that, no problem. He drank too much, didn't he?"

"You know about that?"

"I know he smokes weed, and he goes to parties when Mom thinks he's at a friend's. I'm at the middle school now. That stuff gets around."

As they headed downstairs the phone began to ring. It was Laurel; Cass told her everything. Matt bit at the inside of his lip as he listened.

"Oh my God!" Laurel gasped with every new piece of information. "This is my fault. This is because of me!"

Adam took the phone. "We'll go to the hospital. You stay there with the kids."

Cass hung up and Matt was still standing there. "You can go back to bed," she said gently.

He stared at her. "And do what? Lie there thinking about how we've got two alcoholics in the family now?"

* * *

EARLY the next morning the front door opened. Laurel's arm was tight around Drew's slumping shoulders, guiding him toward the stairs. His face was sickly pale and he avoided Cass's gaze. Laurel had cried all her makeup off, leaving gray smudges in the hollows under her eyes. She gave Cass a brief, grateful smile that seemed to cost her every last bit of will.

Adam followed closely behind. At the bottom of the stairs he turned to Cass, tugging his wallet out of his pocket. He snatched out the whole wad of cash and thrust it at her.

"I can't take money for this. I'm Laurel's friend."

"You're a friend to all of us." He pressed it into her hand and headed up the stairs.

* * *

CASS tried to get some sleep before her ten o'clock AA meeting, but her mind wouldn't settle. She stared at the curtains luffing in the slight breeze. Out that window, over the lawn, in the house next door there was a family in terrible pain. Wealthy, smart, well connected. And still miserable and scared. She wondered if there was such a thing as an easy life.

She went downstairs, and Scott came down shortly after. "Kesslers were out pretty late," he said with false innocence, as if she'd snuck out for some sort of rendezvous after Adam and Laurel had come home. She was tempted to make something up in retaliation, but the truth was worse than any lie. It was how his brother had died.

"Drew went to the hospital with alcohol poisoning last night."

Scott blanched, and she felt a stab of sympathy, despite his snide comment. "Is he okay?"

"He's home, so he's out of the woods. But he didn't look too good. None of them did."

"Geez," he breathed, shaking his head. "He could've . . ."

She nodded. *Died.*

The unsaid word swirled around them in the silence of the kitchen, uniting them in the anxiety that remains after a narrowly avoided tragedy, and in the sorrow they shared over the tragedy that had not been averted. Ben had died only six months earlier; so much had happened since then. And yet Ben was still very much with them, a rascal ghost with a cautionary tale.

"What time did it happen?" he asked.

"Around ten thirty, I guess."

"The game was over by then."

Who cares about the stinking game?

"Oh," she said. "How'd it go?" She didn't watch his games anymore. She needed a break from the whole concept of Scott—not like she ever truly got one. But still, it helped not to have to look at him when he wasn't physically in the room.

He blinked a couple of times, absorbing this news about her not watching. But it wasn't the game he was referring to. "I'm just saying you could've called me. I would have answered."

"Oh, I, uh . . . I just assumed you were busy."

"Could've left a message. It's important, something like that. They're a good family."

She'd never heard him speak so positively about the Kesslers before. But this wasn't about the Kesslers; it was about him wanting to be someone who got called. Unusual for Scotty, who'd always gold-medaled at avoiding other people's business, she thought. But maybe things were changing on that score—not a major shift, just a slight recalibration.

She remembered him joking about his house turning into McGreavy's Home for Lost Women and Dogs. Maybe he'd seen that it could be nice to have people in your house. And when their kid nearly kills himself, you want to be told.

"I should've called you," she said.

He shrugged and went for the Cocoa Puffs.

When Cass left for her AA meeting, Laurel was pulling up in front of the house. She waited for Cass to get into the minivan.

"I wasn't sure if you'd make it," said Cass. "How's he doing?"

"Sleeping. The doctor said he was lucky. It could have gone the other way." She drove slowly, as if her nerves were so shredded she wasn't sure her limbs would obey her commands.

"How are *you* doing?" Cass asked.

"Other than feeling like I've committed a heinous crime and have no right to live?"

"Yeah," Cass said gently, knowing that to debate it would be useless. "Other than that."

Laurel took a deep breath and let it out. "Of all the stupid, horrific things that have happened because of my drinking, this is the worst. And it's the only time I haven't felt the urge to drink more because of it. I know we're supposed to take it one day at a time and everything . . . but honestly, I don't think I'll ever miss a meeting again."

* * *

CASS was in the office when Scott peeked in. "You all right? You've been parked in here so long, I was starting to wonder if something was up." He sidled up to the desk and eyed the screen. "Schoolwork?"

"Yeah, I'm a little behind."

He glanced out the window toward the Kesslers' tidy lawn. "Watching the house?"

"Not really."

His look was skeptical but softened by a hint of sympathy.

"They have everything," she said. "Everything. And still . . ."

He nodded. "Makes you wonder if anyone has a normal life."

* * *

LAUREL called the next morning. "I'm not going to the meeting," she said. "I just can't leave him home alone. He's still so tired and headache-y. Are you okay to walk?"

So much for never missing another meeting, thought Cass. "Sure. Maybe you can make it tomorrow."

"Oh, I'm going to a meeting, I'm just waiting for Adam to get home."

Cass sighed with relief. "For a minute I was worried—"

"I wasn't being clear. But believe me, inside I *am* clear. Painfully so."

Cass offered to sit with Drew while Laurel went to a noontime meeting. Laurel met her at the door. "He's watching TV. Not talking much, so don't be offended. I'm letting the rude behavior slide for now." She hooked her turquoise purse over her arm and headed for the car.

Cass went into the family room where Drew was watching *World Wrestling Expo.* Someone named "Bone Crusher" was repeatedly slamming someone named "College Boy" headfirst into the mat. Drew slumped aggressively into the microsuede couch and didn't look up.

It's like a superpower, thought Cass, sitting down next to him. *This kid could ignore someone to death.*

After a while, Bone Crusher seemed to feel that College Boy's brains were sufficiently scrambled and stopped to strut cartoonishly around the ring. Cass let out a little chuckle.

"She paying you?" Drew muttered snidely.

"Paying me?"

"To babysit. You should demand extra. Combat pay for watching the fuckup."

"No, she's not paying me. But you're right, I should ask for a little something for watching this crap."

"I like it," he said. "Maybe I'll take a bunch of steroids and join up. Hell of a lot better than living in Wortherton," he snorted. "More like Worthlesstown. Wo-town. The town of Woe."

Cass remembered feeling the exact same way at his age— angry and hopeless and willing to do anything to escape. But she'd been in a foster home where it took all her wits just to stay one step ahead of a pedophile. She'd stopped eating and had to be hospitalized. She'd felt like the fuckup then, but looking back, she realized now that it had been an effective strategy.

Drew's situation certainly seemed less dire. But she'd learned from AA that dire was in the eye of the beholder. And maybe having a barely recovering alcoholic for a mother, and a mostly absent authoritarian for a father, and feeling responsible for three little brothers was enough to qualify, even if you did live in a nice house.

She gazed at him, wondering what she could possibly say that wouldn't sound trite.

He turned toward her suddenly and sneered, "You said you'd help me, but that was bullshit. Which is nice because it means you fit right in with this worthless town."

She smiled. "Yeah, Wortherton is just crawling with unwed, pregnant, broke, recovering alcoholics." He did not smile back, but she could see it had thrown him off his rage game. "Drew," she said. "You've got my attention. And you've certainly got your parents' attention."

"So?"

"So what do you want to do with it?"

"Maybe I just want everyone to leave me alone!"

"If you wanted everyone to leave you alone, you wouldn't have done something so stupid and dangerous. What do you want, Drew? Everyone's listening now. But you gotta say it." She wanted to hug him, sitting there all pale and sick and sad. She wanted to pull him onto her lap the way she had taken little Timmy and cradle him and make him believe that things could get better. It was a silly thought, but it helped her keep calm in the face of all that rage and sorrow.

"Say what you need, buddy," she murmured gently. "It's the only chance you have of actually getting it."

Chapter XXX

It was a weird sort of holding pattern. Scott was silent but po-
lite, in his rough-around-the-edges way. Occasionally they'd get
hungry at the same time, or one of them would be watching TV and
the other would stand beside the couch for a few minutes, drawn in
by something interesting or funny on the screen. But mostly they
avoided each other. It was as if they were each driving a car without brakes, just trying not to crash. Cass wondered ruefully how
two people so often able to complete each other's thoughts generally
spent the rest of the time misunderstanding each other.

Then Scott got sick.

Cass didn't know what time he'd gotten home the night before.
These days she tried to be asleep before he came in. It was early
morning, the birds still loud and boisterous, their calls mixed
with the sounds of heaving coming from Scott's room.

Drank too much, she thought, and rolled over.

But before she could get back to sleep there was another sound,
a low moan. And she remembered that Scott rarely drank enough
to get buzzed, much less to the point of vomiting.

She got up and went to his room, knocking lightly on the closed
door.

Another moan.

She opened the door a face width and peeked in. He was not in
bed. In fact, he wasn't in the room. "Scott?"

A weak "Yeah," then coughing.

She found him crouched on the floor of the master bathroom wearing only a pair of blue plaid boxers, elbows on the toilet rim, his back curling spasmodically with each heave. When he finished, he sat back on his heels.

"You look green."

"I feel like a hundred and ninety-seven pounds of mold."

"Drink too much?"

"Two scotches, maybe three."

"So this is a bug, then."

"Bug, nothing. It's a freaking tarantula." He leaned back against the Jacuzzi tub. His jaw began to quiver and he wrapped his arms around himself. "You put the AC on?"

It was late September, cool and dry, and she had put the heat on before going to bed.

Am I supposed to take care of him? she wondered. *He basically hates me. Probably can't stand having me see him so weak.* She was sure he just wanted her out of there. But he looked so helpless.

At meetings they often talked about not assuming you know what others think or feel, and erring on the side of kindness.

Okay, she thought. *Here comes some kindness. It's up to you to throw me out if that's what you want.*

"Do you own a thermometer?" she asked.

A wan yet sarcastic smile. "Yeah. There's a defibrillator around here somewhere, too."

She came closer, grimacing at the sour smell, and put her hand against his forehead. "You're like a furnace."

She offered to help him to bed, but he preferred to stay where he was, and she got him a pillow and blanket to rest with between bouts. She took a T-shirt from his dresser and helped him into it, pulling it over his head and tugging it down over his long torso like a child. His feet were cold and she got him a pair of socks.

He sank back onto the pillow in the middle of the dark-tiled floor, and she covered him with the blanket.

"Sorry about all this," he said, voice barely above a whisper now.

"It's okay. Try to get some rest in between."

The morning wore on, and she checked on him often, giving him sips of water and wiping the toilet bowl with a soapy rag. "Shouldn't you call the team doctor?" she asked him once.

"Not yet" was all he said.

She felt bad leaving him for her meeting, but she got a dissertation from Laurel about how to handle stomach bugs. They stopped at a convenience store and got some Gatorade and saltines for when he was able to hold things down.

Around noon the phone rang. It was Kate.

"I did it."

Whatever it was, she didn't sound happy about it.

"Did what?" Cass was tired from the early rise and hours of nursing duty. She hoped this was a small "it."

"Went to the police this morning."

A very large "it." Cass sank down onto a kitchen stool. "How'd it go?"

Brighton police station. Cass could picture it easily, having waited outside the yellow brick building with the globe lights on the various occasions when Ben had been taken in for questioning. A couple of times she'd had to answer questions herself. It seemed a lifetime away from her current upstanding citizenship in Wortherton.

"They gave me this woman detective from the Sexual Assault Unit to talk to," said Kate. "She was really patient and nice when I got upset a couple of times. She had to ask some hard questions, she said, to make sure I wasn't just trying to get back at an ex or something."

Kate told the detective everything. "Then she asked how I got out of the motel and where I went. I had to tell her, Cass. She said if I withheld information, she couldn't proceed with the case." Kate took a deep breath and let it out. "She wants you and Scott to come in."

"What? Why? We didn't see anything."

"She said you're—hold on, I wrote it down. Percipient witnesses. You didn't see it happen, but you saw me right after and saw what's called fresh complaint evidence." Kate gave a humorless chuckle. "I guess the assault was fresh and I complained to you about it."

Scott is going to flip, thought Cass. *Just what I need. Another reason for him to hate me.*

"I'm wicked sorry." Kate's voice trembled with regret.

"Don't apologize," Cass said. "You didn't commit a violent, hideous crime. They did, and they should go to jail for it. And also have their dicks cut off. With toenail clippers."

"But Scott likes to keep a low profile . . ."

"He'll live." Cass could hear him throwing up again. *Or maybe he'll puke himself to death, and I won't have to tell him.*

The rape kit evidence had been sent to Brighton Police as soon as it was collected, along with numerous pictures the nurse had taken of Kate's injuries. According to procedure, it had been kept as a "Jane Doe" kit in case the victim wanted to press charges at a later date.

"I told the detective I was sorry I waited so long, but she said it was really common, and two months wasn't even that long. Sometimes women wait years, and then the rape kit is sitting right there in the police department with the evidence they need. It'll take a long time to get the DNA analyzed, but the pictures and the medical report should be a good start, she said."

The detective searched the police database for the guy's name to see if he had any previous convictions. Then she had Kate look at a photo array of eight different men.

"All the pictures looked a lot alike, but I picked him out right away. She was pretty impressed. And she said they already had DNA evidence on him from a prior arrest."

After reviewing the pictures and the medical records, the detective had called back. "She said, 'I'm so sorry this happened to you.'" Kate started to cry. "I said, '*He's* the one who should be sorry!' And she said, 'If you're telling the truth, and we can find him, I think he's going to be.'"

Since Kate didn't know the names of the other two men, the detective said that they would try to get that information from Breen when he was brought in for questioning.

"So the next thing is for you and Scott to come in tomorrow to make statements."

"We'll go over in the morning," said Cass, "before Scott goes to Fenway."

"Thanks," said Kate. "Thanks so much."

"I'm proud of you for going after them," said Cass. "It takes a lot of courage."

They said good-bye and hung up. Cass heard footsteps in the hall. A moment later, Scott appeared in the doorway wearing a clean shirt and a pair of jeans. "Who was on the phone?"

"Kate."

"I heard you say something about going somewhere before I have to be at the park." His face was gray and slightly sweaty, and she suspected he still had a fever.

"How come you're dressed?" she asked.

He leaned against the doorjamb as if he could barely manage the effort of standing. "Batting practice."

"Scotty, you couldn't swing a bat to ward off masked intruders right now."

"I never missed a game."

"Well, you're missing one today. They'd send you home anyway to keep you from infecting the whole team. Now go back upstairs before you pass out, and I'll bring you some Gatorade."

He let out a weak laugh. "What are you—practicing?"

"For what?"

"Motherhood. You sounded like such a mom right there."

* * *

CASS checked on him a couple of times, but Scott seemed as comfortable as he could be, passed out in his bed now that the vomiting had subsided. The fever made him mumble in his sleep. She wished she knew what he was dreaming about.

At about nine she locked up, set the house alarm, and headed up the stairs for the last time. The day had begun so early she could barely keep her eyes open any longer. She had just crawled into bed when there was a knock, and then her door opened.

She flipped the light back on, and he flinched at its brightness. He looked so pale, like some cave creature that never saw the light of day.

"You okay?" she asked.

"Yeah, uh, I never got a straight answer from you about going somewhere tomorrow."

Cass sighed. She had really, *really* wanted to wait until the morning to tell him, hoping that after a good sleep he might be just slightly less pissed about going to the police station.

"Kate reported the rape."

"Good. Fuckers oughta have their heads bashed in. But jail's okay, too, I guess." He rubbed his face. "Wait, what's that got to do with . . . ?"

Cass explained about percipient witnesses and fresh complaint evidence. "She talked about pressing charges when we were at Fenway, but I didn't know if she'd go through with it."

"But then she did, and you didn't tell me."

"That just happened today! I wasn't going to bother you, with the state you're in."

"But you knew hours ago! Were you waiting to spring it on me at the last minute?" He shook his head, fury animating him out of his fever-induced fog. "Jesus, Cass, I'm on a major-league sports team, and this could end up in the fucking papers, like pronto. You get that, right?"

She wanted to remind him that he wasn't a suspect. In fact, he had done something good. But he hated feeling exposed, and no amount of convincing was going to change that. "I'm sorry. I just wanted you to get a good night's sleep—"

"Good night's sleep, my ass. I've done nothing but show up for you, and you still keep me in the dark as much as you can. For the life of me, I will never understand how I deserve that."

* * *

SHE tried to talk to him the next morning, but he wasn't in a listening mood. He wasn't feverish anymore, but he was weak and looked like he hadn't slept much. He wanted to get the trip to Brighton done in plenty of time before batting practice, and he didn't seem to care if she had to miss her usual ten o'clock AA meeting and walk five miles to a later one.

The inside of the Brighton Police Department station was only vaguely recognizable to Cass, having had a good buzz on the handful of times she'd been there in the past. Ben had needed her to corroborate his whereabouts occasionally, and she'd been brought in for questioning about a friend of theirs once. She had no record, but it still made her feel like a criminal.

She and Scott were ushered into separate rooms to tell their versions of the night Kate was assaulted. The detective who sat across the table from Cass had a jutting forehead that formed a ledge over his eyes. She wondered if there were hats that would fit him. Or maybe he didn't wear hats. Maybe his own forehead was enough to keep the rain off his face.

She answered all his questions cooperatively until Officer Ledge

Head asked, "So is it even remotely possible that your friend was a little bit, you know . . . into this?"

"Into being raped by three guys and beaten beyond recognition?"

"Well, you say it like that, but some of these girls these days, they like it kind of wild. They're looking for that *50 Shades of Grey* experience, you know what I mean? Spices things up for them."

Cass winced in disgust.

Ledge Head got defensive. "All I'm saying is that some girls might think they want that, and give the signals, and then change their mind when it gets out of hand."

"No one wants their ankle broken or their face so bruised they can only see out of one eye! So no, she did not want—or even *think* she wanted—any of what happened that night."

Ledge Head's hands went up in surrender. "I have to ask these things."

"There's something else. Kate said he threatened her that if she told, he'd kill her and everyone she loved. If he finds out she reported it before you pick him up, what then? She's in danger, right?"

The man's thick fingers gripped the pen as he scribbled this onto his notepad.

"Right?" said Cass.

"Everyone's in danger all the time," he muttered offhandedly without looking up at her. "It's the way of the world."

* * *

WHEN she went back out front, Scotty was standing with his arms crossed while some guy tried to talk to him. "*Finally,*" he said, taking her by the elbow and guiding her out toward the car.

"What was that, a fan?" she asked.

"No," he said tightly. "He's from the *Globe*. Snooping around for some other story, and he finds me in the lobby like a sitting duck! Shit, I'm gonna be in the fucking paper."

As they drove home, Cass ruminated on Beck Breen's threat. Kate was self-loathing enough to chance jeopardizing her own life. It was the everyone-you-love part that had kept her from reporting it right away. She'd been worried about her cousin Melanie's family.

And me, Cass realized. What if Breen found out that she was Kate's closest friend—and that she'd provided witness testimony? Could he find her?

"What."

She turned to look at him. "I didn't say anything."

He continued to stare straight ahead, maneuvering the car through Oak Square and out toward the Mass Pike. "Yeah, but you're wound as tight as a spring. That cop give you a hard time?"

"No, it's just . . . It's dumb, but Kate said something. That the guy threatened to kill her if she talked, and everyone she loved."

Scott's face went hard. "Did she mention you to him?"

"No. I mean probably not. She didn't say she did."

"But she was wasted, so who knows what she said."

"I'm more worried about her cousin. She has little kids."

He was silent for the rest of the ride. But when he pulled into the driveway, he said, "You should hang at Laurel's tonight while I'm at the game."

She had thought of that. Over the course of the car ride, Breen's threat had ballooned into palpable danger in her mind. "I just hate to bug her after everything they went through with Drew."

He turned to look at her for the first time all day. "Don't argue."

* * *

WHEN Cass called, Laurel said she was happy to have the company. But she didn't look happy when she opened the door. The house was strangely quiet.

"Where are the boys?"

"Timmy's napping, and the older boys aren't home from school yet. I need to talk to you." Laurel strode back toward the kitchen, and Cass followed, hoping desperately it was an interior design crisis, or a cleaning crisis—anything but a real crisis.

Laurel poured a glass of milk and set it on the table. "Drink," she said, sitting down. "Babies suck the calcium right out of your bones."

Cass took a sip. "What's up?"

"The guidance counselor at Drew's school is strongly suggesting family therapy. *Strongly suggesting*." She jabbed her finger at the table with each word. "As if I can't be trusted to do everything in my power to help my son!"

"Well, maybe he just doesn't know you that well. A lot of families probably want to sweep something like this under the rug."

"I am not sweeping!" Laurel let out an exasperated sigh. "I *should* be sweeping—or vacuuming. Heck, this should make me want to dust-bust the whole neighborhood."

Cass smiled. Laurel had finally gotten fully on board with AA—she certainly had the self-deprecating humor down. "So you're going to do family therapy?"

"All that mucking around in the past. The kids will have to talk, too." She closed her eyes. "It's all going to be about me and what a terrible mother I've been." She looked at Cass. "Remember the Prescott Center, when you asked how badly I'd screwed them up?"

"Oh, God, Laurel, I didn't even know you then, I was just reacting to—"

"Yes, but you were right. That's why I hated you so much."

"I never should have said it. You have no idea how bad I felt."

Laurel waved it away. "I was baiting you about not going to a doctor. I was so ashamed, I had to make someone else look worse than me. Buying my innocence with your guilt."

It was true, Cass realized, and she had to hand it to Laurel for admitting it. "Can you believe that we're such good friends, after the way we started?"

Laurel patted her hand. "Frankly, it's shocking."

Cass sighed. "Now, I have something to tell you." She explained what had happened and why she had to stay out of the house until Scott came home. *If he comes home*, she thought.

"And now he's mad at me. It's not like I was trying to keep things from him—I was only waiting until he wasn't delirious with fever. And then there's a *Globe* reporter at the police station. Like I have any control over that!"

Laurel considered this for a moment. "I think he's scared."

"Yeah, well, I'm scared, too, and I have a lot more reason to be."

"No, I think he's scared for you."

Cass rolled her eyes. "If he's so worried for my well-being, why's he treating me like dirt?"

"Some guys are like that. Anger is easier than fear. It makes them feel less helpless."

"He should be angry at the criminal in this scenario, not me!"

"I'm sure he is. But he's also angry at you because you're the reason for the fear."

* * *

WHEN Scott pulled into the driveway late that night, Cass went home.

"How was your game?" she asked him.

"Sucked," he said.

"Sorry."

The message light was blinking on the answering machine, and Cass pressed the play button. Scott stood in the doorway to hear it, too. It was Kate. Based on their statements, the pictures, and Kate's medical report, the police got the DA to issue a warrant for Beck Breen.

"Now we just have to wait for them to get the bastard," said Scott. "I got a series in Tampa starting tomorrow," he went on. "Can you stay with Laurel?"

"I can ask."

"Let me know. If not, you're going to a hotel. Even with the alarm and all, I don't want you alone in the house."

Protective. Maybe Laurel was right. She looked Scott in the eye, and for once he didn't look away. "I wasn't trying to keep things from you, Scotty. You have to believe me on that."

Chapter XXXI

"Cass, you have to stop calling me," Kate murmured furtively.

"I'm just checking in!"

"I know, and thanks for that, but I'm working. I'm getting more shifts now."

"A couple of weeks ago you barely had any."

"Right, but then the manager—you know, the chronically annoyed one who didn't like mutts?—she quit, and the assistant manager, Dev, the one with the titanium leg, he got promoted, and we're buddies, so he loads me up. Okay, I gotta go. I'll call you later."

Cass tried to focus on her schoolwork, but with Beck Breen on the loose, the fear that had smoldered in her gut since her mother's death burned even hotter than usual. She could feel the liquor cabinet calling. One little drink would blunt the serrated edges of her fear. . . .

The cursor seemed to move across the screen of its own accord. It clicked on the drive that held the girls a cappella CD. *Blackbird singing in the dead of night* . . . Mary's voice curled around Cass like a soft blanket, and she felt her hopping pulse decelerate slightly.

She was finally making some headway on an article on brain development when there was a sudden motion in her peripheral vision. She startled and sent the computer mouse flying off the desk.

"Geez, you're jumpy." Scott was standing in the doorway. She gave him a warning look and he put his hands up and said, "No, hey, not like you shouldn't be."

She took a deep breath and tried to quiet her jangled nerves. "What's up?"

"Put your shoes on. We're getting you a cell phone."

On the drive over to Shopper's World, she made a weak attempt at saying it would cost too much. Scott replied simply, "Don't."

Back home again, Scott went upstairs to pack for the Tampa series. Cass was reading the booklet on her new phone when the landline rang.

"Hi, can I speak to Scott?" The voice was friendly, almost familiar. But then she remembered that no one who actually knew Scott used the landline.

"Who's calling, please?"

"This is Craig Meskie from the *Globe*. I'd like to talk with him about helping that girl."

Cass hung up. Then she went straight upstairs and told Scott.

* * *

CASS woke early in the Kesslers' guest bedroom the next morning and padded quietly out to retrieve the paper. There it was, in the Metro section under *New England News in Brief*.

RED SOX PLAYER COMES TO AID AFTER ASSAULT

Police are in search of a Brighton man on charges of aggravated assault alleged to have occurred at the Beauty Rest Motel in Brighton on July 18. A friend of the victim and Red Sox third baseman Scott McGreavy claim to have aided the victim after the assault, bringing her to the hospital and then to their home to recuperate. Neither could be reached for comment.

She hoped Beck Breen wasn't a *Globe* subscriber. Or if he was, he was only a headline reader. Because if he came across this little tidbit, he now knew about Scott. And if he could find Scott's house—and let's face it, with the internet, you could practically locate Sasquatch's home address—he could definitely find her.

From the Kesslers' living room window, Cass watched several cars pull into the cul-de-sac over the course of the morning. The driver would usually head up to Scott's empty house and ring the doorbell, notebook in hand. One had a microphone and was accompanied by a cameraman. A couple of them even went around the side of the house, trying to peek inside.

They know Scott's not home—all of Boston knows the Sox are in Tampa. They must be looking for me. It was strange, watching people looking in your windows to see if you were home. She called Scott and told him about the article. "Only three sentences," she said. "There's a picture of you playing third base, but it's not that big and your face is kind of hard to make out."

"Oh." He almost sounded disappointed.

"Hey, if you want me to send in a better one . . ." she teased.

"Yeah, you do that," he said, chuckling.

She told him about the reporters. "It's good you're out of town. The story will be old by the time you get back."

"We'll see," he said. "So how're you feeling? You and Hallie been under a lot of stress the last couple of days."

It tickled her to hear him refer to the baby as Hallie, the inside joke a remnant from happier, closer times. "I'm okay," she said. "I'll feel a lot better once they have him." He didn't need to know that her heart seemed to pound constantly these days.

"Stay away from the house."

"I will. I forwarded the landline to my cell phone in case the police call."

"Good thinking. And get a lot of rest."

"You, too."

"Ah, don't worry about me."

* * *

LATER that day Cass's cell phone rang. She checked the caller ID to make sure it wasn't another reporter calling the landline, but it said McGreavy so she answered, "Hey."

A woman's voice, heavy with contempt. "Who are you? And where's my son? And who answers the phone, 'Hey,' like some kind of barn animal?"

Cass was dumbstruck. "Uh—"

A snort of disgust. "Never mind, don't tell me your name. You won't be there long enough for me to need it again, and then I'll have it in my head like some jingle from a product they don't even make anymore. Just tell him to call his mother." And she hung up.

It was well before game time, so Cass called Scott. "Your mother just called the house."

"She's like a dog with a goddamned bone. She's tried me six times today and I can't deal with her now."

"Why does she keep calling?"

"It's that damn article. She gets the *Globe* so she can brag to her friends. Except baseball-wise, there hasn't been much to brag about lately. Me in the paper for rescuing some girl is like hitting the lottery for her. But it's a small article, and good bragging requires details," he muttered. "I just keep reminding myself she's in Hawaii, thank God. It'd take something bigger than this to get her on a plane."

* * *

CASS made plans for lunch with Patrick, and she was nearly caught up with her schoolwork. She could almost make herself believe that things were getting back to normal. Whatever that meant at any given moment.

"I just want Scott to come home. I feel safer with him around."

Patrick nodded. "He looks out for you."

"Plus, he's kind of on edge all the time anyway. When something pisses him off, his anger hits the surface like a torpedo. That's a handy friend to have when someone might be after you."

Patrick gave his tea a few extra stirs.

He's trying to figure out how to react, she thought. *Poor Patrick. He's too sweet and well dressed for all this.*

"Sometimes you get the brunt of that, hon," he said gently. "And you don't need any more stress in your life."

She laughed. "Yeah, ya think?"

"How's the craving?"

"It's up. Sometimes I feel like I'm going to have a heart attack, and a drink would calm all that down."

He gave a commiserating smile. "No more trips to that bar, I hope."

"Not so far." Cass stared down into the dark tea. "You know what I keep thinking about? How I used to be at least half in the bag all the time. Like *all the time*, Patrick. Looking back, I can see . . just what an awful waste it was. Useless and ugly." She shook her head. "Much as I want a drink—and I do, believe me—I can't imagine living like that again."

"You've got a taste for sobriety. It's a good sign, but don't let it fool you into thinking you'll never go back to being that half-buzzed girl. That can happen any day of the week."

* * *

AT three A.M. that night, Scott got home from the series in Tampa. Cass had just come back from one of her nightly trips to the Kesslers' bathroom and saw the headlights trace across the guest room wall. She tossed her stuff in a plastic shopping bag, left a note for Laurel, and walked across the dew-damp grass in her nightgown. The light was on in the kitchen; he was flicking through the mail, his eyes surrounded by filaments of tiny worry lines. He looked up when she entered, taking in the nightgown and the plastic bag. "You need an overnight bag."

"Hopefully soon I won't need one."

"How come you're awake?" he asked.

"I was waiting for you to come home. Laurel's is nice, but now that you're here, I'd rather be in my own bed. I just feel safer." *With you*. But she didn't say it.

"This was my last road trip. Season's over on Wednesday." He walked her up the stairs.

"Sorry you didn't make the playoffs."

"Yeah, well . . . wasn't our year. Night, Cass."

"Night, Scotty."

* * *

ON Tuesday she had a pregnancy checkup, and Ana was not happy. "Your blood pressure is too high, *mi hija*. Are you doing too much? Running around to get ready for the baby?"

Cass felt a wave of guilt. She hadn't done one thing to get ready. There was no car seat, no baby clothes, not even a package of diapers. Of course, she wasn't sure where she'd be living when the big day finally came. . . . But she and Scott seemed okay at the moment. He hadn't said anything more about her finding somewhere else to live, and she sure wasn't going to bring it up.

"I'm just stressed out," she said.

Ana urged her to find ways to relax. "We don't want your daughter to come out biting her tiny nails from worry!"

When Cass returned to the waiting room, Scott stood up and tucked his phone away. "How's she doing?" he asked.

"Ana?"

"The *baby*."

"Her heartbeat is louder than ever, really strong, so I guess that's a good sign."

"Oh, you got to hear that?" He looked away, rubbed his arm.

"Did you want to come in?" It hadn't even occurred to her to ask, after the last appointment when he'd chosen his stupid phone over her.

"Nah, that's okay. Maybe next time."

* * *

WHEN Scott was ready to leave for the park that afternoon, Cass was reading an article on object permanency in young children for one of her classes.

"Come on, Cass!" he called from the mudroom. "You gotta go to Laurel's."

"I'm just finishing up!" she called back. "I'll go over in ten minutes."

Heavy footsteps, then he was there, eclipsing the office doorway. "You can't stay here."

"I know, I'm almost done."

"I'm gonna be late for batting practice." Annoyance rose in his voice.

"Just go." She squinted at the screen. "I'll be done before you're at the end of the street."

"You're pissing me off."

You're pissing yourself off, she almost shot back. But then she remembered Laurel's comment. He gets mad when he's afraid. Reluctantly, she clicked out of the page and stood up.

As Cass walked across the lawn, Scott rolled the black SUV slowly through the cul-de-sac. When she reached the Kesslers' door, he picked up speed, gunning the engine a little harder than necessary.

Message received, you big jerk, thought Cass with a smile. The one thing he wouldn't protect her from was his own frustration.

Laurel was on the phone and waved Cass in. "We can't do that night," she told the caller. "No, I'm sorry, but my husband is out of town . . . yes, and the next three nights after that, too . . ." She put her hand over the receiver and mouthed *therapist*.

Cass went into the kitchen. She stroked Bunny's silky ears and leafed through the *Wortherton Townsman*. An item in the calendar section caught her eye: an author talk at the library on *GPS Set to Joy: How to Reprogram Your Life to Locate Happiness*. It set off a ping of memory . . . where had she heard of that?

Then it came to her. It was one of the books Scott had given her when she was waiting to get into rehab. She had tossed it aside at the time; the title had seemed to mock her, as if to say you *could* make a normal, happy life for yourself . . . but you're so screwed up, you *won't*.

Now the book aroused her interest. She had tucked it away on the shelves in Scott's office, next to all those classics he'd never read, and she suddenly wished she could leaf through it. Maybe she could take it to the library and get it signed by the author. The thought of being somewhere other than Chickadee Circle for just one night was so appealing. She hadn't been to a free performance in a long time, and Ana had urged her to do things to relax.

Laurel was still on the phone when Cass slipped back out and crossed the yard to Scott's. She found the book quickly, the bright colors of its spine practically lit up next to the faux leather tomes on the shelf. It was right next to *Jane Eyre*.

Jane Ear. Cass smiled, remembering Scott's butchered pronunciation. She had read it twice: once quickly for English class, and then slowly to savor all the unpredictable ups and downs of Jane's life. Cass pulled it from the shelf and flipped through the pages. It took only a few moments to find her favorite passage, where Jane's employer, whom she loves, tells her he is sending her away. Devastated, she replies:

"Do you think, because I am poor, obscure, plain, and little, I am soulless and heartless? You think wrong! I have as much soul as you, and full as much heart!"

The poor girl was losing everything, but she could still claim her own worth. *She would've done well in AA*, thought Cass.

The house was quiet, and Cass wanted to curl up in one of the leather armchairs and give *Jane Eyre* a thorough rereading. But Scott's admonition about being alone in the house still rumbled in her mind, and she suddenly felt anxious to get back to Laurel's. Tucking the *GPS Set to Joy* book under her arm, she locked up the house and hurried back across the lawn.

Dinner at the Kesslers' was always an exercise in self-control for Cass, as she tried to keep from laughing at the boys' antics and Laurel's near despair at their manners. Timmy climbed out of his booster seat a dozen times, Matt made gagging sounds at Luke's choice of mustard on his peas, and Drew let his long legs meander under the table like an octopus while asking to be excused every other minute. Laurel finally gave up and set them free.

As Cass cleared the dishes, she asked Laurel about giving her a ride to the library at 7:30 for the *GPS Set to Joy* event. "It should be over by about nine."

"No problem at all," Laurel said, scurrying after Timmy to get him in the bath. "By then the younger ones should be all tucked in."

Laurel dropped her at the library with a few minutes to spare, and Cass sat on a bench enjoying a moment of peace in the early evening breeze. The sky at the horizon was still pale blue, growing darker high in its sapphire dome, a few stars just beginning to prick the darkness. It was October now, she realized, the change of months eluding her in all the anxiety of the past week.

The last baseball game of the regular season would be played tomorrow night. It had been a lackluster couple of months for the Red Sox, and she was sorry for Scott, but glad that he'd be home now. She wondered what he did in the off-season. He didn't travel or play golf, and he had no family to spend time with, atoning for six months of road trips and late nights.

A few more people were heading into the library now; Cass followed them in and took a seat. The librarian introduced the author, Anthoula Giakoumakis, who seemed to compensate for her tiny stature by wearing blindingly colorful clothing—a neon-yellow skirt with a white blouse that pulsed with large red flowers. White teeth gleamed behind the shine of raspberry lipstick. "Hello, hello, everyone!" she trilled, hands circling the air in a wild double wave to the crowd.

Cass looked around. Including the librarian there were six people in the room. A few responded with little one-handed waves of their own. Others looked anxiously toward the exit.

"Sooooo . . . happiness." Anthoula Giakoumakis sighed joyously. "Where is it? Is it here?" She bobbed her head behind the podium, then popped up again. "Is it under your chair?"

Gag, thought Cass. *This is worse than mustard on peas.* She was tempted to sneak out, but then she would have to wait an hour and a half for Laurel to pick her up.

"Happiness," said Anthoula, "is like space—out there, made up of who knows what. Only a feeling, one that comes and goes, completely impermanent. And yet we seek it like it's a winning lottery ticket! People say, 'I just want to be happy.' It's baby talk! Ga, ga, ga!"

One brave soul raised his hand. "So, um, I don't mean to be rude but . . . why is the name of your book about locating happiness?"

"It's a joke! It's funny! Also, my publisher said the word 'happiness' sells books. You're *here*, aren't you?" She let out a delighted laugh.

Holy crap, thought Cass. *She's wacko.*

"Let's stop talking about this stupid concept of happiness and talk about building a life that makes sense. To you. Your life does not need to make sense to me. It needs to make sense *to you*. So here's another word we're going to throw out the window: normal."

She heaved an imaginary object toward the windows to her right. "Bye-bye, normal. You stink."

That caught Cass's attention. As nutty as this woman seemed, could she possibly have an answer to the problem of normal?

"Now, you are going to divide your entire life into two categories: the things that make sense—the parts that work well—and the ones that don't. Okay, got that? Is everyone with me?" Anthoula took a moment to make sure all six of them were with her. "Make a list of three things that fit who you are, that feel good and right. Maybe not *normal*, but right."

A woman took a pad of paper from her purse and began to scratch at it with a pen.

"No, no, no, no," cried Anthoula from the podium. "Not a *list* list. A *mental* list. That paper will go out with the recycling in a day! A mental list stays with you always."

Penitently the woman slid the paper and pen back into her purse.

"Quickly, people!" shouted Anthoula. "This is not a trick question!"

Cass thought quickly: *1. Being in recovery. 2. Being pregnant. 3. Living with Scott.*

She let out a mental groan. Living with Scott was not something she wanted on her list. Living with Scott was not likely to continue. She exchanged it for *3. Taking classes.*

"Okay, enough," Anthoula said. "That's not what you're here for, is it? You're here for the other category." She clapped her hands together. "Okay, make a mental list of the things in your life that don't make sense. Top ten. Go!"

1. No home. 2. No income. 3. No job . . .

"Okay, enough. This list could be as long as your arm. Maybe you should write it down. Ha, ha!" Anthoula pointed at the woman with the paper in her purse. "Now we're going to break that list down into the things you can do something about and the things you can't change, like your eye color, or your parents. You get what I'm saying? Yes, of course you do. You are all smart people—you came here to do something about your life, and that is brilliant!"

Anthoula put her hands on her hips. "Now, I'm smart, too, so I'm not going to tell you everything in the book. You have to buy it and find out for yourself! But here's one activity for the list of things you can change. Take your smallest thing. Maybe it's a bad habit, like drinking too much coffee or biting your nails." She put a cupped hand to the side of her mouth as if to tell a secret. "Stop doing that."

She laughed wildly. "I'm serious! It's a small thing—you said so yourself! Stop doing that one small thing, and improve your life in a small way. It will give you confidence to take on something bigger. You see how smart that is! There are many smart things like that in my book, the one you are now going to buy. Okay? So line up over there by that nice lady selling the books, and I will sign them for you. Buy several copies—they make excellent gifts!"

She started to walk back to the table loaded with books, when the lady with the pad of paper raised her hand. "What," said Anthoula.

"I just . . . well, does your book have any advice about . . . the other things?"

Anthoula put her hands on her hips, face flat with annoyance. "What other things."

"The things we can't change."

Anthoula let out an aggrieved sigh. She eyed the woman suspiciously. "You are very wily. You are trying to get all the answers out of me."

"No, not at all!" the woman said, flushing with alarm. In Cass's estimation she seemed to be the least wily person on the planet. "I was only asking . . . I just wanted to know if . . ."

Anthoula went back to the podium. "Okay, this is a very smart crowd. I can see that now. I will tell you one more secret for the sensible life." She nodded, as if agreeing with herself that this was the right decision. "There is so much we cannot change. How we were raised, terrible things that have happened to us. This is the human condition." Her tone was subdued. Cass had the sense that Anthoula's mental list of things she could not change might be rather long.

"Have you ever heard the saying 'You can't unring a bell'?" A few people nodded, but others looked confused. "Once a bell has been rung, it has been rung. There's no way to make it unrung. Do you see? Those terrible, senseless things cannot be undone. There's no going back in time to make it happen another way.

"But the human mind is a very powerful thing. It has power beyond what we can imagine. Isn't that funny? Our minds are so powerful that we can't wrap our powerful minds around it. And so here is what I say to you." Her voice was low, but not with the false sideshow tone she had used before. It was filled with long- ing and hope—for herself as much as anyone else in the room, it seemed to Cass. "You must unring the bell."

"How?" whispered the woman with the paper.

"By using the power of your mind to create a life without those terrible things in it. To let them go, the way the sound of a bell drifts away, into the air, into nothing. And then it is as if the bell has never rung at all."

Eyes cast down, Anthoula seemed to be pondering her own words. "Please be clear. What I am suggesting is impossible. And yet the impossible has been made possible countless times in the course of history. You can do this impossible thing. You can un- ring the bell of your unhappiness. With your mind and with your heart. In your own way. For yourself."

Chapter XXXII

Cass walked out into the soft night, her signed book cradled in her arm. "To Cass, carrying a wonderful new bell inside her. Warmly, Anthoula." The other people filed out, each with several books, and they nodded or smiled at her as they headed to the parking lot. One said, "Good luck," and Cass wondered if she meant with the baby or with everything. With unringing the unhappiness bell and building a life that makes sense.

She called Laurel for a ride home. Drew answered. "She might be a while," he said. "Timmy woke up with a coughing fit and she's got him in a shower for the steam."

"It's nice out, and the walk is so short," said Cass. "I'll be home in twenty minutes."

As she walked, she thought about kooky Anthoula Giakouma-kis. Her suggestions hadn't really been so brilliant. Stop doing things that don't make sense in your life. "Unring the bells" of the bad experiences you've had . . . somehow. Nevertheless, Cass felt as if she'd been given something, if only a reminder that she *could* make changes and move beyond past misfortunes. It was basically the same message as AA, told with attention-getting wackiness.

But it had also given her that relaxed, free-performance feeling. The baby's foot moved under the surface of her pumpkin-size belly, and her maternity top bubbled out from left to right. She would be born in less than two months. It was time to start getting ready.

Time to get a place of her own.

Much as she loved Scott—and she did, deeply, she realized—she couldn't keep walking on eggshells, hoping he'd let her stay a little longer, and then a little longer after that. It was no way to build a stable life for her baby. The money didn't seem to be much of an issue for him. Maybe he'd be happy to pay for an apartment not too far away. Maybe her small bad habit was to keep shuffling along when she should get up the guts to ask him for the money to move out.

Rounding the corner to Chickadee Circle, she knew she'd miss living here, but the time had come. Her friendship with Scott was in a relatively good place. If she could keep it that way, she could always come back and visit. The cul-de-sac came into view, and Cass picked up her pace, anxious to tell Laurel her revelation.

As she started across the Kesslers' yard, her phone rang in her purse, startling her—she still hadn't gotten used to having one again. When she pulled it out and checked the caller ID, it said Kate Kelly. This was either good news or bad.

"They got him!" A state trooper had pulled him over in northern Maine for a busted taillight, checked his plates, saw the open warrant, and took him in. His arraignment would be the next morning. "It shows he's a flight risk, so they'll probably hold him without bail. And they'll lean on him to give up the other two guys."

"Oh my God, Kate, that's huge! That's—"

Cass's foot landed on something in the grass, something hard and round—a ball? a chew toy?—and suddenly her legs were out from under her, her body flying forward. She hit the ground flailing, an arm wedged under her belly as she slammed into the lawn, pain searing into her ribs and back. She let out a scream of pain that seemed to reverberate across the neighborhood.

Her phone had landed a few feet away, out of reach, and she could hear Kate's panicked voice. "Cass! CASS! Jesus, what the— I'm calling an ambulance!"

And then another voice calling out to her from farther away. "Cass? Is that you?" Laurel was at her side in the next moment. "Oh my God, are you okay?"

With the wind knocked out of her, Cass couldn't speak for a moment, but she could feel the pain ebbing a little.

Laurel turned back toward the house and yelled, "Drew! Call an ambulance!"

"No, I . . ." Cass gasped. "I think I'm . . . okay."

In a few minutes, sirens were blaring in the distance, approaching them. Then the sky filled with lights flashing red, blue, red, blue. Thumping footsteps in the grass coming toward her; a man's low voice. "Ma'am, are you okay? Ma'am, can you speak?"

Cass pushed herself up into a sitting position. Laurel knelt on the lawn beside her and helped to stabilize her. "I'm all right. I just tripped."

The EMT said, "Let's just double-check, shall we?"

With his help and Laurel's, Cass rose slowly and moved toward the ambulance. Inside, the EMT took her vitals, checked for fetal movement, made sure her arm wasn't broken or sprained. "You seem okay. Blood pressure's pretty high, but that's common with a scare like this. Even so, I don't think it would be the worst idea to take a little ride to the hospital."

"I really feel fine," said Cass. "My shoulder's just sore. But thanks."

He eyed her. "You sure?"

"Absolutely. And thank you so much."

"Okay, well, we'll all be here for another few minutes filling out the paperwork, in case you change your mind."

As she and Laurel walked up the front path to the house, she noticed all the vehicles. Not just an ambulance but two police cars and a fire truck, too. "Wow, they really emptied out the station, didn't they?"

Laurel chuckled. "The officer told me they got two separate

calls on this—Drew's call and someone else's. It was probably the most exciting thing to happen all day in this sleepy little burg."

"It must have been Kate. I was talking to her when I fell. She'd called to tell me they got the guy."

"Oh, Cass, that's the best news! You better call back and let her know you're okay."

She still felt so shaky. "Would you mind calling her? I just want to sit for a minute."

"Of course." Laurel took Cass's phone and placed the call as she walked upstairs to shoo the younger boys back to bed.

Cass sat down at the kitchen table, pressed her hands against the smooth cherrywood, and tried to quiet herself for the baby's sake. She closed her eyes to slow it all down—her pulse, her racing thoughts, her throbbing shoulder. She heard the front door open and thought the EMT had come back to check on her one more time. In another moment Scott loomed in the kitchen, hair still damp from his postgame shower.

"Why are there about forty emergency vehicles out front?" he demanded.

"Sit down," she said.

"Just tell me."

When she was done, he said, "Goddamn it, Cass! What were you *thinking* walking home alone?"

That was the part he was focusing on? And what could she say—*I was in such a good mood it just didn't seem like anything bad could happen?*

"Were you drinking?"

"What? No!"

"It's the only thing I can think of that would make you act so irresponsible."

"Look, I know you're mad, but you don't have to—"

He put his hands up. "Hey, it's none of my business . . ."

Laurel came in and padded quietly across the floor. She laid her hand on Cass's shoulder. "Everyone's a little fragile right now, Scott," she said. "Let's talk about this tomorrow."

He blinked at them, Cass shaky and pale, Laurel beside her. "Are you coming home?" His voice was flat, and she knew he was working hard to sound like he didn't care either way.

"You can't yell at me," Cass said wearily.

"I won't."

They said good night to Laurel and started across the yard. Scott took her elbow, the one that had gotten twisted beneath her, and she winced.

"That's it, we are going to the hospital," he said sternly.

"I'm fine. I just need to rest."

"Cass—"

"I *know*, okay?"

"Yeah, okay," he said, "but, Christ, you scared the hell out of me!"

She almost smiled. Finally he'd admitted it.

"Fucking cop cars with the lights going," he muttered. "For all I knew you were dead."

She slid her hand under his arm and let him guide her in. "I'm sorry for scaring you."

Just the exertion of climbing to the second floor made her so weary she could have slept standing up. She leaned against him, put her good arm around him. "Thanks for caring so much, Scotty. You're a true friend."

He put his arms around her, gently so as not to squeeze her shoulder. "You can't do stuff like that to me," he murmured.

She closed her eyes, let her temple rest against his chest. His oxford shirt had the same crisp cotton feel as her pillowcase.

Without letting go, he moved her with small rocking steps into her room.

It's like slow dancing, she thought. When was the last time she'd slow danced? She couldn't even remember.

"You want to change into your nightgown?" he asked.

"No. Too tired."

He pulled back the covers and helped her into bed. He tucked the sheets and blankets around her and left, closing the door behind him. As sore as she felt, sleep came quickly, gentling her into its embrace. There was a bell there in the edges of a dream, a bell called Beck Breen.

And it was not ringing.

Chapter XXXIII

Cass's shoulder woke her, pain pulsing up into her neck when she accidentally rolled onto the bad arm. The late morning sun streamed in, giving the room an unfamiliar, harsh glow. The clock said 10:15. She hadn't woken this late since she'd stopped drinking.

Downstairs, Scott was eating granola.

"Hey," she said groggily. "Getting healthy?"

He shrugged. "We're all out," he mumbled.

"What?"

"We're all out of the stuff I like. You haven't gone shopping in a while. I mean, not like you could, with everything going on."

"You should've told me."

"I should've gone myself. I got spoiled with you doing it all these months."

Cass reached up for a glass in the cabinet, but the pain in her back from even this small gesture made her suck in a quick gasp of air before she slowly lowered it to the counter. "So you want to go grocery shopping? I've already missed my meeting."

"Laurel came by to pick you up, but I told her you were sleeping." His gaze followed her as she shuffled to the refrigerator. "You think maybe you should get checked out?"

"I've got an appointment tomorrow anyway," she said. "It can wait until then."

* * *

S𝖼ᴏᴛᴛ went food shopping by himself. "The way you're moving, it'll take all day," he said, shoving the list in his pocket as she sat with her feet up on the couch.

"You just want free rein to buy junk food."

"Yeah, because I can't do *that* anytime I please. What am I, a five-year-old?"

"No, you're a full-grown man who eats like one."

He aimed his gaze at her belly. "Sorry to break the news, Hallie, but your mother's a health food freak. Stay in there as long as you can, because you're only gonna get broccoli and spinach out here."

He returned later with three bulging shopping bags swinging from each hand, unloaded them into the cabinets and fridge, then trudged upstairs to collect his gear. It was the last game of the season; the Red Sox weren't going to win any pennant this year. There was something profoundly futile in playing such a game, which didn't matter either way. Might as well be a pickup game at the town park.

"Laurel's around, right? Case you need something?" he said when he came down slinging his big sport duffel over his shoulder. It was the same bag he'd loaned her to take to the Prescott Center. Now he needed it to cart home all the stuff from his clubhouse locker.

"Yeah, she's around. They've got family therapy later. She already warned me she'd be by after, and I'd better have some of my best encouragement ready."

"Family therapy." Scott shook his head and gave her a baffled look.

"I know, right? For us it was more like 'suck it up and stop whining.'"

"My father would've punched the therapist and said, 'How'd ya like *that* for therapy?'"

She smiled at this sad little joke, but empathy surged through her, and it was all she could do not to tell him how sorry she was. But that was not the deal. The deal was that he could reveal his pain as long as she didn't look at it too hard or too long, or worst of all, feel sorry for him. Which she did. So terribly sorry that his child's body and tender heart had been battered by someone whose job it had been to protect those very things.

He held her gaze for longer than she expected, as if he'd built up some stamina for being . . . known. For having her be privy to his secrets. This was not a faded thing, his abuse as a child. Its gangrenous color still pulsed. That bell still rang.

She couldn't take a chance on words. *I know*, she told him silently and gave the smallest little nod. The wadded muscles along the ridgeline of his shoulders seemed to release slightly, and the strap of the duffel bag slid down. He hitched it back up and said, "Don't bother watching the game tonight. Go to bed early. You need the rest."

"We'll see," she told him. "I'm feeling better. I might stay up. Have a good game."

"As if it matters," he grumbled as he left.

After a while she was hungry and got up to fish around in the fridge. He hadn't done so badly. Of course, there was a squeeze bottle of Cheez Whiz and a four-pack of artificially flavored Frosted Sugar Cookie pudding cups. But there was also a bag of apples, several containers of the yogurt she liked, and, displayed conspicuously on the top shelf, a bag of spinach. Cass took a yogurt into the study and ate it while doing the review for her next test.

She was feeling better, though the strangely sharp pain in her back still ached. Looking up from her studies and out the window, she saw all six Kesslers pile into their minivan. Laurel had complained that it would take a joint act of God and Congress to get Adam home in time to make a five o'clock family therapy appointment. But he had done it. Cass suspected that Laurel was secretly hoping he wouldn't, and the appointment would have to be postponed.

The minivan now out of sight, Cass's attention retracted from the cul-de-sac and into the den, where her eye caught on the dust bunnies that had congregated along the edges of the wallboard. Tired of studying, she tugged the vacuum cleaner out of the closet with her good arm.

She had vacuumed her way through the living room and into the study, when the pain in her back seemed suddenly to pinch harder. And it wasn't so much in her back, she realized, as behind her stomach. Then she noticed a sudden warm swampy feeling between her legs.

Cass pulled her maternity pants down right there in the study. In the crotch of her panties was a splotch of red, alarmingly bright against the white cotton. She stared at it, her mind ricocheting desperately from one absurdly harmless possibility to the next . . . *some sort of minor bruising from the fall last night . . . a little spotting like the pregnancy book says in the first trimester . . .*

She got the book and riffled agitatedly through the pages until she found something that said *Call your doctor immediately if you experience any vaginal bleeding in the third trimester.*

Cass called the clinic. "Can I speak to Ana, please?"

"Ana's gone home already. The clinic is about to close. You got something wrong?"

"I . . . I'm seven and a half months pregnant, and I've got . . . I'm bleeding . . ."

"Okay, now you just hold on—I'm going to find somebody."

The silence in the house seemed to expand as she waited, until Cass felt like she was the only person on earth.

The receptionist came back on the line. "If you're bleeding, you got to go to the Emergency Department. Nurse says it could be serious. Don't fool around now. You need to go."

The nearest Emergency Department was at Woodland Hospital, in the next town. How would she get there? Laurel was at the therapist's office; Scott was in the middle of batting practice, neither of them even reachable, much less able to drive her. Cass hadn't set up a rideshare account on her new phone yet, so she called a cab.

The cabbie, an older man with a ruddy, pockmarked face, struck up a conversation. "You follow the Sox?" he asked, eyeing her in the rearview mirror.

"Yep," she said, her voice flat and uninviting, hoping that if she stayed perfectly still, she could somehow halt the progress of whatever was happening inside her.

"Boy, they suck this season. Never seen such a bunch of spoiled, overpaid babies."

Seriously? thought Cass. *I get this* guy?

"They got no bats, and the fielding . . . sheesh. My aunt Millie could do better. And what they pay these guys! Scott McGreavy oughta be the Bionic frickin' Man for what they're shelling out, and he's had more errors in the last month than any other player on the team."

Oh, God . . . poor Scotty. Cass had had no idea it was that bad. She could feel her heart start to pound. "Do you mind not talking?" she said.

"What?"

"Do you mind, you know, like . . . shutting up? I need a little quiet right now."

"Huh," he snorted indignantly. "Sorry for living."

"No, it's just—"

"Hey, I get it. Why listen to a guy who actually *works* for his paycheck?"

He thinks I'm from Wortherton. Cass almost laughed.

The cab pulled up in front of the Emergency Department. Cass gave the guy a twenty and said, "All yours," so she didn't have to wait for change.

"Screw you," he muttered under his breath. But he kept it.

Cass didn't stay long in the waiting room. Soon after she told the triage nurse she was bleeding, she was in an exam bay, in a hospital johnny, with two nurses taking her vitals and strapping a monitor around her belly. A doctor came in, a tall Asian woman with her black hair bobbing from a clip at the back of her head.

"Okay, Ms. Macklin," she said, squirting Purell on her hands and rubbing methodically. "It appears that you're stable, though your blood pressure is higher than we like to see it. The baby's heartbeat is regular, and vaginal bleeding is minimal—both very good signs. We're going to transfer you up to Labor and Delivery. That's the best place for you right now."

The doctor stepped outside but was apparently stopped by someone a few feet from the door. Cass could hear snatches of conversation. "Pregnant" and "bleeder" seemed to be the operative words. In minutes a nurse and an orderly were wheeling her gurney down the hall and into an enormous metal-walled elevator. "Is there anyone with you?" the nurse asked.

"No, I took a cab."

"You might want to call a friend or family member."

Cass felt stupid. She should've told someone, but it had all happened so fast, and she'd been so scared and hadn't formed any plan other than *Go to the hospital.*

Scott would be mad if she didn't tell him—no, actually he would *act* mad when what he really was was hurt. She didn't want any more hurt between them. Life was hard enough.

She tugged the cell phone out of the plastic bag with *Belongings of* printed on it with an empty line below and left a message. She tried to keep it neutral, not wanting to alarm him and ruin his last game. "I'm having a little bleeding so I'm getting checked out here at Woodland. I'll probably be home before you are. But just in case . . . I wanted you to know."

The nurse's eyes slid toward the orderly. The look said, *This one doesn't have a clue.*

Chapter XXXIV

The Labor and Delivery room had wires and lights, screens and blinking things, and a huge blue rubber ball in the corner. Cass wondered what on earth that was for.

She'd probably know if she had started labor classes, as Laurel had bugged her to do. But Cass had dragged her heels. The problem was the "coach." She didn't have one. The usual suspect—the baby's father—was obviously unavailable, and what were her options? Kate or Laurel, she figured.

Kate didn't have a car, and public transportation could take too long. Also Kate's most recent hospital experience had been pretty traumatic. How would she feel being back in that very same hospital, sitting through hours of labor? Cass couldn't bring herself to ask.

Laurel was the obvious choice, of course, but Cass was hesitant. Laurel was a bit of a know-it-all about pregnancy and babies. What if Cass wanted to do things differently? And if Adam was away when Cass went into labor, how would Laurel juggle everything? When she'd urged Cass to sign up for the classes, she hadn't offered to coach. Maybe she didn't want to.

Cass didn't even like the word *coach*. It was so sporty. As if squeezing a large item through a normally small opening in your body was some sort of competitive activity that you could be "coached" to "win."

What she thought she might actually want was the opposite of coaching. She might want someone who would just hold her hand and shut the hell up. There was someone who was ideal for that job, but how could she possibly, ever, in a million years, ask him?

Nurses were poking a needle into her arm, strapping and attaching things. She wanted to ask them what that huge blue rubber ball was for, but it didn't seem appropriate. Like asking *Where's the nearest ice cream store?* in the middle of a hurricane.

The doctor came in, a trim, middle-aged man with thick silvery hair and a shave so close it seemed as if he'd been waxed. He looked like a TV doctor. Could a man that smooth and handsome really be capable of handling a misbehaving uterus?

"Ms. Macklin, I'm Dr. Norton." He smiled and shook her hand. "I know you've probably answered these questions down in the ER, but I need to ask them again, if you don't mind."

"Sure, no problem," she said, knowing full well that a man like this, so deftly confident, might ask if you didn't mind something, but that your minding had no real bearing on whether he would go ahead and do that very thing. He would.

"Have you had a blow to your belly or fallen down recently?" he asked.

"Yeah, I fell pretty bad last night, right onto it."

"And your blood pressure's been high for how long?"

"A couple of weeks."

"The bleeding began when exactly?"

"At about five o'clock." The clock said six. She'd been losing blood for an hour.

"I've ordered an ultrasound—the cart should be here any minute. I suspect we'll find a partial placental abruption, in which the placenta has started to detach from the uterine wall. It can be brought on by high blood pressure or a blow to the abdomen, both of which you've had."

The placenta, source of all oxygen and nourishment for the

baby, pulling away from the uterine wall where it gathered up those very things? There was no way this could be okay.

"Is the baby . . . ?"

"The fetal monitor shows a normal heart rate, which tells us the baby is doing fine at the moment and indicates that if this is an abruption, it's only partial. However, if it were to become a complete separation, that situation would be emergent."

Emergent. That was a Ben word. He'd liked it because it had several meanings—emerging, like rising or coming to be, or it could mean urgent. An emergency.

Dr. Norton kept talking. Cass heard phrases like *immediate cesarean section* and *fetal death* and *maternal jeopardy.* They glazed together like raindrops on a pane of glass.

People came in. Scrubs, lab coats. A machine on a cart. One of the cart's wheels squeaked and Cass found herself listening to that rather than to Dr. Norton's emergent talk. She wished she could be two people: Listener Cass, standing upright, asking appropriately probing questions . . . and Pregnant Cass, slumped on a plastic-y hospital bed, listening to everything but.

The room was full of people now, six or seven at least, staring furrow-browed at the ultrasound screen as the wand roamed aggressively across her belly. Cass didn't know where to look. She couldn't see the screen, but she would have averted her gaze from the sight of her placenta abandoning its post, going AWOL when her baby's life depended on it. She stared at the big blue ball and wished for a friend.

She should've left a message for Laurel, who'd be home by now and would come right down. Her bossiness would be a blessing. But Cass's cell phone was in that *Belongings of* bag in the narrow closet across the room. Everyone was so busy, she didn't want to ask for it.

Scott would be coming in from batting practice, eating in the clubhouse with the team, prepping for the game. All those errors . . .

she wondered if he was even in the lineup. She wished he were here, not because he would be the least bit useful, but because he would fully understand her fear. He would be in it with her, and the safety of his nearness would be enough.

The wand stopped pressing into her stomach, and she looked up. A few of the lab-coated people were slipping back out of the room. Dr. Norton had a stiff smile on his smooth face. "What we're seeing is a fairly significant abruption, Ms. Macklin. The team will be coming up with a treatment plan shortly, and I'll be back to let you know what we recommend."

Two nurses bustled around her. Cass couldn't focus on them. She felt like her vision was becoming unreliable, her eyes wandering directionless around the strange room.

"This feel okay?" one of the nurses asked, adjusting a strap across Cass's belly.

Cass didn't know if it felt okay.

"Ms. Macklin, you all right?" Cass could hear the concern prickling in those words, but she couldn't respond. The pain in her belly was starting to move, to swell, to get louder . . . the feeling was so . . . loud . . .

The nurse pulled the sheet away from Cass's thighs and let out an inadvertent gasp. A blur of movement, forceful words . . . *Dr. Norton to room 6 STAT . . . all available nurses . . .*

The other nurse was saying things to her in a soft, reassuring tone, belied by her bruising grip as she stuck another needle into Cass's free arm.

Then the room was in motion all around her, faces staring down, lights overhead rolling past as if on some sort of pulley, strobing into her eyes.

Chapter XXXV

Cass started to make sense of things in the shower. Or was it a bathtub?

She was in a reclined position, so maybe a tub. The shower curtain was very tall and wide, and seemed to wrap all the way around. The tub was soft . . . Okay, maybe it wasn't a tub.

Someone was standing near her. Cass blinked. A woman was touching her, doing something, but Cass could only see arm movement. She couldn't feel the corresponding results.

"Ms. Macklin," the woman cooed softly, "you're in recovery."

How does she know that? Cass wondered vaguely. *It's supposed to be Alcoholics* Anonymous, *for godsake.*

It came to her like a slap. The hospital, the baby . . . She put her hands on her stomach, which was suspiciously squishy, not taut and round like the last thousand times she'd touched it.

"Your baby's doing fine. She's in the NICU."

"The . . . ?"

"The Neonatal Intensive Care Unit, where they take babies who need a little extra help," said the nurse gently. "The anesthesia really hit you, but that should be wearing off soon. The baby's father is here."

Ben? Ben is here?

Another face came quickly into view.

Not Ben.

But familiar.

"Hey," he murmured.

"Scotty." Her hand wandered out of the snowbank of blankets to find his. He grasped it, enveloping it. His other hand circled her wrist as if to keep her from floating away. Which was good, because she felt as if she might do just that.

"Sorry," he said. "I thought they might not let me in if I didn't say I was . . ." His eyes shifted momentarily to the nurse, who raised her eyebrows. "The baby's father is my brother and he's dead." It was his *you-wanna-make-something-of-it?* tone.

"I need him," Cass told the nurse.

"Fine by me." The nurse gave a little shrug. "Your incision's cleaned up now, so I'm going to let you two be. The doctor will be in to talk to you, and then you'll go to your room."

When she left, Scott pulled the one lone chair up to Cass's bedside and took her hand again. "What happened?" he breathed.

She told him as much as she could remember. "What time is it?" she said.

"About eight."

"Did the game get rained out or something?"

"No, it's going."

"Right now? Why aren't you there?"

He laughed incredulously. "Uh, because I got this insanely calm voice mail about how you were *bleeding* and in the freakin' *hospital*. But oh, no worries, you'd be home before me."

"You left?"

"I told Rogie and he told one of the coaches. Hopefully."

"Scotty, you walked out on a *game*?"

"Yeah, and you had a baby. Can we talk about that now?"

There was throat-clearing outside the curtained walls of the recovery bay. Then a woman parted the fabric and entered, tall and muscular, her bony wrists sticking out the ends of her lab coat. "I'm Dr. Abayo." She gave Scott's hand a sharp pump and patted

Cass's limp arm. "I'm the neonatologist from the NICU. You've got a nice healthy girl, there. She's got some growing to do, and she'll be with us for a while, but she's a real champ after what she went through."

Cass let out a little gasp of gratitude. Scott squeezed her hand. "She's in good shape, then?" he said.

"Yes, absolutely. And big! Almost five pounds."

Cass froze. "Not even five pounds?"

"Oh, trust me, that's huge for the NICU. When they're ready to let you travel, you'll come up and see for yourself." She turned to Scott. "You can come up in an hour or so, once they've got her all settled in." She seemed about to leave, but then she hesitated. "I just have to say, I'm a huge fan, Mr. McGreavy. I know it's been a tough season, but hey, that's all part of the Red Sox experience, right? We're up, we're down. Next year we'll be up again."

Scott gave an uncomfortable smile and said, "Let's hope so."

"And congratulations on your baby girl. We're going to take good care of her."

"Uh, thanks very much." The doctor left, and Scott's fingers traced along the blanket at the edge of the bed. "Sorry," he said. "I didn't feel like explaining it all over again."

"I really don't care," Cass said. "I'm just glad you're here."

* * *

CASS was transferred to the maternity ward, and it was a relief not to be surrounded by quite so many machines and wires and blinking lights. She still had plenty, of course. An IV on one arm for fluids, a transfusion bag on the other arm for blood. Tied to the railing of the bed was the button for her PCA pump, so she could give herself a dose of painkiller when the throbbing ache in her gut accelerated from uncomfortable to toe-curling. The pump limited the dosage, however, so Cass didn't have to worry about her alcoholic's instinct to overmedicate.

Scott waited in the hall while the nurse got her set up and the doctor looked at her incision. He was young and scruffy and a little too hip. "Wow, this is a good-looking cut for a crashed section," he said, bobbing his head in emphasis. "Props to the doc on this one."

When he left, Cass asked the nurse, Tamara, "Is he a real doctor?"

"Resident." Tamara gave a little eye roll. She had short black hair and skin the color of root beer. Her movements were efficient but gentle. Cass liked her immediately.

When Tamara left, Scott called, "All clear?," from the shadow of the doorway.

"Safe to enter," she called back, tucking the blanket up across her chest.

He was still wearing his uniform pants, though he had a normal short-sleeved shirt on.

"I left the clubhouse kinda quick," he explained, settling into the rocking chair next to her bed. "I grabbed a shirt and changed at a stoplight." Then he started to laugh. "At the next light I pulled out my athletic cup. I look over and there's this old lady on a bus, staring right down into my window. I thought she was going to drop her teeth. She sees a guy yank a big hunk of plastic out of his drawers, and she's probably thinking 'What is this world coming to?'"

Cass started to laugh and at first it felt so good. It had been over a week since she'd found anything remotely humorous, and the visual of that poor old lady watching Scotty pull what must have looked like a triangular soup bowl out of his crotch was the funniest thing she could imagine.

The clenching of her severed gut muscles hit her like a punch. She pressed a hand against her stitches and reached for the PCA button. But she couldn't stop laughing and the searing pain made her cry.

"Are you okay?" said Scotty, jumping up. "Should I call the nurse?"

In another moment the medication wended its way into her bloodstream, tamping down the worst of it. Cass let out a grateful breath and unclenched her teeth. "Don't make me laugh."

The world went cottony then, as the meds continued to soften the edges of her senses and she closed her eyes. "Sorry, baby," she heard him say from a long way off. "I won't do it again."

She needed to sleep. Actually sleep was imminent whether she wanted it or not.

"Scotty. Go see the baby."

"Uh-uh," he said. "Not till you do."

"Just go check on her."

"She's fine. The doctor said."

"Go home, then. Get some rest," she told him.

She could feel the blanket being tucked up under her chin. Had Tamara come in?

"I'll be back tomorrow," said a dreamy, Scotty-like voice. "First thing."

"'Kay." Was she speaking aloud? It hardly seemed to matter. "Love you."

Something smooth and soft brushed her forehead. And then warm, woolly darkness wrapped itself around her like a shawl.

* * *

THE next day had a foggy quality. Sights, sounds, and sensations were filtered through the misty drizzle of pain medication, anxiety about the baby, and a sort of waterlogged feeling.

Scotty came in with a bag of mostly useless stuff—clothes she couldn't wear, and her *GPS Set to Joy* book, which she didn't have the mental focus to read.

"And here's your hairbrush," he said.

"That bad?" Cass asked.

"Yeah, it's full of knots."

She smiled at his brutal honesty. Why *not* tell someone who'd just been through a slash-and-grab C-section, and hadn't even seen her baby yet, that her hair was messy?

"Sorry, but it is," he said defensively.

Laurel came in after she got the boys off to school and dropped Timmy at his morning nursery program, just as Scott left to clean out his locker at Fenway. It was as if sitting in the rocker next to the bed were some sort of tag team activity. Cass didn't like to see him leave.

Laurel wanted to hear the whole story in minute detail, and at first Cass found this taxing. But as she recounted it, Laurel would nod and say, "Good thinking," or "Whew, that's a relief," and Cass felt just a little less traumatized. The terror of the previous day began its journey toward past tense and the volume on her alcohol craving fell to a manageable decibel level.

Laurel had to pick up Timmy at noon. When she left, Cass heard voices in the hallway—not actual words, but she recognized Scott's low voice by its timbre. He came in carrying a sack of takeout food. Cass said, "You guys synchronize watches or something?"

"You been through a lot, and a hospital is . . . well, it's a hospital. We don't want you to be alone." He squeezed her toe. Then he sat down in the rocker, the wood squeaking just a little under his weight. He ate his lunch, they talked, she slept, they talked some more, he dozed.

She studied him slumped in the rocker, head lax against the backrest. He looked older than his thirty years—older than Laurel, who had a decade on him. Even in sleep his face had a hardened look, as if he'd spent his adulthood on the night shift at some factory instead of outside playing baseball. She wondered if sadness and anger and isolation could change the contours of your face, just as people grew to look like their dogs or their spouses; and might the hardness mellow somewhat if he were able to stop his own bells of misery from ringing?

Kate called. "Oh, my God, I just got the message from Laurel. How *are* you?"

Cass found herself telling an abbreviated, sanitized version of the events. Kate's own terrifying medical experience was clearly leaking into her concern for Cass. She kept saying, "You must've been so freaked out!" She offered to visit, but the thought was exhausting.

"I should be out of here in a couple of days," Cass said. "Why don't you come over to the house sometime next week when you have a day off?" Kate seemed relieved. Cass certainly was.

Then the nurse came with the wheelchair, and the three of them headed up to the NICU. In the elevator, Scott took out his phone and began flicking at it agitatedly. Cass was already worried about seeing the baby. "You have an important text coming in?" she said, annoyed.

"I can't find the stupid camera. Laurel told me to take pictures, but I never used it before." The nurse glanced over. Scott handed her the phone and said, "Be my guest."

At the reception desk, they were given wristbands identifying them as belonging to Baby Girl Macklin. Scott continued to pose as the baby's father, glancing at Cass for approval. She didn't care—it was the least of her concerns. A NICU nurse greeted them at the door. "I'm Hilde," she said. "I'm on your daughter's primary nursing team, so we'll be seeing a lot of each other." She was short and round, with hair so bleached it seemed like a doll's.

Hilde led as Scott pushed the wheelchair down the hall and into a large room with four clear capsulelike things on each side. Most were at least partially covered with blankets. "Bright light is hard on a preemie's immature senses, so the blankets keep it dark until light is needed."

At the end of the row on the right, she stopped. "Can you stand?" she asked Cass.

Cass struggled to her feet. She felt Scott's hands on her rib cage from behind.

"You've got her in case she starts feeling a little wobbly?" Hilde seemed concerned.

"I'm a ballplayer," said Scott. "I catch things for a living."

Hilde pulled back the blanket from the top of the capsule in front of them . . .

There she was, Baby Girl Macklin.

She was so small! And tubes everywhere—in her nose, in her arm. Wires attached to her chest and her foot. Naked except for a tiny cap and a diaper the size of a cocktail napkin.

"Isn't she beautiful?" said Hilde.

"Oh, God . . ." Cass put a hand to her mouth. Her eyes filled.

"Cass, she's okay," Scott murmured from behind her.

"Is she?" Cass demanded of the nurse. "Is she okay?"

"She's fine," said Hilde. "She's smaller than full term, but she's a lot bigger than most of these kids. The tubes and wires look scary, but they're normal for a preemie."

Dr. Abayo approached, towering over short, stocky Hilde. "I see you're getting acquainted," she said, sticking her hand out to shake Scott's. Cass felt him let go, but his hold on her resumed as soon as the handshake was over.

"Would you like to touch her?" asked Dr. Abayo.

Cass hesitated. Emotions swirled through her: ecstatic, mournful, terrified. She felt crazy.

Scott's hands urged her forward. She stepped up to the isolette and slowly slid her hand into one of the openings, fluttering with tension.

"It's okay, baby," Scott whispered. She wasn't sure if he was talking to her or to the infant. But the low growl of his voice, the warmth of his breath by her ear, steadied her.

The baby's belly was soft and warm. "Hi, sweetie," she murmured. "I'm your mom."

Mom.

Tears cascaded down Cass's face. What she wouldn't give for her own mother to be here, seeing her granddaughter. Touching her. Holding Cass. Making all of this—everything—better.

The baby's face was small, but her cheeks were round, her eyes closed, her impossibly tiny mouth pursed slightly. Her chin was strong, like Ben's and Scotty's. Downy peach-colored hair peeked out from one edge of her knit cap. Despite all the tubes and wires, Baby Girl Macklin was heart-stoppingly beautiful.

I will never be the same, Cass thought. *Now that you're here, the world and everything in it is new. Even me.*

She carefully withdrew her hand, turned her face into Scott's chest, and wept.

Scott's arms were tight around her. He didn't say anything, but she could feel his chin against her hair, and smell his clean, salty smell. Her crying slowed. He stroked her back. The nurse handed her some tissues. "Sorry," Cass said.

"Very common reaction," said the nurse.

"We get a lot of tears in here," said Dr. Abayo, adding quickly, "happy tears!" An awkward silence followed. Certainly not all the tears cried in the NICU were happy. Some were despairing. To distract from this truth, Dr. Abayo said, "Okay, Dad, it's your turn."

"Oh, uh . . ."

"Come on now," Dr. Abayo prodded jovially.

Cass looked up at him. "You helped her get here almost as much as I did."

He gazed back at her, and a faint ripple of pride crossed his face. Still holding on to Cass with one arm, he reached his big mitt of a hand in and gently stroked the baby's belly. His thumb was as big as her thigh. Her mouth moved, a little grimace that looked like a smile.

"She loves her daddy," said Nurse Hilde.

Cass felt the little catch in his breath and looked up to see the sorrowful smile, gone in an instant. He looked down at her. "Time to get you back to your room. My arm's getting tired."

Nurse Hilde's eyebrows went up at this, but Cass understood. Emotion was overwhelming them both. She slid back into the wheelchair. "Bye, baby," she said.

On the elevator back down to the maternity floor, he said, "Damn."

"What?"

"I forgot to take pictures. Laurel's gonna have my ass."

"Scotty, do you have any pictures of you as a baby? Because I sure don't."

"My mother might have a few, if she didn't throw them out when she moved to Hawaii."

"Why would she throw them out?"

The elevator doors opened, and Scott pushed the wheelchair into the maternity ward hallway. "She kept talking about starting a whole new chapter. Didn't want to bring any of her old stuff with her. Had to have new furniture, new clothes, everything."

"She's a piece of work, isn't she?"

He snorted. "That doesn't even begin to cover it."

When they got back to the room, he took her elbow and steadied her as she got into bed.

"You're pretty good at this," Cass said. "You could have a second career as a nurse."

"You're assuming I have a first career." He slumped into the rocker.

"Oh, geez, I forgot. What happened about you walking out on the game?"

"Nothing. They fined me. But I think it was more about the fact that I just left. If I'd stayed and waited for permission, it probably wouldn't have been too big a deal."

"Is it a lot?"

"It's just money, Cass. I know we weren't raised like that. But if

I had it to do all over again, I still wouldn't wait around for some idiot to give me the okay to go."

Such a good guy, she thought. *Such a good, stand-up guy.*

"Hey," she said, "that was funny what you said up in the NICU about catching things for a living. You never tell people what you do."

He shrugged. "People either know, or telling them makes me sound like a bragger."

"Yeah, but you told that nurse."

"I wanted her to know I wasn't gonna drop you!"

"And you didn't," Cass said with a smile.

His gaze was soft but he wasn't smiling. "It wasn't hard."

It was quiet for a while, except for the gentle creak of Scott rocking the chair, the *skritch, skritch, skritch* of rubberized clogs going up and down the hall, and the general hum of a building with an impressively high ratio of electrical devices per square foot.

Then Scott said, "Baby needs a name."

"I know. I've been thinking about that."

"What's it gonna be?"

"I'd like to name her Margaret, after my mother. But we'll call her Maggie."

"Sounds good." Scott nodded. "What about her last name?"

"Well, I thought . . . I was thinking that it might be best if she had my last name. You know, so people would know I'm her mom. I mean, not that they wouldn't know, but it would be easier. I wouldn't have to keep explaining it all the time." She found herself justifying this for some reason, when all she had to do was say "Maggie Macklin," and that was the name.

"What about Ben?" Scott said.

It felt like a cheap shot. "Ben's not here," Cass said coldly.

"That's my point. It's the only connection she has to him."

"I'm not going to pretend he never existed, if that's what you mean."

"That's not what I'm saying—"

"But I do wonder what I'm going to tell her when she asks things like, what did my dad do for a living."

"Tell her he was a stockbroker." An obvious attempt to lighten the mood.

"It's not funny, Scotty. You're making a joke out of the fact that there's almost nothing I can tell her about her father that isn't going to make her feel sad and ashamed." Cass felt her throat tighten with anger and the threat of tears.

"Hey," he said gently. He wanted her to look at him, but she couldn't. "We'll tell her he was really smart and loved crossword puzzles. And he tried a bunch of different jobs but never found his stride."

Ben. Cass felt hot tears fill her lids. *He should be here . . . but if he were here . . .* She had to admit that she almost certainly would never have made it this far. In fact, it had been his absence that had made her sobriety possible. And if Cass hadn't been sober, Maggie wouldn't be the relatively healthy baby she now was. If she were here at all. Cass had had no choice in the matter. . . . But if she *had* had a choice . . . she would have chosen Maggie over Ben.

The tears spilled down her face.

"Cass . . ."

"I hate crying!" she growled through clenched teeth.

"Laurel says the hormones can make you a little nutty after the baby's born." His tone had a hint of wariness, and this infuriated her even more.

"That's bullshit. *You* started this."

He took a breath, exhaled slowly. "Should I leave?"

She snatched a tissue from the bedside table and blew her nose loudly. "I really don't care."

"Okay." He pushed himself up and out of the rocker. "I'll see you tomorrow."

"Whatever."

He left and she wanted to scream after him, *See, I can say "whatever," too!*

And then she broke down sobbing.

Nurse Tamara came in. "Hey, what's going on?" she crooned. "What's all this about?"

"My stupid boyfriend died, and I live with his brother, and I love the guy, but I fucking hate him!"

"Okay . . ." Tamara soothed. "You need some sleep, darlin'. I'm going to go get you something to help and I'll be right back."

Cass let loose a string of loud gasping sobs that hurt her belly and made her feel like some howling, crazy-haired mental patient, like the insane wife from *Jane Eyre*.

But then it passed. And she felt better.

But also a little guilty that she'd basically kicked Scotty out.

But not that guilty. He'd recover.

Maybe he was in recovery now. This made her chuckle, the thought of Scott in recovery from her yelling at him. Maybe there was a twelve-step program he could join.

When Tamara returned, Cass was laughing, her face still wet with tears.

Tamara smiled patiently and shook her head. She handed Cass a glass of water and a tiny paper cup with a pill in it. Cass took the pill, and Tamara checked her vitals and tucked her into bed. She sat in the rocking chair and waited for Cass to doze off.

Cass liked that. With her eyes closed, the creak of the rocking chair made it sound like Scotty was still there in the room.

Chapter XXXVI

Blue-gray light filtered in around the window blinds. The clock said quarter to six.

Tamara came in. "How we feeling today?" she asked.

"We're feeling a little less like something out of a horror movie."

"How nice for us."

"Can I go up and see her?"

"Of course."

Cass showered and changed into clean johnnies; Tamara brought a wheelchair just in case, but Cass preferred to walk. She didn't break any land speed records, but she made it.

They stood there by Baby Girl Macklin's isolette, watching the little girl blink and kick her foot. Cass put a hand in and rubbed her belly. "Maggie," she sighed. "My Maggie. Tamara, you touch her, too. I want her to know how many good people there are in the world."

Tamara smiled at the compliment and stroked Maggie's hand, the size of a nickel.

A NICU nurse came and Cass asked her to put Maggie's name on the isolette card. Baby Girl was crossed out, and Maggie was written in. Macklin stayed the same.

"You'll be seeing a social worker today," Tamara said lightly, as they rode the elevator back down.

"Why, because I went psycho last night?"

"Well, you got a lot on your plate. C-section, baby in the NICU, stress in your living situation. You'd be seeing a social worker in the NICU anyway."

"I really don't hate Scotty," Cass said.

"Every woman I know hates the man in her life at some point, darlin'. Even if it's only for a minute."

* * *

SCOTT didn't show.

Laurel walked in at about 9:30, and Cass was so relieved. "I think I really scared him."

"A little," said Laurel.

"You talked to him?"

"He called to let me know he was giving you some breathing room this morning."

"I should apologize."

"Well, that wouldn't be the worst idea, but honestly, Cass, after everything that's happened, you deserve all the slack in the world. Scott understands that."

"Because you told him so," Cass said knowingly.

A sly grin. "I may have suggested it."

"You'd make an excellent counselor, you know that? Hey, how did family therapy go?"

"Surprisingly well. Of course, it was mostly about my drinking. And cleaning! Apparently that really gets to them. Those boys will all marry slobs because of me." She gave a little head-shake. "But then the therapist asked if there was anything else they wanted to talk about, and Drew said, 'I'll tell you what I really want.' He turned to Adam and said, 'I want you to get a job where you don't leave all the time. It's not good for Mom and it's not good for us.'"

"Holy smokes, he did it!" said Cass. "I told him it was up to him to say what he needed."

"Oh, my gosh, Cass." Laurel reached out to squeeze her hand. "Thank you."

* * *

THEY went up to see the baby, and Laurel got misty-eyed and said she was the most beautiful baby girl she'd ever seen, and snapped an absurd number of pictures with her pink-cased iPhone. The social worker came by and asked if this was a good time for them to meet. Cass looked at Laurel.

"Perfect timing," Laurel said. "I need to be on my way." She hugged Cass. "You're doing great," she whispered.

The social worker, a pale young woman named Ruth, dressed in monochromatic beige, led Cass to an office nearby. They exchanged pleasantries, and Cass thought it was a breeze until Ruth said, "I'm glad to have the chance to talk with you alone, without the baby's father."

A tingle of anxiety ran across Cass's scalp.

Ruth continued in her neutral tone. "I understand you were feeling angry with him last night. First let me say that anger is a perfectly normal emotion when a person is under the kind of stress you're experiencing. But I need to ask if you feel safe at home. Are you fearful of him for any reason—either for what he's done in the past, or for what you think he may be capable of?"

"To be perfectly honest," Cass said, "home, with Scotty, is the *only* place I feel safe."

As they talked, Cass surprised herself by being unusually frank about her upbringing and her alcoholism. Ruth assured her that the conversation was confidential unless there was concern that Cass might hurt herself or the baby. Even this was said with such wan dispassion, Cass wondered if Ruth had ever kicked up a fuss about anything in her whole life. Besides, Cass was too exhausted to lie. She even admitted that Scott wasn't the baby's real father.

Ben would have been furious with her for spilling all those secrets. But Ben wasn't there.

When the session was over, Cass went to see Maggie again. There, staring into her isolette, was Scott. He looked up, then turned his gaze back to the baby.

"She's active today. See how she's moving her arms?" They watched the baby slowly bend her wrists and elbows, as if the air were water, and she were a little fish learning to swim.

"Sorry I flipped out," said Cass.

"I shouldn't have pushed about the name."

"I didn't really want you to leave."

He turned to look at her. "You hid it pretty well, then."

Nurse Hilde came up behind them, bleachy hair gleaming harshly under the fluorescent lights. "I was just about to check on our girl. I see she has a name now. Maggie, how nice!"

As Hilde checked Maggie's vitals, she explained about each of the wires and tubes: an IV for fluids in her arm, an oxygen saturation gauge on her foot, echocardiogram wires on her chest and belly, a gauge to make sure her body temperature was normal, and a gavage tube in her nose for feedings. "We're giving her preemie formula until your breast milk comes in, and then you'll pump and we'll give her that. Eventually she'll be able to nurse from your breast or a bottle, and the gavage tube will come out. I'll just finish up here and then you can hold her."

Cass stiffened. She wanted to, but without much experience with babies, even a chubby full-term newborn would have felt daunting—all that floppy unpredictability. Hilde pulled up a padded rocking chair, and Cass sat obediently. The nurse regarded her with a measured eye. "Okay, first take as big a breath as you possibly can. That's it, now hold it, hold it . . . All right, let it all out, every last bit." Cass went limp with the effort. But she felt less tense.

Hilde opened the isolette and lifted Maggie out, bringing her—
wires and all—to lie snug in Cass's arms. "Hi, Maggie," she whispered. "It's Mom."

Hilde pulled over a chair for Scott and went to care for another
baby. Maggie waved her little arms and flexed her legs. Her eyes
traced across Cass's johnny, and up to her face. It was hard to know
how well the baby could focus, but to Cass it felt as if the baby's
dark blue eyes were holding her gaze, looking right into her.

"You did it." Scott didn't mean just holding the baby, she knew.
He meant all of it.

Her gaze slid momentarily to his. "Couldn't have done it without you."

"You could've."

"It would have been harder, Scotty. Way harder."

He smiled and leaned forward to put his finger in the path of
Maggie's gently fluttering hand. She grasped it, and he seemed for
a moment to be as content as Cass had ever seen him.

"It's not just about Ben—the name thing," he said quietly. "I
want her to understand . . ." He hesitated, struggling to express
himself. Words had been Ben's playground, but for Scott even
English was a foreign language sometimes.

"She should know," he started again, "that I'm hers, too. And
she can come to me if she needs something. It's her right. She'll
never question that if she has my name." He glanced up at Cass,
fixed her with a purposeful gaze. "Think of the difference it
would've made if you'd had an uncle to turn to."

It would have been life altering, Cass knew. And what if something happened to her now? The thought of this tiny, vulnerable
child suffering a similar fate . . . it was unthinkable.

Scott's words were no less powerful for their simplicity. In a
couple of short, noncompound sentences he'd effectively added
himself as the second planet orbiting the baby's sun. It was an
indisputable argument. Ben would've been proud.

As Cass pondered this, Nurse Hilde wandered back. "Is it your turn now, Dad?"

The look of certitude on Scott's face quickly turned to one of vague fear.

"Don't you want to?" asked Cass, her implication clear: *All this big talk about being her uncle, and you don't even want to hold her?*

"'Course I do," said Scott, his cheeks going pomegranate beneath his afternoon stubble. "I just never held a baby before."

Hilde reached for Maggie and said, "It's a lot easier than catching things out of the sky."

Cass switched places with him, and he soon had the baby cradled in his massive arms. Another nurse had a question for Hilde and she moved away again.

"How's she look?" Scott said, squinting uncertainly at Cass.

"She looks fine. You look like you're wearing your shoulders for earrings, though. Just relax." Cass reached out and pressed down on the ridgeline of his shoulders. "Pretend your hand is a mitt and she's the ball." This seemed to make sense to him, and he settled into a more comfortable position. They watched Maggie wriggle and sweep her little arms around, and they had to untangle her from her wires once. Then she grabbed onto his shirtsleeve and held it for a while.

"Why do you care so much?" Cass asked.

Scott seemed to understand that this wasn't a challenge. She simply wanted to know.

"Lotta reasons."

"Like?"

"Like she's my brother's kid. And granted, I wanted to punch some sense into him most of the time, but . . . you know. When we were young . . . he was good to me." Scott shook his head. "Even when he was a falling-down drunk he was probably the best friend I ever had." She could hear a tremble of emotion vibrating below his words.

He sighed, composing himself. "And let's face it; I'm not exactly housebroken when it comes to women. There's a good chance I'll never have kids of my own."

Maggie had stopped waving around, and her eyelids began to droop. Scott shifted, letting her sink a little lower into the nest of his arms. He set the chair to rocking gently.

"When you first came to my house, you asked me to make an investment. Remember that?" He was looking at the baby, but it was clear to whom he was speaking. "Well, I did. Over and over again—against my better judgment most of the time," he said softly. "I kept expecting things to fall apart, but they never did, at least not too bad. You kept up your end of the bargain. So now"—his eyes flicked over to Cass and then back to the baby in his arms—"I'm invested."

Chapter XXXVII

When Hilde returned to help get Maggie back into her isolette, Cass asked her for a pen. She took the name card and after *Macklin* she added *McGreavy*. She showed it to Scott, who tried to keep from smiling too widely.

As they waited for the elevator, he rested a hand on her opposite shoulder, his thumb against the nape of her neck. She laid her hand on the small of his back. They stood there silently until the elevator doors opened. When they broke apart to enter, Cass felt as if she had been unplugged from some important source of nourishment. Those two points of contact—the palm of her hand and the nape of her neck—felt warm all the way down to the maternity floor.

After lunch, Cass realized it had been a week since she'd checked in with her sponsor.

"I was starting to worry about you, quiet girl," Patrick said when she called. "I've been leaving messages at the house. Are you okay?"

"Yes, I'm fine." She smiled and fingered her hospital bracelet. "Patrick, I'm a mom."

"What? Oh my God! Dennis!" His voice was aimed away from the receiver. "She had the baby!" He wanted to know everything, of course, and she recounted the events with a growing efficiency, mentally noting the parts she left out, like the surly cabdriver, and the parts she emphasized, like waking up in the recovery bay to see Scott, and how he'd left the game for her.

Scott had closed his eyes and let his head loll against the rocker's backrest, but she could tell he wasn't sleeping. He was listening.

"And what's our miracle girl's name?" asked Patrick.

"Margaret Hallie Macklin McGreavy."

Scott's eyes flew open and a laugh burst out of him. He grinned over at her and shook his head. She smiled back, nodding. "We call her Maggie," she told Patrick.

"We?" said Patrick.

"Everyone," Cass replied quickly. "The social worker told me they have AA meetings right in the hospital, so I'm going later this afternoon."

"That's terrific, hon," said Patrick warmly, but she could sense the edge of concern in his voice, too. They made plans to get together when she got home and said good-bye.

"Hallie?" said Scott. "You're serious?"

"I like it," she insisted. "And now you can't ever complain, because you gave her as many names as I did."

"Me, complain?" he said with false innocence.

"Oh, no, not you," she said snidely. "You're Mr. Easygoing."

* * *

AT four, Cass gingerly put on the maternity clothes Scott had brought, grateful that they were loose around her C-section wound. The pain had decreased steadily in two days, and she was sick of wearing johnnies, but she was still a bit sore.

At the AA meeting on the second floor, however, several people were in johnnies. One elderly man in a wheelchair had an IV bag hanging from a pole and an oxygen tube at his nose. Cass wondered how bad off she'd have to be before she gave up and started drinking again.

Most of the sharing centered, not surprisingly, on health issues.

One man had had to have three fingers amputated because he'd gone on a bender and smashed them (he still wasn't sure how) and an antibiotic-resistant infection had set in. He was a concert pianist.

Cass had heard plenty of tough stories before, but there seemed to be a higher percentage of truly hopeless ones. She didn't want to talk. By comparison her story seemed too hopeful. The woman next to Cass, smartly dressed in tan slacks and a cream-colored sweater, seemed perfectly healthy, and Cass figured she'd been holding out for the same reason: too happy.

Let her talk, Cass told herself. *I'm not going to be the too-happy girl.*

Finally the woman began to speak. "I used to come here every day."

She stopped, and it seemed as if she were done. But she was so still, Cass realized she was holding her breath. The woman exhaled raggedly. "My baby was in the NICU for 119 days, and every day I'd sit with her and then I'd come to this meeting. It was my routine." She looked down at her hands; a fat diamond ring sparkling on her finger shook slightly. "I started to forget what life was like without a baby in the hospital. It was . . . comforting.

"She seemed to be doing so well, and then she stopped progressing and she got weak and then she got sick." Another silence. Another gasp. "Twenty-nine days ago, she died.

"I came back here because I don't know what else to do. I can't seem to find a new routine. I quit my job when she was born. My husband goes to work every morning and the house is just . . . empty. I get dressed and sit in the living room and wait for him to come home. I don't think he actually likes coming home anymore.

"So many years of not being able to get pregnant was what tipped me into alcoholism in the first place. But finally, on the sixth IVF try, an embryo implanted. And it was her. My baby."

Tears began to roll down her smooth cheeks. "I didn't drink

a drop. Didn't even want to. And now she's gone. I want to start drinking again. I really do." She let out a sharp, painful-sounding laugh through her tears. "I *really do*. But I'm stuck in this not-drinking routine. Which I guess makes me a failure at everything. Even alcoholism."

Everyone was crying, even the man with the oxygen tube, and Cass thought he might die right there in the room. The leader, a middle-aged woman with a *Thank a Nurse* pin on her collar, could barely collect herself to start the Lord's Prayer. Cass held the woman's hand, so smooth and cool it could have been a mannequin's. After the group finished choking out the last words, hands were dropped, and people began to straggle away from the room like survivors from a shipwreck. The woman stood there. Cass couldn't leave her. "I'm so sorry," she murmured.

The woman took in Cass's loose maternity clothing. "You've just had a baby," she said.

"Um . . . yeah."

She forced a smile and whispered, "Good luck."

* * *

SCOTT wasn't there when Cass made it back to her room. She burrowed down under the covers and cried. Exhausted, she eventually dozed off. When she woke, Scott was in the rocker.

"Where were you?" she asked.

"I went up to see Maggie. Then that Dr. Abayo came by. It must have been a slow day on the unit or something, because she stood there talking baseball with me for a good twenty minutes. She played softball in college. Knows more about the game than half the guys I've played with." He chuckled. "We're going for beers later."

"Really?" Cass's heart sank at the thought of being abandoned after what she'd been through at the meeting, and she was also weirdly jealous. She'd watched a heck of a lot of baseball this season and understood the game better than she ever had before. But clearly she wasn't in this woman's league.

"No, not really," Scott scolded. "I was kidding!"

"Well, you could, I guess . . ." Easy to be generous when you knew your bluff wouldn't be called. "It might be nice to go have a normal evening."

"A normal evening? I don't . . . even . . ." he sputtered. "And anyway, I'm pretty sure she's playing for the other team."

"Yeah, I kind of got that sense." She wasn't jealous of Dr. Abayo romantically. She was jealous of her . . . sportsically.

He stared at her, then shook his head. "Okay, moving on. How was the meeting?"

"Really sad." By the time Cass had finished telling him about it she was crying again.

He tugged the rocker closer to the bed. "Listen to me," he said. "That is not you. You are never going to be that woman. Maggie's a good strong baby—the doctor said. She's going to be out of here in a month or so, not a hundred days."

"But things go wrong, Scotty," she said, still crying. "You can't know for sure."

"Hey, have you seen those other babies? Maggie's the biggest one on the unit. I'm telling you, she is kicking newborn ass up there."

Cass let out a snort of a laugh. He handed her the box of tissues. "You got a little . . ." He tapped his nose. "And what'd you spill down the front?"

Cass looked down. There were two round wet spots at her nipples. "My milk's in!"

She hit the button for the nurse, who came in looking distracted. "Yes?"

"Um, my milk came in. I think I'm supposed to pump or something."

The nurse's face fell slightly. "We're a little crazy right now. I'll bring you a pump, but I won't be able to help you with it till later." She strode quickly from the room, then bustled back with something that looked like a small, soft-sided cooler, and set it on the tray table.

Cass eyed the bag. She looked at Scott.

"Well, don't look at me," he said. "I never even milked a cow."

"You don't have to put it like that!" she snapped at him.

"You want me to open it?" he said.

Cass was worn out from crying and worrying about Maggie. "Never mind," she said.

"Let me just look at the instructions." He tugged them from the bag. His eyebrows went up, and he turned it to show Cass. On the cover was an attractive woman, naked from the waist up, a clear plastic cone suctioned onto each of her enviably-size breasts.

"Wow," said Scott. "That does not look comfortable."

"Give me that." Cass snatched it out of his hands. The whole thing was embarrassing and overwhelming, and she felt like killing him or weeping again, or both.

"You want me to leave?" he asked quietly.

"I don't know!" she screamed.

He took the booklet from her, packed it back into the bag, and put it on the floor out of her view. "It's almost dinnertime," he said. "Let's just watch a little TV."

Cass pressed at the pillow over her C-section, her fingers digging into the white cotton case. Scott flicked expertly through the stations until he found *Yukon Men*, a reality TV show about people living in Tanana, Alaska. An older guy with a scraggly ponytail was explaining that they were nearly out of meat and it was "fawty degrees below zero."

"You hear his accent?" said Scott softly. "That guy's from Boston."

The man further detailed their peril if they weren't able to kill some elk soon, and Cass could hear his half-forgotten *R*s.

"Geez, think of it," murmured Scott. "Moving to East Freakin'

Egypt, Alaska—*from Boston.* I bet he's having some second thoughts about *that* decision right about now."

"Boston's not the center of the world," Cass said peevishly.

"Damn near close. Who'd want to live anywhere else?"

"People in Paris might beg to differ."

"Let 'em beg all they want," he said. "I'll take Boston any day of the week."

They watched the show: the wind barreling through the scrim of trees against an icy landscape, the men desperate to catch up with a herd of elk, the dogs yelping as they pulled the sled, and Cass felt her breathing slow and her muscles unclench. She was warm and fed. Scott was nearby. And though he drove her crazy sometimes, she loved him. And she knew that deep beneath his fortresslike exterior, in his own way he cared about her, too.

Tamara came on shift at seven and was pleased to meet Scott, though she was clearly taking his measure. Then she told him, "You look hungry."

"Nah, I just had a sandwich from the caf. But thanks, anyway."

"Okay, let me put it another way. Our friend here needs a little privacy while she's getting the hang of things." She tipped her chin at the breast pump bag on the floor.

Scott was on his feet and heading for the door without further prodding.

"Okay, now, darlin'," she said to Cass, unpacking the pump. "It might seem like a wild beast is trying to devour you at first, but you're a smart girl. You'll pick it up quick."

Tamara was right about the wild beast part. But when Cass saw the first drops of milk fall into the attached bottles like liquid pearls, she felt accomplished and grateful. She knew breastfeeding didn't work for every new mom. "And that's how it's done," said Tamara, smiling proudly. "Your baby girl is going to get the best that God and boobs have to offer."

She showed Cass how to disassemble and clean the pump, and

they left for the NICU. Scott was right outside the door, leaning up against the wall, arms clasped across his chest.

"You the bouncer?" Tamara teased.

"I guess you could say that," he said with a chuckle.

Up in the NICU, the nurse attached the breast milk to Maggie's gavage tube that traveled up her nose and down into her tiny belly. Scott put an arm around Cass's shoulders and squeezed. "Nice work," he murmured. Cass smiled broadly. She was feeding her baby.

It was a happy moment. And yet Cass couldn't quite get the image of the woman from the AA meeting out of her head. She had spent over a hundred days in this very room. It had been her comforting routine.

Cass didn't ever want to get that comfortable. And she was privately terrified that, despite Scott's insistence, she could end up just the same way—without a baby or any hold on her life.

Chapter XXXVIII

The next day, Cass was released from the hospital. It felt strangely sad to leave the fluorescent-lit room. Her whole life had changed here. Of course hundreds of other women's lives had changed in that room, too, each welcoming a brand-new person to love and worry about. But Cass could only think of her own obstacle-strewn course toward motherhood, and how it had culminated here amid the industrial-grade furniture and blinking medical equipment.

Scott came and gathered up her bag, bottled milk, and discharge papers, and they went up to the NICU to see Maggie.

"When was the last time you pumped?" Nurse Hilde asked Cass.

"About an hour ago."

"That's recent enough. Maggie needs to practice her sucking skills, but she's not ready to actually nurse yet, so empty breasts are perfect."

Cass sat in the padded rocker and unbuttoned her shirt. Scott squinted out the window at the cloudless sixth-floor sky. Cass guessed "empty breasts" was not a concept he wanted to think too hard about. Hilde tugged over a chair for Scott. "Come on, Dad. You'll want to see this!"

It was abundantly clear that Scott did not want to see this. *What single guy would?* thought Cass. And yet it annoyed her. When

Maggie came home, she'd be nursing all the time. Was Cass supposed to hide out in her room to protect his delicate sensibilities?

She eyed him and ticked her head toward the chair. Chastened, he slunk over and sat.

It was nice to have Maggie's bare skin snuggling against her own. Her cap was off and her downy red hair felt like a cloud of silk against Cass's arm. She tipped Maggie's head toward her breast. After a few confused moments, Maggie began to suckle—tentatively at first, and then with increasing vigor until Cass whispered, "Holy crap—it hurts!"

The panic on Scott's face almost made her laugh. "Is . . . is that normal?" he asked Hilde.

"Very," she said. "In fact it's an excellent sign. Maggie's got a strong sucking reflex, which means she'll be ready to try breastfeeding soon. It's good practice for Mom, too."

When Cass was ready to stop, Hilde said to Scott, "Your turn! Unbutton your shirt. Skin to skin contact is very important, especially for preemies, who spend so much time in isolettes."

Scott's eyes cut to Cass, and she couldn't help but smile. He wanted Maggie in his life, but so much of this was more than he'd bargained for. She murmured, "Second thoughts?"

He set his jaw and started undoing his buttons. When his chest was exposed, Hilde tucked the little girl into his shirt. She wriggled against him, her hand grasping at the scattering of chest hair. He grinned at Cass. "It tickles."

Cass tried to keep her eyes focused on Maggie and not on Scott's impressively muscular chest. *It's just my crazy hormones.* But she was only half convinced.

Eventually it was time to go. Hilde gave Cass a pump to take home, and they said good-bye to Maggie, who slept peacefully in her little plastic pod.

In the car on the way home, Cass felt her spirits sink.

"You okay?" said Scott.

Cass sighed. "I just want her home with us."

"Me, too."

"You'll have to deal with seeing me nurse her, Scotty. You can't be a guy about it."

"Hey, I never saw it before, okay? I was kinda freaked. But after the first few minutes it just seemed . . . I don't know. Normal. It's what babies do."

"It's what *boobs* do, too."

"Hey, I'm all for the many uses of boobs," he said. "I am staunchly pro-breast."

She whacked his shoulder with the back of her hand. But she did feel a little better.

An hour later, her spirits plummeted again, and she lay down on her bed and cried. The house felt weird. She was the new Cass; she had entered the sacred realm of motherhood. She was completely different . . . but the house was exactly the same.

Laurel came over. "You're depressed," she told Cass. "Every cell in your body is screaming that you're supposed to have a baby in your arms. Your hormones are wild, you have to deal with this stupid pump and a painful scar. Nothing makes sense!"

Cass burst into tears. "And I HATE CRYING!"

"We need to get you to a meeting."

Cass went upstairs to get her purse. Laurel was murmuring to Scott when she came back down. Cass wanted to yell, *Stop talking about me!* But maybe they weren't. And if they were (what else would they be talking about—sports?), it was only for her benefit. Still, every nerve felt stripped bare.

The meeting was in another town, and they didn't know anyone, and the room smelled of Lysol. But after Cass pressed out a few sentences describing what she'd been through in the past four days, she thought, *No wonder I feel crazy.* And she felt less crazy.

After Laurel dropped her off, Cass found Bunny the dog waiting at the door. "Why's *she* here?" Cass whined at Scott. "Did Laurel rope you into dog-sitting?"

"Laurel thought she might be good company."

"I don't need company!" Cass snapped. "I need my baby."

"Just go sit on the couch with her while I make dinner."

Cass galumphed to the leather sectional, the dog close at her heels. "What's for dinner—Pop-Tarts and Cheez Whiz?" Bunny hopped on the couch and put her head in Cass's lap.

"Pet the damn dog," said Scott.

When Cass ran a hand over Bunny's back, she snuggled closer. "For a scaredy-cat, you sure are a noodge." She stroked the silky fur, as Scott clanked around in the kitchen behind them.

She woke to the smell of burned tomato sauce. Dinner was grossly overcooked. The pasta was pasty, and the broccoli was olive green. "I didn't want to wake you," said Scott.

"You were *afraid* to wake me."

"You said it, not me."

She sighed. "Sorry I'm so awful. This is great, Scotty. Four food groups and everything."

He smiled. "It was a big day for me. I saw a baby nurse and I cooked a vegetable. I might try space travel next."

She wanted to hug him. She wanted to crawl into his lap and bury herself in his chest. She wanted to sleep wrapped around him like a blanket.

Whoa, girl.

"You're the best," she said. "NASA will be lucky to have you."

* * *

FOR the next couple of days, Cass and Scott took the pumped milk in to the NICU and cuddled Maggie against their bare chests, and it started to feel almost normal. But not like a routine. The woman from the hospital AA meeting was never far from Cass's thoughts.

When Maggie was a week old, Dr. Abayo said it was time to try actual nursing, not just sucking on empty breasts. She took to it easily. "She's a champ!" said Dr. Abayo.

Cass was so proud. She smiled and murmured to the suckling girl, as Scott and Dr. Abayo lapsed into an analysis of the summer's Red Sox trades, and whether losing a solid center fielder in exchange for an aging catcher and a middling designated hitter was good strategy.

"Management," Scott said, shaking his head.

"Who knows what they're thinking," Dr. Abayo concurred.

* * *

THE next day, something seemed off. Maggie was wan and sluggish. Her dark blue eyes didn't seek out and focus on their faces with the same intensity. Cass's anxiety rose. When the nurse came by, she said, "Maggie's not eating very much. And she seems a little warm."

The nurse checked her temperature gauge and frowned. "I'll put her back in the isolette, where the temperature is controlled. That should help. Why don't you two go grab some lunch?"

"I'm not hungry," said Cass, feeling as if she'd just been told to go out salsa dancing and leave her baby with the coat check girl.

"You need to eat." The nurse used a practiced, placating tone as if to pacify an overtired child. "Breastfeeding burns calories. You have to keep your strength up for your daughter."

Cass's face burned with anger, but before she could let out a molten retort, Scott grasped her arm and guided her to the NICU entrance. "That bitch," Cass snarled in the elevator.

"Easy, girl. It's their ballpark, we have to play by their rules."

When they got back, Dr. Abayo was waiting for them. "I'll say one thing," she told them. "Your instincts are good. We would have caught it soon enough, but sometimes a mom has a sixth sense about these things." Cass felt her blood pause in her veins.

"Caught what?" demanded Scott.

"We took a blood sample and Maggie's got an elevated white blood cell count. The culture will come back in forty-eight hours, telling us more, but we suspect it's a staph infection. We've started her on a course of antibiotics. In all likelihood she'll be looking better in a day or two."

"Likelihood?" said Cass, her voice pinched with fear.

"Well, I need to be completely honest. Preemies are, by definition, not quite ready for the world. They're immunosuppressed, so they tend to pick up germs easily and have a hard time fighting them when they do. Her chances are good, but I'd be lying if I said this was nothing."

Chapter XXXIX

Cass spent the rest of the afternoon with her hand in the isolette, lightly stroking Maggie's belly or leg. She tried to nurse, but Maggie was lethargic and wouldn't latch on.

Cass's shirt got damp. "You need to pump," said Scott.

"I don't want to leave her."

"I'll stay with her."

"*I don't want to fucking pump!*" Cass hissed under her breath.

His face went stern. "You gotta do it."

Cass went to the pumping room, but her body was so tight with anxiety, she didn't produce much.

Mom, she thought. *Oh, God, Mom, what am I going to do?*

* * *

WHEN they got home that night Scott made peanut butter and jelly sandwiches. Cass only ate a half, then she went upstairs and got into bed. She could taste how good vodka would feel—like cool salve on a blistering burn. Just a sip or two to take the edge off her throbbing panic. She'd almost forgotten how strong the craving could get.

I should call someone, she thought. *I should be a good little alcoholic.*

But she was too tired and scared. Too ashamed to reveal herself. *I'm a mother now.*

I'm a mother now. There's no excuse for this crap.

She bullied herself into staying in bed but couldn't stop her spinning thoughts about the woman whose baby had died after 119 days. Cass had felt so sorry for her. But Maggie was only eight days old. If she didn't make it . . . 119 days would make the other woman seem lucky.

*   *   *

THE next day Maggie was worse. Pale and limp, she didn't grasp their fingers or even try to nurse. Dr. Abayo told them that it could take up to two days for the antibiotics to start winning the fight, but Cass's frantic brain went to the worst-possible scenario. At the end of the day Scott nearly dragged her out of the NICU. "You're exhausted," he said. "You need food and sleep."

Cass felt she should stay. But a little part of her wanted to go, too. The sight of the sickly baby was becoming more than she could bear and she needed a break; but this inflamed her guilt.

At home, Cass took a long shower, the near-scalding water turning her skin a feverish pink. Woozy from the heat, she crawled into bed and fell into a fitful sleep.

She woke with a start in the dark room, a vision of the woman holding her dead child flickering like a faulty TV image across her addled brain. Panic brought on a pain in her chest so sharp it felt like open heart surgery without anesthesia.

There was no baby in her belly to kick some sense into her this time. Her baby was miles away. Sick. Maybe dying.

Just one drink.

In moments she was downstairs by the liquor cabinet. Where had he put the key? Her fingers traced along the tops of windows and picture frames. It wasn't in any of the kitchen drawers, but she found a tiny screwdriver, its flat head so small and thin it was the perfect size to jimmy the lock. She never saw Scott drink anymore. It could take weeks or even months before he realized the lock had been broken. By then it would be over.

One way or another it will all be over.

She slid the thin metal tip into the lock, and hope surged through her. But then it stopped and no amount of twisting and wiggling would budge the bolt. She pressed her hand against the glass. In the dim light the bottles seemed to sparkle like costume jewelry behind it. She looked up. Scott's prize bat, the one signed by all his high school teammates, lay on two small wooden arms that protruded from a plaque. Cass took it and tapped at the lock with the butt of the bat, hoping to force it. She knocked lightly at first, but when this did no good, hit it harder.

She never heard him approach, but suddenly he was looming over her.

"What the hell are you doing?"

As if he didn't know. As if it wasn't completely obvious.

She stood up. "I need a drink. Just one. Where's the key?"

"I'm not giving you the key!" he said, incredulously. He grabbed the bat, and she fought him for it, because now all her options were slipping away. No key. No bat. Her brain was a heat-seeking missile trained on one thing: the warmth of a stiff drink going down her throat.

"Are you crazy?" he said, wrenching the bat from her grasp.

"Am I crazy? Yeah, Scott, I'm crazy. You've said it a million times. I'm a crazy, screwed-up drunk, and now my baby is at death's door. And I have *nothing*. Not *one fucking reason* not to have ONE DRINK. So open this fucking cabinet before I throw a chair through it!"

He stared as if he barely recognized her, this snarling predator before him.

"Okay, I'll open it." Suddenly he raised his arms, and the bat came down on the liquor cabinet with a shattering crash, the glass top splitting and splintering, the bottles in its path bursting in a spray of red and amber. Cass cowered away from the flying shards, but then stepped toward it, desperation wailing like a wraith in her ears to rescue just one sacred bottle.

Scott's arms rose again, and the bat descended like a pickax into a gold mine.

"DON'T!" she screamed. But he wound up again and slammed the bat into a bottle of Glenlivet scotch that had been teetering on what was left of the second shelf.

His favorite scotch. And he didn't care. That's what it meant not to worship alcohol.

He continued to pound at the mangle of glass and chrome, shards mingling with booze that swept toward their feet like a tide. The sharp sweet smell of alcohol rose heavily into the air.

One last bottle, dark and round—she had no idea what it was— Grand Marnier?—rolled toward her through the ocean of booze, and she reached for it.

Crash! The bat came down, and brown glass flew like shotgun scattershot.

She stared at the wreckage he'd made in his own house. His breathing was heavy beside her. Then he reached up to one of the wooden arms that had held the bat against the plaque; when he turned back to her a tiny key dangled from a ring around the tip of his finger. He let it slide off and splash into the spreading sea of glass-infested booze on the floorboards.

She threw herself at him, fists flailing at his stomach and chest, and he grunted in pain before grabbing her, spinning her so her back was against his chest, crisscrossing her arms and restraining her like a human straitjacket.

"Mean bastard!" she screamed, wrenching back and forth.

"You calm down right now," he growled in her ear, "or you'll bust your stitches."

"Make me!"

"Oh, I'll make you," he warned, cinching her arms a little tighter across her chest. "I can stand here all night."

Her shoulder, the one she had wrenched only a week ago, was practically combusting with pain. She wanted to fight, to inflict the same damage on Scott that had been done to her. By her mother, up and dying right in front of her, and that pervert in foster care, by Ben and his insane risk-taking, and by Scott's relentless mistrust.

His stance was wide, but she could have found a shin to kick or a foot to stomp. But the violence seemed to sluice out as fast as it had engulfed her. Her struggling slowed, and suddenly hurting Scott seemed pointless.

It all seemed pointless.

"You want this booze so bad you're willing to eat glass?" he snarled in her ear.

No. She didn't want anything anymore.

"And don't think you can play me by going all limp and submissive. I'm not letting go of you for a second."

"If Maggie dies . . ." she whispered.

"Stop that," he ordered. "Nobody's dying." But somewhere in his words she sensed the smallest seed of uncertainty.

Tears began to roll down her cheeks. "If Maggie dies . . ."

He let go of her arms and spun her around in front of him. "No," he said. He gripped her shoulders and bent down to look into her face. "No way."

"It could happen. What if—"

"We're not doing this." He shook his head, taking control again. "We're not playing what if." He turned her, guiding her out of the wreckage of the dining room. Tears blurred her vision. It was as if he were leading a blind person.

He took her to the big leather couch, lowered her onto it, sat next to her.

"I'm so scared," she whispered.

"'Course you are."

"No . . . I mean I'm scared all the time. Like *all the time*, Scotty."

"I know."

She wiped her face with her sleeve. "How could you possibly know?"

"I was an abused kid, Cass. You think I don't know what fear looks like?"

"I hide it."

"Not that well," he said. "Not from me."

Exhausted, she let her head fall against his shoulder, and they sat there for some time before he nudged her away and got up. In a moment, he was back, holding out the phone to her.

"Call your sponsor," he said.

"I'll call tomorrow." She was too embarrassed to talk to Patrick now, with the whole thing so recent and awful. Later she would know how to explain it. Now she still felt too crazy.

"Call him." Scott tossed the receiver into her lap and walked away again.

"Why?" she asked wearily.

He paused by the dining room door, holding a broom and a dustpan. "Because I can't handle this by myself, Cass. You got someone to call. Call him."

Cass dialed Patrick's number, knowing it would wake him, cringing at what she had to confess. But when he answered, and she told him, he said, "I'm so glad you called, hon."

"I didn't actually want to. Scott made me." She could hear glass scraping across the floor in the next room.

"Smart man," said Patrick, sounding impressed.

"Smarter than I deserve."

"As smart as any of us deserves."

Scott walked through several times, getting a trash barrel from the garage, hauling the mangled chrome back out, getting a mop and bucket. When the call with Patrick was over, Scott was on his way to the sink to empty the bucket again. She said, "I'll help you."

"I don't need any help. Just sit there and don't move."

When he was done cleaning, they went upstairs. In the hall-way outside her bedroom, he said, "I know you're scared to death. I am, too. But I swear, if you leave that room before morning, I'll put you and your stuff on the lawn."

He went into his bedroom and closed the door.

Chapter XL

Cass had lain awake for some time, his words ricocheting around her head.

On the lawn.

Homeless. It was her greatest fear, or had been until Maggie got sick. She knew he meant it. Much as he cared about her, he would not put up with one ounce of alcoholic bullshit. He'd done that for too many years with Ben.

She must have dozed off eventually, because it was after nine when she came downstairs. Scott was gone. There was a note on the counter.

You don't go anywhere before you go to a meeting. Laurel will pick you up at 9:45. If you're not ready, you'll have to wait for the next one.

That was it. No indication of where he was.

When Laurel pulled up, her face said it all.

Cass said, "Scott told you."

"Yes. I'll take you into the hospital after the meeting."

"What about Timmy?"

"Adam's working from home. I'm free all day."

Cass had never heard of **Adam** working at the house before. "Does he do that often?"

"The company agreed to let him take a position with less travel and office time. It means less money, but we all talked about it, and we decided it was worth it."

When they got to St. Vincent's, Laurel said, "Make the most of it." And Cass did. She told them all about her desperate, insane attempt to get booze, Scott bashing the hell out of his own liquor cabinet, and his threat to put her out of the house. No one said a word, but there were a lot of nods. *Lucky girl*, their faces seemed to say. *He's a keeper.*

When they got to the NICU, Cass could see the difference right away. Maggie was just a little pinker, her arms and legs a little more active, her face more responsive. The sight of those dark blue eyes blinking up at her was the most beautiful thing Cass had ever seen.

She called Scott's cell phone but he didn't answer. She left a message. "Hi . . . uh . . . I just wanted to tell you she's better. Come and see her if you want. I'll be here all day. Oh, except I'm meeting with the social worker and I'm going to another AA meeting. But other than that . . ."

I love you, she wanted to say. *And thank you for doing what you did. And I'm so sorry.*

But she could not convey the depth of that by voice mail. She hoped to God she'd see him before long. Before it became set in his mind that he couldn't put up with her anymore.

Ruth the social worker was dressed all in gray. "How are you doing?" she asked wanly.

"I've been feeling a little crazy," said Cass.

"Just a little?"

A joke, thought Cass. *Miss Bland made a joke.*

"It's fairly common for parents of preemies to feel depressed and somewhat out of control," Ruth went on.

"Oh, trust me—it's way past 'somewhat.'" Cass described the last few days, culminating in the utter madness of the previous night. Ruth focused on Cass's proactive coping strategies: going to AA meetings, studying for her classes, spending time with friends. "You have a lot of strengths," she said. "Not every parent I see has so many."

"Really? How about the obsessive desire to drink—you probably don't see so much of that, either, I'll bet."

"Actually it's very common, even for nonalcoholics. The stress of a sick child can breed all kinds of maladaptive behaviors."

"But I *am* an alcoholic. We're not talking about an extra glass of wine at dinner."

Ruth gave a tepid smile. "No," she said. "We're not."

"And I can't go off the deep end every time she gets sick or hurt."

"You're right. You can't."

This was getting a little annoying. Ruth was supposed to be the one with the answers. "What do you suggest?"

"My suggestions are meaningless," said Ruth. "Children get sick. Bad things happen. You know that as well as anyone. What's your plan when something makes you want to drink, Cass? This is no different from any other time."

* * *

AFTER lunch, Nurse Hilde thought it might be good for Cass to try breastfeeding. The baby latched on, and though she didn't nurse for long, it was far better than she had done in the last two days. Laurel clapped her hands. Cass said, "I wish Scotty was here."

"He needs some time," said Laurel. "His nerves are pretty frayed, too."

"He said that?"

"No, he never says much. But he usually makes himself pretty clear."

When they left the hospital, they went to another AA meeting. Then they stopped at a grocery store and Cass bought steak, potatoes, green beans, and ingredients for chocolate chip cookies. Cooking was another strategy she'd identified with Ruth. Also, she needed to do something nice for Scott and start to make amends.

He wasn't home when she got there, and this made her anxiety expand with the speed and toxicity of a mushroom cloud. Where could he be all this time? Was he ever coming home?

Stop steering the bus toward crazy town and cook the damn food, she told herself.

He came in as she was taking the last batch of cookies out of the oven. He was red-faced and sweaty, his shirt damp, his sport shoes muddy. He scanned the room the way he used to when she first came, as if there could be contraband around every corner.

"Hi," she said. "Go for a run?"

"Yeah."

"I've never seen you do that before. Is it an off-season thing?"

"No, I just felt like it."

"Oh." She took a glass from the cabinet and ran it under the tap. When she handed it to him, he made eye contact for the first time, his face hesitant and wary.

Keep calm, she told herself. "Steak for dinner," she said. "I'll put the broiler on now and it'll be done by the time you're out of the shower."

He frowned. Clearly this kind of functional behavior was not what he expected. "I'm not hungry," he said. But he didn't sound sure.

"That's okay. Let me know when you're ready. Have a cookie, though. They're better when they're warm." She lifted one off the pan with the spatula and held it out to him. He stared at it for a moment. Finally he took it off the spatula, then turned to go up the stairs.

"Thanks," he said over his shoulder, a beat too late, as if he'd only just remembered to treat her with courtesy.

He came down later, showered, in clean clothes. He sat on one of the kitchen stools. She stopped scrubbing the cookie pan, dried her hands on a towel, and sat down next to him.

"I am so sorry."

He stared down at his hands resting on the countertop. "How's the baby?"

"She's a lot better. The meds really kicked in."

He nodded. "Good."

"Scotty, I know you're furious with me, and you have every right to be. I was insane last night. I broke all the rules."

He shrugged and picked at a reddened callus on his hand. She guessed it was from lifting his dumbbells for too long. He must have spent the day trying to sweat out his fury.

"I just want you to know that I'm truly sorry, and that I'm back on track. I went to two meetings today, and I saw the social worker, and I'm dealing with my fear in a healthier way."

He nodded. "That's good to hear."

"And I'm sorry I dragged you down like that. It won't happen again."

His head came up and he looked straight at her for the first time. "It won't happen again? What are you talking about? Of course it will."

Cass's jaw dropped. "What?"

"You made it pretty damn clear. You said your baby's at death's door and you didn't have any reason—I believe you said 'any *fucking* reason'—not to have a drink."

"I . . . I wasn't thinking straight . . ."

"Right. And you probably won't be the next time something bad happens to her, either. And what if—God forbid, but what if the worst happens? You won't have any reason at all not to get wasted and go back to your old ways. What would keep you sober then?" He glared hard at her. "Nothing, that's what."

Oh, God, she thought. *He's right.*

They talked about this all the time in AA, and she had missed it completely. You can *get* sober for someone else, but it's no way to *stay* sober. You can only stay sober for you. She thought of Jackie, the woman she'd met at her first AA meeting. Thirty years of sobriety down the drain—she'd been staying sober for her husband.

People come and go. They're born and they die. The only thing that's fixed in the equation is you. You have to be worth your own sobriety.

"You're absolutely right," she said.

He looked away, the muscles in his jaw pulsing as he clenched his teeth against his anger.

"I got sober for Maggie, and I've stayed sober for her—and for you, Scotty. I love my life here with you. But I have to change my thinking on that. Because if you and Maggie went away, I *still* don't want to go back to drinking. There's nothing for me there. That's what I have to focus on now. Staying sober for me."

His jaw stopped clenching, and he turned back to eye her warily.

"Scotty," she whispered, "you're brilliant."

Chapter XLI

Cass felt so much lighter after that, relieved of a burden she didn't even know she'd been carrying. It wasn't entirely about other people anymore. It was about self-respect and being a good enough reason to stay sober in her own right.

She worked harder than ever—at being a responsible mother, a kind friend, a successful student—but now it was more for the joy of feeling competent and helpful, not so much to avoid the shame of failing in other people's eyes. The perspective shift helped her enormously.

Maggie made a full recovery. By the time she was three weeks old, the gavage tube was out and she was breastfeeding during the day and bottle feeding with Cass's pumped milk at night. Her pale peach-colored down grew into auburn-red hair. "She's her mama's girl," Scott would murmur, brushing it with a finger. Maggie's blue eyes began to go brown, like Ben's. Cass had half hoped they'd stay bluish gray, like Scott's.

Gradually he stopped watching so closely for Cass's every misstep. Strangely, taking the focus off keeping him happy . . . made him happier.

It was ironic.

Ben would have loved that.

* * *

LAUREL brought her old baby equipment over; Scott emptied out one of the bedrooms and set it all up. "For a tiny little thing, she's got more gear than a major-league team," he said. One night he came home with a rocking chair like they'd had in the hospital. He pretended it was for himself—"I may just live in it"—but he put it in Cass's room. Cass knew better than to say thank you, but she hugged him anyway.

Kate visited with Cass and Maggie in the NICU. She was now assistant manager of Hair of the Dog Grooming Center. She confided to Cass that she had a crush on the manager, Dev, with the titanium leg. But she wasn't going to do anything about it. Not yet, anyway.

Cass completed her two online classes with final grades of B and B plus. She'd hoped for better, though with all that had happened, she knew her expectations had been too high. Nevertheless, she felt her chances were improved for landing a day care job when the time came.

Whenever that was. There had been no talk about her moving out since Maggie's birth. Once when Scott was giving her a driving lesson through a neighboring town they passed a sign, APARTMENT FOR RENT, on the lawn of an old Victorian. Cass slowed to get a better look.

"You have to keep up your speed," Scott chided, "or the guy behind you is gonna end up in your back seat."

She didn't know if he'd seen the sign. She wanted to say something. But the small part of her that was still a scared, motherless child was loath to point out the obvious: that she was a temporary guest in his home. That this holding pattern could not go on indefinitely.

* * *

ON November tenth, at almost six weeks old, weighing seven pounds, and able to hold her head up for several seconds at a time, Maggie Hallie Macklin McGreavy came home to Chickadee Circle. Scott carried her in, sleeping in her car seat, and set her on the speckled granite countertop of the kitchen island. He and Cass sat in their usual stools, watching as her eyelids fluttered with a dream, her lips puckered momentarily as if suckling and then relaxed, her cheeks smooth and pink. They glanced at each other and smiled, then went back to baby-gazing.

Maggie was home. And it was all that mattered.

That evening, the Kesslers came to welcome the newest resident of the cul-de-sac. Each boy took a turn holding Maggie, even little Timmy, with Cass snuggled next to him on the couch, buttressing his best toddler intentions. Laurel took endless pictures. Scott and Adam stood next to each other, arms crossed, watching the proceedings like a pair of bodyguards.

"Tough season," said Adam.

Scott shrugged. "How's the new job?"

Adam shrugged.

It was Laurel's turn to hold the baby, and the younger boys crowded around as she made little surprised faces at Maggie so she would smile. A cheer went up at every drool-laden grin.

Drew stood in the doorway a few yards off. Cass came over and stood beside him. "How's it going with your dad at home more?" she asked.

"It sucks. He checks up on me way more than Mom ever did." Drew mimicked his father's low, serious voice. "Where's your homework, let me see it, let me look it over for you." He let out a snort of disgust. "It's killing me." Cass gazed at him passively. Drew rolled his eyes. "You don't feel sorry for me at all, do you?"

Cass gave a slow headshake. "In fact, not only do I *not* feel sorry for you, I feel jealous of you."

"It's official," said Drew. "You're a mom. Moms ruin everything, even complaining."

Though she knew he would hate it—and he did, his body stiffening in horror—she hugged him, imagining that somewhere in there, the little boy he once was, and maybe even the man he would become, didn't mind so much.

* * *

A couple of days later, Scott had something to tell Cass, and he didn't look happy about it. "I've been holding off," he said. "I just wanted us to enjoy having Maggie home and settled."

"What is it?"

"My mother's coming."

Chapter XLII

"I f she didn't come for her own son's funeral, why's she coming now?" Cass asked Scott as they changed the sheets in the remaining spare bedroom.

Scott gave the blanket a hard yank and jammed the flapping end under the mattress. "I told her about Maggie." He shook his head.

"What's wrong with that? She should know about her granddaughter."

"And that's why I told her." He gazed at Cass for a moment then shook his head again. "Just . . . don't let her throw you. She goes for the drama any way she can."

Gilda arrived a week before Thanksgiving, and Scott insisted on going alone to the airport to pick her up. "I gotta let her complain at me for a while before she sees you and the baby," he explained. "It's like letting a pitcher with a wild arm throw a few balls and wear himself out a little before you start swinging."

When Scott returned with his mother, Cass was wearing her best postpregnancy clothes—a brown skirt with tights and a pumpkin-colored cardigan that went nicely with her auburn hair. Maggie was dressed up in a sage-green velour dress and matching headband on her peach-fuzzy little noggin. The house was immaculate. Laurel had suggested baking something to create a welcoming smell, and Cass had made Irish soda bread from a recipe she'd found online.

She watched Gilda stride up the front walk. She was tall and powerfully built like Scott, but not heavy. She carried a paisley-patterned purse from the crook of her elbow and surveyed the house with an assessor's eye. Scott hauled several suitcases up the walk behind her.

Cass opened the door. "Very nice to meet you, Mrs. McGreavy," she said, holding out her hand to shake, cradling the baby against her with the other arm.

Gilda gave her hand a perfunctory half grasp and said, "Nice to see you again. We've met before, but you may not remember. You were a little . . . under the weather."

She stepped past Cass and into the house. Cass looked at Scott. He gave her a fake-bright smile and murmured, "Play ball!"

* * *

GILDA appeared to pay no attention to the baby at first, though Cass could see her glancing out of the corner of her eye. They sat in the living room with tea and Irish soda bread, which Gilda declined because "peasant bread is all carbs and butter." Scott sawed off an enormous slice and practically swallowed it whole. Cass was afraid he might choke.

Finally Gilda turned her attention to Maggie, as if she had descended out of thin air into Cass's arms. "Well, she certainly has red hair."

Cass glanced at Scott. He tipped his chin. *Go on, you can handle this one.*

"I had hair like this when I was little," Cass said. "Then it turned auburn when I got older."

"None of the McGreavys ever had red hair. None of my people ever did, either." Gilda took a sip of her tea and set it down. "I had eleven brothers and sisters and not one of them had a single red hair on their heads."

"Eight," said Scott.

"Excuse me?"

"You always said you had eight brothers and sisters."

"I didn't used to count the ones that died, but now I do. I realize how important it is to respect the dead." She eyed Cass, as if Cass were a grave robber or a conductor of séances. "Besides," she said to Scott, "how would you know—you never met any of them."

"You were on the outs with them long before I came along."

"I wasn't on the *outs* with anyone. They all just lived far away."

"Holyoke," said Scott. "It's not that far."

"And not a redhead among them." Gilda shook her head. "What do you make of that?"

* * *

GILDA went up to her room to rest before dinner, and Cass went into her own to nurse Maggie. She liked to sit cross-legged on the bed while Scott sat in the rocker.

"She thinks Maggie isn't Ben's!" Cass hissed, fearing Gilda could hear through the walls.

Scott rocked as if he were trying to row upriver. "Is she Ben's?"

"*What*? Of course she is! You know I never slept with anyone else."

"Then what do you care what Gilda thinks? Besides, maybe she thinks it and maybe she doesn't. One thing's for sure, she's throwing all the knuckleballs she can."

Cass had gone all out for dinner—swordfish and wild rice and a lush green salad with crusty bread. She set the kitchen island with place mats and full place settings, something she never did for just Scott and herself.

Scott was taking a bag of trash out to the garage when Gilda came in. "We're eating in the kitchen?" she said. "Like the help?"

It hadn't occurred to Cass to set the dining room table. She'd never eaten in there before. She hadn't even been in the room since the night Scott had busted up the liquor cabinet, but now she moved each place setting. There was a dark line along the wallboard where the liquor had seeped into the edge of the floorboards. The sight of it made her feel slightly sick.

"What's that smell?" Gilda seated herself at the head of the table. "It's like a barroom."

Scott sat across from Cass. "I broke a bottle of wine in here a while ago." He passed the swordfish to Gilda, but she just passed it on to Cass.

"I don't eat fish," she said.

"Since when?" said Scott. "You love fish."

"I've been reading up on it. Too much mercury." She glanced at Cass. "Goes right into the breast milk, no doubt."

Cass passed the plate back to Scott. She didn't have much appetite anyway.

"I was one of twelve, as I said." Gilda took up where she left off, as if the reference had only happened a moment ago. "It was terribly hard on my mother. She was weak, always had some sort of ailment, always in her bed. I don't think I ever saw her smile. I was the youngest, and my older sisters raised me. They resented it, I'll tell you. They'd lock me in the boiler room for hours so they could see their boyfriends, and I'd bang on the door till someone let me out. I can't blame them, really. I would've done the same." She took a bite of bread and raised a finger, putting the conversation on hold while she chewed. "But my point is," she said finally, "they didn't have birth control back then. Well, maybe they did but people didn't use it. But if my mother had only had two, like I did, the family would've been much happier. My boys had a far nicer childhood than I did. I made sure of that."

Scott looked as if she'd backhanded him.

Gilda turned to Cass. "I understand your baby was *unplanned*."

Cass blinked back at her, dumbfounded.

"Even welfare mothers are smart enough to get on the pill these days." And she took another bite of bread.

* * *

"Scotty, she's *awful*," Cass whispered later that night in her room, as she held the baby over her shoulder and burped her.

"Yeah, it's kind of like getting stabbed with a fork over and over. It probably won't kill you, but it's gonna leave some very weird marks."

* * *

As if to mirror the tension in the house, Maggie was up more than usual in the night, fussing in her bassinet next to Cass's bed, her duckling squawk demanding an answer.

"What is it?" Cass asked her for the fifth time. "Why are you so crabby?" Maggie just stared back at her, her little lips drawn down like an overturned boat in high seas.

Bleary, Cass went down to the kitchen later than usual the next morning, hoping that Gilda had already eaten. But there she was, cup of coffee in hand, sitting at the kitchen island.

Lying in wait, thought Cass.

"There's that beautiful baby!" Gilda took Maggie right out of Cass's arms. "I'll hold her for you while you eat." Cass felt as if she'd been baby-jacked. And where was Scott?

Gilda cooed at Maggie, "Your uncle thought you were sleeping so he went for a run."

Coward, thought Cass. She poured some cereal and was about to sit down when Gilda got up and left with Maggie in her arms.

It's probably all right, Cass told herself. *What could she do?* But then Cass realized that she didn't really know what Gilda was capable of. She could do anything.

Cass followed her into the living room. Gilda was at the window pointing out birds in the yard, talking in baby talk. "See that blue jay? She's going to get a nice fat worm for her baby." It seemed harmless, grandmotherly even, and Maggie appeared content. But shortly after Cass entered, Gilda walked out, taking Maggie into the study. When Cass went into the study, Gilda went into the dining room, all the while cooing adorably. There was nothing actually wrong.

Except it felt all wrong.

Cass heard the mudroom door open and dashed toward it. Scott came in, sweaty and red-faced, his hair sticking up at odd angles as if he'd run to Rhode Island and back. "Get the baby," Cass hissed at him. "She keeps walking away from me. It's freaking me out."

Scott headed toward the baby talk in the dining room. "There's my girl!"

"I'm holding her," said Gilda petulantly.

"She needs a diaper change." He took the baby forcibly from his mother's arms.

"You're all sweaty!"

"She doesn't care, Ma. She's a baby."

Scott carried Maggie upstairs, with Cass at his heels. In the baby's room he closed the door. He handed Cass the baby and pulled off his sweaty T-shirt. "She's cat-and-mousing you. She takes what you love most, and she never really does anything with it, she just wants you to come after her."

"For godsake, *why*?"

"Attention. She scores it like junkies score crack," he said, rubbing his shirt across his damp chest. "Did it to us all the time when we were kids."

"What did she take of yours—no, don't tell me. Your baseball mitt."

Scott tapped her nose with the tip of his finger. "And Ben?" he asked as if it were a quiz.

Cass gasped. "His crossword puzzle books!"

"At first. But then he one-upped her."

"How?"

"He just stopped caring. About anything."

Chapter XLIII

Scott took Gilda shopping to get her out of Cass's hair for a while. Then they would go to the old neighborhood in Brighton so she could show off to the few people she still knew there.

Cass took the opportunity to invite Patrick over. He'd stopped by when Maggie had first come home and brought a nearly life-size stuffed dog with long silky ears and soft fur. It actually looked a lot like Bunny.

"That'll tide you over till we can convince Uncle Scotty to get a real one," Cass had whispered to the baby.

But today wasn't a baby visit. Cass served tea and the rest of the Irish soda bread so quickly, it was like a fast-food drive-through. Patrick patiently buttered his slice.

"She's a complete nutjob!" said Cass before she even sat down. "Everything I do to try and please her she turns into something bad."

Patrick nodded. "Dennis has an aunt like that. He was her favorite of all the cousins until he started liking boys. I still can't make that woman happy."

"What do you do?"

Patrick gazed at her and smiled.

Cass laughed. "Nothing. You do nothing."

"Exactly. There's nothing I *can* do except bring my best self to the situation. What self she brings is up to her." He sipped his tea. "How are you holding up?"

Cass thought for a moment. "Actually, I'm pretty good. I'm worried about Scott, though. She twists the knife like nothing I've ever seen."

Patrick shook his head. "Ain't family grand."

"Maybe I'm lucky Maggie's my only real family."

"There's the family you get and the family you choose." He patted her hand. "Choose wisely."

* * *

"IT was pretty pathetic, really," Scott told Cass when he and Gilda got back. "Old Mrs. McIntyre is practically blind, so she couldn't even see the new scarf and cashmere sweater."

Cass marveled at how he seemed to know all his mother's tricks, and how to give her just enough to keep things on an even keel. The only time his mother had gotten the best of him was when she referred to his childhood as happy.

At dinner, Gilda turned to Cass. "So you have big plans for Thanksgiving!"

Scott flashed Cass a warning. "Our good friends the Kesslers invited us over," he said.

"Sounds like quite a party," Gilda said, still addressing Cass. "Where do they live?"

"Next door."

"That huge house? I'll bet their dining room table is miles long."

"Ma, I told you. They invited us and we said yes. It's rude to invite someone else."

"It's not rude if it's your mother and she has nowhere else to go!" She turned back to Cass. "Could you ask them?"

"Ma, you have loads of friends in Hawaii. You're never alone on Thanksgiving."

Cass thought he'd finally had the last word until Gilda said suddenly, "Remember Thanksgivings at our house? Dad used to carve the turkey—he was so good at things like that."

Scott drank a long gulp of his water.

"He was handy. I'll say that for him," Gilda went on.

Scott stabbed a piece of chicken with his fork but never brought it to his mouth.

Gilda sighed. "He certainly knew how to fix things."

Scott put his fork down, and Cass could feel it coming, like an earthquake deep on the ocean floor, causing the whole ocean to swell.

"He also knew how to hit his kids."

Gilda shifted in her seat. "Well, you boys, you were incorrigible. Thick as thieves." She wagged her finger for emphasis. "The two of you banded together and nothing could get to you."

"He could."

"Well, he was rough with you, I'll admit that."

"Ma." Scott glared down at his plate. "He beat the shit out of us."

"That's how it was back then. Spare the rod. And who suffered most? Me, that's who. All the yelling and crying. It hurt me, that's all I'll say." The wagging finger came up again. "It hurt me far more than it ever hurt you or Benny."

Scott looked at Cass, face blank but somehow also wide open, as if to let her see how it was to be inside his skin. *This is where I come from*, he seemed to say. *This is what it was like.* And for a moment he seemed to want to crawl into her gaze, as if he might find safety there. As if it was the best hiding place of all.

"You should let me cook tomorrow," said Gilda, drumstick held between the tips of her fingers. "I'll show you how *I* do chicken."

After dinner, Cass carried their plates into the kitchen. Scott followed with the serving platters. For a moment they just stood there. She wanted to put her arms around him and say *I'm so sorry for what you went through.* But he didn't like pity. "She's crazy," Cass murmured.

"Batshit crazy," he said. "You don't even know." He shook his head, but it was coming, she could tell. "One time . . ." His body shifted uncomfortably with the memory. "I was twelve, and I was just starting to see that I might have something. I could throw faster and farther than any kid on my team. My arm was really good." His face went hard. "That was the arm he broke."

"Oh, Scott," she breathed.

"Mother of the year in there took me to the emergency room. The doctor was this young guy, so tired I don't think he could even see straight to notice all the old bruises. Anyway, he told her he'd have to cast the arm. 'I'll have to look at all that plaster for the next month?' she says. 'Can't you just put an Ace bandage on it?'" Scott's chin quivered with emotion. "The old man broke the best thing about me, and she didn't even want to get it fixed right."

She could feel him falling into the memory, a black hole pulling him down into the abyss of his parents' abuse. Without a thought, she slid her arms around his waist, laid her head against his shoulder, and hugged him. He held on as he never had before, arms tight around her, cheek against her hair, as if the realness of her was the only thing that could break his fall.

The dining room door squeaked. "Well, what's all this about?" Gilda's voice was sour with disapproval.

Scott's arms loosened but he didn't let Cass go. He looked down at her, gathering himself for a moment. Then he aimed his sights at his mother. "I was just telling Cass about the time Dad broke my arm and you told the doctor to put an Ace bandage on it."

Gilda froze. She gave Cass an icy smile. "My goodness, he's gotten so dramatic since you moved yourself in here. He never used to say three words about anything, and now he's dredging up whatever misremembered thing he can. I hope Benny's child won't turn on you the way you've turned my child on me."

* * *

GILDA took a book from the study and parked herself in the living room, an obvious display of being too busy to care what they thought The book was *Jane Eyre*.

She and Jane have grim childhoods in common, thought Cass, and she had a moment of sympathy for little Gilda, banging on that boiler room door, trying to get someone's attention. *But cruelty didn't make her stronger, like Jane. It just made her manipulative and mean.*

Uncharacteristically, Scott followed Cass around for the rest of the evening, and at first she wondered if he was afraid that Gilda's antics might make her want to drink. But it didn't feel like that. Scott wasn't worried about her this time. He just wanted her near.

Late that night, after everyone had gone off to their separate bedrooms and the house was quiet, Cass nursed Maggie and put the sleepy baby into her bassinette. She got into her own bed and sat there in the dim light thinking about what Scott had told her.

He broke the best thing about me.

The bastard broke more than your arm, thought Cass. She'd heard that soldiers sometimes came home with post-traumatic stress disorder. Scott hadn't been to war, but he might as well have. It had the same effect: whatever it was that happened, you were still there, still in it, no matter how long ago it occurred. Sometimes Scott was still there.

In the kitchen, he'd talked about it instead of stuffing it down like he usually did. And he'd let her respond with her body if not her words—in fact he'd clung to her for those few moments. It came to her then, in full force, how much he must trust her. And that as safe as she felt with him, he felt safe with her, too.

Footsteps in the hallway outside her room, a tap at her door.

"Mmm?" she said.

Scott came in and closed the door quietly behind him. He did not go around to the other side of the bed to look at the baby as he usually did, or sit in the rocking chair. He stood in the middle of the rug like a drowning man without a life preserver.

His face was blank, so blank it must have hurt. Cass got worried. Something big was happening. She waited, knowing that to rush him would be to risk an explosion—or a further tamping down of whatever this was.

He crossed his arms, could barely look at her. Finally he said, "I don't know what to do."

About what? she wanted to say. *What is it?*

"I try to keep it in check," he said.

She waited, her own heart pounding anxiously.

"I know you don't . . . you're not . . . You've got the baby and everything, and you're just trying to keep things simple. But I can't . . ."

Oh God, she thought. *Can't what?*

"I can't help how I feel. I've tried." He glared down at the carpet. "Like, every way I can think of, I've tried."

His gaze came up to level at hers and his face wasn't blank anymore. It was apologetic for having any feelings at all. She could see it so clearly. The pain. The embarrassment and frustration. The longing.

He longed for her.

She tried to remember Rule Number Two, but the reasons for it, once so obvious and compelling, seemed to have evaporated. After everything they'd been through, she'd never felt so certain of anyone in her life. Her fingers slid forward on the blanket. "Scotty . . ."

His lips parted and there was a little involuntary intake of air. "Yeah?" He seemed bolted to the spot, watching her, despair arcing hesitantly toward cautious hope.

She slid her legs out from under the covers, over the side of the bed, her nightgown slipping up to her thighs. The hem dropped down again when her bare feet touched the carpet. She moved toward him, because for once he could not move toward her. She laid her hands on his chest, and he let out the breath he'd been holding.

His fingers alighted on her waist, tentative as dragonflies. "I don't want to screw things up for you," he murmured. "That's the most important thing. Like, if I'm stressing you out . . ."

"You're not stressing me out." Her hands slid up to his shoulders and around his neck. He allowed this, still hesitant.

"You got a lot on your plate."

"Are you trying to get me to wave you off?" She leaned closer, her face tipped up, inches from his. "Because it's not working."

"I know I'm not your first choice."

"Yes," she said, looking straight into him, making it impossible to contest. "You are."

She took his beautiful, worried face in her hands and kissed him gently, letting her mouth linger near his. His arms, as if acting against orders, slipped around her, drawing her body toward him. "Really?" he whispered against her cheek.

"Trust me when I say"—her hands slid under his T-shirt—"really." He arched closer, his arms circling more tightly around her. She pressed her hips against his.

"God, Cass . . ." One hand ran up into her hair and the other down her back. She kissed him along his jaw and back to his lips, more insistent now, and she felt her desire for him, locked away in solitary confinement for so long, step out into sunlight.

Yes. This. All of it. All of him.

Tasting him, touching him, feeling the warmth of his hands on her, she wondered how she'd ever had any restraint at all, much less enough to hold something this strong at bay for so many months. She was done with that.

Releasing him, she took his hands and drew him back toward the bed.

"You sure?" he breathed.

"Completely."

As she tugged him toward her, he watched her, reading her as he always had, not by her words but by her gaze, her intentions. *I want you,* she thought at him now. *All of you. Only you.*

This seemed to shift something for him, and he followed her under the covers, wrapping himself around her, kissing her face and shoulders. He started to caress her breast, but then stopped. "Does this hurt?" he murmured.

"No." She kissed him harder.

He was worried about the baby. "She's fast asleep," Cass whispered. He was worried about Cass's scar. "It's all healed," she insisted, gasping as his hand slid below it.

She pulled off his shirt and he tugged off her nightgown, and the feeling of their bellies against each other made her ravenous for every possible inch of contact. She slid her hands into the back of his pajama bottoms and he let out a bearlike moan. He slipped her panties off and she pushed his pajama bottoms away, rubbing her smooth thighs against his thick, muscular ones.

She noticed everything about him, which seemed strange until she remembered she'd never had sex sober before. This made her hesitate, suddenly self-conscious and unsure.

"What?" he whispered, his hands slowing on her back and buttocks.

"I'm just a little . . ."

"What?" He froze.

"Nervous. I've never . . . I've only ever done this . . . drunk."

He exhaled. "You're doing fine. Besides, I don't think I've ever done it without a few belts in me, too."

"Yeah?"

"Yeah. It feels very . . . real."

"It does! I'm feeling everything, and it always used to be kind of hazy."

"Tell me what you like," he whispered.

"You," she said. "I like the way you smell, the way your skin feels."

He smiled. "I love your hair. It always smells like flowers or something."

"Always?"

"I've been noticing it for a while," he admitted.

"How long?"

"Don't make me tell you."

"Tell me."

He sighed. "Since the doctor's office when we found out she was a girl."

"You've been crushing on me since then?" she teased.

His face fell, and she knew she must have said exactly the wrong thing. "It was the same for me," she added quickly, "but I didn't know you were feeling it, too."

She kissed him, but he didn't kiss her back.

"I'm not crushing on you, Cass. That's not what this is."

"That was the wrong way to put it." She put a hand to his cheek. "I love you, Scotty."

I love you, I love you, she thought. It felt so good to finally say it out loud!

"I love you, too, baby." She could hear the same relief in his voice. "So, so much."

* * *

THE first time was slow and exploratory. He couldn't stop worrying that he would hurt her. "I'm not fragile!" she whispered finally, and that helped. He seemed slightly surprised when she came. His own climax was a low muted growl.

Afterward they lay facing each other, her leg over his hip, his nose against her cheek.

"Is this weird?" he whispered.

She thought for a moment. "A little," she said. "But the rest of my life has been weirder, so by comparison it's pretty great." She felt his smile on her cheek. "Is it weird for you?"

"A little. But it's more of a relief. I was kinda starting to lose my mind."

She chuckled. "You're funny."

He was quiet for a moment. Then he said, "Not as funny as Ben."

And there it was—the Ben Question. She had to think about how to respond, how to be honest without disrespecting a man they'd both loved, who'd ultimately brought them together.

"Ben had a sharp wit," she said finally. "But sometimes he thought things were funny that weren't. Like they *really* weren't. You know how he was—nothing mattered except having a good time, and I'd had a bad time for so long before I met him, it was enough. But now it's different. Now I need someone who can be serious, too, and step up when things get tough."

He shifted, running his hand up her thigh, pulling it tighter across him. "I was jealous of you two."

"You were?"

"Yeah. Even though you were so messed up, you had each other. You were even closer to him than I was. And he had someone he didn't have to pretend around."

"Pretend what?"

"Pretend anything."

They lay there pressed against each other, faces and bodies, breathing in tandem, her chest expanding as his contracted to make room. It felt so new, and yet so strangely normal, as if they'd been curling themselves around each other for months.

Then she felt him tense slightly. "I gotta ask you something," he said.

"Okay."

"Don't get mad."

A prickle of panic ran across her skin. "What is it?"

"If you were . . . having feelings . . . how come you went cold on me last summer? What did I do wrong—I need to know."

"You didn't do anything wrong! That was the problem—you were amazing, and I was falling so hard for you. But I just couldn't see how it'd work. You know, for the long term."

"You didn't think I'd stick with it."

"I didn't know if either of us would stick with it. And then where would I be? Out in the cold. Without you."

"You almost lost me anyway. And I think I almost lost you a coupla times."

"Yeah, I know. I was terrified."

"What changed your mind? Now, I mean."

"Oh, God, Scotty, we've been through so much. With the baby, and just . . . everything. So many times you could've walked away and you didn't. And I got stronger. I trusted myself more. Besides, it just got too hard to fight."

"Fight me?"

"No. How much I love you."

"I've been fighting it for months. It's like walking around in a grudge match with myself."

She pressed her nose into his cheek and whispered, "Sorry."

"Nah," he murmured and tugged her closer. "I didn't trust it either. I wanted to walk away. A lot."

"Why didn't you?"

"I loved you too damn much. Plus I think you're the best friend I ever had."

"What about Ben?"

Scotty sighed. "He was great. 'Cept when he was bombed. 'Cept when he broke my heart over and over."

"I broke your heart a little, too, though. Didn't I?"

He thought about this a moment. "You did. But you never left me, Cass. Ben was always leaving me for the bottle."

She felt the fear rise, and she wanted to stop talking, stop getting too deep into this. But she knew she had to press herself forward. Had to be the Cass she'd been aiming for all this time, and tell the truth. Keeping quiet was the old Cass.

"I can't promise that'll never happen with me," she whispered. "I could still fall, any day of the week. If I start pretending like it couldn't happen, it surely will."

"And I could still be a jerk, or blow up over something stupid. But we'll come back to each other, won't we?"

She squeezed him hard. Her Scotty. The strongest, kindest, smartest man she ever knew. "Yes," she said. "Always."

He relaxed then, and she could hear his breath go soft and slow. She felt her own body melt a little more into his.

It occurred to Cass how incensed Gilda would be if she found out about them. She asked him, "Does your mother really have friends in Hawaii?"

"Hell, yeah. She could charm a dog off a meat truck. She has to so she can have an audience. The really crazy stuff she saves for me."

"Lucky you," said Cass wryly.

He kissed her cheek and said, "Luckiest man alive."

* * *

THE second time was more relaxed, smoother, more deeply satisfying. His moan at the culmination was louder, and Cass could feel it run deliciously up her spine.

There was a faint squawk from the bassinette, and then the crying started in earnest. Cass laughed. "You woke her!"

"That girl needs to start sleeping in her crib."

Chapter XLIV

Cass needed to go to an AA meeting. She had skipped the day before because of Gilda, but she was done caring about what Gilda might think. Anyway, as Scott said, who knew what she really thought? Maybe Gilda herself didn't know.

"Where are you going?" Gilda asked through the doorway from the living room, *Jane Eyre* in hand, as Cass got the baby bundled up in the front hall.

"She's going out, Ma. Leave her alone." Scott pulled the car seat out of the closet.

Oh, what the hell, thought Cass. "I'm going to an AA meeting. I'm an alcoholic."

"Oh, I know," said Gilda. "Trust me, I'm aware of that."

"Good, now we're all clear on that point," Scott said snidely.

"Can I come with you?"

Knuckleball, thought Cass.

"Ma, it's for *alcoholics*."

"Yes, but they're very accepting of nonalcoholics. I went to a few Al-Anon meetings, because of Ben. Is it an open meeting today?"

Cass considered lying, but she hadn't in so long, she was out of practice. Besides, there was nothing to do here but bring her best self, as Patrick had counseled. "I think it is."

"It's all settled then." Gilda went upstairs to get her purse.

Cass panicked. "Don't leave me alone with her!" she hissed.

"Ah, geez . . ." Scott sighed and got his coat out of the closet.

Cass called Laurel and said she'd meet her there. "I'll explain later."

* * *

GILDA walked into the meeting as if she owned the place. She was an attractive older woman and the way she smiled at some of the men made them light up like bottle rockets. Cass was starting to see what Scott meant about charming dogs off meat trucks.

Scott carried Maggie in her car seat, and his eyes soaked in the details of the church basement and the velvet AA signs: ONE DAY AT A TIME, KEEP IT SIMPLE, and LIVE AND LET LIVE. Someone offered him a raffle ticket and he pulled a twenty out of his wallet. "That's too much," said the man with the tickets.

"It's really not," said Scott.

People came up to greet Cass and grin at Maggie, some chucking her under the chin or giving her leg a squeeze. Scott pulled the baby's car seat back from this at first.

"These are my friends," Cass murmured to him. "They know her."

Laurel came in and Cass introduced her to Gilda, who gushed, "Oh, you're the one having them over for Thanksgiving!"

Cass gave Laurel's arm a surreptitious nudge. Laurel smiled and nodded.

"That's so kind of you." Gilda emphasized this as if it were a great act of charity.

The meeting was called to order, and the leader began with the preamble. "Alcoholics Anonymous is a fellowship of men and women who share their experience, strength, and hope with each other . . ."

A young woman got up to speak. A tough childhood, drug-addicted parents, time in jail. Driving drunk she'd almost killed someone . . .

Scott's hand slid over to find Cass's, fingers intertwining with hers. He leaned close and whispered in her ear, "How old is she?"

"She looks pretty young."

"I get thirty days," said the girl, holding up her chip. "Best thirty days of my life." The crowd clapped and cheered.

The sudden noise scared Maggie, and Scott reached down to scoop her out of her seat and tuck her into the crook of his arm. He ran a finger over her downy red hair and looked at Cass.

Not our girl, the look said, and Cass nodded.

At the break, Gilda swooped in and took the baby before Scott could protest. Cass gave him an alarmed look, and he was up and following his mother around the hall. She smiled and chatted, using the baby as bait for conversation.

"So," said Laurel. And that's all she said, which meant she'd seen the hand-holding.

"Yes, okay, we're together," Cass admitted. "It's new, though, so I don't even know what it means."

"Of *course* you know what it means," Laurel scoffed. "And by the way, it's *not* new—you've been together for months. You're like cuff and link, the two of you. I'm just glad you're finally getting some physical benefit out of it."

Cass was mortified, but she laughed despite herself.

* * *

GILDA left two days before Thanksgiving, bemoaning the fact that she'd only had six days with her beautiful granddaughter. She never acknowledged the shift in Cass and Scott's relationship, though they didn't hide it. In fact, Scott regularly slid an arm around Cass's waist or kissed the top of her head in front of his mother; Cass was fairly certain he was purposely flaunting it. Not that he didn't do such things in private, too. He could barely keep his hands off her.

That night Cass nursed Maggie in her bed, Scott lying next to them with his hands clasped behind his head. It was windy, and they could hear branches creaking and leaves rustling all around them.

"I should get the gutters cleaned out," said Scott.

Maggie finished, and Cass sat her on Scott's chest to burp her, holding the baby's chin and chest with one hand, patting her back with the other. Maggie let out a loud belch.

Scott smiled. "Way to go, champ."

"Does she need a diaper change?" Cass asked.

He raised his head for a moment and sniffed. "Nah, she's good."

The baby fussed, her eyes half-lidded, face pinched in sleepy annoyance.

"Hold her while I get a drink of water," said Cass.

When she came back, Scott had the baby cuddled belly down on his chest, his large hand spread protectively across her back. Cass slid in on the other side and laid her head below his collarbone. His arm came around her, hand resting on her hip, heart thumping reliably against her cheek. As the three of them lay there snuggled together, listening to the shushing of the wind, Maggie let out the tiniest little baby snore.

This is who we are now, Cass thought. *This is our normal.*

Scott's voice was a whisper so low it almost seemed like a thought in Cass's mind. "My whole life, I've never been this happy." She turned to look at him and saw a tear slide from the corner of his eye.

She reached up and touched it with her finger. "Me, too."

"You were happy with Ben."

"That was different. This is grown-up happy. I never thought I'd have this."

He shifted, pulling her in tighter, whispering into her hair as if to filter his words through something soft. "I'm scared I'm going to screw it up, or you're going to start drinking again . . . something. I don't know. And I'll lose everything."

"We just have to keep talking, Scotty. We have to be honest with each other and not let things build up."

He seemed to ponder this for several moments. "I'm not always good at that."

She chuckled. "Don't be so sure. Remember when you wanted her last name to be McGreavy? You were brilliant. I didn't have a prayer."

She could feel his body relax. "I love you so much, Cass. You have to know that, even when things are hard."

She pulled herself up until her face was against his cheek, kissing him, pressing into him. "I love you, too, Scotty. So, so much."

* * *

THE next afternoon, as she came downstairs after putting Maggie in her crib for a nap, she heard him on the phone in the kitchen. ". . . yeah . . . yeah . . . Ah, for chrissake, the Twins? . . . Shit . . . Of course I'll take it. What am I gonna do—retire?" She stood there waiting for the call to end, waiting to hear how their life would be totally upended.

"Minna-fucking-sota," he muttered when he hung up. "Middle of fucking nowhere, USA." It had been a long time since she'd heard him drop an F-bomb.

She sat down at the kitchen island next to him. "When?"

"Not till spring training, thank God. Gives us some time to figure it out."

"Figure what out?"

"What we're going to do." He sat there, blinking, trying to wrap his mind around it. "I've never been there except for games. You?"

"Me?" She laughed. "I've only ever been to Connecticut, and that wasn't exactly to take in the sights."

He frowned. "Maybe you should stay here with the baby."

"What? Why?"

"I'm not around during the season much, anyway, and you love this house. You've got friends here, and your meetings."

"I'll miss my friends, but I don't particularly love this house. You do, but I don't."

"*I* don't love this house."

"Then why'd you buy it?"

"I don't know . . . I guess I wanted to know what it was like, having a house like this."

"And?"

"And it's expensive."

"It's a lot to clean, I'll say that."

"I thought you loved it," he said.

"I loved finally feeling safe. I loved being with you. I don't need this house for that. And I'm certainly not staying here if you're halfway across the country, Scotty. I'd be miserable here without you."

He thought for a moment, conjuring some long-ago memory. "When I was a kid, all I wanted was my own place. No yelling, no hitting. Just quiet." His focus returned to her. "Now all I want is to come home to you."

Cass felt her eyes go shiny with emotion. She slid her fingers into his and said, "You're my home now, too."

He leaned toward her, rested his face against her cheek for a moment, and kissed her. "Laurel will be really upset," he said. "She's crazy about you."

Cass smiled. After Gilda's comment, Laurel had, of course, invited them for Thanksgiving. "Let's not tell them till Friday," she said.

"Yeah," he said. "Tomorrow, let's just be thankful."

Thankful, she thought. *Yes.*

Epilogue

Maggie's little boot hit a clump of damp grass and she stumbled. At eighteen months, her toddler gait didn't account for uneven terrain, though she could dash giggling across the living room carpet back in their cozy house in Minnesota.

With her hand wrapped securely around Scott's index finger, she regained her balance. It was her preferred mode of travel in unfamiliar places, gripping that finger. Scott had to hunch sideways to bridge the distance between her outstretched hand and his. "I'm gonna grow a hump on my back and get a job ringing church bells," he'd tell Cass with a wry grin.

It was April and the cemetery groundskeeper was clearly not quite up to speed with the lawn maintenance yet. Boston had had a relatively warm, wet spring, and things had bloomed early and with vigor. Cass remembered how gray and lifeless it had looked two years ago. But then her vision hadn't been all that clear.

Two years ago. It was hard to believe.

They had come to Boston for the Twins' series against the Red Sox. They'd been back several times before, but this was their first trip to the Market Street Cemetery. Cass gazed at the headstone, twisting her wedding ring, a soft sadness swelling in her chest.

"Whoops," she heard Scott say, and then their daughter's irritated cry. "Well, don't get mad at me," he chuckled. "You're supposed to hold on."

Maggie was sitting on the ground, her legs splayed out in front of her. She held her arms aloft. "Up!" she whined. "Dada, up!"

He leaned down for her, then tossed her into the air above him, and she squealed in terror-laced delight. It had worried Cass when he'd first started tossing Maggie like that, though nothing worked better to distract her from minor unhappiness. But Scott had said, "I catch things out of the air all day long. What do you think I'm going to do—drop my kid?"

He settled Maggie into the crook of his arm, then strode through the grave markers and came to stand next to Cass. She could feel the warmth of his nearness as she watched beads of condensation slip down the headstone's polished granite plane.

She'd been so drunk when she was here last. And then she'd headed off to cross the vast uncharted ocean of her addiction, terrified and underprovisioned, in search of dry land. It was the greatest risk of her life, getting sober. Greater in some ways than any Ben had taken.

It had been worth it, though fear could still get the better of her some days—when Maggie had had bronchitis, for instance, or when she worried about what they'd do after Scott's baseball career was over. Occasionally the mosquito buzz of her craving for alcohol still grew into the hungry, scavenging hiss of a vulture circling her weakened resolve.

But there was no denying that her long-shot gamble—and Scott's—had paid off. And she was working hard to pay it forward. She was an AA sponsor herself now, and her sponsee was no day at the beach. The young woman could be full of resolve in the morning, then call from a liquor store checkout line by afternoon.

A chubby little finger stretched forward into Cass's line of vision, perforating her thoughts. Maggie pointed at the headstone her parents were so focused on and said, "Dat."

Neither of them responded to her comment for a moment, and

it hung heavy in the damp spring air: how to explain "that" to a toddler. They had discussed it, of course. They would tell her about her biological father but hadn't quite settled on when . . . or exactly what to say.

It was Scott who finally broke the silence and began the conversation. Though he kept his voice light, Cass could hear the bass notes of sorrow in it. "That was my brother, Ben," he said. "He would've loved you like crazy, Mags. Just like he loved Mama and me."

Author's Note

This story is not meant to be a comprehensive review of alcoholism, nor to represent the entire gamut of experience. Addiction takes many forms and expresses itself in a wide variety of mental, emotional, and physical aspects. I hope readers will find the depictions in this novel to be plausible and enlightening.

If you think you or someone you know may have a substance abuse issue, these resources can be helpful.

- **Alcoholics Anonymous, www.aa.org.**

- **Al Anon, www.al-anon.org.** A mutual support program for people whose lives have been affected by someone else's drinking.

- **SAMHSA (Substance Abuse and Mental Health Services Administration), www.samhsa.gov. National helpline: 1-800-662-HELP (4357).** A free, confidential, 24/7, 365-day-a-year treatment referral and information service (in English and Spanish) for individuals and families facing mental and/or substance use disorders.

Acknowledgments

Many thanks to the people, resources, and organizations that provided me with facts and information, certainly, but also with a wider view of the many ways there are to navigate this life.

I'm grateful to Alcoholics Anonymous for the help and support it offers to so many. I first went to open AA meetings and Al-Anon meetings to understand my family better, but the concepts have stuck with me for my own use. It's a tremendously inspiring philosophy that anyone, addict or not, can turn to for hope and strength. Friends and family who have experienced alcohol dependence also gave me great insights and were generous in sharing their personal experiences.

My thanks to Detective Ruth Backman, who answered countless questions about how law enforcement conducts a sexual assault investigation, including interviewing witnesses and how the DNA evidence is handled. My friend Miranda Jones, a former assistant district attorney and assistant attorney general, prepped me on the legal aspects, including the "fresh complaint rule" of evidence. Miranda also throws a really fun book club meeting, but I didn't need to interview her to know that.

My team of medical experts included Heather Starr, a thirty-year neonatal intensive care nurse who gave me a tour of the Brigham & Women's Hospital NICU; Emergency Department

Nurse Practitioner Carla Stafford, who detailed the steps of alcohol poisoning and its treatment; and Dr. Julie Van Rooyen, a gynecological surgeon who talked me through placental abruption and lent me her medical tomes. I'm indebted to these smart women who offer so much to those in dire circumstances.

Katie Stack served as my editorial assistant and was game to dig up all kinds of juicy facts, like what kind of money a midlevel Red Sox player would actually make. She also gave me the benefit of her astute early-reader acumen. A flight attendant who staffs the Red Sox away-game flights provided lots of interesting inside baseball (oh, how I've been waiting to use that phrase) on the players and life on the road. I'm not allowed to use her name, but she knows who she is, and how thrilled I was to get that kind of information!

My writers group, authors Nichole Bernier, Kathy Crowley, EB Moore, and Randy Susan Myers, are not only tremendous writers, but also true friends through thick and thin. Fiction Writers Co-op is indispensable for book shout-outs, industry intel, mutual support, and general irreverence. Early readers Cathy McCue, Megan Lucier, Brianna Fay, and Kristen Iwai gave great feedback and asked all the right questions.

I'm delighted to be back with executive editor Lucia Macro and the team at William Morrow, with whom I published my first novel over a decade ago! Her suggestions truly helped *Catch Us When We Fall* land in just the right place.

It's hard to overstate what a great agent and friend Stephanie Abou continues to be. Her editorial eye, sage advice, and got-your-backness mean the world to me.

Tom Fay, lifelong Red Sox fan through the Curse and World Series champion years alike, served as my in-house consultant on all things baseball. We spent a lot of time at Fenway. Sometimes research is pure fun, especially when you get to do it with someone you love.

About the author

About the book

Insights,
Interviews
& More . . .

Meet Juliette Fay

About the author

Brianna Fay

JULIETTE FAY is the bestselling author of five novels including *City of Flickering Light* and *The Tumbling Turner Sisters*, a *USA Today* bestseller. Previous novels include *The Shortest Way Home*, one of *Library Journal*'s "Top 5 Best Books of 2012: Women's Fiction"; *Deep Down True*, shortlisted for the 2011 Women's Fiction award by the American Library Association; and *Shelter Me*, a 2009 Massachusetts Book Award "Must-Read Book" and an Indie Next pick. Juliette is a graduate of Boston College and Harvard University and lives in Massachusetts. Visit her at juliettefay.com. ᨓ

Writing *Catch Us When We Fall*: A Fluid Process

I woke up one morning on the watery edges of a dream. I can't remember the dream at all, but a lingering image flickered in my semiconscious: the only two people at a burial. One is furious, one is bombed.

At the time I was wading through research for another project, my first rocky foray into historical fiction, and it was not going well. There were just so many facts. I was drowning in all the things one could possibly want to know about the early 1900s, not yet sure of how to home in on what was truly useful to the story. I was also using a new software program that was supposed to magically organize all the different kinds of files writers use (research, sources, interviews, character descriptions, the odd paragraph that didn't fit anywhere but you really wanted to keep, etc.). I was spending more time trying to understand all the tabs and merge functions than actually writing.

The drunk woman and the irate man were far more compelling. ▶

Writing *Catch Us When We Fall*: A Fluid Process *(continued)*

Why was she drinking? What was their relationship? Who was in the casket? I lay in bed for the better part of an hour that morning imagining answers to those questions, and then dashed off a bare-bones chapter. I figured it was maybe something I would come back to one day after I finished the story that was giving me headaches and getting me nowhere.

But a few days later I was still thinking about those two, whom I'd dubbed Cass and Scott for no reason other than those were the names that had popped into my head that morning. Usually I spend a lot of time thinking about names. I research ethnicity and meaning, and make sure they don't start with the same letter as anyone else's. But this story only had two characters, so I was free to skip all of that and just write.

I never bothered to title it anything other than "Cass and Scott" because it was just something I was playing around with while I procrastinated from doing my "real" work of wrestling the early 1900s to the ground. It percolated at the back of my brain, and a week or so later I wrote another chapter just to get it out of my head. I needed to clear the deck for a character named Iris who never really came into focus for me.

Cass and Scott were in high definition, though.

There's a saying that there are two kinds of writers: plotters and pantsers. The former plan everything out. They make charts and lists and story boards; they know every character and plot thread and how it all weaves together; they know the ending. The latter, no surprise, fly by the seat of their pants. They may not know anything other than *Josie's going out for sushi,* and let it roll on from there.

I've always been pretty squarely in the middle I know a lot about the main characters, but rarely the secondaries. I have a general sense of the arc of the story, and a number of plot points, and where it will likely end, but I let things change if the story doesn't end up heeling to my initial plans. My first novel, *Shelter Me,* is about a young woman whose life is upended when her husband is hit by a car. I knew she would eventually seek out the driver and had notes on how she would take him to task. But when ►

Writing *Catch Us When We Fall*: A Fluid Process *(continued)*

I got to writing that part of the story, she had processed her grief to a point where she was able to have compassion for the poor guy, who had come undone with guilt. Plot-wise, it wasn't a hairpin turn—just a course correction.

Cass and Scott found me bushwhacking deep into pantser territory. There was no premeditated story arc—in fact, the research and planning were only ever about a chapter or two ahead of my writing. Every third page took me by surprise. The process was, as they say, fluid.

Okay, Cass is at Scott's house and he's at a game, and . . . maybe a kid comes over to mow the lawn? Sure, give that a whirl. Enter Drew Kessler, who would become the glue for much of the plot. It was thrilling and slightly terrifying.

The one thing I did know for certain was that addiction and sobriety would be the central theme. My father is a recovering alcoholic and I have a number of alcoholic friends and family members whom I love very much. I've seen the misery addiction inevitably brings and experienced the fallout. And I've marveled at the painful beauty of recovery.

I always knew I would write about someone in the grip of addiction; I just didn't expect her to grab me out of bed on a random January morning when I was supposed to be working on something else. Then Cass and Scott showed up, and in I dove. ◠

Reading Group Guide

1. After drinking a customer's tequila sunset at the very beginning of the story, Cass is able to stay on the wagon for the rest of the novel, though she does come very close to drinking a couple of times. What do you think makes it possible for her to stay sober?

2. How do people who were not actually in the story, such as Cass's mother and Ben McGreavy, impact the course of events? How does the setting of Wortherton play a role?

3. What's your idea of a stereotypical alcoholic? Were you surprised that a woman like Laurel, who seemed to have a picture-perfect life, was so addicted?

4. Scott's focus on his baseball career to the exclusion of almost all else borders on obsession. How does he use baseball to

manage the pain that lingers
from his abuse as a child?

5. Are there any bad habits in your
   life that you have a hard time
   stopping, even when you know
   you need to? (Playing online
   games, shopping for unnecessary
   items, eating junk food, worrying
   about things you can't control,
   holding grudges, etc.)

6. Are there any positive coping
   mechanisms that you use?
   How might some of the Alcoholics
   Anonymous strategies explored
   in the novel be helpful?

7. Why does Patrick want Cass to
   avoid having romantic relationships
   for at least six months from the start
   of her sobriety?

8. "Fear and shame. An alcoholic's
   constant companions." Did this
   sentiment surprise you? How do
   fear and shame impact people's
   behaviors? ▶

9. Cass ruminates on how Gilda McGreavy's grim childhood was similar to Jane Eyre's: *"But cruelty didn't make her stronger, like Jane. It just made her manipulative and mean."* Why does adversity make some people more compassionate and others more selfish?

10. What do you think Scott will do once his baseball career is over? How about Cass—will she complete her degree? What do you think each of them would be good at?

11. Just as Cass worries that her alcoholism could cause problems for their relationship in the future, Scott worries that his temper will come between them. If you had any advice to give them, what would it be?

12. When would be the right time for them to tell Maggie about her biological father? ▶

If your book club would like to discuss *Catch Us When We Fall* with the author, Juliette Fay is happy to join you by Skype, Zoom, or other video format with groups of five or more, subject to availability. To schedule, contact her at juliettefay.com. ∼

Discover great authors, exclusive offers, and more at hc.com.